Han Suyin is the daughter of a Belgian mother and a Chinese father who, a Mandarin and scholar entitled to enter the Imperial Academy, had chosen instead at the age of nineteen to travel on a scholarship to Europe.

She was moved by the poverty and sickness she saw around her to take up medicine. She studied Chinese classics and mathematics while waiting for a place at Yenching University. Then, after completing her pre-medical education, she travelled across Siberia to Europe on a scholarship and continued her studies at the University of Brussels. In 1938 she returned to China, married an ex-Sandhurst Chinese officer, who later became a general in Chiang Kai Shek's army, and practised midwifery in the interior during the Sino-Japanese War. From this experience she wrote her first book, *Destination Chungking*, in 1940. In 1942 she came to London, where her husband had been appointed military attache. Three years later he returned to active service in China, leaving Han Suyin to complete her medical studies in London. After her husband was killed in 1947, she spent a year as a house surgeon at the Royal Free Hospital before accepting a doctor's post in Hong Kong. There she wrote the Eurasian love story (her own) that brought her international acclaim and success as a writer. The Sunday Times described *A Many-Splendoured Thing* as 'an astounding love story . . . brilliantly topical, but far more than that, for she handles an eternal theme with power, insight and unfailing artistry.'

Since that time she has written numerous books, both novels and non-fiction. Her combined autobiography and history of China in five volumes, has been hailed as an important contribution to international understanding. Bertrand Russell said of the first volume, *The Crippled Tree*, 'during the many hours I spent reading it, I learned more about China than I did in a whole year spent in that country'.

By the same author

China: Autobiography, History

The Crippled Tree
A Mortal Flower
Birdless Summer
My House Has Two Doors
Phoenix Harvest

Novels

A Many-Splendoured Thing
Destination Chungking
. . . And the Rain My Drink
The Mountain is Young
Cast But One Shadow and *Winter Love*
Two Loves

Non-Fiction

China in the Year 2001
Asia Today
Lhasa, The Open City
*The Morning Deluge: Mao Tsetung and the
    Chinese Revolution 1893–1953*
*Wind in the Tower: Mao Tsetung and the
    Chinese Revolution 1949–1975*

HAN SUYIN

The Four Faces

PANTHER
Granada Publishing

Panther Books
Granada Publishing Ltd
8 Grafton Street, London W1X 3LA

Published by Panther Books 1971
Reprinted 1972, 1976, 1985

First published by Jonathan Cape Ltd 1963
Reprinted 1963

Copyright © Han Suyin 1963

ISBN 0-586-03541-9

Printed and bound in Great Britain by
Collins, Glasgow

Set in Linotype Times

Author's Note

All the personages in this novel, except for the August Presence of Prince Norodom Sihanouk, Chief of State of Cambodia, are fictitious and bear no actual resemblance to any person living or dead. Neither does the Suprême Hotel of the story bear any resemblance to any Cambodian hotel, whose comfort and excellent cuisine have often been enjoyed by the Author in her sojourns in this happy land.

Contents

If only, thought Gion, coercing his ears against the scream of jet fighters, if only the fellow would stop talking about himself.

The dining hall of Donmuang airport, Bangkok, was air-conditioned, but in the early morning the conditioners were turned off, the doors opened. The blare of American fighter aircraft on manoeuvres slammed at his ear drums. This perpetual howl loosened upon all, penetrating every body cell, shattered reason by clamour, produced a jumpy hostile tautness, dredging up the violence necessary for war.

At a long table forty American Air Force men ate breakfast, their jaws chewing, their coffee cups lifted and put down again. The assault of noise set up in their faces a counter-tension: stony jaws, eyes flat as dolls', a buffer of calm against the seething air without, the tension within them.

Next to Gion's table a Siamese Air Force officer in American kit said to a German tourist: 'Thailand is a bastion against communism. We must be prepared.' The jets tore at his words, ripped them into their own screech.

The German nodded, convinced by the screaming jets, their laughing hyena sound of war-to-be.

'I assure you,' shouted Gion irritably, for competition against the jets' raving was like trying to assemble fragments of a torn-up letter in a high wind that kept dispersing the pieces, 'I assure you, Mr—mmm——'

My God, I've forgotten his name, and he must have told me twice.

'—that nobody looks down on Eurasians nowadays. You've got a good job.'

'But I can't become a top executive,' screamed back the young man. '*They'll* keep me from that.'

'You've got a Dutch wife. *She* can't look down on you.'

'She doesn't know what it will be like, once we go back to Holland, on my pension.'

'That's at least twenty-five years from now,' replied Gion, and the young man's lips moved through another excoriating whoop to say:

'Thirty-two and seven months.'

'You've got a comfortable flat, nice children. Nobody would think about your being half-Indonesian half-Dutch if you didn't bring it up.'

'I wish,' said the young man, 'that we Dutch had never left Indonesia. Then we wouldn't have to be fighting communism everywhere.'

Gion, exasperated, half rose then sat down again as another jet savaged the sky. Where could he go, except to the men's toilet, or to wander in the concrete courtyard, already sun-baked, where Buddhist priests stood looking at the out-rushing fighters? The passenger plane Gion was booked on had to wait for the manoeuvres to end before it could leave. If only the young man would talk about something else, anything, except the tragedy of being a Eurasian. Such a petty thing to be worried about, when all around them Eurasian war was being waged . . .

'It's good to see so much equipment,' the young man was saying. 'Those jet fighters, they're the latest. The U.S.A. won't let us down. They'll fight for us. Otherwise I'll lose my faith in human nature.' He swivelled his head again, trying to reach Gion's ear. 'Let me tell you how I feel inside me about all this . . .'

Sheila Manley clapped her hands to her ears, then put her hands down again upon her lap.

Charles Manley, drinking his coffee in sips, shouted across the table: 'Sheila, darling, aren't you feeling well?'

'It's the noise, Daddy. It makes me giddy.' She rose, pushed back her chair. 'I'm going to telephone Princess Sumipoon.'

Charles said: 'I thought she had already left——' A jet took the rest of his sentence. Sheila moved away. Her father continued sipping his coffee, sick at heart as he always was when his daughter ignored him, and with an effort began once again to read the *Bangkok Post*, which splashed on a three-column space: COMMUNISM DEFINITELY CRUSHED BY YEAR'S END, SAYS PREMIER. As big a headline on the other side of the page proclaimed: FILM STAR SLAPS HUSBAND IN COURT.

From the ladies' room at the end of the dining hall Eliza Crawfurd came to him. She is the only woman here with a hat on, thought Charles, immediately composing his features and glazing his eyes, re-entering the placid, professional personality which was the Charles that his wife knew. He rose to draw out a chair for Eliza.

'Where's Sheila? Where's the child?' asked Eliza, with the petulance that was still sprightliness to other men, symbol of youth retained.

And Charles, who thought he concealed what he felt about his daughter from his wife, replied: 'She wasn't feeling too well with all this noise. She'll be back.'

Chundra Das stood in the courtyard of the airport watching the Buddhist monks. Not that they were unfamiliar: shaven round heads, faces smooth above the saffron robes, bag of yellow silk hanging on one shoulder, Buddhist monks were plentiful from Burma to Vietnam. Two of them had cameras slung round their necks, one held a briefcase. All, unmoving, watched the fighter planes gash their way through the air. They stared opaquely, as children look through a window pane at a barren landscape while their minds conjure lovely tales of mythical lands.

Chundra peered towards the dining hall's open doors, as quickly turned his head again. If someone had come up to him, he would have had a gesture of surprise, said: 'I hadn't seen you . . .'

The dining hall, crowded with its U.S. Army officers, U.S. airmen, and some tourists, now shut its doors and the air-conditioners began to hum. The radio announcer blared: 'Passengers via Siemreap, Phnom Penh . . .' Walking sideways, Chundra sidled back into the dining hall where people were rising, collecting hand luggage, walking towards the exit. He trailed after them, not wanting to be seen, and seeing, in the courtyard, a young monk handing a parcel to a girl.

Captain Lederer's shirt was sweat-damp, in spite of the coolness in the small air-conditioned office of the airplane company. He sat alone, waiting for the manoeuvres to end before take-off. Couldn't these bastards find a better time to practise their massacres? They wanted to make people wait, impress them about this war business. And there would be a war now, any day. It couldn't go on like that.

'Take-off,' said the co-pilot, head pouncing into the room.

God, thought Lederer, rising from his chair with the action of a folding rule snapping itself into the perpendicular, I am tired before I begin.

He walked, an army officer's walk, the long corridor lined with plastic seats on one side and the air companies' offices facing them on the other; eyed the sheep-flock of tourists following the Siamese air hostess to the waiting lounge where passports were retrieved before embarkation, surveyed the hostess, short legs, wasp waist, pert buttocks emphasized by the patent leather belt; rapidly stirred, as rapidly felt the ebb of desire. He deliberately went through the wrong exit and on to the apron, with the hot dull sun dispersing a ninety degree temperature at seven-thirty in the morning.

'Fait chaud,' he said, sliding into his cockpit seat and feeling another burst of sweating invade his skin. 'Bring me a drink, someone. Brandy.'

Regulations did not allow pilots to drink before take-off, but Lederer said: 'Merde,' and took a peg of brandy on ice cubes. He could say 'merde' to the VIHEA Airlines Company at any time. They wouldn't get another pilot like him, even if they ransacked Saigon and Hongkong and Manila for one. He'd do what he liked, no damn 'meteque', yellow, black, or brown, was going to order him about. 'Non, monsieur, on parle poliment à Lederer, François.' He thought he was the only one to know that his bravado sickened him with fear, provided him with an ugly vertigo, a fall within himself, like a death, which he needed to prod himself alive. If the VIHEA Air Company took on a younger man (and the Asians were coming up fast), thanked him for past services (they had him on a month-to-month basis now, instead of the two-year contract he wanted), what would he do next?

Crénom, what shall I do? A wife I see twice a week, who costs me the earth, and often I'm so tired it's no use. A son, started too late, my joy and my damnation, the only photograph I carry in my wallet, my life hard labour for him for the next, say, twenty years and I'm not young ... If I'm fired there's the Congo, Laos, or Algeria, if only they don't calm down for then it's the dole and the queue. But there'll always be a war, somewhere, and in a war they need types like me, the hard ones. We know all the tricks, not only how to make machines work, but how to make a man talk, how to drill the same know-how into others ...

But I, said a still, small voice in Lederer, his childhood voice, I never *liked* cruelty. I hated it, before, always did ...

Pick up the chits at the end of the party. Play well-to-do. All the time the terror of the irrevocable plunge, tomorrow disgusting with an empty purse, child and wife to feed. And, my God, do they eat, those two?

Talking of eating, the Congo wasn't attractive now they'd started eating people again. At least in Indo-China you hadn't been compelled to eat what you had mutilated ...

Laos ... but it looked like settling down, which was bad. However, there might be gun-running, and of course the Trade. The Trade wouldn't settle down for a good long while, not with that strong-man of Democracy around, the big General What's-his-name. As for gun-running, things might be looking up in Indonesia. Although now they shot one over there, a white skin no longer made any difference, put you in jail along with the natives, shoot you, as if you were like anyone else on earth ...

He started to check the controls, his mind absent from what he was doing. The co-pilot shouted: 'Let them in.' Behind him Lederer heard the tramping, scuffling noises, the seats thumping back. Tourists. Sometimes he hated them so much he felt like looping the loop up in the blue, tossing a salad of tourists.

Hopping round the world to places where they buy souvenirs, write postcards, snap photos. Might as well stay at home and watch TV. They'd see more.

His hands flicked the switches, eyes upon indicators, ears listening to the co-pilot's drone testing the intercom. Take-off was an interval of pure trance, surge of the plane under him as it left earth; even if it was only a DC-3, when he'd flown Skymasters and Constellations before, it gave him a moment of goodness.

'Ça va.' The plane fled, ambling past the airport tower, stationary, revving, engines crescendo, then in a forward rush gathered speed, leaping into air. And always in that unquiet second Lederer's mind darted back to the past of six years ago, wondering whether he would be able to take off or whether he would crash, as he had crashed on take-off in Hanoi, with all hell and its Sten guns let loose on the tarmac, in that 'dirty' war that had ended in Dien Bien Phu.

The plain of earth spread its revolution round the ascending machine, and Lederer's uncertain ecstasy was over.

Last night he had explained this to the blonde who had come too readily to his bed, almost unasked, lying back after a couple of drinks, so that even he had been surprised. But 'je lui ai fait l'honneur quand même', he murmured, looking for the small stir, tide of himself so desirable in its coming and going, a leap in air of himself. He had tried to explain the satisfaction of this jump into elation to the blonde, the satisfaction of his perpetual defiance towards his own employers. Then it had happened.

By the way, she should be on the plane. He hadn't remembered the blonde in the pasty morning sourness with those screaming jets, had not seen her in the dumb flock of tourists behind the Siamese hostess.

'Heh,' he said to the co-pilot, 'the cute blonde, last night ... see if she's there ... ask her to the cockpit.'

Women liked being asked to the cockpit. Often he had to ask a man, a V.I.P. The list of passengers bore a tick against V.I.P. names. Then there were the V.I.C.s. Those belonged to the Other side. They were never asked to the cockpit, and the air hostess watched them, in case ...

The blonde. He was surprised as his flesh tried to remember its yesterday, and found it as vacant of sensation as a just walked into hotel room. He could not remember, neither his mind nor his body.

Ça, c'est marrant that I should forget—too many, or too much Cointreau.

He knew himself capable of more than this manoeuvred clutching now erased, had tasted a capacity for pain and longing alien to what had taken place, took place often, meant almost nothing, evanescent routine like flying tourists or flicking ash from a cigarette. Nothing was left of the blonde, except this surprise that it was nothing.

I must have been blotto.

Suddenly she was there. He motioned to the empty seat, and took in her hair: texture, length, odour, colour. She was a real blonde, a silky, fine, ponytail one. The face under this hair he could not think of entirely as a living organization, since it was not yet normalized by acceptance. It was an architectural arrangement to scan, the forehead smooth and high, temples and cheek-bones young, a nose delicate and small, a mouth flexible, the lips smooth under lipstick.

O careless love, lost in the planned simplicity of a face I cannot describe.

'What lipstick do you use?'

He shouted it again, in her ear bent forward and diagonally across the space between their seats.

'Dior,' she said. 'Number Sixty.'

'I like it.' With conviction, as if he had recognized it. She smiled, an elastic stretching of the mouth showing no teeth, her eyes looking through the glass at the landscape below. When they came near to Angkor he would swoop round, and round once more, to show it to her, its extent, its symmetry, its ample monumental beauty. He would tell her: 'Angkor is really a collection of great cities, begun in the seventh and ended in the thirteenth centuries, an architectural marvel, many square miles of monuments, temples ... the eighth wonder of the world.'

The co-pilot stood in the narrow gangway behind them. He was a taciturn Brittany man, faithful to his wife. He had not crashed in war, his tranquil nerves did not need to reassure him that he was alive. He did not feel the shame of defeat eating up his insides. 'Every man must be free,' he would say. Lederer would retort: 'You don't know what France means.' The co-pilot would shrug: 'Don't excite yourself,' and go back to his silent, nourishing dream of a little town on the North Sea and a wife who did not wear lipstick.

A river traced its lizard gleam, the radio operator stirred. Among the compact forests rose the stones of Angkor, complexities of the square, formal, precise, gigantic.

'This is what you have come to see. Angkor. Down there.' Lederer suddenly loved Angkor, with the love of the Frenchmen who had resurrected it from the jungle, thought it profanation to show to the thronging curious. Angkor was something to be proud of, something pure. Not like the other things.

The only work we did where we didn't cheat at all.

The blonde peered down studiously at the monuments sweeping below.

'How long are you staying?' He was insolent, but she did not know it.

'Two weeks.'

Two weeks? She was joking. Two days, four days was the tourist limit. Except for the few who fell in love with Angkor, like Bernard Reguet, the curator of the Angkor ruins, or the American woman who had asked that her ashes be scattered by plane over the monuments.

'Then I shall have the pleasure of seeing more of you.' He was hostile. She might hang on, leechlike, make demands.

'I'm with Father.'

He was surprised, then remembered. Last night she had talked about a father. What had she said? And he, what had he talked about?

The co-pilot hovered, they were landing. The girl left. Lederer wanted to ask : 'Qu'est-ce tu en penses?' But the ritual of descent had begun, and again he was gripped by the fear he kept demanding to conquer, every time knowing himself re-born into a security he longed to destroy. Death was a narrow gorgeous moment, a landscape that gaggles of tourists did not go into, and return from death even more satisfactory. For François Lederer, in life there had been Dien Bien Phu, and Dien Bien Phu was a hole in the brain of a good many French Army officers who had fought in Indo-China, and some had not been quite right in the head ever since. Now there was Algeria, and the hard ones from Indo-China had their drug-need for violence there renewed. The O.A.S. was directed, staffed, manned by them ... Lederer, who flew tourists from Bangkok to Cambodia and on to Saigon, spoke of his friends in Algeria 'teaching those bastards a lesson'; meanwhile knew only the small, self-created tremors that he needed to remain alive.

Once out of the plane he asked the co-pilot: 'What do you think of her, eh?'

'Legs too long,' said the co-pilot.

'Crénom,' said François Lederer, grinning, 'can't remember her legs.' And then he was ashamed.

Gion watched the fair-haired girl walk to the cockpit, invited by the twist of her back to the pastime habit of all men, the mental unclothing of a woman. He then carried his eyes back to the airplane window, to rice fields, a river, forest: not the thick, spongy, cauliflower masses seen yesterday coming from Indonesia, but distinct trees, promising salubrious space below their foliage roofs. The plains sparkled dryly, morning sunny. November was the best season to come to Cambodia, the best time to see Angkor.

The Neutralist Congress of Writers he had been invited to attend in Cambodia was his excuse to return to Angkor, a place for which he had conceived a nostalgic hankering on a first visit two years before. The Congress might be an unsatisfactory affair like many of these writers' reunions; for Gion, it was an opportunity to see Angkor once again. He would not be involved in more than a token attendance at the Congress. Gion had been to one or two such conferences arranged by the free world, and so far had found them unprofitable where writing was concerned. A medley of ulterior motives prevailed, and in spite of high rhetoric such meetings of minds often became misty affairs. Larger than real, voices earnest, views passionately stale, writers poured phrases like artistic integrity, freedom, human values, appealed to vision and imagination, phrases become meaningless by reiteration. The voice of the artist bidding the artist be himself can become singularly tedious.

Gion remembered a Congress some years back somewhere in Europe, a shaming farce. Apparently under the auspices of several eminent heads of state (who had sent pleasantly platitudinous messages), it had turned into blatant political campaigning, contrived by Muni Multani, a brilliant and ambitious Indian politician who had typed his way into the *Author's and Writer's Who's Who* on the basis of a tract entitled *How to Save Freedom*. And Muni Multani now sat three rows in front of Gion, in the same plane, evidently Congress-bound.

Multani and Gion recognized each other in Bangkok airport, and mutely decided to remain unaware of each other. Multani wanted every Asian country to fling itself on the side of the West and engage in military pacts and programmes. Indefatigably he travelled, lectured, wrote about The Threat of

Communism. His presence here, on the way to the same Neutralist Congress of Writers, in the neutralist kingdom of Cambodia, might be significant. What was the Congress really trying to promote? Neither the word Peace, which usually denotes the Left, nor the word Freedom, which always denotes the Right, had been used in the invitation which Gion had received. Clearly the letter stated:

> 'Neutralist Congress of Writers
> Cambodia

'Dear Friend,

'Our country, lovely Cambodia, is non-aligned and believes in a positive neutralist policy. We think that writers all over the world who are interested in the future of humanity should assemble in a spirit of strict, impartial objectivity, together examine their world heritage of literature, and devise ways and means whereby conflicting views can reach a harmonious synthesis.

'Writers interested in attending this Congress please fill in and return the enclosed card.

'P.S. All expenses incurred (board, lodging *and* travel) will be the responsibility of the writers attending, and positively *not* of the Congress.

> 'SECRETARY (illegible)
> 'Neutralist Congress of Writers'

Unlike the Freedom conferences which provided first-class fares and best accommodation, this one assumed the writers would pay their own expenses. The Peace conferences, usually more shoe-string, involved certain hardships: some governments had the habit of jailing writers attending them on return to their own country. To make guests responsible for their own expenses ensured that the writers attending the Neutralist Congress would be remarkably few. How many in this spiritually honoured and materially slighted profession could afford the expense? And of those who could afford, how many would come?

Two rows behind Multani, one row in front of Gion, sat Chundra Das, tower of strength among Progressive Writers, whose books had been acclaimed for their proletarian truth.

And indeed, thought Gion, he *is* a good writer, when he forgets to switch on the politicalese. Chundra was white-haired, his chubby face harboured a young candour made of unswerving faith in the Good Society to come, optimism unshaken by whatever went awry in the building of it, for he knew that man was wayward, and no theory was fool- or wayward-proof. But this did not dampen his enthusiasm, for he was profoundly convinced that mankind was on the way up, even though cruelty, violence, and callousness seemed at times as common today as two thousand years ago.

At the airport Multani had turned his back on Chundra, who had smiled pityingly, and majestically opened a book entitled *The Tragedy of Western Interference in Asia*. This book, Gion knew, contained in a paragraph a most unflattering sketch of Multani's political career. Das and Multani at one and the same Congress? Neither of them, Gion thought, could have paid his own expenses. Chundra could not afford it, and Multani was too well backed by Western Foundations to pay for himself. Only Gion, well off by inheritance, could be what is called a 'free agent', making a choice of his own volition.

One never knew, one never knew with intellectuals in the cold war (and the term 'intellectual' now covered a multitude of those who strummed a typewriter keyboard, from newspaper correspondents through novelists to poets). In the winds that blew hot and cold and all at once, many of these wielders of symbols, themselves victims of the words they used, were driven to a fierce, self-tearing search for the Self, became lost in a 'freedom' which left them with neither individual purpose nor social significance, because they felt themselves above all responsibility to their fellow men. They were caught in a Self which rapidly deliquesced towards Nothing, since all it acknowledged was 'self-expression', a meaningless term. Sometimes they became enmeshed in another web, felt only too responsible for ideological leadership, became arrogant because they lost their humility labouring for Ideas noble and good and Mankind's need through the ages, and this earnestness seldom could afford the exercise of humour, for the needs were too large, the ideas still on trial, beset by dangers. Gion thought; I know, and we all know, that we are stumbling our way into a better kind of world, even if it is a hard way to go, but humour can only come with tranquillity. There's no real humour about war.

Some writers, like Lot's wife, turned towards some impossible nostalgically burning town, a Golden Age of the past. Others made money out of a heady mixture of affluent boredom, unrelieved even by sex, or picked their own scabs, uncovered self-made sores, magnifying these into wounds of the spirit. Still others recorded dutifully the appearance of things in formulas that did not trespass, and they too lost themselves, confusing panegyric with dedication, and collective good with chorus docility.

All this went on, a perpetual churning maelstrom of perplexity and debate, the Writer's Position, the Values he might fight for, the Things he ought to be committed to, the Disciplines he ought or ought not to commit himself to. Writers clung to these eel-slippery words, clutched at theses and formulas, revelled if perchance they felt a genuine emotion about some cause, laboured at it till they lost it through over-use, or because there were too many emotions about too many things in a world that galloped headlong either into collective annihilation or a collective reasonableness (and the second alternative seemed so much harder to achieve than the first).

Gion carried within him this querulous, necessary ambiguity, the dialogue of that eternal contradiction, which is why the writer is, but he shrank from communicating it, for verbalizations of his inner states appeared to him, like smoke, to obscure instead of elucidating the issues. He had told himself that he preferred to make up his own mind', and realized that this choosing not to choose was really an escape, a running-away. Sometimes he would come out of his refusal, dispute and argue, hope that by accident someone might point a sure way out for him and others like him, caught in the cross-fire of two economic systems. But gradually he had given up trying to find a way between commitment and non-commitment, content to accept that there should always be, as here on the same plane, Multani and Chundra Das, apparently irreconcilable in their views, who had to live together or destroy each other. He was unwilling to take sides, though he knew this state unsatisfactory and, naggingly, uncreative. But he consoled himself with wisdom. He had done his stint, he had enough ... he expected nothing more. Once again this Congress of Writers might be a cold-war fracas, an exercise in mock belligerence, a frozen witless verbiage, not a meeting of those who strove to solve the many-faced ambiguity of what is real and alive and for ever changes, in form and content, reality of the many metamorphoses, phoenix perpetual. Accommodations were a rule in history and would occur again, but somehow people never got tired of being thoroughly, savagely, pitted against each other first in a demonic exercise of irrationality. And yet, thought Gion, Man for ever walks the tight-rope between Symbol and Reality; at no instant is he sure of the one or the other ... He thus reasoned with himself, yet felt curiously hollow inside; told himself it was better not to choose, yet was desiccated with his freedom from any cause to fight for.

The blonde girl came back from the cockpit. She has nice hair, Gion thought—although I do not really like blondes. At this moment of his life Gion endured a phase of asceticism, of retreat from the world of the senses, in keeping with his lassitude in the war of words. Deliberately eschewing human contact, he chose continence, withdrawal, an abstract mood, rather as others chose drink or sex. He told himself that he wanted to keep his mind clear, observant; knew this partly false; was sometimes afraid that this non-emotion, this lowering of tone and colour in his reactions, meant he was getting old, but reassured himself with a look at his trim figure in the mirror. The result had been an increased non-sensuous pleasure in beautiful things, a connoisseur's tactics in choosing to know more and to read judiciously, the acquisition and treasuring of objects carefully chosen, a few exciting emotions, exciting because removed from human contact, devoted to *things*, such as for instance the monuments of Angkor. He read, wrote, travelled, met a good many people, got out of knowing them too well or too much, avoided involvement beyond a gentle friendliness, a reticent, kind-eyed interchange which placed no burden at any time upon his heart. And having made himself a life free from suffering, studiously walking the delicate elfin way of non-committal, he suffered numbly, all the time, from being with himself, from the unrest brought by the fact that no Absolute remained to bind him fast, save language, words, the ceaseless myth; and this domain was narrowing, he knew himself tedious to himself, the images less easily stirred, the apprehension blunted.

He kept his eyes on the girl as he fastened his seat belt. She reminded him of something, someone. The plane whined descent, he opened and shut his mouth, looking out of the window again, at the fast-growing earth rushing up to fill his sight, braced for the small, satisfactory bump as the plane touched down.

Mabel Despair's legs ached, they always ached since the baby. If anyone had told her: it's because you wear too heavy shoes, she would have been angry. Her feet were something she worried about, and her shoes came from England, had always done so; her English mother had put her in Start-Rites, and she had continued buying English leather shoes, too heavy for the tropics. She could not fold her legs under her, as the man across the aisle did. But then, he was Indian, and she ... well, thought Mabel, nobody would know my father was a Chinese from Burma. Mabel's complex came from the fact that she looked European, which was a handicap in getting a job now-adays in Asia. People didn't believe that she had an Asian soul, that she was emotionally Asian, which meant that everything that happened in Asia mattered to her, and what happened in Europe was colourless and remote from her. But on the other hand she could only speak English. And that meant that she was handicapped, both in competing for a job and in her social life. Now even European firms in Asia demanded secretaries who knew at least two if not three Asian languages, besides English. And socially speaking, if you only knew English, Asians thought you were pro-colonial, and avoided you. Fortunately Mary Faust had understood her, given her something to do, saved her from this terrible feeling of having nowhere to go ... of being useless among the useful, hard-working millions who were working their way up to human dignity ... except return to an England which she had heard her mother call 'home'. And that was defeat, acknowledging that she wasn't, couldn't be, Asian.

'You can study, improve yourself,' Mary Faust had hissed in her enthusiastic voice, tremulous with fervour. 'You can become a useful tool of the Revolution.'

Tool of the Revolution. Mabel Despair had only the haziest ideas on Revolution, had never read Marx, but felt, like all Asians do, part of an unending process of change, and welcomed change because it was a way to a better life. Straight away she had fallen in love with Mary Faust, in a way that she never had for her own husband. It was a pure, wonderful feeling, adoring heroine worship. Mary Faust herself was not Asian. She was American. But she *understood* Asians. More, she knew Asia better than most Asians, since she was making the Revolution in Asia. She had told Mabel this and Mabel believed every word Mary said.

Typing for Mary Faust was working for the Revolution. Her husband Thomas Despair, half Tamil and half Scots, was noncommittal about Mary Faust. 'The woman is a bit cracked,' had been his comment. Mabel had stormed out to do Mary Faust's bidding, leaving her husband to lunch by himself and to wipe the baby's dribble. Mary Faust had withered Thomas with a glance, and said icily: 'Take care, when the Revolution comes ...' And Thomas, who knew he had no group protection, since he was, like Mabel, a member of a very small and powerless Eurasian minority, had wilted and packed Mabel's things for her. Mabel was going to the Neutralist Congress of Writers to take down the speeches of Mary Faust, who would attend the Congress and direct it in the correct ideological channels, towards the Revolutionary future. Mary had said that this was a most significant event, and that she must be there in person in order to see that 'no one deviates from the ideological struggle'.

So Mabel was on the plane to Angkor, to the Congress, with aching legs and many dreams: dreams of meeting a famous author who discovered in her his inspiration, an essence of subtle understanding ...

She went no further in her dreams, for there was Thomas, mild, good with the children, such a good man. They had five children, and the Chinese amah looked after them, They spoke Chinese and English and had picked up Tamil from Grandma. Thomas would housekeep, while Mabel at the Congress would work creatively for the Revolution.

Bless you, Mary, she thought. This otherwise would not have happened to me. She should be willing to die for Mary.

And for the Revolution. She plunged on in her dreaming. There was a plot. Mary had said to her: 'You must be ready to do Anything to Save the Revolution ... even to go to bed with a Capitalist.' Mabel saw herself, sacrificing for the Revolution; being beaten too, by a large Capitalist; which suddenly, in her dream, was not all that unpleasant ...

'In the vastness of Television land,' Chundra Das read in the airplane magazine, 'a visitor finds that TV news and information actually hold only a slender enclave, roughly comparable to Goa wedged into the subcontinent of India. Less than five per cent of the revenues of the TV companies are earmarked for gathering and presenting news ...'

It was remarkable, thought Chundra, how he still feared Mary Faust.

My heart beats, my pulses race. Even assuming the lotus position, to calm and fix my spirit, has produced no quietening of my nervous system.

It was true that Mary Faust seemed to leave behind her an amount of frayed nerves, shattered emotions, and seared spirits, out of all proportion to her own importance. And the fact that Mabel Despair was sitting across the aisle to him was enough for Chundra Das to feel turmoil resurgent, for a glimpse of Mary herself in the morning at the airport, peremptorily seeing Mabel off (Thomas kept at respectful distance from his own wife during the process of last-minute recommendations from Mary, while Mabel jotted these orders down in her shorthand book, at the same time carrying her hand luggage and clenching her teeth on the handle of her handbag), had been enough to precipitate Chundra, head swathed into a muffler suddenly unearthed from his hand luggage, out of the dining hall. He had taken refuge among the Buddhist monks, sacrificing breakfast (paid for by the air company). A little while before perceiving Mary Faust he had watched Muni Multani come in, delightedly had opened a book which he knew Multani detested; but Mary had made him shut the book, shield his face, and flee. And perhaps it was a good thing, for in the courtyard, among the Buddhist monks, he had observed a most puzzling incident ...

Mary was not on the plane. Only this short, tangle-haired,

bespectacled girl with a slightly overfed figure; the exact type of girl or woman who fell for Mary Faust and was dominated by her, typed for her, ran errands, sobbed when she scolded (and how her tongue could lash), and loved the sobbing and the reconciliations afterwards. I still wonder, thought Chundra, why I keep on being upset by Mary? When I know all the answers, when I know she's bogus? It had taken him months to realize that she was a hoax, or, in the Asian political short-hand which he used, an opportunist. Yet, every time, it was the same thing: his heart smote him, he was hypnotized, and panicked . . .

Muni Multani was quite another thing. He knew how to handle Multani, Multani was an out-and-out reactionary. He must fight Multani at the Congress.

He picked up the magazine again. '. . . The scheduling of informational programmes is profoundly affected by the profit motive . . .' He read on, but his thoughts were away from what his eyes read. He bent towards Mabel Despair: 'Would you like to borrow my magazine?'

Muni Multani day-dreamed. His day-dreams were always vivid, his night ones non-existent. He stretched long legs clad in carefully unobtrusive trousers. A rich, dark suit, its status aspect unappreciated by his fellow Indians. Their sense of men's wear he deprecated, secure in his painstakingly acquired knowledge of the elusive snobbishness of texture and dyes.

In his day-dream he manufactured the semblance of the man that he was to meet, for which attendance at the Congress was an excuse. The face of this person was, he had been told, round and jolly; he laughed a lot, was partial to blonde secre-taries, and had money salted away in a numbered account in Switzerland . . .

Seeing Chundra Das at the airport had given Multani a jolt, as he literally said to himself, for Multani, like many Indians of his English education, employed the English clichés of his col-lege days, still the currency of verbal communication at the Gymkhana Club in New Delhi. 'You gave me quite a jolt' and 'By Jove' covered his wife's more colloquial lapses; she, poor thing, still murmured: 'You didn't wish me yesterday' in a strong sing-song, instead of saying—well, thought Multani, perplexed, what did one say to a person who hadn't acknowledged your presence?

Of course, Chundra Das would be at the Congress representing the Other side. 'I must keep cool, calm, and collected,' Multani told himself, as he had been told by his father when he had taken the Cambridge School Certificate examination thirty years ago. Multani's stringently drawn features had a tendency to become bedimmed in a light, porous sweat when excited, but the automatic repetition of the three Cs induced in him a feeling of reassurance. He felt fourteen once again, come out top of the class, his father's proud hand on his shoulder...

In his day-dream he was shaking hands with the round, jolly fellow, saying the appropriate words, then sitting back, savouring what ensued, knowing that he, Multani, had been chosen for this delicate job...

The seat in front of him threw itself back. Multani angrily gave it a push. The occupant, who had pressed the release button too quickly, turned round. She had a hat on, and only tourists wear hats in South-East Asia. 'I'm so sorry,' she said, in a high, arrogant voice, 'd'you mind?'

Multani was immediately squashed. It was the voice, the accent, which had bemused and conquered his youth. The English voice, the tone of complete self-assurance. He answered: 'Not at all. It's quite all right.' And found that the 'r' of 'right' didn't sound right, in spite of all the years abroad.

But the other side of him, the Asian side, the one he called 'the revolutionary' (it made his American friends laugh), was angry as it had not been for a long time. It's always the women. The bitches. Well, *he* knew how to deal with them.

At the Suprême Hotel d'Angkor a stiff new red carpet was being rolled from the main door to end at the entrance of the larger one of the two dining-rooms. The manager, Monsieur Paulet, supervised the rolling. His Serene Highness Prince Sihanouk, ruler of Cambodia, was giving a dinner at the Suprême to a visiting Chinese trade delegation. The carpet would be needed again for dinner with an American delegation the following night. For Cambodia, a neutralist country, deftly balanced by her intelligent ruler between antagonist powers, positive non-alignment was sensible. It implied no pandering to either side, but a realistic appreciation of the facts of international politics. Whoever wanted to help was welcome, but no strings, no commitments to become missile sites for other people's bombs. If one side hinted that Aid would only be given if ... there was always the Other side, ready to help without strings. This cut the Gordian knot of economic blackmail and military bullying. The only really free enterprise left in the world was this economic competition for the goodwill of the uncommitted, the neutral, the non-aligned, a turning of the tables by the small and the weak on hectoring Great Powers. 'I do what is best for my country and my people,' said Prince Sihanouk, 'with me they come first.' Those who found themselves unable to use the loans called Aid to buy themselves another war base or satellite were angry with Cambodia and with its Chief of State, Sihanouk.

'It's a funny crowd of tourists,' said Captain Lederer, surveying the travellers waiting to be registered. It was ten degrees cooler here than in Bangkok, a dry, luminous sun, the sparkling ease of a country where nobody worries about the cold war. Already Lederer felt his tenseness go. But he knew that he could not endure a paradisial unconcern: he needed war, if only with himself.

'It's the Congress.'

'Congress?'

'You were drunk last night,' said the radio man. 'They told you at the Bangkok office. There is a Congress of Writers here, that's why the crowd looks different. Pen-pushers.'

'Your blonde,' said the co-pilot, 'is she a writer?'

'Pillow books,' said the radio man.

'Merde,' said Captain Lederer. 'Keep your wit for your own chicks.' He looked across the hall. Sheila sat between a dignified, ascetic-looking man with bright, sunken brown eyes, and a tall, elegant woman who wore a sleek dress with sprays of large red roses, and a picture hat with a rose on it.

Sheila walked across the room. 'Perhaps you'd like to meet my father, and my stepmother?'

Lederer followed her, aware of his muscles tensing, yet also aware that it was ridiculous to be aggressive about meeting the father of a girl he had slept with.

'My father, Charles Manley,' Sheila said, 'and this is Eliza

Crawfurd, Mrs Manley. Captain Lederer.'

She slumped back in her chair. Lederer disliked Charles Manley and his wife on sight, an elating antagonism. They surveyed him with polite scrutiny, as if to them he was a superior servant.

'How long are you staying here, m'sieur, 'dame?' he asked, suavely impertinent.

'Dear, dear,' replied the woman, in a quick, silvery, arrogant voice, '*everyone* asks us the *same* question.' She inclined her head to one side, purposefully guileless brown eyes upon him. She had a thick gold bangle high up one arm, twenty-four carat, heavy, chic. Lederer wanted to pull the hat's brim over her face.

'It's the custom to ask this question, madame. People remain here two, at most four days.' He pointed to the tourists at the reception desk. 'It is nine-forty a.m. By ten the tourists are in their rooms. At ten-thirty they file down again. A bus is waiting. Pause while they photograph the hotel. They are driven to the ruins, beginning with Angkor Vat, the big temple. The guide lectures. The tourists stand, far enough to take a good snap. They all carry at least one camera, sometimes two and a cine-camera. With that load one perspires easily. The Cambodians know it and have placed chairs and tables under a tree on the roadside. The tourists sit, are given Coca-Cola in big glasses with ice cubes. All drink, many worry about germs, ask if the glasses are clean and the ice sterile. They walk into Angkor Vat, following the guide. Then on the bus to the next stop, the Bayon. Under a tree are tables, chairs, Coca-Cola. They drink Coca-Cola, take snapshots while the guide lectures on the many faces of the Bayon. Then on, to the Terrace of the Elephants. The Leper King. And so on.' He snapped his fingers. 'Two days, you have finished Angkor. Tick it off your list. Another Asian culture done.'

The woman laughed, a blend of trill and ripple which made François Lederer feel savage. 'Fortunately we're not in a hurry, Captain Lederer. My husband is an expert on undeveloped countries. We shall be here two weeks.'

'For the Congress?' said Captain Lederer. 'A most important Congress, I believe.'

'I'm not quite sure,' said Charles. 'A Neutralist Writers' Congress sounds rather odd. I'd like to attend. It might help me to understand Cambodian politics, although it doesn't quite come within my scope of research.'

'Everything is politics,' said Lederer cheerfully, 'especially literature. You must be *very* interested, monsieur, otherwise you would not have come. All the writers are to pay their own expenses. Most unusual.'

Charles stiffened. 'I represent an International Organization.'

'Ah,' said Lederer, 'they pay well, I'm told.'

'Sheila, my sweet,' warbled Eliza, 'do go and ask the chap at the desk whether our rooms are ready, will you?'

The girl walked away, her back straight.

'Excuse me,' said the captain, 'I regret that I must leave you.'

'Good-bye, Captain Lederer. We'll be seeing you, I suppose,' said Eliza.

'Almost certainly,' replied Lederer.

Sheila was at the counter, writing her name. 'Sheila Manley,' she wrote, 'age twenty-one.'

Lederer said to her: 'Thank you for presenting me to your father. Shall I see you at lunch? Or after? I shall be in my room this afternoon. I fly from here to Phnom Penh at four p.m.' He managed to produce an aura, an exudation of contained passion. He'd háve her again, and the hatted woman too. That would teach Monsieur Manley a lesson. A bourgeois like him needed to have his wife and daughter seduced.

'I'll come,' she said, 'after lunch. If you really want me to.'

Her humility shocked him, like a slap. Again he felt ashamed. He saw that she peeled the base of her right thumb, a small girl picking her nails; the skin was off, she plucked at the raw area with the fingers of her left hand. And he wanted to kiss the wound she thus maintained. But he said to himself: 'Merde,' and turned away.

Gion saw his door open, framed in its emptied oblong stood the blonde girl of the plane.

'Oh,' she said. 'Sorry. Wrong room.'

'Thirty-four.'

'I got mixed up.'

'It is confusing.' What a poor liar she was. He stood, hands on his suitcase, expecting her to go away, yet like all people newly arrived at a hotel, lonely in an environment not made his own by strewn personal belongings and the ritual gesture of bed and chair and bathroom, hoping she would linger. 'Staying long in Angkor?'

'Two weeks. Because of my father. He's attending the Congress.'

'So am I.'

'Are you a writer?' She leaned against the door jamb. 'You don't look like one. You're too handsome.'

Pleased, he tried not to be. 'Do sit down for a minute. One's rather lost at first if one doesn't know anybody.' He said it to put her at ease, indicating the french windows open upon the balcony, giving on to a road ribboning between trees, sunlit open spaces to guarantee his non-intentioned affability. 'Would you like a drink?'

'No thanks.' She sat down, and he turned back to his suitcase, half regretting his impulse. Would she chatter, when all he wanted was a presence while he unpacked?

'I was wondering...?'

'What I did?'

'Not only that. What are you? Which country? It's getting so difficult to know these days. I can't tell people's nationalities any more.'

'I am,' he said, trying not to sound theatrical, 'of that new company of airborne and rootless travellers who go round the world, and get paid for writing about it.'

'Oh,' she said, 'a journalist.'

He did not correct her. 'What about you?'

'Me?' She swung her foot. 'I'm nothing. I belong nowhere. I wish I did. Wish I could attach myself, somewhere. But I can't. I was at school in Switzerland, married in New York, got a divorce in Reno like everyone else, and now I'm travelling with my father and his wife. My father is Charles Manley, and he studies under-developed countries, and gets awfully well paid for it. I'm travelling with him because I've had a nervous breakdown and been psychoanalysed and travel was recommended. Charles is taking me round, and Eliza Crawfurd is taking him round. Or so she tells people. Though it isn't true.

My father came because he wanted to. He can do what he likes, you know, so long as he writes a report about it. Daddy's very clever, of course.'

'Who's Eliza Crawfurd?' asked Gion, amused by her candour, startled by the switch of words, Charles, father, daddy. He opened a drawer, laid his shirts in it, closed it, opened the cupboard, started to hang his suits. He always carried portable hangers because even the best hotels lacked a sufficiency. As he smoothed the cloth, making the coat shoulders fit the plastic curve, he suddenly saw himself. How organized he had become, how meticulous about trivia. He spared himself, not giving wildly any more, even in generous moments finding a reasonable argument for giving; careful of his emotions, holding on to the non-attachment he had achieved. It was security, to know oneself not easily moved. One felt on a pinnacle, watching the flood sweep its corpses by. One could, of course, do a lot to help others, because one's mind kept its clear remoteness. He watched himself and also the girl, watched her with replete detachment as he would a spider or an animal, caged in its own life, to be looked at, not to be intervened with in any way. That was the main thing, not by untoward action to disturb others. He would not move a finger towards her, but neither would he hurt her. This would be a pleasant, shallow meeting, with its slight, gay comfort. If she was in trouble she might tell him, and he might help, because her telling would be an indication for action; but afterwards he would withdraw, non-involved.

He could see himself hanging his clothes, the blonde girl in the armchair, in the Cambodian hotel room, and it was trivial yet portentous, insipid but with a will of its own, a beginning.

'What are you smiling at?' said the girl. 'Is it funny that Eliza should be my stepmother? Actually my own mother was her sister. Eliza hated her, and I hate Eliza.'

'Oh.' Gion was nonplussed. What could he say? 'I've never heard the name of your stepmother, Eliza Crawfurd, I'm afraid.'

'She's the famous fashion correspondent for *Mascara*. Created the Genuine Oriental Look in clothes. Daddy is brilliant but academic, nobody knows him because nobody bothers about academic people, they're not News. But lots of people know Eliza. She's the face that launches a hundred thousand tourists into the right clothes every year. Daddy's here for research, and Eliza to catch the antique, exciting essence of Angkor. We were in Bangkok ten days catching Siamese sauvity. There's a photographer coming too. Peter. He's pansy. He adores Eliza.'

'And what do *you* do?'

'Nothing. I *believe* in wasting time. And ruining my life, as *they* tell me I do. But I hate Eliza——' with that flashing, raucous candour of hers Gion was beginning to like so well— 'hate hate hate her. And she hates me too.'

'You say "hate" so positively,' said Gion, removing his ties off the bed and laying them in a drawer in some silk paper brought with him.

'Do I?' She opened her eyes, which she had shut on the last word 'hate'. 'I like talking to you. Usually I don't like to talk to the men I meet. I only make love with them.'

Gion remained unsurprised, knowing her intent to shock, wondering why he suddenly had the feeling that she would say exactly what she had said a second before she said it. How lonely she was, as lonely as anyone so young could be.

'You're lonely, that's why.'

'That's why what?'

'Why you do as you say. Make sex. Call it love. Or think you do.'

'Why,' she said, 'what else is there in life? I ask you, what the hell is it all about? I'd like you to tell me. You're a writer. Even the best writers nowadays find nothing but boredom to write about.'

'I don't know what life is,' he said. 'That's why I write, to try to find out. At least, to pretend I do. It gives me a countenance.'

'And what d'you write for now?' she flashed at him.

He replied: 'I don't know. I thought I did, but I don't know any more. Perhaps I've stopped asking myself.'

Yes, he thought, suddenly gone into the far-away mood of writers, who forget their surroundings, drop them with automatic unremembered gesture like a glove or a book on a familiar table, I don't know what life is about, I've never known; at one time it seemed important to find out. Every book I wrote would be, I thought, a discovery of what life was about. I was on the verge of an answer, every time. And then the answer became a non-answer, the urge to find out lessened. I had money. Money is wonderful, but it's also terrible because it gives one freedom, and freedom means no more questions to someone like me, because I have nowhere to give myself ... I can travel, do what I like. Whatever I write, I sell. But this freedom which I now have, and which is due to money, has made me more careful than when I had no money, for if I ask too many questions I might turn out, like Chundra Das, to be labelled 'political' and lose my public.

So now Gion wrote the kind of light, glib story that needed travel to bring his backgrounds and people to him. He made money, and did not remain riveted to one place, one city, one atmosphere, one kind of people. He need not become, as he saw so many become, provincial, knowing the rest of the world only at second-hand, tossed by TV-controlled emotions whose lifespan endured a week at the most. He knew all the faces of truth about Tibet, Suez, the Congo, and chose not to take any side. For whatever happened, time dulled the indignation, muffled the throb, the event slid into its allotted slot, where it became accepted past. Few writers really bothered to *understand*, to find out what exactly happened, and why, Gion knew, because he travelled, but refrained from acting upon his knowledge. He felt pleased at having escaped, through money, the worm's eye view, the immediate assault of indignation, but at the same time he had missed participating in the event, proclaiming a stand, giving his own judgment. The flood had passed him by, and he had turned away from the corpses. And yet, had he escaped?

You've escaped a good many absurdities, a good many attitudes of the moment, but somewhere, somehow, haven't you also left something undone?

'The only freedom left,' he said, sardonic, 'is to be able to get away from it all.'

'That's what I said,' she replied. 'You don't believe in anything, so what is left for you, I wonder? Sex too, like me? Or boredom and frustration, like some make a kind of end to end all of? Or Zen? Or what?'

'I don't know. It isn't sex. I don't believe you can just isolate sex, or boredom, or anything. From the general context, the whole personality, the environment, I mean. It's true some people tend to refugee themselves into sex, because it's possibly the most intimate thing about the human being.'

'Intimate my eye. Isn't sex really the best way of not having to face up to knowing people? You don't have to talk when you make love. You don't even have to pretend that you *like* each other. It's so easy to tell, when its over, that you really loathe each other, isn't it? It's so easy to get up and go.'

'Perhaps.'

'Sex is really the most unprivate fragment of what we are, don't you think?'

'I suppose so.' How quickly she's got me down to an essential stripping, to discussing Being itself. I don't even know her name. I feel we might casually lie down together now to test her assertions. It's a challenge she is throwing at me. But I'm not going to take it up.

'Bed, the great resolver,' she said. 'Doesn't give an answer, only holds back a lot of questions, so it looks like an answer.'

'But can't you ask the questions, even in bed?'

'No. Somehow it's more shameful to ask questions than to flee together into dreamland,' she said, suddenly sounding flat, trivial, a child tired of a long story. 'And then, when it's over, they go away from you, recoil as if you were a leper. I'll know when a man really loves me. When it won't happen that way. That's why, you see.'

'I don't see.'

'I don't see,' she mimicked. 'Haven't they told you I'm a nymphomaniac?'

'You may be,' said Gion. 'We in Asia aren't as preoccupied about sex, don't work ourselves up into an absorbing interest in it, because we've got so much else to worry about. Survival. Hunger. Economic problems. Disease. Illiteracy. Social change. We need the assurance of the next meal, not the distraction of the next coitus. We don't need to find ourselves alive in the sex act, because our bowels gripe, tell us we're hungry and alive. So we have Revolution in the air we breathe, rather than Intercourse to kill time.'

'Nobody's going to read you in the West if you write about Asian Revolution,' she said, dogmatic. He was so detached, shutting the cupboard, storing the suitcase under the bed ...

this excruciating neatnesss of his irritated her with a sense of familiarity, as if they had been married a long time. 'At least, not where I come from. Where I come from we're mortally afraid of Revolution. We're frantically worried about Asians and Africans getting up and demanding the things we have, so we always call it Communism and become all moralistic about violence, only to put off the evil day when we'll have to share, equal to equal. Bored with revolution, or we pretend we're bored, we don't want to hear about poverty, hunger ... we can always give money to buy a child back from hunger, can't we? Haven't you seen our best magazines carry these items? "Buy a child, buy a baby——" Korean or Vietnamese or even on the moon, so long as it's well away from us? And we haven't got love or passion any more, because we read about it, see it on TV, know it by words before we feel it; we've only got boredom. A Big Nothing. Take me. I'm a case. I've done everything, everything. Whenever I tried to find out what something really meant, to *me*, I found it in a book, written up, analysed, mashed for me into a pulp of words. So then I had to start again, trying to find what is really *me*. I'm not like Eliza. Eliza doesn't feel anything unless she's read it somewhere first, and doesn't think it nice to feel or know anything that isn't written down in a woman's magazine. I want to feel it first, and words destroy it for me. That's why I want to know: what is really true? What do *you* live for? Do you know?'

'I don't know,' said Gion. He thought: this is the question of all the young of today, in Poland as well as in England. It hasn't reached us in Asia, for most of us know only that we must live to secure tomorrow's rice, and that seems to be the answer. Afterwards, we shall see. But as for myself, I too have been deprived of the answer by affluence. And so I too am tempted, like a child, to end this unbearable question in her arms and bed for the usual fray of endocrines. How curious, he thought, detachedly. This talk is a prelude, alerting me in spite of myself, making me want her ... The ultimate contact, or is it the escape from contact through intimacy? For a moment he had an absurd vision of a cocktail party in the year 2000, when it would be good form for the guests to rub each other's exposed privates, while their faces were carefully shielded by masks.

'Shall we have a drink?'

Ordering a drink was the next gesture of the ritual of escape, of hiding the face while uncovering one's lower parts without the shame of nakedness, impropriety excused since the mind could plead alcohol to cavort away from the body's function. She was right. Sex was the only safe subject.

'I don't know whether they have drinks at this hour,' he added, pressing the bell button. He would drive with her to the edge of whatever abyss she wanted to fall into, but he would not fall.

'It's always drinks,' she said, 'but I will.'

He ordered a brandy bottle from the Cambodian waiter, and knew all newness drained beforehand, the scene in front of him already withered. That was how it was with her, and she had succeeded in conveying it to him: the pre-knowledge of meaninglessness. She knew all the off-gestures, all leading straight, as she had said, to the same enactment, abysmal like a yawn.

They sipped, knowing in their acceptance of all that had succumbed to her harsh truth the moment reduced to its own unsubstantial shadow, the comfort of having nothing to say; warriors resting, day already done.

Then he could look at her and see her as she was, a lanky graceful girl with blue blue eyes, a Siamese cat's eyes, because at times she appeared to squint very slightly. And in her very youth a timeless disorder, compelling the mind to similar disarray. And she looked at him and saw him as he was, an ordinary man, middle-aged, slim, not unattractive, not pleated with the wrinkles of self-importance; a little younger-looking than his age, a little desiccated with self-containment, not trying to be strong, or masculine, or anything but what he was; as lost in his composure, in his meticulous self-possession as she was in her search for something that she called herself and which eluded her.

'What are we going to do?'

'There is one thing we can do.'

She looked up as he rose, expecting the usual things that are to do about a face and neck, already discouraged, yet willing to try once again.

'You and I,' he said, 'will take a taxi and go to Angkor Vat.

I want to look at some of the carvings there. With you. And then...'

'And then what?'

'Then I'll bring you back for lunch.'

Relieved, outraged that he should have circumvented her, she found another shocking thing to say. 'I can't lunch with you. I've got an appointment. And after that, another one with Captain Lederer. He wants me to sleep with him again this afternoon.'

Gion did not reply. He took her hand, walking with her to the door. Hand in hand they walked down the stairs into the waiting hall, past the reception desk.

She had walked into his room, into his care. Now he had to take her need in his hands. Years of carefulness gone, in a moment. He heard the duologue of himself. One voice saying: 'Are you prepared to get entangled?' The other: 'Pretty girl, perhaps you can——' The first: 'You bloody liar.' The second: 'Am I my sister's keeper?' No, yes, no, yes ... the voices shouted, drowning each other out, as he entered the taxi after her. God knows what will happen, he thought, except that I don't believe in a god.

He lay back into waiting: I shall take her to Angkor. I won't push anything. But do not let her ask too much of me, for I do not want to hurt her, and I do not want to be hurt. But this also was not quite true, nothing was really true, nothing was truly real, except to sit quietly waiting for what was to come.

Muni Multani slammed down the room telephone, opened the door, hurtled downstairs to the reception hall.

For ten minutes he had tried to telephone Bud Kilton, whom he had been told in Bangkok to get in touch with 'speediest'. He had met Kilton once before. It made things more plausible. A rigorous appearance of the coincidental, a reassuringly normal behaviour, was important.

Never go out of your way to do things. Always appear casual. All serious business was transacted over drinks at a bar, lunch or dinner; most important business was always murmured in a rowdy cocktail affair with lots of strangers invited, ignorant of what was going on, their hoarse laughter covering the whispers.

He descended, fuming visibly (the pearly dim sweat upon his fine brown skin that gave him a bronze, oiled statue appearance, and enhanced his hawklike profile), upon Mr Lee, the receptionist-clerk-secretary.

Mr Lee Souvan was Chinese, assimilated Cambodian, completely assimilated as are many in Cambodia. His name had been Khmerized,* his daughter had married a Khmer, his sons spoke fluent French, Khmer, Siamese, Malay, and English. He himself spoke seven languages and owned three houses and two wives, his Number One being Officer in Charge of a regiment of Royal Socialist Youth (Female). Mr Lee was on call for everything at the Suprême much of the day and night. His face was moonlike, he smiled a dazzling row of teeth as if handing Multani an ivory chair.

'You desire, monsieur?'

'The telephone in my room doesn't work. I had to come down to make this call. I want Mr Kilton, who is registered at Siemreap 299, please.'

Mr Lee seized the telephone and spoke into it in Khmer, handed Multani the receiver. 'Here, monsieur, is your friend.'

'Allô, allô,' said a voice. 'La Conservation. J'écoute.'

Multani said: 'Idiot. Get me the manager. I wish to see the manager immediately.'

'All at once, monsieur,' said Lee Souvan. He undulated to a door with the word Manager written upon it. Out came Monsieur Paulet, satisfied with the red-carpet rehearsal.

Multani explained: 'I want to telephone to Mr Kilton, telephone 299 Siemreap.'

Paulet turned to Lee Souvan: 'Alors, Lee Souvan, qu'est-ce qui arrive?'

Lee Souvan muttered something in French to Monsieur Paulet, whose brows suddenly met, then parted company.

'Monsieur,' he said, with hauteur, to Multani, 'is it the telephone you want, or the gentleman?'

'I want to speak to Mr Bud Kilton,' said Multani, 'and all I get is some lingo I don't understand.'

Monsieur Paulet drew himself up to reach the top of Multani's shoulder. 'Monsieur, in the Kingdom of Cambodia, due to

* Khmer—Cambodian

38

the high vision of its leader Prince Sihanouk, even our telephone operators are efficient. The lady at the switchboard, sensing you wanted Mr Kilton, and not his telephone, has put you through to him where he is now, which is not at his home but at the Museum.'

'Conservation,' said Mr Lee tactfully, 'the French school for the restoration of the monuments. The Museum.'

Monsieur Paulet departed, and Multani, a little abashed, took the receiver from Mr Lee. 'Hallo,' he said, 'is that you, Kilton?'

'Monsieur Kilton? Un moment,' said a voice at the other end, and then Multani heard Kilton's voice:

'Bud Kilton speaking, friendship motivation plus.'

'Bud Kilton——' said Multani (what should he say, having seen Kilton only once?), 'how are you, Bud? Long time no see. This is Multani, Muni Multani. You know. Just in from Bangkok.'

I hope he gets the drift, hope they warned him beforehand.

'Who? Who's that? I can't quite——' began Kilton.

'I'm a great friend of Sanger,' said Multani rapidly. 'You'll remember Sanger, we were together. Dear old K.P.,' said Multani, hoping the code signal of K.P. had been clear enough.

'Why, sure, sure, why ... yeah, I get it. Saludo, what do you know, dear old Modegni!'

'Multani, my name's Muni——'

'Why, sure, sure. Magnani. Of course. Sorry, friend, couldn't catch your name at first, this phone. I'll be right round, as soon as I've finished over here. You at the Suprême?'

'I cabled,' said Multani, with a sinking feeling that Kilton wasn't at all in the know. 'From Bangkok, yesterday.'

'Get here tomorrow,' replied Bud. 'You know how things are. I'll be right over.'

Multani replaced the receiver, suddenly doubted that he would recognize Kilton. Glancing round, he saw Chundra Das studying tourist objects in a glass case: silver ash trays, ivory paper cutters with carved handles, plaster figures of Cambodian dancers, silk *sampots*, the Cambodian skirts. 'Spy,' muttered Multani, loud enough for Chundra to hear, and sat in an armchair at a table strewn with magazines. Unfortunately they were all either in Khmer or in French. All at once the edifice of stratagems, the reasons for his coming to the Congress of Writers, appeared, in the tranquil hotel, with the cheerful voices of the taxi-chauffeurs and *samlo*-pedallers spurting laughter from outside, ludicrous idiocy. Here was another world, in which the sun outside was light and warmth, the sky contained clouds and a child's kite, and there was a lack of tension, of impending danger, which vaguely irritated Multani. He looked sourly upon the waiters with their happy-go-lucky leisureliness, the Cambodian sales-girl in the tourist shop chatting and laughing. Here were no military preparations, no planes tearing the air, no dramatic headlines, no alarm prepared and planned to keep the nerves on edge, producing terrorizing noises to give a semblance of rationality to what might otherwise be known as madness. His nerves, no longer pitched to apprehension, now left his body unstrung, uncomfortable, as if someone had played a joke on him and an invisible audience was laughing at him, Muni Multani. What he had come to do, which had seemed so vital, a dangerous mission, a mission to preserve peace, in this tangible peace became absurd. And if this feeling was true, then Multani's actions became meaningless, his speeches were gibberish, the whole purpose of his life one stupid mistake.

This peace is a delusion. This country's neutrality is dangerous to us. We must save Cambodia, in spite of herself.

Multani saw Kilton before the latter saw him. He did not realize, until the heavy figure darkened the sunlit doorway, that he remembered Bud Kilton. A square face, an overlap of jowls, a buffer of joviality carried like excess luggage, an uneasy man.

Kilton walked in, with furrowed brow and a large smile, as if the upper and lower portions of his face were unrelated. Multani waved a magazine.

'Well, well,' said Kilton, 'if it isn't my old friend Magnani? Say, I never knew you went in for Italian silk suits.'

'My last book sold rather well,' said Multani modestly. 'They bought it for the series *What You Should Know About Communism*. I thought I'd come for this Congress. Sounded interesting.'

'You bet it is,' said Kilton loudly and heartily. 'Everything's fascinating here. I love it. Just LOVE it. Shall we have a drink?' He looked round, perceived Chundra Das and Mabel Despair chatting with Mr Lee, lowered his voice. 'Probably tomorrow night. A taxi will pick you up here. Comprenez?'

'Righto. Well, how are things?'

Kilton gave his push-button open and shut smile, which convinced people until they caught themselves doing it. 'Fine, fine. God-wise we've made big strides. We'll have real conversions any day now. *Any day*. Religious-culture-wise I'm starting a million-dollar campaign for books in the Khmer language. "In every hut a Bible." That's our motto. Say, that was smart, catching me at the Conservation.'

'The operator kept putting me through. I thought it was the wrong number.'

Kilton's upper face corrugated more deeply, while the hilarity of the lower structures increased. 'Smart, those girls.' He lowered his voice. 'Keeping tabs on everybody. Can't move without someone reporting. Always following me round. Not only the Khmers, but also the French. They hate us, the French. All the French businessmen out of South Vietnam pouring in here now. Whenever they can, they try to do us down. And they're supposed to be our allies. This country's neutral, you know. That means everyone can come in. Can't start anything without someone or other getting to know it and throwing a spanner in the works.'

'Pretty tough.'

'That's why we've *got* to rock the boat,' said Kilton. 'This neutrality business is immoral, like someone said a while back. Got to fix things up so they'll do it *our* way. The democratic way. We're on the spot. *We* know the score better than those guys up in the State Department. They're beginning to go soft. Beginning to think there's all kinds of neutrality. And that'll be the end of *us* in South-East Asia if we go soft.' Kilton hunched in an Atlas shrug, preparing his shoulders for a worldsize load. 'The guys here figure they've got something on me.'

'I hope not.'

'Not what you think. That's O.K. I'm experienced. Got to be, out here. Everybody smiling and sweet, then, zoop, they let you have it. Never trust anyone, especially not waiters. Say, boy, you're learning pretty fast,' he told the Khmer waiter benevolently as the latter, without being called, came up with another drink and removed his empty glass.

'You always take three in the morning, monsieur,' the waiter told him in French.

'See what I mean?' said Kilton. 'Notice everything. Now someone's got me in a jam, or so he thinks. Personal, strictly personal.'

'Can I help?' Multani exuded brown glitter to suggest sympathy.

'Forget it, friend. A snag. Thing I got to face, thanks.'

Multani said: 'You're highly thought of, I know that.'

'Good to hear it. I get my hardship allowance, of course, but money isn't everything. By the way, I've got something I'd like you to take care of, something personal. Keep it with you, don't leave it lying around, until I can get it processed. Will you?' He got to his feet, waved his hand in a ta-ta child gesture. 'Will be seeing you.'

Left alone, Multani looked at his Bulova watch. He walked to the reception desk and took his key. All the keys were laid out in a neat row on the reception desk. He would unpack, shower, change. After lunch he'd go sightseeing, take pictures. He tried humming lightly as he went up the stairs, feeling his leg muscles work, arching his instep. Something personal, Bud said. He could guess. Those ex-missionaries always were collectors. And managed to smuggle the loot out pretty well.

Eliza Crawfurd rested, little pads of cotton-wool soaked in lotion upon her eyelids. She stretched her arms as far up as they would go. At forty she was agile, slim, graceful.

'Ageless,' Peter Anstey said. The word enhanced the satisfactory endurance of her skin and flesh. 'Ageless.' She whispered the word. It felt like petals touching her lips.

Regular exercise, massage, massively nourishing creams, conserve efficiently, but the best youth preserver is admiration. For lunch she would wear the pale blue Siamese silk suit with shoes to match, and a Bali silver necklace. The hat with the rose, the roses on the Swiss cotton dress, had been right for the morning, gay, *prime-sautier*. After lunch and a small siesta she would wear the pale olive skirt, pencil straight, with the Italian silk jersey, an off-beige which picked up the pinks and mauves of sunset. Then she would shop for the local silks. Both she and Charles had declined to join the morning sight-seeing tour, Charles because he said he wanted to unpack, and Eliza because her beauty routine was stern discipline, not to be departed from.

Eliza went to the mirror, examined herself, and started kneading and pounding her hips at their vulnerable middle third. Then she slapped her hands on the floor, up and down, a dozen times, and feeling tautened lay down again to get the slight swelling induced by air travel out of her ankles.

Eliza had been tossed into fame by a blanket in Mexico. It was Peter Anstey, the Photographer, who at that time worked for *Classic*, the man's magazine, who gave her the idea of a personal column on fashion for tourists. The 'Eliza Crawfurd look' was a feature of both *Classic* and *Mascara*, its female counterpart; it had made *Classic* the most eagerly sought after man's magazine in all the world airports, not only by men, but also by their wives. In Mexico Eliza had draped a *huipil* about her shoulders, Peter had snapped a picture, together they had provided the paragraph:

'*De rigueur* for a visit to the picturesque bazaars, the traditional *huipil*, here worn by Eliza Crawfurd (wife of the well-known economist, Charles Manley). Thrown carelessly over one shoulder, drawn over your coiffure as a hood, trailing in the golden dust of this glamorous city, woven by hands trained in centuries of craftsmanship, you will glow with new confidence, sightsee with the calm assurance that you *are* at your best, looking your best, ready for the best . . .'

The series had caught on: *cholis* of India, wafer-thin sandals with upturned toes of Karachi, *mumus* from Fiji, wearing silver anklets astride an elephant in Nepal, '*de rigueur* for a tiger hunt with the Maharajah of Tipoor'.

Peter Anstey, the photographer, who had prospered through this collaboration, had recorded an international parade of wigs in Tokyo, was flying in from Hong Kong, and would be in Angkor in a few hours to do with Eliza a series: *What to Wear in Cambodia*.

In these stampede days of universal automatic tourism, cosmopolitan hair-dos, heels and lip sheen, like airports, dispense a dreary uniformity. It was genius to resurrect a mummy for its head-gear, ransack a temple for a skirt. This piracy of the past induced in those whose affluence was infected with a sense of inadequacy the thrill of communication with esoteric cults and exotic cultures. The tourist paid to acquire without hardship the feeling of being one with exhumed Beauty and Art through the medium of a Greek scarf, a Babylonian shoe, an Ethiopian belt, a weave, a pattern, a shade preciously different.

The Peter Anstey–Eliza Crawfurd combination would now explore the fashion resources of Cambodia, while Charles pottered about with the Congress and his researches on under-development. Originally Eliza had planned to go to Saigon. But Saigon was a wee bit tiresome: bombs at odd corners, no one could get out of the city; the countryside overrun by guerrillas, and everyone said the best troops were kept to protect the President's life. There wasn't much will to fight the communists and even on the airport one could hear the rattle of machine-guns from the guerrillas. Eliza had decided to accompany Charles to Cambodia instead. Though she had heard that Cambodia wasn't democratic; it was neutral, and someone in Bangkok had told her that being neutral was being Red. She had expected the usual paraphernalia of war-to-come. But there were no planes and no soldiers around. In fact, nothing more exciting than a dinner tonight with some Chinese trade delegation or other.

It might be fun to see the Prince at dinner tonight. I'll wear the silver-grey frock.

Charles had been rather nervy lately, due to that wretched child of his. Eliza had long ago decided to stay detached from that relationship. Too emotional. Emotion produced wrinkles on one's face and neck, the neck even more revelatory of emotional indiscretions. It had been so with Jacqueline, Eliza's sister, whom Eliza adored with deep, fervent hatred. Jacqueline and Eliza had both been models, Jacqueline successfully, and for three years Eliza's rack had been pictures of her sister on the cover of fashion monthlies. The day had come when Jacqueline could only be photographed for lingerie and underwear. 'My legs are still good,' she had said. Her face had begun to show the wear of feeling, corroding the imbecile perfection of a model's face. Only the very young can afford to weep, smile, and yet maintain features the better for the squall. After a time the skin, the muscles beneath, show the marks of a responding spirit, and that takes you off the first-class covers. Came the day when Jacqueline's legs could no longer be used for stocking ads. Then silly Charles married her, thinking he was in love with her. Jacqueline, still beautiful enough, was now started on pre-lunch dry martinis, and gin is poison to the complexion, expecially the round-the-nose pores which just beg to start dilating. The child, Sheila, Jacqueline's daughter. The other men, the drunkenness. The divorce. Jacqueline taking sleeping tablets, killing herself ... and Charles had married Eliza. Eliza, by then, had learnt to guard herself against love, and conquered the fashion world instead, having watched Jacqueline long enough to know what not to do: to eschew not only gin, but also passion, and the dangerous grace and favour of love clawing away at one's features.

Charles and Eliza's marriage had been a sensible arrangement. Both he and Eliza earned money. Not that Charles wasn't well off, but there was that wretched child to provide for, and psychoanalysts were so expensive. What a good thing Charles and Eliza had separate accounts. Dear Charles. So satisfactory, but for this daughter of his.

Actually, if only Sheila could get herself married ... Charles couldn't really bear to part from her. He was absurd in his love for his daughter. Sheila should be settling down, instead of trying everything from beatniks to Bedouins and nervous breakdowns. Now Charles had insisted on taking her along on this trip, though heaven knows he couldn't control her in the least, she was always getting into other people's beds. What a good thing people didn't associate the girl with the beautiful, successful Eliza Crawfurd. Sheila was always up to something. Like her mother, Jacqueline ...

Eliza sighed, patted cream on her face, gently round the eyes, briskly on chin and jaw. She was sure the captain—what was his name? Lederer?—had slept with Sheila. Foolish girl, ruining herself. And Charles let her. So long as she called him Daddy, threw her arms about his neck ... Sometimes, though, he got quite angry; then he would walk and walk, up and down, in his room ... But Eliza was not going to worry. What was it that delightful maharajah had told her in Calcutta (terrible, ugly place, Calcutta, so many filthy, wretched people in rags, lying about, not even *trying* to smile, not *at all* interested in Beauty)? 'Madame, you must always think beautiful, noble thoughts. That is the Secret of Eternal Youth.'

After scented almond oil on her shoulders came her underwear, a pale blue caress to harmonize with the Siamese silk suit. Shoes, sheer stockings, then back to her face, rouge, the eyebrows with a brown pencil, hair by hair, cream powder, eye shadow, mascara, lipstick. She chose rings, a small choker of milky opals, not very good quality but so marvellous with the suit.

'You are indestructible, Eliza, because your *bones* are so lovely.' It was Peter Anstey, of course, who had said that. Trust a homo to have perception. Most men treated women as if they were steaks for immediate consumption, their compliments tainted with the drooling gusts of appetite. Dear Peter. He was an aesthete. Only homos really *know* women. If only Peter could bring himself to be a *little* normal. But he was so susceptible. Eliza had now developed an eye for the kind of young man Peter fell for. Sometimes dear Peter fell so hard that he spent more time taking pictures of his latest find than of Eliza. That of course was tiresome, especially when he took his latest love around *with* them.

She bent to smile at the dressed total face in the mirror, twisted to admire her waist, her body supple; no one would think her forty. Peter would photograph her in front of the temples of Angkor, stepping down from a *samlo*, the three-wheeled vehicle, man-propelled, in use in Cambodia. The contrast between her poised elegance and the sweaty face of the man whose pedalling legs were the vehicle's engine, was the essence of the picture's appeal, subliminal fillip, fulfilling every woman's yearning for a triumphal trampling of something underfoot. Peter's fashion pictures were successful because they often carried this contrast: the beggar boy shoeshining Eliza's delicate brogue, the work-and-baby-worn dropsical Egyptian wife fingering a radiantly slim Eliza's skirt ... and every tourist, dressing docilely to Eliza's suggestions, buying the Eastern treasures of bags, shoes and stoles selected by Eliza Crawfurd's impeccable taste, felt beautiful and kind, like being at the smartest Charity Ball of the Season.

Someone knocked.

'Come in, Charles. I'm ready.'

But it was not Charles, who occupied the room next to hers (there were no communicating doors).

Eliza stared. 'You? You?'

'Yes, Eliza. How kind of you to recognize me. I want to talk to you.'

'Get out, go. I don't want to see you.'

'You want me to tell Charles, Eliza? About Jacqueline?'

'He won't believe you. It's too long ago.'

'Nothing is too long ago, Eliza. You know that.'

Then Eliza Crawfurd's face began to change for, in spite of discipline, at forty a face cannot withstand emotion as well as at twenty-five.

'It isn't anything difficult, Eliza. I just want to ask you to do me a small favour. For old times' sake.'

Charles Manley returned from his visit to Sheila's empty room, unlocked his suitcase, flung his clothes into drawers, hung two suits, placed his briefcase in the wardrobe, and clad in a shirt and twill trousers marched out into the sunlight.

He saw the tourist bus drive off, with its load of tourists going out for the morning circuit of some of the monuments. Sheila was not among them. He wanted to walk in the sun; wanted to get away from Sheila's empty room. Wanted to walk away the rankling pain in his chest when he thought of Sheila.

Sheila. He had seen the look of François Lederer upon her, her vacant look at him. How well he knew those eyes of hers. Another one, another ... Each time hell, so that he had to walk, walk, like a madman, until exhaustion took over, numbed the pain.

Oh, Sheila. My little girl.

She never guessed how he cared. How he had felt ever since she was fourteen, and had been found after three days' search in bed with this man of forty-five. One of Charles's colleagues. It had been hushed up. Then later, fifteen, sixteen, other men, more men, parties, psychoanalysis, one marriage, divorce, breakdown, more psychoanalysis.

Sheila, my little one, my darling ...

Powerless, he had watched her on this trip, in Cairo, in India, in Bangkok; the research tour he, Charles Manley, had undertaken on a grant, to study the fall in revenue of cash crops in under-developed countries in the last five years, with relation to the amount of Aid given to these countries, turned out a trail of beds for Sheila. Even hotel waiters.

Nodding over rows of rubber trees, trampling down young rice in paddy fields (with photographers present to snap pictures of him, the expert, as if immediately the rice crop would increase, the rubber flow more abundant, the ever-increasing gap between rich West and poor East suddenly disappear), Charles had heard nothing, felt nothing, except Sheila, Sheila...

God knows, he had tried, tried looking after her, tried; marrying Eliza had been part of this effort. No one could say that Eliza was beastly to Sheila. Not at all. Those were the years he had been busy, so much away. And then, all at once, everything seemed to go wrong with Sheila. Never a hint of anything, and then the old man of forty-five, and ever since ... how many?

'My dear Charles, your daughter is Jacqueline's daughter. Need I say more?' Eliza had said it, and Charles hated Eliza for having said it.

Sheila, beautiful, healthy, normally intelligent ... and all those men. It was no use telling oneself that young girls were like that nowadays, that in Denmark or Sweden it might even be normal. It hurt. He had stormed at her. It had gone on. Two years ago he had struck her once. This time he had succeeded, all through this trip, in keeping silent, because Sheila was ill and it might drive her away from him altogether. Then she would no longer turn to him with those shadows of weariness, that crushed look on her face, put her arms round him as she did sometimes, saying: 'Hold me tight, Daddy,' as she had done ever since she was five. And though she came to him from the arms of other men, yet still, she came back to him...

He was walking into some forest now, unconscious of where he went. He strode among trees, and they let leaves fall upon him.

It was thus he came to the small village among the trees not far from the main road. A huddle of about twenty houses on stilts in a small clearing, a twisting path among the houses leading to a new, clean, white-plastered Buddhist shrine, a *stupa*, raised on a stone platform, with its benign gilded wood statue of the Lord of Compassion.

Under one of the houses a woman pounded rice in a wooden vat, another bundled hay for two buffaloes with shining brass and silver necklaces round their necks. A handful of children ran together to watch him, an old man squatted near an iron pan, under which were hot charcoal embers, cooking a syrupy looking liquid which might be palm or coconut sugar.

The woman pounding the rice left the wooden shaft standing in it, and came to peer at him. She had a stone-white eye. She smiled, uncovering a mouth red from betel, and returning to the vat scooped some of the pounded rice and gave it to him on her palm. He picked at it and ate it. It had a strong flavour of yeast, chewy, a little like popcorn.

With laughter a child came to touch his sleeve, and then another one, to look at him close, to smile. He returned the smiles. One man brought a small wooden stool, so low that he had to stretch his legs in front of him to sit. He sat. The sun was gentle upon him, and there was a breeze caged away among the tree-leaves. The men and women returned to work, leaving him quiet, sitting facing the shrine. Then a young man came with a container of bamboo, and gave him some palm wine to drink. He drank, feeling the pain leave his chest.

Eliza crossed the corridor to Sheila's room, opposite hers. That girl never locked her door.

Now she was in the room, sniffing Sheila's scent, a woman in another woman's room, hostile to the other woman's smell, to the careless clothes flung on the armchair, the suitcase bulging open. That girl's things were always in a mess. She must have just dumped everything and gone out.

There was the box of chocolates. Sheila had left it in the open suitcase. It was really too simple.

She took the box under her arm, and left the room. A minute later she was back, carrying a box of chocolates, putting it exactly where the other had been placed.

Always the same dream, in exact sequences of mystery, dread, to end with an apocalyptic burst of ... not exactly happiness, but something near to it, which woke him up. Gion wondered at his dream's persistence, for it recurred, had recurred, off and on, for some months, and its end was always the same. Thinner, darker, naked but for a loin cloth, he stood, a blossom of stone in his hand, in a desolate plain where the dry stalks of a field burnt dry meant death was about its harvest. He heard a voice, his own, say: 'Now I understand.' And he knew that he was going to die. But he was not unhappy. On the contrary, it was like a sudden Illumination. He was happy.

Now, in the bare, gleaming sunlight that sprayed them, lacquered Sheila's golden hair as they crossed the man-made moat round the big temple of Angkor Vat, followed by children with smiles like small white suns in their dark faces, he was transported into his dream again. It only lasted a few seconds, and again it was day, silence emphasized by the intermittent call of some jackdaws, the sparrows' off-and-on jabber, an elephant hoofing the dust, walking in the aroma of his own odour, the not unpleasant elephant smell that one comes across so often in Cambodia.

'What's the matter?' said Sheila. 'You're mumbling to yourself.'

'Am I?' This was disconcerting. It cut off the small desire to tell her about his sudden day-time lapse into another world. 'I feel haunted in Angkor. Pleasantly so.' Perhaps the grey stones of Angkor Vat, so much like the grey luminosity which filled the landscape of his dream, had evoked it.

'You've been here before?'

'Yes. Once. I spent weeks here, roaming about each temple. I dream about this place,' he added, hoping for a resurrection of his wish to tell her of his dream. But there was the suspicion of a frown upon her forehead as she looked at the raised columns and arches, the five towers heaped upon the mountain of galleries and staircases covered with a lacework of carvings.

'It takes time to get used to this kind of art. It's so different.'

'Yes, it takes time.'

Her lack of enthusiasm was an axe, chipping his own pleasure away. What was my reason for bringing her here? Why should I think that this magnificence would move her, as it moved me?

'This is terrific,' exclaimed Sheila. 'What is it?'

'The battle between the armies of Hanuman, Lord of Monkeys, and the armies of the King of Ceylon. The king kidnapped the beautiful Sita, wife of Rama. With the help of Hanuman, Rama got her back. It's from the *Ramayana*, as important as the *Odyssey* to your civilization. The whole of South-East Asian art is based on this Indian epic. You must have seen it acted at the Siamese theatre in Bangkok.'

'I never saw any theatre. Once I nearly went. A Siamese prince wanted to take me, but we finished up in bed instead. Eliza bought lots of Thai silk and appeared on TV, and daddy lectured about under-development. I think this is like the temples in India.'

Gion was annoyed both by her reference to the use of her time in Bangkok and her confusion between Khmer and Indian art. 'Khmer art is quite different. Nowhere in India will you find anything like Angkor.'

'Well, it's much more sexy in India,' she replied, with the candid obstinacy about her pet subject which he now felt she used to irritate him. It did. Irritate and stir him. But he wasn't going to touch her.

'Eliza was shocked in India,' Sheila went on. 'The only backgrounds she could be photographed against decently were the Taj Mahal and that sort of thing. In the north.'

'Mogul,' said Gion. 'Islamic. Different approach to the Vision.'

'Vision? What a funny word.' Sheila laughed.

They walked into the bat-infested, ammonia-scented interior of Angkor Vat, with the perpetual twitter of bats in the dark narrow ceilings of stone. Don't let me get angry with her, thought Gion. Anger is involvement. The most stupid involvement. Let me remember that she is European, cannot understand the theology responsible for these monuments, that it may appear as repulsive to her as the idea of the perpetual suffering of Christ, nailed to a cross to compensate for the pleasures of this world, seems barbaric to me. Pain to redeem the joy of living was ever an obsession with Man. Even the Buddha did not abolish Hell.

They walked the courtyards, Sheila's blue eyes staring without reverence or comprehension, and Gion felt he had committed an impropriety, as if he had given her a venerated relic to desecrate. They walked in silence, and his anger abated. In the semi-fluid obscurity cloaking them, his dream seeped back, its sadness and fatal irresolution, the sight of himself holding the stone lotus, while death waited to deliver him in the ruined field.

He said to Sheila: 'Let me show you what I wanted to show you.'

'Hope it's exciting.' She sounded disappointed. Nothing sexy, he thought, nothing to titillate her.

Past the princes and the warriors, the gods and the priests, the monkeys mouthing fangs into limbs of men and striking skulls with stones and tree trunks, past the elephants, the parasols, to the gallery where thirty-two heavens and thirty-seven hells stood recorded.

'Here it is.'

Along the sixty-metre gallery, ascending piously, the wealthy, the fat, were carried in palanquins to paradises of delights; the replete, the hypocritical, the smug, took elevation towards a slovenly beatitude. Below them, foundations of their bliss, grovelled, writhed, suffered, with gaping mouths and numbered ribs, the mobs of the damned, the unworthy and the poor, condemned by Yama, Lord of Justice, who presided matter-of-factly over the scene. They had hungered and worked, condemned in life, damned in hell, torments commemorated in stone polished by the hands of those who centuries later came to peer at their tortures. The granite shone with a dark glow of human skin, oil left by the palms of those who touched it. But no one had left this oily linger of humanity upon the prosperous riding befeathered and silky to gorgings in heaven, they were too high for reach.

Two years ago Gion had been fascinated by this scene of Hell and Heaven, although equivalent portrayals of torture and agony in European museums left him unmoved. Here he identified, there not. A similar logic of crime and punishment had perpetuated these horrors in medieval West and medieval East. Committed to the print of photographs and films were similar collective horrors, going on, unchanged, in the world. And humanity had accepted them, one and all, past and present, real or carved, in this world and in another ... In Christian hells the torments were eternal, to the end of time, each being had but a single chance to save himself. In Buddhist lands these beatings, disembowellings, hangings, crucifyings, dragging of women with ropes threaded through pierced noses and gashed breasts, burnings, impalings, were transient agonies; rebirth, another salvation, the steady stream of life unending, received the human spirit in another time, another place: for man was not a single individual, but a continuum of different selves through the ages, with many chances to fulfil his sum of good and evil through aeons of lives. Of those that had at last freed themselves from rebirth, some, looking down in pity, chose life again, with its suffering, pain, and toil, to help others gain Beatitude. And these were the Buddhas. There was no God, but only perpetual life, and that could become a Hell from which only Total Awareness could save mankind.

'It's rather awful, isn't it?' said Sheila.

'I wanted to show it to you. It's Hell, but not for ever.'

'Why not for ever? I thought we never had a second chance.'

'In Buddhism one has many chances.'

But Sheila, abruptly shaking her head, as if at a buzzing fly, said, flippant: 'They haven't got anything sexy in this place.'

Bitterly, he felt like leaving her there, going away. Shallow, sneering Sheila. Nothing in her would begin to respond to anything outside of her body and its preoccupation, and this was her Hell. Gion saw her savagely as one of those women condemned to lust, and lust again, and again, climbing the tree of lust, for ever.

And then, as she shook her golden head, like a child, he felt for her a great pity, and said: 'Come and look at the beautiful *apsaras** carved on the walls. You'll find their head-dresses fascinating.'

Sheila was delighted. 'Eliza will be photographed here, no doubt with a replica of the skirts they wear. But she'll have to wear a bit more on top.'

They rounded the upper terrace, where the massive five towers, silver and grey in sunlight, forbidding, obstinate, disfigured by the wind, reared their mass of uncemented stones. They peered through the chiselled bars of windows at the placid

* apsaras=female deities or spirits.

landscape, which Sheila observed was pretty with lots of trees. They paced more corridors with bats in the vaults, the ground rank with slippery excrement in tiny pellets littered upon the large stone pavings Sheila made exclamation and comment. Gion answered her equably, imparting information. Finally he said: 'Let us go back. Time for lunch.'

He helped her down the narrow, steep stairs, felt her arm's flesh between his fingers. In the taxi she began to weep. The tears rolled on her cheeks unwiped. He ought to have asked (the rest of his life he would regret that he had not): 'What is the matter?' But he could not. He sat on, silent, letting her weep, feeling it a good thing that she should weep, feeling that if he interfered something might go wrong with them, their odd new relationship. And also, dreading involvement, dreading argument ... He let the tears roll, offering only silence. And when the taxi stopped she jumped out, made her way into the hotel, not looking back.

At lunch Gion sat at a table in the dining-room. At another Eliza, Charles and Multani were lunching with Bernard Reguet, the French curator in charge of the ruins, Sheila was not there. Of course. She had told him of another meeting for lunch. And Lederer, laughing with the co-pilot at a table in a corner, expected her in his bed for the afternoon.

It's nothing to do with me, I can't stop her.

He made a strong effort to watch Eliza, whom Sheila hated so much. Eliza spoke French very well, Charles with a strong English accent, Multani badly. Multani wore a striped Indian handloom shirt, and had placed a shiny new leather camera case on a chair by him. He was going to tour the monuments after lunch, he announced. Bernard Reguet was obviously fascinated by Eliza. She gave him the ageless attention of a woman enthralled by a man's intellect, and he responded. She was beautifully dressed. Gion thought her face tense, her voice too high. Multani argued, and as always with Multani the argument was political controversy.

'Non, monsieur,' Bernard Reguet was saying, 'neutralism is *not* a vicious Red trick, but a natural, spontaneous desire of most Asian countries to discover their own identity, to choose what is best for them. Cambodia is a small country of five million, and neutralism is the only way it can remain Cambodian and not be swallowed up.'

'But anyone who compromises with communism will be engulfed. One's got to take sides.'

'Democratic ideals are abstractions that do not exist in Asia. They do not even exist in many parts of Europe. They are fast declining in France, and even in England. In Cambodia the Prince does not like democratic threats.'

'My dear sir, I was only warning. There's no such thing as non-communism. One can only be pro or anti. There is no Middle Road.'

'Oh,' said Eliza, coquettish, 'do tell me all about the cult of the God-King, Monsieur Reguet, in old Angkor. How thrilling those centuries must have been.'

'Go to the Bayon, madame. There, in the many-faced towers, you will be able to grasp the idea of Infinite Power turned upon itself.'

'The temple with all those faces?' asked Charles. 'I saw a picture of it. Rather gruesome.'

'A picture can give you no idea of its magnificence. It is architecturally insane and sublime. After eight years here I do not know whether I love it or hate it. You cannot *like* the Bayon. It is Idea made stone, the God-King petrified in contemplation of the world, the world turned to stone in the eye of God, grandiose, immutable, a monument whose megalomania overwhelms. And it also represents a gigantic lotus, flower of Buddha's Compassion.'

'I think it will do wonderfully as a fashion background,' said Eliza.

Like other French archaeologists who had reconstructed Angkor stone by stone, Reguet was unquenchable about it. 'Think, madame, of the labour. Those immense blocks of stone, quarried forty to sixty miles from here, brought here by hundreds, thousands of workers ... It always seems to me that it is the architects, engineers, the artists whose names should have come down to us, rather than those kings whose *grandeur* exhausted itself in these works. Yet the builders have remained anonymous, and no doubt many died young. Only their work remains.'

'They had a faith,' said Charles. 'They did not build for

themselves, but in an effort towards immortality.'

'Immortality?' said Reguet. 'Why should human life be worth little in the face of the illusory immortality of a king? Why? Why must thousands, hundreds of thousands, toil and perish to leave behind enduring witness of man's desire to immortality? It is folly. Megalomania. Why not direct this effort to the happiness of mankind as a whole instead?'

'But Angkor did ennoble mankind. It left something for us to look at, to admire, not like the bigger and better bombs we have nowadays. I prefer the old kind of megalomania to the new one, the one that is constructive to the one that plans only to destroy.'

'Oh,' said Eliza, 'it can't have been so bad being a slave in those days, carving lovely things in stone. Quite fun, really.'

'Anyway,' said Multani grandiosely, 'they were creating Culture, and we are now preserving it against communist destruction.'

'Ah,' said Reguet, with perceptible irony, 'humanity may not be there to enjoy its Culture. I understand we've got a clean bomb now, that will only kill people and not destroy property.'

The food, Gion had thought, leaving the restaurant, was French in name, but tourist in fact. I suppose it can't be helped, he thought. Many of the tourists would not like the genuine cuisine. It compared favourably with that served at the Hilton in Cairo, at the Peninsula in Hong Kong; and of course there was a bottle of tomato sauce on every table, for the Americans.

I am getting old, I am getting old. Small things annoy me more.

He decided that he would take all his meals at the market at Siemreap, from the Chinese stalls which served excellent Cantonese dishes, cheaper than the Suprême.

As he walked down the corridor thinking of the implications of his new fastidiousness, he was hailed by a bright-eyed little woman in a Cambodian skirt.

'Oh,' he exclaimed, 'Sumipoon! When did you arrive?'

Said Sumipoon: 'We came by my cousin's private helicopter about ten minutes ago. And you?'

'Plane from Bangkok this morning.'

'Why didn't you get in touch with us in Bangkok?'

Sumipoon was a slight woman, half Siamese, quarter Cambodian, quarter French, vivacious, clever, fluent in five languages. Gion had been in love with her when he and she were both adolescent. A vague kinship had kept them apart, for Sumipoon's mother was against consanguine marriage. Sumipoon then eloped with George Rolland, a penniless Frenchman who had wandered east as a painter and remained there, painting atrociously and happily. Sumipoon had taken to writing novels published in the newspapers in serial instalments, and she had become a popular, best-selling authoress. Since the cold war George, floating above revolutions and coups, acquainted with everyone both European and Asian that intrigued and counter-intrigued in South-East Asia, had taken a job as Cultural Officer for MESSO. MESSO was an economic and military body supposed to counteract communism and spread democracy in South-East Asia, and culture was part of its psychological warfare section. George's present work in MESSO consisted in making a collection of folk songs of Asia. Sumipoon said that George hated MESSO, but that one of her uncles was in it, a prince with a clear vision of the fluidity of all situations, since he had abetted at one time a Japanese invasion and been knighted a few years later by the British for services rendered.

'MESSO is an anachronism disguised as an organization, so inefficient that George is quite happy in it. Anyway,' Sumipoon stated, 'as a princess myself I know how to change sides gracefully. It doesn't do for princes to be too definite about anything. One must swim with the current of history.'

Besides writing novels, Sumipoon had five children, numerous love affairs, none of which had interfered with her happy family life. She had also adopted another twelve children of various races, maintaining her household in happy chaos and making it easy for Rolland to proclaim that they did not have a *tikal* in the bank. 'Only an overdrawn overdraft,' said Sumipoon, 'but as a princess no bank dare refuse me a loan.'

'Sumi,' said Gion, 'you look younger every time I see you.'

'It's because we have a new baby,' Sumipoon beamed. 'George found him. Look.'

She pointed to George, who came up, a slim man with Spanish eyes and gentle hands, cradling in his arms an enormous flaxen-haired little Hercules of two.

'Found him on the steps of the Buddhist Association for the Maintenance of Moral Principles,' said Sumipoon. 'Illegitimate. Can you believe his father was a Tamil? That's what the records say. He looks so Scandinavian, doesn't he? Or Dutch. How handsome he is.'

Sumipoon and her children were small and dark, and Sumipoon had always felt a great attraction towards fair, blond babies.

'Sumi,' said Gion, 'would you marry a handsome Dutchman?'

'I have too many relatives in Indonesia, some of them might cut me dead. You should have seen us, packed tight in the helicopter this morning,' she continued, 'Astarte and Orion, our two eldest, our new baby, and Mary Faust, an acquaintance who hates George. Mary has lots of luggage, all priceless manuscripts, she tells me. Always travels with the complete works of Lenin in Esperanto, and that's twice as bulky as in any other language. They arrested her in Bangkok, of course, but I made them release her. She's already been through the hotel guest list, and found a writer she knows, and gone off to look for him. She was staying with a cousin of mine in Uganda, where she was trying to organize an Institute for Progressive Tribal Chieftains, and that cousin gave her a letter for me. I shall write a novel about her, and make lots of *tikals*.'

'Mary Faust plays at revolution because Hollywood doesn't make that kind of film,' said George.

'Oh,' said Sumi, 'I do *hope* something exciting happens. Writers' Congresses are so *dull*. Nobody can really *talk* about writing. Of course George has to attend, culture is his job. He is supposed to write confidential political reports on all the writers who attend, for the cultural files of MESSO. As if George could spy on anybody. He simply can't ever make out who's what. Anyway, who can tell nowadays? Especially with writers.'

'Not as bad as politicians,' said George. 'They're born polyfacetic in South-East Asia.'

'I haven't seen anyone from the Congress as yet,' said Gion.

'There's a circular about the Congress pinned up by the front door,' said Sumipoon. 'I think it was put up by Mr Lee Souvan.'

Above the glass case where tourist objects were spread for inspection a piece of paper was pinned to the wood. Gion now saw, in French, English, Cambodian, Chinese, and Thai, the following message:

'TO ALL AUTHORS ATTENDING THE NEUTRALIST CONGRESS AT THEIR OWN EXPENSE, WELCOME AND AGAIN WELCOME. Please present yourselves at 7 to 8 p.m. on Sunday, November 12th, evening, at the desk marked Neutralist Congress in the Manager's Room of the Hotel Suprême. The first gathering of the Congress will be at 10 a.m. on Monday morning. To keep yourselves in full knowledge of current events in Cambodia and the world, read my newspapers: *The Trumpet of Siemreap* (appearing every two days) and *The Voice of Angkor* (every Monday).

'(Signed) ULONG SERAP

'Secretary of the Neutralist Congress of Cultural Workers (Section Literature), Author, Poet, and Journalist, Manager of world-renowned newspapers.'

'Who is Ulong Serap?' asked Gion.

'His Eminence is my seventh step-uncle by marriage,' said Sumipoon. 'A very nice man, a very good businessman; used to be a general and a politician, but gave it up and became a monk for three years. He meditates and tells everybody their past. The children will be delighted to meet another relative. Astarte and Orion love having relatives everywhere because they're mad about sleuthing. They want to start a private detective agency, and they want all their relatives to become their agents. Such a good idea, isn't it?'

Sumipoon was sure all her children, born or adopted, would be writers, painters, musicians, lawyers, engineers, or doctors. 'And I hope some will be communists and others capitalists, so whatever happens we shall be safe. I am reading *Hamlet* to him' —she pointed to the blond boy— 'he likes it. I think I shall call him Laertes. Laertes Souphanavoring Rolland. He *might* become a film star.'

With promises to meet at four, Gion left them, feeling glad that Sumipoon was here. He had not called on her in Bangkok because his airplane had come in too late the night before. And also, he had not really wanted to see her. Last night he had been wholly enclosed within himself, refusing contact. Sumi, because of their old love, was contact, and it always hurt a little to make the effort. But now it had happened without effort.

He fingered his diary. Wrote down: 'Arrived Angkor 9.20 a.m. Saw Angkor Vat with S.M.' Then: 'Schizophrenia Gross and sustained impairment of emotional relationships with people. Either aloofness or empty clinging. Also abnormal behaviour towards other people as persons. Using them or parts of them, impersonally.' He stared at what he had written. 'Using them, or parts of them.' So many 'sane' people used others, or parts of others; millions of people were used, impersonally. Wiped out, impersonally. The whole world in which he and Sheila lived was mad. A world of lunatics, used by or using other lunatics, all living under this permanent threat of total extinction. 'Sheila: she is wrapped in herself, drowned in herself, in her own death fulfilled, closed to the sun, hermetic in all-fulfilling blindness.'

Words, he thought, words, and they apply to all of us, not only to Sheila. What have I come here for? What do I live for? What, in the words of the young, is the Meaning of Life?

He threw himself on his bed and shut his eyes. But he could not rest. He left the room, walked round the hotel, watched by the delicately derisive eyes of the taxi-drivers and the *samlo*-men as he strode the three o'clock heat of the afternoon. Sheila must be with Lederer, he thought. In a cool, cool room, full of shadows. 'Stupid woman,' he said aloud, 'I won't have anything to do with her.' And he paced the grass, as if by treading on it he could tread Sheila's existence out of himself.

At one-thirty, lunch over, Charles Manley walked out of the hotel with Bernard Reguet, leaving Multani who announced he was going to take some snapshots of the ruins. 'No siesta for me.' Eliza alone would siesta.

'I want to show you some of our latest finds,' said Reguet. He was pleased to have found Charles Manley to talk to. 'That insufferable Indian,' he said, talking of Multani to Charles, 'who is he?'

'I don't know him well. A political writer. Attending the Congress.'

'Ah yes, the Congress,' said Reguet. 'A most extraordinary assemblage. But good fun, no doubt. Everything turns out happily cock-eyed out here. His Eminence Ulong Serap is also like that. He predicts the past.'

'Predicts the past?'

'Yes. He was granted Illumination. He can recall the past lives of many people. According to him I was a Khmer in the tenth century. A maker of statues for the King. That is why I find them so easily, and I'm to become a Cambodian again in my next life. To be a Cambodian is to be the absolute top in humanity's ladder. I am duly grateful.'

'All the French seem to like Cambodia,' said Charles.

'Not all. Some of the businessmen still look back to the old colonial days. Others are quite happy to make what profits they still can make. And here they can still make a very good living. This country is hospitable. Too hospitable, sometimes. We have some very trying people round. A man named Kilton, for instance. A Dale Carnegie type of missionary. I believe he is a friend of Mr Multani's. Here we are.'

They had crossed the tarmac road, walked about two hundred yards of it to the entrance of the grounds belonging to the Conservation where Reguet lived in a small whitewashed brick bungalow set in a large, unkempt garden, so unkempt that it was indistinguishable from the forest beyond it. In a concrete pond a baby crocodile lay, stuporous and unblinking. A young tiger with wild yellow eyes paced, restless, a very large chicken-wire net cage. A couple of baby elephants, some fantail pigeons, and two gibbons, were also about. On the ground floor was a large archaeological store-room. Upstairs were Reguet's quarters, dining-room, living-room, bedroom, and a small private working-room with locked cases containing small statues, on the walls some rubbings of the Angkor carvings, and in a corner a beautiful wooden statue of the Buddha, glowing with worn gold, a desk and a swivel chair in the middle of the room.

'Let me show you this.' Reguet rummaged in a large crate.

But Charles was not looking. He stared through the open window which gave upon the road.

Sheila was coming out of a taxi, which stopped near the Suprême and then drove off with someone else inside it to whom Sheila waved her hand. Then Charles saw her walk along the roadside, turn the corner, walking the few yards towards the hotel.

Captain Lederer, back from lunch into the penumbra of his room, raised one eyebrow, contemplating the man who heaved himself over the side partition of the verandah. At the back of the hotel the verandahs ran continuous with each other, only sloping cement partitions stood between each private portion. It would be easy for an agile person to get from one verandah into another.

Lederer watched the man flick the dust off his clothes, walk into his darkened room, where, perceiving Lederer lying fully dressed on the counterpane, he stepped back.

'I do beg your pardon. I did not know you were in.'

'Even had I not been in, this is intrusion. Have you lost your key, do you not wish the manager to perceive you, or are you an agent of the police?'

'Nothing of the kind,' said Chundra Das, for it was he. 'But a woman has penetrated into my room, which is next to yours, and I wish to avoid her. At least, until I am ready to meet her. She is ... how shall I say, she affects my nerves. I was fortifying myself, and she arrived unexpectedly. I may have a nervous breakdown about it.'

'Is it the well-rounded little woman you were talking to this morning?'

'No, that's her secretary,' said Chundra, sitting down on the armchair and completing the cleaning of his coat and his jodhpurs. 'I spoke to her to find out what the plans of her employer were. I am a writer, I'm sensitive to personal auras.'

'You must be very sensitive,' replied Lederer. 'I, however, am not a writer, and I am expecting a lady at any moment. You will have to take refuge elsewhere.'

'Well, all right,' said Chundra Das. 'Sorry I intruded. But you don't know what she does to me. I ran away when I heard her at my room door. Just bolted. But I shall be all right once I nerve myself to face her.'

'Is she beautiful?' asked Lederer, scanning the table top for something to drink. The laws of courtesy held true, even for this portly Indian with the candid face and the shock of Russell-ish white hair that proclaimed his thinker's vocation. He could not be anything else but a writer, and a progressive one. In Paris I'd hurl plastic at him. He would be lynched in Oran. Sexually full of sense, gullible in nothing, his candour, an apparent naïvety, hiding Brahman astuteness, he would still be lynched, his mop of white hair bloodied. Lederer detested him kindly. He was amusing. If the story were true ... but what an incredible story: it was much more likely that he was a spy. If so ...

'Beautiful? Like an evil genius, like a snake. She haunts. And she does it because she combines American puritanism with the most sweet knowledge of how to rouse men. And does it all in the name of politics. All she does which is most selfish she proclaims to be for the good of all. And people believe her. They confide in her, and they're lost. When they withdraw, bruised, excoriated, licking their wounds and impotent, it's too late.'

'My dear chap,' cut in François Lederer, with concern, 'surely this is most serious? I am sure a trip to Saigon ... I know some sweet and gentle creatures who will restore your self-confidence——'

'Oh, I don't mean that,' said Das, *that's* all right. She couldn't do that to me, oh my, no. I mean, look at the *mental* mess I'm in, trying to avoid her now. Yet I know I can't avoid her for ever. Actually neither Mrs Despair nor I expected her until tonight. All of a sudden after lunch Mrs Despair burst into my room. "She's there, and NOTHING is ready. She's furious. Oh, Mr Das, save me." "Does she know I'm here?" "Yes. She's gone through the guest list. She's upstairs now." I heard her knock at the door, and fled. Give me a breather, will you? Until your lady friend turns up? I'm discreet, I assure you.'

'Breathe as you wish,' replied Lederer. 'As for myself, I shall go out in the corridor, perhaps catch a glimpse of your Mata Hari.' Throwing a glance at himself in the mirror, Lederer went out. He had been waiting for Sheila, wondering where she was. He had better warn her. Then, in the corridor, he thought: suppose this is a trick? Suppose—— He returned to his room, opening the door softly and suddenly. Chundra was sitting in the chair, he appeared not to have moved at all. 'I can't see signs of any woman around. Surely the best thing to do is to face the dragon and tell her to leave you alone?'

'Let me collect my spirits first. I'll go in a minute.'

There was a knock at the door, and without a pause it opened for a tall woman with bronze hair, a beautiful face with deep brown eyes, and a determined mouth.

Chundra sat rooted in his chair.

'Das me-boy,' said the woman, her voice ringing with the habit of command, 'you here? I was waiting for you. How dare you keep me waiting? Who's he?' She jerked an imperious chin towards Lederer.

Captain Lederer drew himself up, and found he reached up to the newcomer's nose. He felt like savaging her, on the spot. 'Capitaine Françoise Lederer, at your service.'

'You're not at my service. I don't need you.' She looked again at Chundra. 'Nothing is done. Nothing is done right. I need *you*, Chundra. You *must* help me.'

As if hypnotized, Chundra rose. He cast a desperate look at Lederer, but the latter was not looking at him. Das said feebly: 'Well, thank you, Captain.'

Mary Faust shut the door firmly after him.

Bitch, Lederer thought. Then he went to his suitcase, locked in the locked wardrobe. Untouched. All was well. But he still didn't believe the story. The man must be a spy.

Mabel Despair was wiping reddened eyes when Mary Faust, followed by Chundra, re-entered his room. She stumped to the desk, her heavy-soled shoes noisy in the silent afternoon.

'Well,' said Mary Faust, sitting down in the armchair, 'now that Das is back in the fold, let's get to work. Das me-darling,' she said, suddenly tender, her face reflecting all-enveloping concern, 'why do you run away from me? You know I can do nothing if *you* don't help me, don't you? You *must* help me. You know it's for the future of the world, for mankind, for the good of all, don't you?'

Mary went on, her siren voice pouring: 'I had a feeling you

were behind that chap's door. Although Mabel wouldn't tell me where you were at first, even when I pinched her.'

Captain Lederer, holding his briefcase, walked to the head of the stairs and saw Sheila coming up the stairs. He stood waiting, a little angry.

'I've been waiting for you.'

She looked at him as if her eyes could not focus. He felt her changed since that morning in the plane; changed since the obliterated hour of night he had entered her body and not known her; different from the little girl who peeled her thumb at the reception desk.

'I went for a drive,' she said. 'It's beautiful outside.'

'Good idea,' he said, 'fresh air is good for one. I have to fly on to Phnom Penh at four. Would you like a drink at the bar? Or coffee?' He was releasing her of the compact which might have brought their bodies together once again. And, he thought, to what end? Perhaps he would know her better over a drink, talking with her. Intercom instead of intercourse, he thought, ribald, both words debased.

In the siesta afternoon young flies meditated upon the bar counter, where a waiter dutifully slept. Only tourists, with a programme and a schedule to tick off their itinerary before they left next day, stamped around a revving bus, exhaustedly determined not to miss some of the eighty-odd monuments spread out over a hundred square kilometres which make up Angkor.

Captain Lederer woke the waiter and ordered two Camparis *à l'eau*. He glanced at his watch. Two-forty. An hour and a quarter with Sheila. Would an hour and a quarter of sensual contact have solved their ignorance of each other? Would seventy-five minutes of untouchability, exchanging words like pelting gravel, do better? How did one get to *know* someone else? Come to it, did he really know, say, his wife? The mystery of knowing another human being ... He was more embarrassed in Sheila's presence, clothed, sitting in public, waiting for her drink, than if naked she had lain by his side. The necessity of self-exposure, in silence or in talk, in comradeship, this beginning knowledge of the Other One, was more demanding, also more dangerous, than the intimacy of love-making, the signs and endearments which confessed nothing, revealed nothing, and perhaps meant nothing. Suddenly Lederer knew this, and in the moment of understanding he said: 'Aux beaux yeux de ma Sheila,' looking at her now, Campari in hand like a gladiator's shield, yet looking at Sheila with discovery. She was evanescent, would forget him the moment he looked away, for he was not real to her; in a crowd he would not recognize her because she would not know him. 'I would like to *know* you better.'

'There is nothing mysterious about me.'

He looked at his watch, pretended to ease the wristband, said: 'Your father is a famous writer, I believe?'

'Daddy's an economist.'

'I think your father must love you very much.'

'Yes,' she said. 'He loves me, loves me very much. You don't love me. That's good. I do not matter to you.'

'You are very beautiful,' he said, 'many men must care for you, as I do. Sheila, je t'aime bien, tu sais.'

'You've slept with me, you can't remember what it was like.'

'I do remember, but...' He wanted to say: 'You are more desirable, you mean more, a landscape glimpsed, to be searched for again, yet much of me refuses the effort because it would hurt. I have been hurt before, as one gets older one gets less tough, less callous. Only the young, like you, are too young to know when they're hurt. But I am afraid. I must defend myself against you.'

But he could not say it. Instead, raging at the insipid formula: 'I am a married man, I have to go back to my wife. I am afraid to fall in love with you.'

'It doesn't matter. It's so awful to be loved. By people like you. People who run away all the time.'

She is like a cat scratching.

'I have deserved this. But let us part good friends.'

Oh, those ready-made phrases, they come up to the lips like vomit.

'I think I *am* in love. With someone ... someone I have never slept with, never will. Someone who tried to make me understand.'

He was jealous, hurt as once as a child when he had seen the sun go down. He felt a gesture called for, a last parody of truth. 'I am glad for you,' he said, looking again at his watch. 'If you will excuse me, I *must* get ready. The plane. I fly to Phnom Penh. All my wishes for your happiness.'

'I hope,' she said, 'you crash and I never see you again.'

He bowed, a little stiffly. I won't crash, not this time. Then he remembered his wife. He would sleep with her, think of Sheila at one time or other during the night. And then he would forget.

At four o'clock Gion knocked on the door of the suite which the Rolland family occupied.

'Oh,' exclaimed Sumipoon, when she saw him, 'I haven't got a watch, and George never knows the time by the sun. It's the right hour to go to the Bayon, isn't it? And coming back, when the sun sinks, we shall watch the towers of Angkor Vat "resplendent with gold", as the Chinese travellers used to describe them eight hundred years ago.'

Gion felt like telling her that it wasn't the towers of Angkor Vat, but those of some other edifice, which had been thus described, but Sumipoon rushed on. 'We wanted two suites in the hotel, actually, because MESSO is paying for all this. But Mary Faust has taken one, and another writer has booked the remaining one, so we're all in one suite.'

'Beware of Mary,' said George.

'Because once she asked you for money,' retorted Sumipoon. 'George always feels astonished when people ask him for money. He withdraws like a snail into his shell. But I don't mind.'

'Sumipoon gives to anyone who asks her,' said George. 'Many people take advantage of her.'

'What would you have me do?' said Sumipoon. 'Refuse, and find out later that someone genuinely needed the money and I didn't give it? I'd rather be cheated nine times out of ten than cheat someone else, prevent the development of a destiny by my niggardliness.'

'Buddhist,' said George. 'She'll be a Buddha, after she's given herself to eat to a poor, starving tiger, as the Lord of Compassion did.'

'Don't ask me to cultivate a cautious heart, a fenced-in little backyard for myself alone,' said Sumipoon, suddenly angry.

'That is not living for me. Anyway, I'm not *that* merciful. I'll write up Mary as a character and make money.'

'A much attenuated one, I'm afraid,' said Gion. 'You can't bear to be really nasty to anyone in your books, Sumi. Even the wicked have a blessed reprieve.'

'That's why people *like* my novels,' she replied. 'No utter condemnation. Let's go.'

Orion and Astarte, Sumipoon's fourteen and fifteen year olds, were called away from a game of chess, and greeted Gion with their striking good looks and ceremonious bows. They were both politely indifferent to grown-ups, convinced of their own superiority over anyone as ghastly aged as twenty-five. Astarte considered her mother excessively childish; she assumed command of the expedition by saying that she would drive the car. The taxi-driver obliged by sitting next to her, and held Laertes on his knees, charmed with the baby's fairness.

The afternoon forest held all the greens and yellows of the world among its leaf-edged horizons. A small wind caught high in the high branches made paradise. Why am I today so sensitive to what is around me, so overwhelmed by small things? thought Gion. And the answer, shipwreck stone jutting out of a sea, was Sheila. An image floated, dapple on his consciousness, like those shadows leaves stroked on his face as the car drove on: Sheila and Lederer, sitting in the hotel bar. He had seen them as he paced the hotel garden, and had rushed back to his room, telling himself he didn't care. And now, in this featherweight moment, it was no more than a passing sadness, light as the shadow of a leaf in the wholeness of a forest.

And Laertes laughed when leaves fell upon him, for they had thrown back the roof of the car. Orion sang, turning on the radio loud to the Khmer music which trailed an unending melody, gay, unemphasized, and Sumi said: 'This is music according to the Confucian scholars: a regulation of one's moods, a beat of time, a hierarchy like this forest.'

Upon them came the four-faced towers of the outer wall of Angkor Thom, a mile away from Angkor Vat, a city of monuments in the centre of which was the Bayon. On both sides, across the usual moat, a bridge lay between its double row of genii, good and evil, each side pulling a huge naga snake in perpetual tug-of-war. Reguet and a few Khmer workmen were there, measuring some boulders of laterite dug out from a corner of the moat, and waved at them as they passed.

They plunged into the gateway, sunslit narrow, between the lotus uprooting three-headed elephants that supported the enormous staring four-faced head above them. The sun caught shadowy smiles round the mouths, and Gion's hands tingled with remembered carving.

'Mamma,' sang Astarte, as they drove into the avenue in front of the Bayon, 'there's going to be a coup. Everybody says it.'

'You've been listening to Mary Faust,' said Sumipoon.

'No, Mamma. It's the waiters. Orion heard it too.'

'These children,' said Sumipoon. 'They know more about what is really going on than MESSO does.'

'The Prince will win. Nobody can beat him. Want to bet, Father?'

'Me? Never again,' said George. 'I lost too much over the last Siamese coup, Army against Navy. The Army won, I'd bet on the Navy.'

'Gambling is forbidden in Cambodia,' said Sumi. 'People used to bet on the weather, and some lost their shirts on the rain.'

'Oh, Mother, do stop being moralistic. All life's a gamble,' said Orion grandly.

'Don't use clichés,' said Sumipoon severely. 'In any language they make my skin creep.'

The Bayon was in front of them, fifty-nine enormous towers standing stiff as the strong full petals of the lotus, straightest and most dauntless of all flowers. Fifty-nine towers, each one four faces seven metres high, eight eyes looking to all points of the horizon, encompassing the world with sight, for sight is command, possession, achieving immortality through awareness, memory in stone.

They stared, Gion and Sumi, George and the children, at the monument that stared back with all its eyes, all its faces watching them. The whole edifice underwent multitudinous metamorphoses: one moment a compact and enormous lotus stretching towards the sky, ascending the air in the final invocation of its central highest tower; at another moment, menhir disfigured by centuries of wind, prayer made stone; at yet another, a sagging, crumbling heap of leprous granite; or an absurd motley of faces crowding to protrude eyes at passers-by; or a mastodontal spider brooding, crouched over its web of earth.

'Wonderful place for a murder,' said Orion. 'All these squashed corridors and dark corners.'

It hurts, thought Gion, hurts as it never has. (O inept and stupid girl, whose awkward vulgarity has wakened me as no brilliance has done for years, I bless you.) Sheila, what have you done to me?

'Let's come and see it again by moonlight, Mamma,' said Orion, as they slowly walked the snake-sided monumental bridge to the first galleries. 'Mr Le Souvan says it's full moon tomorrow night. There will be dancing at Angkor Vat tomorrow night. But let's come here afterwards.'

'There's going to be a party tonight,' said Astarte. 'Mamma, may we go up to the Prince and ask for his autograph?'

'Of course,' said Sumipoon. 'I always long to put Prince Sihanouk into one of my novels. He has real moral courage. But then MESSO would probably fire George. They don't like Prince Sihanouk, he's a thorn between two roses to them because he goes his own way.'

'Sumipoon hero-worships him,' said George. 'Quite the wrong thing for the wife of an official of MESSO.'

'What do you do in MESSO, George?' asked Gion.

'He collects Asian folk songs,' said Sumipoon.

'Quite wrong, I collect erotica,' replied George, 'but MESSO doesn't know it. Can't think of a better investment at the moment. Building up a really first-class collection of erotica is *so* important. And we've got excellent air-conditioned libraries in MESSO, just the thing to keep valuable stuff.'

They circled the first galleries, where naval combats, battles with elephants, war in all its panoplied aspects spread on the carved walls. And always, at the lower level of each high design, between the feet of warriors and their steeds, or below the seas of armadas strewing slaughter, came little men and women and children, eating, sleeping, carrying packs, or driving bullock carts, playing and washing and sleeping, cock-fighting or cooking or consulting the doctor or delousing each other's hair, within a landscape of palm and coconut trees, houses and bullocks, exactly the same landscape as in the villages of Cambodia today; and their faces were life itself, with pouts and smiles and sorrow, excitement and humour and patience, quite unlike the set masks of those about the dreadful business of tyranny, of obedience to glory and grandeur and destruction.

'Like the cathedrals of Europe,' said George, pointing to his children. 'I'll take you to see them next year, Astarte. There also the workmen put themselves in, between the feet of the saints, carving their own or their fellow workmen's faces, as they have done here. It's wonderful to find the same impulse animating a Khmer workman and a French one, both working about the same centuries in history and having never heard of each other.'

'Except that the people here are much more beautiful,' said Sumipoon firmly. 'You can still see many women today with the same mouths and eyes.'

The children, like agile goats, ran in the sombre corridors, leaping up the steps, while Sumi and Gion followed more sedately, and George stopped to attend to a small want of Laertes'.

They walked the slippery, fungus-laden steps. George carried Laertes, Gion found himself listening to Sumipoon's light, gay voice. She bubbled over, talking of many things, all good-natured and gracefully worded. Could he tell her about Sheila? Sumi never really approved of high-flown sentiments. Tragedy, under her pen, was always a little funny, the pathetic wore a built-in smile. And Gion was half ashamed of the emotions he felt, for he had lived self-approvingly, cautiously, and was now raw and hungry as a schoolboy, raw with unanswered questions prickly as cactus jutting out of him, his past a farce, the future unknown, obsessed by a girl who was silly and a nymphomaniac, who had stepped into his room and wept in a taxi. Of his store of years and accumulated choice experiences, placed like antiques in the rooms of his spirit, he had nothing left that he *liked* to contemplate at the moment, except an absurd and silly dream about Angkor, an absurd and silly girl called Sheila, half his age.

If only Sheila had been someone he could admire, but she

confused his spirit's movement with the trivialities of her talk. And yet he could not forget her tear-stained face, and between her face and now he had felt raw, in pain, as if he were bisected partly, say down to the navel.

I have to start again from the beginning.

He had a totality of himself to remake, but he did not know where to start.

'Oh, Sumipoon——' he said, but did not go on, while she turned her head to smile at him a little abstractedly, her round eyes looking beyond him at her children, gone into motherhood.

And then she snapped back, the woman aware of the man Gion. 'Something has happened to you, Gion. Is it important?'

'I don't know yet. I have dreams, or rather a dream, about Angkor. I dream it quite often.'

'Ah,' said Sumipoon, 'how wonderful, Gion, that the stone which remembers should yield its memories to you.'

'Yes, Sumi.' Of course, Sumipoon was a Buddhist, dreams for her reality, with no acknowledgments to Freud or Jung.

They walked round the upper terrace, on all sides surrounded by the faces, profile and front and three-quarter.

'Two craftsmen,' said Sumipoon mockingly, 'contemplating the work of other craftsmen. What did *they* work for, Gion? That in future men would come here to muse and delight and draw fresh life from their handiwork? I always wonder. Do you know?'

'A writer doesn't give answers, Sumi. Only asks questions. Always the same questions.'

They gazed upon the monument's deformities, obliteration of space by mass: a filling of abhorred emptiness with embroidered granite. And the compact idea of the God-King, asserting itself in mountains of stone to its own glory, appeared to them a part of the confused menace, the madness that clamoured for death, unceasingly. For it was said that the Khmers had spent so much time producing this art in stone that they had neglected their irrigation canals, so that the fields were either flooded or went dry; they had employed so many workers and craftsmen that the country was depleted of labour and talent. But others said it was not so: a flood, epidemics of cholera, the plague, had swept the land, and wars had raged up and down the plain. And thus Angkor had been destroyed, its monuments abandoned to the jungle, its peoples had fled, and the past had been forgotten, so that even today the Khmers in the villages spoke of the monuments as built by the Gods, having forgotten that it was the handiwork of their ancestors. And would it be so again? But on a world scale this time? Would mankind, after a nuclear war, gaze upon its own works of a pre-nuclear age, and reverently ascribe them to Immortals, for men might have become too mutilated in spirit or body to conceive of any such work as done by beings like themselves?

'A solemn lesson, isn't it?' said Sumipoon. 'All species die of hyper-specialization, an idea carried to excess. The dinosaurs did. They got hyper-armoured and their brains became smaller and smaller. So shall we possibly, with our ever more enormous bombs and our smaller and smaller capacity to trust each other. It's being too sure that one is right which finishes one off.'

'Perhaps there won't be a war. Perhaps there will be a total renaissance,' said Gion. 'Renewal.'

Inside the recesses of the galleries bats cried their saw-pitched screams in the darkness.

'Not likely,' replied Sumipoon. 'Mankind was ever unable to become wise through Reason. Only through Fear.'

He took her arm. 'Perhaps.' With the bats vibrating in the thickness of ammoniac twilight, near to Sumipoon, small-boned, round-faced, gentle-eyed, he contemplated the going away of his old life, the yet unknown renewal coming to him, the accessible body of Sheila which was no way to her self, but only false entry to a false self.

I must never touch her, that would break everything.

'All Congresses should choose monuments such as these to hold their sessions,' said Sumi, starting up another flight of steps. 'It would have a good effect. Drive the more loquacious writers to silence. Though I imagine quite a few would still go on spouting, in spite of all this silence watching them. Why did you come to the Congress, Gion?'

'I really came back for Angkor. But it also sounded intriguing, a Neutralist Congress of Writers.'

'I wonder why Uncle Ulong Serap thought it up? Whether it's really Buddhist inspiration, or whether he's got something else up his sleeveless garb? Because he's clever as well as religious.'

'Now, now, darling,' said George, 'you're becoming like Mary Faust, suspecting everybody, even your revered seventh step-uncle.'

'Whom I haven't seen for ages,' said Sumipoon. 'We must call and pay respects tonight, darling. By the way, I wish *you'd* take Mary Faust in hand, Gion. Such a beautiful girl, absolutely frustrated.'

'Mary Faust is neurotic,' said George. 'She has a consuming passion for her own advancement. Her cause has the many faces of Mary Faust, and she serves it with devotion.'

'You're unfair,' said Sumi. 'Every woman loves herself, some more, some less. And when a woman loves a man she's still contemplating herself in diverse roles: in his arms, or cooking for him, or as a mother. But Mary is brilliant, and really wants to use her surplus sex energy doing something else. I've seen another girl like that, Sheila Manley.

'Sheila——' said Gion. 'Oh, you know her?'

'We met her in Bangkok,' said Sumipoon. 'And when I went down to order six bottles of Vichy for us and milk for Laertes, I saw her in the hotel bar talking with the captain of the plane. And he left her abruptly, so she must have given him the brush-off, and I had a few words with her. I like Sheila. She had an affair with a friend of mine in Bangkok, a Siamese prince. A very nasty fellow. But she is a sweet girl. I wouldn't be surprised if she became a nun one day. But about Mary, she's so involved now, righting the world's wrongs——'

'All the time it's her own way she wants,' interrupted George.

But Sumi shrugged. 'Sometimes I wish I could take myself as seriously, *believe* in *doing*. I've lost the knack. Too many children, George, a mechanical facility for writing words that sell about people who have no worries but love, all terribly, terribly bourgeois, Mary tells me. When she talks about my writing, contempt just oozes out of her and I feel like burnt toast, darkening at the edges. But I can't help being bourgeois, all my heroines and heroes faintly resembling facially, but with an Asian cast of feature, the film stars of all lands.'

'But your *tikals* will buy my soul's independence, my darling,' said George. 'The only true freedom in our kind of world is founded on a bank account. I'm quitting MESSO as soon as I've built up my library of erotica.'

'It's true,' said Sumipoon, 'that if MESSO fires George we can carry on now. And you too are lucky, Gion, to be well off. I knew a chap, a poet, English. Tall, thin, a little like ... like'— she hesitated, rummaging in her international mind for a hero to fit—'John Gielgud. Or Yves Montand. Or Eiji Okada. He was really down and out. Fired by the British Council for writing a poem about a minor revolution in a small Asian country where he was professing in a university. Nobody minded at all, in fact the revolutionaries were delighted, and the counter-revolutionaries even more so, but the British decided it was tactless to *notice* that a revolution was going on. He came to stay with us. Wanted to go to China, but didn't get a visa. Spurned by both worlds, he thought himself quite extraordinary, because those were the white and black days, when to be neutral was worse than being anti-Brecht. I began to think myself in love with him, though it would have been a mother-act, clearing up his emotional messes. I talked it over with George.' She gave her husband a fond accomplice look. ' "My dear," George said, "I don't mind, of course, but have you noticed his ears?" I looked, and knew what George meant. Ears too soft and pale, making one think of sea-borne sluggish things. Very off-putting. After a time he got a job in the U.S.I.S. He's a professor somewhere for Cultural Freedom. But he isn't happy. He wouldn't have been happy on the other side either. He couldn't co-exist with himself entire in a divided world, and that's what we all have to do now. Co-exist with ourselves.'

'Well,' said George, 'when was it that creative talent flourished only under one kind of government? It's not true, is it? There's only more or less creativeness, depending on a lot of extraneous conditions, but man is an accommodative creature, who's only just begun to worry himself sick about himself. It boils down finally to the handiwork, the art, the beauty he leaves behind. The more he forgets himself, the better he works. Look at what he did when he was Neanderthal, Angkorian, or Renaissance. It's only now that he's started making death on a large scale that he's worried about Art, isn't it odd?'

'To go back to Mary,' said Sumipoon, 'I was saying . . . what was I saying? That you should take Mary in hand, Gion. A beautiful woman, in love by default with an image of herself as a political leader. There must have been many things in her life she's tried not to know, she's so self-defensive. I told her after George left MESSO I'd help her in any revolution she wanted to start, but not now. Do look after her, Gion, she'd be so happy reforming you, she'd brainwash you into *something*. You don't care for anything very much, do you?'

'And what would you say if I suddenly did care, very much, about something?' asked Gion.

'I would say that you'd fallen in love with life again, and be happy. But I'm afraid you've become too wisely selfish,' said Sumipoon. 'You must bestir yourself, Gion. You must suffer again. You've been asleep long enough.'

'Good evening, milady,' said Mr Lee Souvan. 'I trust you have had a pleasant journey from Phnom Penh? The airplane was on time?'

'Marvellous,' said Lady Ada Timberlake. 'D'you know if my friend Mr Das is here?'

'Mr Das is at the moment in the back garden, measuring his footsteps against the wall of the hotel,' explained Mr Lee. 'Shall I tell him you are here?'

'Yes, do ask him to come to my room as soon as possible.'

In her room, Ada went to the dressing-table mirror, surveyed herself, patting her hair, the gesture of a slightly massive, grey-haired woman, drawing in her abdomen automatically, bravely.

There was a knock on the door, and she called: 'Come in.'

And Das, arms outstretched, came in. 'Ada . . .! Did you get my message?'

'Yes. Now, why did you want me here?' asked Lady Ada.

'I'll tell you,' said Das. 'Come out in the garden, and I'll tell you.'

On the same afternoon plane from Phnom Penh to Angkor, which landed in Angkor when Lederer's plane, flying from Angkor to Phnom Penh, had taken off, other passengers arrived.

Mr and Mrs Fumikaro, from Japan, registered their names in neat, meticulous handwriting. Mrs Fumikaro described herself as 'lightning calculator'.

'Lightning calculator,' read Mr Lee slowly. 'You calculate the storms, yes?'

Mr Fumikaro explained: 'My wife is mathematician and novelist.' His own profession was 'businessman and poet'. Both declared the Purpose of Visit: 'To attend Congress'.

A slim, good-looking European, and a handsome Chinese with shiny dark hair came next.

'I'm Anstey, Peter Anstey. Mrs Manley must have reserved a room for me.'

'Oh,' said Mr Lee, 'you photograph the fashions.'

He watched while Peter Anstey signed his name: 'Peter James Anstey, Nationality Australian, Profession Photographer.'

'Teo Kon Teck, Nationality Malayan, Profession—what do you want me to write for profession?' queried Teo of Peter in clipped Malayan English.

'Write poet, my pet,' said Peter. 'You are a poet, after all.'

'We have a good many poets already attending the Congress, monsieur,' observed Mr Lee.

Teo wrote 'Poet', his mouth stretched back in laughter, showing very white teeth. 'My parents would give it me if they caught me writing poet. I'm to become an accountant and go into my Daddy's Bank.'

'How horrid. When you're such an artist, Teo.'

Mr Lee gave them a double room. 'We have no more singles, monsieur. The second and third floors are booked for the Buddhist Ladies' world tour, and the Roman Catholic visiting delegation to South-East Asia.'

'Buddhist Ladies?' exclaimed Teo. 'My Aunty is in it. I didn't know she was coming here. My, I'll catch it from her if she meets me attending a Writers' Congress and not doing my accountancy.'

Peter said: 'You mustn't let your genius be cramped by your family background.'

'That's true,' said Teo. He had had one four-line poem printed in a freshman magazine in Malaya and been told by his friends that he was Shelley. 'But I don't want Aunty to be angry with me. She is a millionairess.'

Then the last of the guests from Phnom Penh had gone upstairs, leaving Mr Lee Souvan meticulously copying the list of passengers of the day into another ledger in his sloping hand, his ball-point sometimes pausing over an 'a' or an 'o' or a 'u' as he checked the passports left with him for control by the Tourist Bureau.

That Sunday evening the main hall, two dining-rooms, and bar of the Suprême Hotel were crowded.

The glass doors of the larger dining-room reserved for the Prince's banquet were shut, and in front of them correspondents jammed. 'Why,' they asked, 'was not the Chinese Delegation received at the Prince's villa, but here at the hotel?'

'Does that mean that Cambodia is moving away from the Iron Curtain countries and adopting a pro-West attitude?' This world-shaking possibility, which could be built up into a major event, had already alerted half a dozen newspapers, from Tokyo to Barcelona.

'I assure you, monsieur,' said the Public Relations Officer manning the doors to prevent the correspondents from installing themselves inside the dining-room before the Prince's arrival, 'it is nothing of the kind. Monseigneur's villa is being repainted. You can see the scaffolding from here since Monseigneur's villa is four hundred yards away, across the road.'

'Is this the time at which villas usually get repainted in Cambodia?' severely asked a *New York Times* veteran.

'All I can say is that it is being repainted,' replied the Cambodian. 'There is no meaning or intention to——'

'You leave the meaning and intentions to US, it's Our Job to interpret facts,' retorted the correspondent, sprinting away to the cable office.

Gion caught the look of worry on the Cambodian's face. 'Don't get upset,' he said. 'People don't remember the next morning what they read in the papers the day before.'

An agitated Monsieur Paulet bustled about, confusing the placid waiters with orders and counter-orders. The red carpet had been swept, and swept again; the waiters, barefooted, hovered on both sides of it, inspecting it with anxious fingers and eyes, frowning and removing invisible hairs; the writers took little leaps over its impeccable surface. A concourse of musicians marched in, walking upon it, shooed away too late, and a dozen waiters went down on their knees to handbrush its surface once more to specklessness. With smiles of Angkorian benevolence at Monsieur Paulet's ire, the musicians settled behind some flower pots, which Lee Souvan had arranged in a kind of archway leading nowhere. Then in dashed, at the double, half a dozen soldiers, unarmed and grinning broadly.

'My carpet——' cried Monsieur Paulet, raising fists to head in agony.

The soldiers were shoeless, their sneakers had been removed at the door. They now crouched respectfully, making themselves shorter out of courtesy to the guests, peering with concentration at the potted plants, walking round them suspiciously; they squatted under the chairs and tables, removed and pounded cushions, ran their hands along the edges of windows; a few reappeared behind the bar counter to frown sternly at the bottles.

'What are they looking for?' asked a woman tourist.

'Plastic bombs, concealed weapons, madame,' replied Mr Lee. 'A little plastic makes a great deal of mess.'

'My, my, and I thought this place was safe.'

'Madame,' said Mr Lee, 'we are neutral, we cannot guarantee to be safe.'

Meanwhile, the correspondents snorted: 'Call that security measures? With that big crowd around? Why, anyone could throw a grenade. They should look at the women's handbags.'

'And in the camera cases.'

'Why cases only? No cameras should be allowed.'

'Frisk everybody. Throw a cordon around. Call that security?'

The Chinese delegation walked down the stairs, and the talk subsided while the five smooth-faced, lounge-suited men ranged themselves on one side. The musicians swung into a polka. A small group appeared at the hotel entrance, two A.D.C.s in uniform, two secretaries in lounge suits, and then, cherubic, cheerful, happy round face carrying its famous dimpled smile, Prince Sihanouk.

A sigh escaped the woman tourist. 'My, look at that smile.'

The music burst into the gay melody of the Cambodian national anthem, the Prince and the Chinese shook hands, and they all walked to the dining-room along the red carpet.

Mr Lee, proudly following the Prince with his eyes, said: 'His Highness is a most accomplished saxophone player.' He had gone down in a low, knee-bent stance as the Prince passed, as all the Cambodians present had done.

Mary Faust was now discovered planted well in front of the row hedging the red carpet. Gion saw the smile upon her face as the Prince walked forward. As he came up to her she extended her hand, at the same time achieving a very slight flexion of one knee. The Prince shook her hand, and dropped it pleasantly. A ripple of envy went through the correspondents.

Now the doors shut upon the Prince and his guests, and everyone else began to move about. Sheila was with her father and Eliza, a decorous family trinity, the remoteness of the well-to-do about them. Gion, watching Sheila, knowing the uncertainty white-anting its way into her smooth appearance, elbowed his way to them, stood by her, said: 'Good evening.' She muttered 'Hallo' as if, for a moment, she was going to brush past, but suddenly changed her mind and called: 'Daddy, I want you to meet ... Mr Hari Gion.'

They shook hands.

'You're a writer, aren't you?' Eliza said. 'Someone pointed you out to me. Of course, I haven't read anything you've written.' Eliza clutched her small silk handbag, matching her dress, between thin, veined hands, hands revelatory of the years.

Charles said: 'We are to register ourselves for the Congress.'

They went to the manager's room where, at the desk temporarily vacated by Monsieur Paulet, a Cambodian sat. Registration was simple: no credentials were necessary; the name, the writer's claim to being a writer (books published, newspaper affiliation); and a card was issued.

'How do you know whether someone isn't a fake?' Sheila asked.

'We prefer to trust. Time will tell.'

'What a charming philosophy,' exclaimed Eliza. 'May I

attend the Congress? I haven't written anything yet, I'm afraid.'

'Intentions also count,' replied the Cambodian.

'I've been to lots of Congresses,' said Das cheerfully to Gion. 'Usually it's the same thing: a minority of writers, a lot of padding by journalists and other nondescripts, political agents, spies, and personable young women reporting on or hanging on to the writers. And then there's lobbying and arranging matters beforehand. At the last Congress of Cultural Freedom they asked me to come. "But I'm on the other side." I said. They explained people got tired of their trotting out the usual exponents of freedom for the writer. "We've always got the same batch of anti-communists, Koestler, Sorrell ... we want some genuine Asians." It restored me in funds, and was most pleasant. They'd chosen a marvellous little town in Germany, with the best food I've ever eaten, and lovely *mädchens* winding about between the desks. Comely and willing. I've never regretted going, even though it was the Other side, for me.'

'I don't think this is quite the same thing,' said Gion.

'You're right,' replied Das. 'It's only because I'm in funds that I could afford to come. I wonder who will attend this Congress, and why. So many issues are involved in writing, aren't they? Politics, of course. It is absurd to demand of a writer to be non-political, as well ask him not to breathe; the Cold War, and all that.'

'I don't understand what he means,' said Sheila, pouting like a child omitted from conversation.

'I think I do, but don't let's bother. Will you have dinner with me, and with your parents of course?'

'Oh, don't call them my parents, it's too awful,' she said. 'I'll go with you.'

'Let's go out and eat at the market, then. I don't like European food out of Europe, anyway.'

'Let's.' She waved at Charles. 'I'm going out with Mr Gion,' she said. Gion wondered at the intensity of Charles's stare as his dark eyes turned to them.

Now they were out of the milling dozens of the hotel, out in the cool night sprinkled with opalescent moon and stars like burrs, walking along the road to the little town of Siemreap. They passed the Prince's villa, a small building with some scaffolding around it, and Gion remembered the repainting. They walked along the river, under the trees, orderly trees clipped with the French regularity which lingers about the gardens and the parks of Cambodia still, as well as about its architecture. They stopped to watch the water-wheels which turned in the river, scaling slices of moonlit water, the splashing women and children bathing from the shores. A cinema blazed neon lights and strident music; the *samlos* rang bells and called to attract pedestrians; little boys with large baskets walked about, calling: '*Painpain, painpain,*' selling fresh buns and bread; unhurried, a small wind ruffled strands of Sheila's hair across her face. And Gion remembered Sumipoon's words: '... in the hotel bar talking with the captain of the plane. And he left her abruptly, so she must have given him the brush-off...' and he was happy.

The world-famous writer, Ashley Basildon, and his secretary Joan Warburton, sat propped on bar stools, causing nearly as much stir as the Prince, but in a different manner.

Ashley Basildon was one of the few writers in the world who have made a fortune by writing. His face was a mask of agony. Whatever emotion assailed him, mirth, doubt, suspicion, perplexity, gaiety, or lust, it was expressed in a grimace which plicated the same folds of flesh upon his face, so that it was impossible to know whether he was laughing, tortured, bored, or amused ... all carved the same grinding wretchedness.

As for Joan Warburton, if Eliza's was the chic of the ageless woman, hers was the full-blown languid arrogance of the young mistress of a famous man.

Two Cambodian writers interviewed Ashley in French. The Cambodians had never read him, but they were earnest, young, and in the traditional manner of Asia thought that he might teach them a 'technique' from which they might profit.

'Do you write in social-realist style, Mr Basildon?'

'Lord, no,' said Ashley.

'Ah, self-expression, then?'

'Give me another brandy, will you?'

'How do you think of your plots, Mr Basildon?'

'Easy. Sex, the guilt complex, a sniff of religion. That's

enough.'

This puzzled the Cambodians. One of them audaciously put another question. 'Pardon, Mr Basildon, but what is the guilt complex?'

'It's the reason why books sell. No guilt complex, nothing to write about. D'you really mean to say that you don't know what it is? Joan, can you tell them?'

'What shall I tell them, darling?'

'That you're my guilt complex, and that without it I couldn't enjoy anything, least of all sex.'

'Darling,' said Joan, 'that isn't very nice, is it?'

'God,' cried Ashley Basildon, 'it's the very foundations of our Christian civilization. Write that down, you two.'

The Cambodians wrote it down.

Ashley Basildon looked at their smooth and happy faces with envy. 'No guilt complex,' he muttered. 'I can't stand it. Joan, let's leave by the first plane tomorrow.'

'Can't, dearest. You promised your producer you'd wait for him here. You're supposed to write a film script based on Angkor.'

'So I am.' Ashley asked for another brandy. 'This place is too happy. No guilt, no inhibitions. How can I write anything here?'

At nine o'clock on Monday morning the larger of the two main dining-rooms, which had served for the banquet of the Prince and the Chinese delegation the night before, was transformed. An array of desks, a table raised on a small wooden platform facing the desks and flanked by three chairs, and a label, NEUTRALIST CONGRESS OF WRITERS, in French, English, and Khmer on the entrance doors, gave it unaccustomed gravity.

Four young Khmer poets went round, asking amiably: 'Are you a Rightist or Leftist writer?'

Multani replied: 'My dear chap, I am pledged to freedom of speech.'

'Well organized,' said Das, who had answered: 'Left, as all writers should be.' 'There's paper and pencils. I once attended a congress in India where there were not even mats on the floor. We brought our own. Comfortable for us, but an Australian writer slipped a spinal disc jerking himself up after thirty minutes of trying to sit.' He fingered the paper. 'Good paper, too. In Venice at a Congress two years ago I stocked up for a year on good paper and envelopes.'

Sheila came in with Charles. And Gion, looking at her and feeling no elation, no surprise, was disappointed at himself. It was a stranger, in a pale blue linen dress, who walked, shook her golden hair. And then, slowly seeping, gathering an avalanche momentum, gladness engulfed him. Oh, he did love her. He was still capable of loving. Would she sit next to him? But Sheila did not (though he saw on her face a brief smile addressed in his direction, and smiled back), she sat with Charles.

Mary Faust entered, with her secretary and the handsome Chinese boy, Teo, who made a movement towards Peter, but was called by Mary Faust: 'Teo, come here!' Meek, unsmiling, Teo sat by her side.

Peter turned round. 'I say, Teo, we're starting work as soon as the morning mist goes. Like to come?'

'I'm afraid he can't,' replied Mary. 'I have an important

document to be translated from the Chinese *immediately*.'

'But I don't know any Chinese, I'm telling you,' said Teo.

Mary Faust, as if she had not heard, opened her briefcase, extracted some sheaves of paper, and gave them to Teo, saying: 'Now don't waste my time. Read this, anyway *try* to,' then began dictating a letter to Mabel; while Teo, flushed, glared at the pamphlet which, as an English-educated Asian, he could not read.

'Stop fidgeting, Teo, I can't concentrate,' Mary said sternly.

Two solidly-built men and one woman came in, a delegation from a socialist country (it turned out to be Rumania). Their clothes were expensive, the woman's hair chic. They were followed by three Americans, the two men in loose cotton shirts and Indian slippers, the woman in a Cambodian *sampot* and blouse; they sat together and conversed in Chinese.

'New Frontier,' whispered Das. 'Now the socialist brothers dress like capitalists, and the Americans pretend to be one of us.'

Sumipoon came in, and George without Laertes. Sumipoon went to sit by Sheila, while George tried to say good morning to Mary Faust, only to be greeted with an icy stare and an 'I'm busy.' He shrugged his shoulders, and sat by a Pakistani writer, who shook hands and said: 'My name is Ahmed Fouad, and I am from Lahore.'

'Ah,' said George, 'I once spent a summer in Lahore. It's a city full of poets, even the hotel waiters recite poetry on Radio Pakistan.'

In saffron robe, with shaven head, a pair of rimless glasses masking half his face, a diminutive Buddhist monk climbed on to the platform, stood behind the table, and said in French: 'Ladies and gentlemen, welcome to the Neutralist Congress of Writers.'

This was Ulong Serap, millionaire, vegetarian, devout Buddhist, and seventh step-uncle of Princess Sumipoon. And with his appearance the Congress, until then a misty improbable affair, assumed a surrealist reality.

Gion, looking round, wondered, not at the small number, but at the number of Europeans attending this Congress. But then, most Asian writers were so poor, it was understandable that few could come at their own expense. Apart from the

Cambodian poets, himself, Sumipoon, Multani, Teo, the Pakistani, Das, and a Japanese couple, the others were European, unless Rumania counted as East.

Das, engaged in the same speculation, said: 'Charles Manley, Ashley Basildon, my friend Lady Ada—the Commonwealth. The British are really neutralist at heart. They alone could bridge the East–West gap, if they did not choose to go sailing upon a sea of Europeans. I'm beginning to believe that it's a racial crypto-feeling which decides for the Common Market against the Commonwealth, as much as the Big Trusts.' For Das, as all of his countrymen, was afraid of what the Great White League would do to the struggling countries of Asia.

Ulong Serap, coughing twice, indicated that he was beginning a speech.

'Welcome,' said Ulong Serap, 'to our peace-loving, positively neutralist, small, but spiritually great country, Cambodia.'

Everyone clapped, except Multani who folded his arms across his chest.

'The Governor of this little town of Siemreap, General Vam Barong, was to address you and welcome you, but he has been taken ill and cannot attend. I present you with his apologies.' Here Ulong Serap coughed again, and Gion sensed a slight stiffening of the neck among certain members of the Congress, an undefinable emotion, gone quickly as a whiff of cologne. He saw Sheila turn her head, look at him, turn back.

Ulong Serap continued: 'You know that under the wise leadership of our revered Prince Sihanouk, Cambodia follows her own true line, true to her national self and her dignity, of independent and positive non-alignment. Not to the Left, not to the Right, but in the Middle, judging each event on its own merits, with logic, clarity, and awareness. This is in accord with the Middle Way preached by the Lord Buddha. I have for the last three years studied and meditated, and before that also known action in the world. I decided to call a small congress of writers of goodwill to examine together the questions facing writers today. Is it possible for a writer to be a positive neutralist? Is not what is applicable to countries also applicable to individuals?

'These are questions, I suggest to you, that you may debate

and perhaps, through discussion, arrive at some useful, fruitful conclusions. The Buddha said: "Questions are more important than answers." This Congress is a free, neutral forum, where as friends we may debate any question.

'I shall now,' continued Ulong Serap, as a murmur of interest rose, 'read the letters and cables of some famous writers and writers' associations who could not be present at this Congress, but whose messages will hearten us in our debate. The first comes from the Writers' Federation of the Peoples' Republic of China: "May the solidarity of the peace-loving peoples of the world be strengthened, and may your Congress with its correct views on co-existence resolutely blast the lies of the Imperialist cliques——" '

'I object,' shouted Multani. 'I object to this message, clearly intended to——'

'Down, sir, down,' Chundra Das sang. 'Let His Eminence proceed.'

'The message continues: "Our writers are busy in the fields and the factories, learning from the working masses, but we are sending two observers to your Congress in token of our friendship." They have not yet arrived,' said Ulong Serap.

At this moment there was a small noise at the door, and two travel-worn Chinese appeared and were greeted by handclaps from the Cambodians.

'Just in time,' beamed Ulong Serap. 'You came in on this morning's plane?' The two nodded confirmation. 'Welcome to our Chinese friends.'

The Chinese bowed to Ulong Serap, brushed their hair back with their fingers, shook hands with the Cambodian writers, and sat at the back of the room.

'This message,' continued Ulong Serap, 'comes from Mr Koenig, of the Committee for Cultural Freedom. "Regret none of us able to participate your Congress since no guarantee given that writers attending live up to their responsibilities by denouncing Hungarian atrocities, Tibetan atrocities, and Berlin." '

Multani shouted: 'Hear, hear,' and started clapping hands, while Mary Faust cried: 'What about Angola?' and the Rumanians 'Lumumba', and Das 'Algeria' and 'South Africa', and the Pakistani's voice, louder than all the rest, shouted:

'Suez!'

'I say,' the voice of Ashley Basildon was heard, 'd'you by any chance have any opium in this country?'

The Cambodians stiffened with anger, too polite to turn their heads. The Chinese muttered to each other, but one of the Rumanians got up. 'We suggest that colonial writers, representative of Imperialism, who have come to make trouble, should be asked to leave.'

At which one of the Americans rose, and in a rather sing-song, careful French, said: 'We demand to know what is the agency behind this Congress, and whether the assembled writers can truly testify that each and every one of them is not associated with any pro-communist or undercover communist organization.'

This made a hubbub of murmurs and clappings, except for the Japanese couple who tut-tutted. Mrs Fumikaro rose and said: 'The gentlemen who spoke are not altogether acquainted with our Asian minds, perhaps...' and sat down again, to loud applause from Sumipoon who understood the innuendo, for the Japanese are very polite people.

Charles, quietly imposing, the Englishman in front of a green baize table, accustomed to bargaining and compromise, stood up, and in a tone, solemn yet not pompous, asked whether 'this somewhat uncontrolled exhibition of political acerbity is in keeping with the aims of the present gathering, the respected garments of our host, His Eminence Ulong Serap, or, indeed, the whole lofty purpose of our assembly?'

The rotundity of phrase cowed everyone. There was prolonged clapping.

'This is going to be a good Congress,' murmured Das happily. 'I can feel it in my bones.'

Ulong Serap raised his hand, and said: 'I am grateful to Mr Manley for restoring a sense of proportion. It is certain that these remarks are not helpful, for they are not within the framework of our present meeting. I shall now continue to read the messages, ladies and gentlemen.'

His face held a puckish glee, and Gion thought: he is having a secret joke. Perhaps Ulong Serap had organized a Congress in order to enjoy, with the humour peculiar to his people, the verbal controversies. For here in Cambodia, in the presence of down-to-earth sanity, the enormous, agitating words, for which men were presumed to want to die, looked what they were, portmanteaux of emptiness. And it took a slightly mad reunion like this to puncture the overpuffed solemn conclaves held elsewhere. Gion laughed, a trap-door issue of laughter, jinn out of pomposity's bottle. He said as much to Chundra Das, now relaxed and happy, as if the battle of words had already been won.

. But Chundra said: 'Yes and no, Gion, but you say this because you want to stay non-committed. Not all words are empty, but we *make* them so when we use them out of context. We, the writers, who should be responsible for keeping the stuff of reality in words, we are the ones who help to empty them, by equating two different things and making them look alike. We call it aggression, whether it is England and France attacking Suez, or India retaking her own territory of Goa, yet the two episodes are completely different, aren't they? We say atrocity, whether the O.A.S. chops up a few Algerian children on the streets of Oran, or the Chinese stop a few Tibetan landlords from gouging the eyes of the serfs ... and we don't stop to inquire the difference. Ignorance, my dear chap, ignorance of the precise issues, the precise, actual, and exact facts, and a strange laziness on the part of the writer to educate himself in the modern world, as if a knowledge of the sound of words was enough, as if a concoction of private torments was enough, for the world we live in today.'

'You are talking of Western writers,' said Gion. 'Asians are not like that. We've still got social responsibility, commitment.'

'Not all,' said Das, a little malicious. 'You haven't. But commitment anyway must be spontaneous, voluntary. Social responsibility *must* become part of ourselves, integrated in our own self-expression, not at variance with it. The truly great writer speaks for all because he *feels* that way, not because he wants to feel or is told to feel. And how many are there in any generation? How many?'

Mary Faust turned round and said severely: 'Das me-boy, don't argue with that bourgeois,' and threw Gion a look of stern contempt.

Ulong Serap resumed reading messages. Congratulatory, exhortative, rhetorical, grandiloquent, restrained, they came from Nigeria and Peru, California and Japan. One, from an Englishman fond of Siamese cats, who had confused Cambodia with Thailand, produced dutiful mirth: 'I understand that these graceful felines are no longer bred in your country. I hope the Congress will promote an Association for their welfare so that these delightful companions of man, the true native of your ancient land, will continue to enrich this sad world with their proud beauty.'

When Ulong Serap had finished he beamed at the assembly. 'Now, gentlemen and ladies, I have invited you here——'

'At *our* expense,' Ashley Basildon put in, and there was laughter.

'—because the world, especially the intellectual world, needs what Cambodia has discovered, positive neutralism. Following in the footsteps of the Lord Buddha, I was granted a modest Illumination. I saw the Lord Buddha's life as the purest example of positive neutralism. Since Cambodia is Buddhist, it is natural my beloved country should follow so closely the precepts of the Light of the World. I felt my mission was to make this clear to writers, so that they in turn may persuade others, and all follow the Noble Path, the Middle Way, which is the Lord Buddha's Way. Positive neutralism is the political counterpart of the Noble Path. It is the expression of the individual within the social context, and as such effects a synthesis between apparent contradictions.'

'Your Eminence,' said Multani, 'we cannot accept that neutralism has anything to do with a religion such as Buddhism. Neutralism is a politically dubious and——'

'I say,' said Ashley Basildon, very loudly, 'any *pretty* neutralist girls around?'

'Mr Secretary,' said Mary Faust, 'I demand that these interruptions, with the motive of sabotaging the Congress, be stopped immediately.'

'Stopped?' sneered Multani. '*I* know what's going to be stopped. Communists like you.'

The Americans glared at Multani in shocked protest. The Fumikaros again tut-tutted gently. Mary Faust held her head high, immensely pleased.

George Rolland rose. 'I suggest, Your Eminence,' he said to Ulong Serap, 'that two committees be formed, one to discuss the role of the neutralist writer in the modern world, the other to study the implications of the words "positive neutralism" as applied to writing.'

This led to prolonged clapping, and Ulong Serap said: 'I agree. Shall we reassemble after the siesta to consider this proposal? Meanwhile, to calm ourselves, one of my colleagues will now recite his own poetry in praise of the Lord Buddha.'

One of the Cambodian poets then read in a sing-song tone what appeared to the listeners to be long litanies, while another translated them into French.

At last the poems were over. It was nearly eleven o'clock, and everyone was hungry, and tired of sitting. 'We shall meet at four-thirty p.m.,' said Ulong Serap.

Sumipoon said to Gion: 'We've imported the Cold War with us. How tiresome.'

The bar of the Suprême, where the writers assembled for drinks before lunch, was the scene of continuing tension, waged between hosts that seemed to mix in amity but were already drawing their lines of battle.

'Perhaps that is what Ulong Serap had in mind,' said Gion. 'Can writers *be* non-aligned in the world today? Does it not mean for a writer judging each issue on its merits, which means a total moral responsibility? It really means total commitment, doesn't it, being neutral? It's a paradox. Neutrality means precisely its opposite, when applied to a writer, because it implies moral responsibility.'

'The moral un-neutrality of Art,' said Das, delighted with his C.P. Snow-ism.

Gion found himself with Das and Ada Timberlake, Ahmed Fouad the Pakistani, and Sumipoon, and a diffident George perhaps conscious of his ambiguous position in MESSO. 'I'm supposed to spy on your thoughts to fill up the cultural dossiers of MESSO,' he warned them, 'but don't worry.'

Charles Manley and Eliza, Peter Anstey, Ashley Basildon and his secretary talked small talk of the theatres in London, as the British do when they keep their moods secret. Peter Anstey threw angry looks at Teo, who had tried to escape Mary Faust, when she had marched up to the Rumanians to engage them in fraternal converse. But they eyed her with suspicion and answered her with stony silence.

'Shall we go to lunch?' This was Das, implacably gregarious, herding as many as he could get together to the dining-hall. Gion managed to pass near Sheila.

'Lunch,' he let fall briefly. And it was Mary, quicker than Sheila, who lifted her head with a sudden, radiant smile, and replied: 'Coming. Now, where's my little boy? Teo, where are you? Come over, we're going to lunch.'

'I'm lunching with Peter,' Teo called back, defiant. And Peter stared into space, triumphant.

Mary shrugged her shoulders, and said: 'Well, bring Peter along. I don't mind.' She looked at Peter with scorn. 'What do *you* do with yourself?'

Subjugated, Peter followed her.

'She's a born dictator,' said Gion to Sumipoon, still conscious of Mary's vivid smile at him.

'She is very sure of herself. That's why people are hypnotized. So many of us are unsure, looking for leadership, and therefore easily obeying dictatorship because it *sounds* so sure of itself.'

Sheila said: 'Mary makes me feel guilty. I've done nothing with my life, she's done so much...'

'What does she want of you?' asked Ada Timberlake.

'That I should help her in her project. A fund for contemporary Asian literature. I think it's a good idea, but I don't know anything about Asian literature.'

Gion said: 'I don't think she does either.'

Sumipoon said: 'Can anyone tell me why so many writers today avoid the really big issues, in the West and also in Asia? The "new wave" of the French, the "angry young men", in spite of their preoccupation with the disamenities of life for the poor young writer, flee what is the very heart and core of the matter where writing novels is concerned: which is that most of our social systems are antiquated and do not correspond to the needs and demands of the One World which science has made of us. There's something terribly wrong when writers become so introverted, distinguish themselves merely by the minuteness of their observation rather than its amplitude.'

Das said: 'I disagree with your "most writers" thesis. We in Asia understand the necessity for realism in writing, because we are going through a Revolution. But where there is upheaval, the times are bad for a novel which reflects deeply, since all values are upset. Writing becomes reportage, swamped by events, rather than a piece of deep philosophical pondering, picking out the main trends, unbogged by detail.'

Ada Timberlake drank soup, wiped her lips, and said: 'Das, in England too, the social theatre, the play about contemporary reality, is already returning. There's Shelagh Delaney and Arnold Wesker. And others. The young ones. They're beginning again.'

Ahmed Fouad, rolling terrible r's, said: 'In the West, writers don't dare face up to the fact of a coming Rrrevolution. And in the East we are so preoccupied with the Rrrevolution already here that we can't see its total face, only fragments.'

'There are two different kinds of revolution in the world,' said Sumipoon. 'The one in Europe will be the automation revolution, the one we're doing in Asia is still the Industrial Revolution. We're two hundred years behind.'

'Do you really believe the Lord Buddha would be in favour of non-alignment in writing?' George asked.

'Certainly. But doesn't it depend on what you mean by non-alignment? C. P. Snow talks of the moral un-neutrality of science. Would he approve of an unmoral neutrality of Art? Certainly not. Neither would Buddha. Buddha certainly was one of our first social scientists. He evolved the idea that the most constant law of nature was change, the continuum of life, and that all of us were responsible, not only for ourselves, but also for others. So of course he stands for commitment, for what the French call *engagement*.'

'I think a writer's first preoccupation is to write, and so his first book is a search for himself usually. After that comes trrrouble,' said Ahmed Fouad, 'because he has to find out what he means by the self, and where he stands in relation to what he is going to picture. All the questions come *after* he's described himself.'

'This is truly Colonial talk,' said Mary sharply. 'You've still got a colonial, department mind, I'm afraid.'

Ahmed Fouad reddened with anger, and Das hastily said: 'Mary, you haven't understood our friend.'

'Self-expression,' said Mary. 'I loathe this bourgeois terminology. What does self-expression mean, anyway?'

'It's a favourite term used by university students in India of the English Literature Departments, who write poems and short stories, mostly inspired by T. S. Eliot, in the student magazines,' replied Das. 'They don't quite know what it means, either.'

'Same in Pakistan,' said Ahmed Fouad. 'Whenever talk about writing comes up, the English Lit. B.A. are on the defensive, jumping in with "self-expression above all". And they only know English Lit., they don't know a thing about how their own people live. They can't even read their own language. They're true colonial. They talk about their writing reflecting the writer's personality first, and the only personality they have is that of their lecturers in the English Literature Department, whoever happens to be in charge. Well-meaning people, no doubt, but unacquainted with Asian literature, they produce bad pseudo-writers.'

'Real talent escapes even the impediments of education,' replied Das.

'Das,' cried Mary, 'you, a veteran of the war against fascism, to speak like that. Art for art's sake. I think you're degenerate. I thought you would see how important it is for us in this Congress to give correct views, agree on a clear position, and——'

'Mary, you don't understand what I say——'

But Mary, who never listened, having learnt that not to listen was a strength in itself, swept on. 'We must organize an Asian Literature Fund, we must form an organization to provide money for the publication of works to reinterpret history, literature, and——'

'Oh, madam,' said Ahmed Fouad, 'people are doing that. We haven't waited for you to tell us.'

'Who will run the Fund?' said Ada. 'You, Miss Faust?'

'Of course,' said Mary. 'I have proved my bona fides. Dare you question them, Lady Timberlake? Are you trying to sabotage my work, the bringing up of the masses to a proper evaluation of their own glorious traditions, trampled underfoot by the most savage exploitation——'

'I never heard so many clichés in such a short time,' said George. 'Mary, you should get a medal. From MESSO, preferably.'

'Have you tried speaking to the Chinese?' said Sumipoon. 'Because they've already done a lot of work about all this.'

'They cold-shouldered her,' said George 'Also the Rumanians. The comrades work and don't talk.'

'They're dogmatists,' said Mary contemptuously. 'But I see I'm wasting my time talking to a pack of pseudo-intellectuals who only wish to retreat from the struggle.' And, heaving with repressed sobs, she rose and left.

Sheila said: 'You've upset Mary, and she really is a fascinating girl. She makes me feel——'

'She works on your guilt complex as she works on Das's,' said Ada briskly. 'Don't worry, she'll come back and finish lunch. I've never known someone like her to pass up her food yet.'

'Oh, dear,' sighed Das. 'I'll go and console her and bring her back. She's so emotional, like a child.' And off he went.

'Pass the butter,' said Ada in the embarrassed silence that followed. 'Dear Das. That's *his* English Lit. background returning, though he's kept it down in his writing. I find Asian men so much less hard-boiled than our own, don't you? And Africans are even more susceptible. Show any woman, preferably a blonde, to some of those new young politicians in Africa, and eight out of ten of them forget all about their principles and come out with state secrets. It's immaturity, also the complex of the White Woman, which still spells Conquest to them, as if sleeping with one of them was an assertion of their equality. Sex has far more to do with politics than one thinks.'

'I don't think we should talk behind Mary's back,' interjected Sumipoon.

'She's always talking about you behind your back, dear,' replied Ada. 'Said you were a slimy novelist grovelling in the filth of bourgeois ideology.'

'That's her way of expressing herself. She's got absolutely no originality in her diction.'

Das returned with Mary, who not only did not appear angry, but smiled amiably.

'As I was saying,' Das immediately took up the conversation again, 'no writer ever really wrote for art's sake. This is a figment of the non-writer's lack of imagination. The creative process is so many-layered that it's no use at all trying to enclose it in sterile formulas.'

'It's the searching that counts,' said Ahmed Fouad. 'Trying to say something, not only within our own dimension, but with all our various consciousnesses aware and alive ... and social consciousness, a sensation of belonging to a culture, a national spirit, a sensation of being the spokesman for ideas, the demands of a people, are just as important a part of the self as the self-expression we were arguing about. Multiplicity is the writer's self. It can't be faked, or simplified.'

'That's why all the *must* schools fail,' said Das. 'When authors are told that they *must* write with social consciousness, responsibility, socialist realism, a commotion occurs within them. For most authors in the revolutions in China and Russia were authors of the bourgeois periods, in revolt against the turpitude of their own systems. A process like a revolution is an avalanche of events, an avalanche of a speed, an amplitude, which the individual consciousness cannot grasp in its wholeness. Years must elapse before the process of assimilation shows some results. Authors are like cows who have three stomachs—they chew the cud of history slowly. In a revolution, authors become journalists: they must produce, because the demand is there; produce and produce for those who have never read before, and although it may appear revolting, yet at the same time this attitude has its justification, for hunger (whether of the stomach or the mind) is an enormous reproach, an insatiable demand, like the beaks of baby birds for ever open, forcing the parents to exhaust themselves in search for food; and for a time what is given them is uni-dimensional, because it hasn't been processed, and ripened and matured ... and because, in a time of revolution, when the total structure, the very framework of our lives, is altered, there must be discipline, control. Control upon the writers is performed by people who haven't the faintest idea of the complexity of the creative process, who suspect all criticism as "reactionary", who will only be smoothed by unilinear panegyric.

'This out-of-step, limping advance between what is offered and what is required persists, it may even become worse, for a time, with a "revolt of the clerks", manifest or covert, as the contradictions between that spontaneous, unconscious process which has to go on in the depths of the writer's being, and the strain of pushing himself into describing or feeling what he *as yet* neither knows nor feels in his bones, his muscles, becomes acute; the strain of writing fulsome praise, when he knows it is not always true. The strain of a long, patient wait, while bureaucrats count the number of words, tamper or distort. This is the testing time, when the writer either falls or goes on, either gives up, or bides his time and nourishes himself in solitude. Finally the pace of revolution slows down, as it moves towards accomplishment. Wisdom and balance return, stability permits criticism and humour. The fanatics melt away, the victims are resurrected, the past discussed, the panegyrics appear ridiculous.

'But on the writer's side, too, an assimilation has occurred. The dimensions of his self are changed: the process becomes understood in its direction, criticized in its errors, but also accepted, in its inevitability and success. The writer's "self-expression" is no longer in contradiction with the achievement of his own people, his system has integrated him, and he has integrated the system, so much so that he can now laugh at it, take pot-shots at it.

'Maturity has come, fearlessness, objectivity and humour once again raise their heads. And after all the toil, the blood, the mistakes, mankind has taken one more step forward—enriched, given new life to literature. That is how I see it.

'Those writers who refuse to understand, who bolster themselves up with the narrowness of their selves against the large movements of history, are compelled to a perpetual fleeing from the real, the vital issues of the day, or to describing an ever narrowing scope of individual appetites. That way lies impotence and oblivion.'

'Come, come,' said Ahmed Fouad, 'you summarize too much, you over-simplify. What about those communist writers who also found themselves out of step?'

'Surely,' said Das, 'the great Chinese writer Lu Hsun also predicted this. He wrote: "Our intellectuals think themselves very progressive, but when the revolution is accomplished, they will find themselves just as unhappy, if not more; for a revolution gallops on, like a torrent, heeding nothing, not even their self-conceit." '

'He himself would have become a victim,' said Ada, 'had he survived, to the Revolution he so ardently longed for.'

'I doubt that,' said Das, 'for Lu Hsun was a scientist as well as a writer. He had detachment and humility. May I remind you that it is not in communist countries alone that the margin between protest and treason is very thin for writers and scientists alike? It is becoming so even in England, where Ban-the-Bomb marchers are tried under an Official Secrets Act, as if their protest were treason. And is not this a perilous come-down from the ideals of democracy? As for the Pasternak case, of which so much has been made ... well, what actually *did* happen to Pasternak? He outlived many other writers; was furiously criticized, but lived on, and made good money. Are there no persecutions of writers in democratic countries too? Can you not remember what happened to writers and artists in Hollywood during the McCarthy era? No, my friend, this is not a black and white question. The writer, the bearer of the creative process, continues, *in spite* of everything, in spite of terror, ignominy, bureaucracy, to grope his way through every system. As my friend Faiz writes, "the ship of pain goes on, towards the silent heaven where lives the unknown, invisible star, it's anchorage at last ..." '

Sumipoon's eyes were luminous with tears. She was easily moved. The candour of her face gave her now a resemblance to Das, the resemblance of those who, at times, will risk everything for what they feel deeply.

But Mary, impatiently, said: 'Escapism. The real issue at stake is this Writers' Congress, which must be guided into the right channels.'

'I think,' said Sumipoon, 'that writers' conferences are exercises in futility. But they do take place, and we come to them. Some of us with prepared speeches, others with a programme. In principle, it is a good thing that we should gather to take a look at ourselves and our fellow artists, indulge in verbal ballistics. But it is a pity that so few of us are really aware enough of the history, geography, and economics of what we discuss. The dialectical necessities at the back of our own motivations are also not clear to us. When the world is so inter-communicating, we only succeed in frightening ourselves and confusing everyone else.'

Put him at a machine and he would be accused of sabotage. As a politician, the routine grind of patting babies and telling lies would lay him low. In any society, any system, under any philosophy, the artist was separate and not separate, representative but not of everything, not even of himself. He was the perpetual doubter, nonconformist, and rebel, always out-manoeuvred, always out-manoeuvring; his habitat between land and sea, never at home in either, his isolation a paradox, for when most alone he organized his best material, understood the tempo of the people he wrote for. Adulation was his poison. He could never be but in eternal ambiguity to himself and others . . .

Lunch over, Gion said to Sheila: 'Let's go for a walk.'

'It's too hot,' she said.

'Then let's go swimming.'

'But I promised Mary——' And then: 'All right, I'll take my swim suit.'

With a feeling of victory, Gion walked upstairs with Sheila, so frightened to lose her that he hovered round her closed door while she was in her room, and thus saw Charles Manley coming up the stairs with Multani.

'Meeting at four-thirty p.m.,' said Charles.

'We'll be back in time,' Gion replied, and again wondered why Charles should look at him with such piercing strangeness.

I won't sleep with his daughter, if that's what he's afraid of.

'Miss Manley and I are going swimming.'

Then it occurred to him that he could marry Sheila, and take care of her. The idea was so tempting that he started dreaming, seeing himself asking Sheila . . .

Then she stood in front of him, saying: 'Gion, I'm sorry, I can't go. I'd forgotten something else I have to do.'

'Oh, I see. Is it very important, what you have to do?'

'I can't tell you now.'

She shut the door; he stayed looking at the closed door, under the impression that she had said no to his marriage proposal. Marriage? Had he really thought to marry her? Yes, he had. He wanted to knock on the door, to say: 'Sheila, will you marry me?' Then he decided against it, went to his room, threw himself on his bed and shut his eyes. What was the other thing she had to do? Who with? Not Lederer, he was not there. Who?

He must have fallen asleep, for now he saw the Bayon, the four faces looking out to all points of the compass, no longer the benevolent image, the power-mellowed visage of Jayavarman VII, King of the Khmers, builder of the Bayon, but the faces of people he knew. And they revolved, presenting to his eyes Mary Faust, Sumipoon, Eliza ... but the fourth, the last face of all, was blank, as yet uncarved.

He woke up with a bitter mouth, a sour and weighty heart, finding the room too hot.

'As I was saying,' Gion heard Das's voice even before he reached the conference room in which the gathered writers were to start their debate, 'we haven't got publishers or printing presses or anything of the sort here in Asia on a large scale. I know writers who not only pay presses to print, they pay a shop for shelf-space.'

'To hell with the world.' This was Ashley Basildon, with Joan Warburton by his side.

'Don't you think we should first state clearly what our problems are?' Ahmed Fouad was talking.

Gion walked into this writers' babel, and Charles Manley greeted him again with the shock of his eyes. There was an inquiry in them which Gion did not understand.

'We are waiting for you, you're late,' said Mary Faust. 'Where's Sheila?'

'I don't know,' replied Gion, and felt the skin of his face burning slowly. 'I haven't seen her since after lunch.'

'She promised to come and help me in some very important work, but she didn't turn up.'

'Well,' said Ada Timberlake briskly, 'the girl is free to do what she wants.'

'She promised to help me——'

'My dear woman,' said Ada, tartly, 'do stop asking everyone to run errands for you. And now that we are all together, supposing we find out who are the real writers among us, and who—shall we say—are merely willing aspirants to the title?'

Multani said: 'I agree. This is a slight upon our personal

character which———'

'I suggest,' Sumipoon said, 'that we nominate two sub-committee chairmen and proceed with whatever questions we want to debate.'

'There's no agenda.' That was Multani. 'I've never seen such a Conference. Usually there's an agenda.'

'Well,' said Gion, suddenly exasperated, 'it's left to us to decide what to talk about. No already contrived platform. I think it's rather good.'

'And, as usual,' said Das, 'we start by quarrelling. Writers are notoriously disorganized.'

Ashley Basildon said: 'Suppose we talk about *Lolita*? Is there any book like *Lolita* written in Asia?'

Mr Fumikaro politely replied: 'In most of our Asian countries such book would be deemed excessively comical, perhaps.'

'So-so-so . . .' muttered Mrs Fumikaro.

'Comical?' said Ashley Basildon. 'Then what about *my* books . . . what do you think of them?'

There was an uneasy silence. Ashley looked round him. Gion said: 'I haven't read them.'

Multani said: 'I have. They're first-class, first-class.'

Mary Faust looked hatefully at Multani. 'What about your tract, Mr Multani?'

'Look,' cried Multani to her, 'you've never written anything I heard of.'

Sumipoon said: 'Please can we rise above personalities?'

'The point is,' cried Ahmed Fouad, suddenly aroused, 'that we're not representative of anything. So how can we talk?'

'We represent ourselves—that's good enough.'

'And who are you? I never read anything from *you*.'

'You never read anything in Pakistan,' sneered Multani, suddenly thoroughly Indian.

'And you've never got beyond *A Passage to India*,' Ahmed Fouad shouted back.

'Oh, Lord Buddha,' moaned Sumipoon, 'are we going to have Kashmir all over again?'

At this juncture one of the two Chinese rose, and holding his shorthand notebook on which he had been taking down every word, said in perfect English: 'My name is Chang.

Never mind the rest, because you would not be able to pronounce it. I have written two novels and three volumes of poems. Never mind what their names are, because I don't think any of you have read them, since they are in Chinese. Before the Revolution I was near illiterate. Now I write, and every day I am full of gratitude to the Revolution which liberated me from my blindness. I——'

Multani interrupted: 'We don't want any propaganda.'

'It's not propaganda,' said Das. 'Mr Chang is trying to tell us about himself. Let us listen.'

'I only want to say,' said Chang, 'that my colleague and I have come to see if we may learn anything new. We are interested in hearing the problems and difficulties of other writers. But we feel that among us are people who have come with certain aims which are contrary to the spirit of the Conference——'

'Speak for yourself.' From Multani.

'He's right,' said Das.

'He's not right.' From Ada.

'What rot,' said Ashley Basildon. '*I* did not need a revolution to become a writer.'

'You,' said Ada Timberlake, 'were born in the Establishment, went to a public school, and will die a perfectly proper conventional rebel in the Establishment.'

'I don't think we'll ever get anywhere this way.' From Sumipoon.

Charles began: 'Suppose we elect two chairmen who will select the members of their respective committees——'

Multani interrupted: 'But we must not have chairmen who represent a communist ideology which . . .'

'This is going to be a good Congress,' repeated Das happily. 'A very good Congress.'

Gion, Das, and Ada walked about in the hall. With them was a thin, very thin and pale young man with Arab eyes and beautiful hands, who had not uttered a word and whom nobody had noticed until now.

Mary looked in the direction of the young man, and asked, with that mixture of aggressiveness and allure which was so stimulating: 'Who are you? I suppose you've come to find material for a novel?'

Das sighed a protest, but as always when Mary Faust was close to him half his jocularity and two-thirds of his assertiveness evaporated.

The young man looked at Mary thoughtfully, as if she were a curious object to examine, and she walked away, without quite managing the sweeping movement she affected. 'I've got work to do. Come, Mabel.'

Gion said: 'Aren't there enough problems and questions without complicating them with people like Mary Faust?' He thought: I wonder why Sumipoon has ever thought of my taking Mary in hand.

'Queer,' said Das, 'Mary always makes me feel I haven't done enough.'

'Perhaps,' said the young man with Arab eyes, diffidently, 'that is because you haven't yet quite got over being colonized.'

'Perhaps,' replied Das. 'Unconsciously, I'm still dominated by *their* unconscious assumption that they know best. I am dominated by Mary. It's something stronger than reason.'

'It's sex,' said Ada unkindly. 'Nothing else, Das me-boy,' she mimicked Mary.

Sheila, thought Gion, why should I feel as I do about Sheila? It isn't sex. It isn't her being a European woman. Can I explain? Not a bit.

> *What was your name, what was my face,*
> *What were we doing, strangers to each other,*
> *Not knowing who I am, not knowing who you were?*
> *Yet here you are, love that I do not know,*
> *A weeping face, a door which shuts ...*

Yet stronger, for the moment, than anything else.

'I think,' said the unknown young man, 'all words out of date. I never find one that exactly means what I want it to mean.'

'Is it so?' Das was perplexed. 'I belong to an older generation in vocabulary than you do, perhaps I don't feel it.'

'You retranslate the events in your own sentences of the past, that is why,' said the young man. 'But for me there is no past, and I find the present difficult to put in words, to say nothing of the future. All the words should be redefined.'

'I know they do sound a bit stale. This constant living with radio and television. We don't distinguish any more between the shouting out of the TV and the real screams of someone being murdered in the street. Or rather, both have become equal shadows that cross our sight. A world of shadows and make-believe infiltrating real events until one partakes of the dream-intangibility of the other.'

The young man shook his head. 'I don't look at TV and I don't listen to the radio. I read detective stories. That's my only contact with the authentic. For me, there's been too *much* reality. I've been in a guerrilla war for the last three years, and I've seen so much that words are all empty. I don't know how to put it.'

'May I ask,' said Chundra, 'who are you?'

'I'm Algerian,' said the young man. 'My name is Ibrahim Malek.'

'Oh.' A happy smile spread on Chundra's features. 'Your wonderful struggle for national liberation...'

'It's not over,' warned the young man.

'Tell me,' said Chundra, 'have you been here long?'

'I was in the war ... three years ... wounded ... Here for a rest. All the words went away. What happened was something that had no words to describe it. Only "death" final, incorruptible. Before the war I wrote. Poetry.'

'Why were you not at the Conference this morning?' said Ada.

'I was. All of you so busy, nobody saw me.'

Chundra was envious. 'I wish I were young again. I also manned the barricades, then.'

Gion thought, I've never manned any barricades, as yet. And he felt ashamed, as if he lacked something essential.

Charles Manley and Mr Fumikaro joined them. After a debate they felt the words 'neutralism', 'commitment', and 'self-expression' meant so many different things that they called for a general debate the next morning.

In the evening Monsieur Paulet, the manager, was once again in evidence with a red carpet rehearsal, and Mr Lee Souvan appeared with gold engraved cards for each member of the Congress. On them was an invitation by His Royal Highness, Prince Sihanouk, to participate in manual labour the next morning at seven a.m. at the new railway track, and to lunch and collective dancing afterwards.

'By Jove,' exclaimed Multani, when he received the card, 'manual labour! Why, it's completely communistic.'

'You'll enjoy it, monsieur,' said Mr Lee. 'A nation can be saved only if hand and head unite themselves.'

'The Red virus has bitten deep into this country,' said Multani. 'Manual labour? I thought we were having a session of the Congress tomorrow. Where is Ulong Serap anyway?'

'Meditating,' replied Ashley Basildon.

'Monsieur, His Eminence asked me to tell you that he will meet you at the field of labour tomorrow morning.'

'My carpet——' Monsieur Paulet, hands to his baldness, rushed to save the immaculacy of the red carpet.

Already the newsmen were assembling. Night fell quickly, a guillotine effect, no long-drawn lingering between light and darkness.

Gion again walked upstairs to Sheila's door, was going to knock, then heard the voices: 'Not this man, Sheila, not this one. D'you hear?'

'But, Daddy——'

'Sheila, I can't stand it any longer. I'll really do something if this goes on. Anyone else, but not this worn-out pseudo-intellectual.'

'Daddy, I love him. I've never loved anyone else.'

'Sheila, I've had enough.'

'I love him.'

Gion knocked.

'Come in,' cried Sheila.

Charles was there, under the orange glow of the electric light, a Charles he did not know, face ravaged, head thrust forward, one hand on his chest.

'I'm sorry,' said Gion. 'I was wondering whether you'd have a drink with me, and Princess Sumipoon and George Rolland.'

'Love to,' said Sheila.

'What about you, Mr Manley? If you and Mrs Manley would care to join us ...'

If Gion had not seen his face a few moments before, he would not have believed that the placid man in front of him slowly filling his pipe with tobacco, pushing the finely chopped leaf into place with gentle prods, was the same Charles.

'No, my dear chap, count me out. Eliza will be back any moment from her photography session. Spent the afternoon out shopping and photographing with Peter Anstey. I must go and do some work of my own. I don't think I should have accepted to come to this Congress. It's all so vague, isn't it?'

'Aren't writers' meetings always vague?'

'It's like the United Nations,' said Sheila. She had dabbed lipstick, atomized some perfume, unconcerned while the men talked, and now tucked her hand in Gion's arm. 'Let us go to Sumipoon.' And then, as suddenly, she dropped her hand, went to her father, threw her arms round his neck, 'I promise I'll be good. You see, he doesn't know.'

'That's my little girl,' said Charles, awkwardly and horribly off dialogue, and kissed her on the forehead. Then, bantering, to Gion: 'Take care of her, will you? She's very precious to me.'

'I will,' said Gion, uncomfortably. This scene, with its sham affection—were they mocking him? Sheila was in love. In love with someone. Who? Lederer? Or someone else? A pseudo-intellectual, Charles had said. So that was why Sheila had not come out to swim with him that afternoon. This was the end of his tenderness of two hours ago, when he had wanted to shout through Sheila's shut door: 'Will you marry me?' She was in love with someone else. But it made no difference, he told himself, no difference at all. He would take her out to dinner, as last night; exactly as last night there would be a moon, small wind lifting her fine, soft hair.

And when Sumipoon opened the door of her suite, the long black hair she was combing streaming down her back, her children behind her, he said: 'Sumipoon, I've brought Sheila. Let us all go out together to dinner at the market place.'

That afternoon at Angkor Eliza had posed for photographs. She had posed, as if crucified, between pillars alive with dancing figures, in front of hooded snakes, looking up, looking down, and the billows of silk from the *sampots* she and Peter draped fostered about her a thousand diminutive suns. A crowd of children watched. Peter Anstey and Teo busied themselves with photographic apparatus.

'Do hurry,' called Eliza. 'I'm getting so tired.'

'I'm going as fast as I can,' replied Peter.

Eliza's irritation made him awkward. He avoided looking at her. In the strong light, she was almost haggard, though carefully poised, and she knew it. 'Do you think it's necessary to concentrate so much on the face? After all, Peter, it's the dress we're interested in.'

'I'm doing my best, angel child. Teo, dear boy, do come and help me with this wire, will you?'

Never again, thought Eliza, never again. I'll go as soon as Peter's finished this series.

Most irritating, as if posing all afternoon against the hot stones, pinned into and out of the heavy silk, was not nerve-racking enough, there was Peter being an ass over Teo. Mary Faust was also making passes at Teo. Only Teo himself did not seem perturbed. He seemed happy helping Peter, squinting critically at Eliza, while she raged silently, raged, and was frightened, and kept saying: 'Do hurry. I'm awfully tired.'

Then it was over, and in the taxi Peter was trying to warn Teo against Mary. 'She'll get you arrested, Teo. She's a subversive person.'

'Not me,' said Teo. 'I got Family. My Aunty is a millionairess, my Father too. My Uncle is a Minister, and I've got three lawyers, two doctors, and two tin mines in the Family. That will look after me. I wanted to go into the Opposition. But my Daddy says no, I've got to take over the Bank.'

Eliza turned the key in her room door. She would have a cold, cold shower, lie down flat, relax in the way the yoga teacher had taught her.

The figure on the grey verandah turned to greet her. 'Hope you had a good time being photographed, Eliza?'

'What is it now?' said Eliza. 'You've had your chocolate box, haven't you?'

'Yes, that wasn't hard.'

'Why can't you leave me in peace? I'm going tomorrow.'

'I've left you in peace all these years. Now you're here. But you won't go tomorrow. I may need you again. You'll go next week.'

'I don't understand. I don't understand.'

'It's good that you should not understand. If you did, Eliza, it would be dangerous. But as it is, you have nothing to fear. I really came in to see how you were, talk over old times.'

In the little town of Siemreap, population twenty thousand, the architecture is colonial French, the shopkeepers Cambodian and Chinese, the streets wide as boulevards, Mediterranean with trees, the river weaves smooth changing colours into its days and nights. The market place is a broad shed in the town's centre, under which are many stalls. Eddies of hawkers cluster, selling food, under gasoline lamps. The Chinese shops remain sleepily open till ten at night, and the proprietors, smooth, fat chests overlapping their trousers, perch on small stools in front of their shops, giving the street inventorying glances as they slap mosquitoes off their backs and thighs with palm-leaf fans. At the small cinema the wooden doors burst open like shutters, letting out an occasional young man, or two girls, and a volley of music, abruptly cut off as the doors shut again.

Sheila and Gion, Sumipoon and George and the children, sat at one of the market stalls run by a Cantonese husband and wife, he skeletal, she enormous. Chickens, defeathered, hung by the neck on hooks, as did cabbages, chillies in strings, garlic, and sausages; in a small aquarium fish swam. The ubiquitous iron pan on a charcoal fire gave off pungent fragrance. In it, one by one, all the dishes were cooked, a procedure which took very few minutes since everything, meat and vegetables, was chopped in small pieces before being thrown in boiling fat.

'All the art of Chinese cooking is in the slicing and the chopping up,' said George. 'That's the first thing lost when a Chinese cook exports himself to London. One day he slices meat not quite fine enough, the chicken pieces are slightly too large, the dish no longer tastes the same. He then descends to chop suey, and the Europeans eat with gusto. He makes a fortune, and retires to a cottage at Egham.'

Astarte and Orion returned from a tour of the market with some Cambodian salad, in which sweet and sour tastes prevailed over the soy-beans, ground-nuts, and pumpkin, mixed with raw chilli.

'Mamma,' said Orion, 'did I tell you there was going to be a coup here in Siemreap day after tomorrow?'

'You told me, Orion. I don't believe it.'

'But it's true.'

'It may be true, but I still don't believe it.'

Sheila ordered a bowl of chicken noodles, and the dexterous cook made his frying-pan spit and hiss, banged it with his iron spoon, and swivelled its round bottom in the glowing embers. A little boy brought them Five Star beer, made in China. 'It's as good as lager,' said George, 'but you can have American or English beer, or German, if you like.'

'I don't like beer, usually,' said Sheila, but she sipped it reflectively, dipping her upper lip over the thick glass as if it were champagne. Suddenly she said to Gion: 'I'm not afraid of you ... as a person, I mean. I'm not.'

'There's nothing to be afraid of, with me.'

'Oh yes there is, there is. Look at her, over there, coming here. What is she after now?'

Gion turned and saw Eliza on the opposite side of the street, peering at the neon-lit shop windows. She was with Charles and Bernard Reguet, and it was strange that he had not heard her voice for it was loud enough.

'Look at her,' said Sheila, 'carrying that big bag. And she only stops to look at herself in the glass of the shop fronts. Why, that's strange: she's carrying the same bag as this morning at the Congress.'

'Looks as if there was a dead baby inside the bag,' said Astarte, 'the way she clutches it.'

And Sumipoon said: 'Astarte, you're ghoulish.'

The noodles arrived, and Gion said: 'Stop worrying about Eliza. It's morbid.'

'Now look who comes,' said Sumipoon. 'The whole Congress seems to be eating at the market tonight.'

Das with Ada Timberlake, and a thin Arab-looking man whom Gion identified as Ibrahim Malek, the Algerian, arrived together. Das as usual was talking, as he never seemed to stop doing except with Mary Faust, before whom he exhibited a constrained look like a little boy caught putting a finger in the jam-pot.

Kilton appeared, his shadow dancing lightly behind his heavy body in the lamplight, and waved his arms about, executing a small Indian war dance and screaming: 'Whoop, whoop!' which astonished the inevitable children firmly insinuated among the stalls. A little girl burst out weeping and ran to her mother. Two small boys cried 'Eyah!' with mock terror.

'Well, well,' shouted Kilton, 'Brains Trust. Meeting of minds. May I join you? Why, hallo there . . .' He waved at Bernard Reguet. 'My old friend. This is a pleasure, a real pleasure.'

He sat next to Sheila, put a hand on her elbow in a father-jocular way. 'Young woman, I'd like to say something to you.'

'Like what?' Sheila's candid eyes looked straight at Kilton.

'That it makes one's heart young again to see someone like you attending a Congress of Writers. Yes, indeed. Our future is with youth. But it isn't enough. Do you know what you're missing? You're missing a most inspiring meeting, which is going to be held in exactly'—he squinted at his watch—'three-quarters of an hour, at our Friendship and Trust Auditorium. A true meeting of East and West in Friendship and Peace. I hope you'll all come? Eight-thirty sharp. That's why the Lord guided my steps here, I feel sure. I went to the hotel, and already delivered the glad tidings to those I met there, then God told me to come here, and I knew He had a purpose. I never act without God's guidance.'

'Does He talk to you?' asked Sumipoon. 'I once met another chap like that, came from Tibet.'

'Any special time of day?' inquired George. 'Or does it happen any time?'

'Any time,' said Kilton. 'The Lord gives and takes away, He talks or is silent, but I walk in His shadow. I know you sophisticated people will laugh at me, but not for ever, not for ever.'

'We haven't been introduced,' said Astarte, 'so I can't laugh at you.'

Sumipoon said: 'My daughter has an off-beat sense of humour.'

'Now, isn't that a smart girl,' beamed Kilton. 'My name's Bud, Bud Kilton. I run the Friendship and Trust classes, and I'm inviting you all to attend our meeting tonight. You'll love it.'

'Is that where the coup against the Prince is being organized?' asked Orion, picking the red chilli out of his chicken.

Kilton's whole face seemed to wobble and congeal at once. 'The—what? What do you mean?'

'My children,' said Sumipoon, 'are writing a detective story.'

'Why, that's good,' cried Kilton. 'That's wonderful. Pulling my leg, were you? Nearly as good as my friend Reguet, over there, who's making up a story about my having stolen some priceless work of art from him. As if Bud Kilton could ever lay his hands on anything not his when God is so near, watching everything. Come on over, Mr Reguet.' He waved at Reguet, who with Eliza and Charles was not a yard away, while the restaurant owner, elated with the sudden flux of clients, wrested trestle tables from neighbouring stalls belonging to the same Trade Union.

'Good evening,' said Bernard Reguet.

'Won't you join us?' cried Sumipoon. 'We're expecting the rest of the Suprême Hotel any time.'

Charles said: 'We'd love to. Actually'—turning to Gion—'you did ask us, but I was waiting for my wife, didn't know what she would like to do. Hope you don't mind if we join you now?'

'I *love* the market,' said Eliza. 'We spent hours here shopping, Peter and I, before going on to Angkor for some photography.'

'Well, now,' said Kilton, 'can I expect all of you at my place at eight-thirty?' Again he looked at his watch. 'You've got heaps of time. I tell you what: I won't budge from here until you've all finished. No, sir.'

'I didn't think you would,' said George. 'But, unfortunately, our family is going to the Royal Ballet dancing at Angkor Vat tonight.'

'We mustn't miss that,' said Sumipoon.

'Do come to our meeting. Only for ten minutes,' pleaded Kilton. 'You'll still be in time for the ballet.'

Charles said: 'It must be quite something. I'd like to go to the ballet. Will you come too, Sheila?'

Kilton said: 'You can see it, and still attend our meeting. It's the Third Anniversary of the Foundation of our Friendship and Trust Association, a most important session. Then we can all go on to the ballet.'

Orion said to Eliza: 'Please, madam, why do you carry your bag as if there were a dead baby inside?'

At which Eliza said: 'Oh!' and rose and walked away quickly, not looking back.

'Orion,' said Sumipoon severely.

'Eliza's a bit under the weather,' Charles said, 'it's the heat.' He looked at Sheila.

Mouth full of noodles, Sheila said, 'Oh, do leave her alone, dad. She'll be all right.'

But Bernard Reguet rose, and said: 'With your permission, monsieur, as I told you, I've already had dinner. I have a call to make. Excuse me.'

Then Sheila laughed, and Charles looked at her, at Gion, then looked away.

Multani strolled about the hall of the Suprême Hotel, envying the American Economic Delegation at dinner with Prince Sihanouk and his ministers. As on the previous day, security precautions seemed by Western standards slack and perfunctory.

'You see,' the Cambodian P.R.O. explained, 'His Highness knows not fear. He goes among his people without guard at all.'

'But something might happen.'

'Oh, yes, our enemies have tried once or twice, but His Highness says: "I am quite ready to die, but I don't believe it will happen so long as my people are with me." '

The journalists retreated to the bar. Multani strolled, waiting for the hour of eight-thirty when his mission would begin.

He was ready. In his jacket, against his chest, on both sides and at the back, well evened out, was a half-million dollars in notes. On his arm was slung his camera case. As for the little something which Kilton had confided to his care, that was concealed in the false bottom of the camera case which had previously held the money. Carefree of aspect, he walked about, looked casual.

The car was a large taxi, in no way different from the taxis that stationed for tourists in front of the Suprême Hotel. Multani stepped in, said loudly: 'To Angkor, the Ballet,' as

Kilton had told him to do.

The moon was a clear-cut disc in an opaque sky. Cradled by the smooth-running car, Multani dreamt: saw his own photograph on the cover of a world magazine, 'one of the prominent young leaders of Asia', saw himself organizing a nucleus of wealthy men, financiers, a few intellectuals, some Army officers and generals, than which no more formidable combination exists: when one has Army backing, everything is possible in Asia. An army needs money, and the financiers were there. A party needs egg-heads, if only to form a ministry of culture and a department of information. He might select among the intellectuals some kind of opposition, preferably calling themselves socialists. There were always youngsters who wanted to be socialists, especially if they came from good, solid families. It was part of their hate-your-father Oedipus complex, but really they were quite solid inside, solid because they couldn't stand much hardship, not really; one watched them for a bit, assessed them; those that really meant business, one eliminated quietly; the others one built up into a kind of benign opposition. That was the real, good way of preventing a real revolution: having small escape valves of pseudo-revolutionary proceedings. His Excellency, Muni Multani, the Prime Minister...

Confusion, that was it. So long as one confused the issues, didn't make them too clear-cut, one could keep the power smugly in one's own hands. He, Multani, would be able to do so...

The chauffeur suddenly turned into a side road. There was gravel, too small a garden, parterres of flowers, and bushes, a two-storied suburban villa, the harking voice of soldiers. Multani stepped out of the car, and was ushered in by a young man who waited by the gate. 'Par ici, monsieur.'

The hallway he stepped into was screened from light by thick silk hangings, so that when the front door had closed on him he was in a dark corridor, until another silk curtain lifted and he stepped into a large, resplendent room, blowzy with French furniture, clocks, mirrors, gilt vases, marble statues, crystal chandeliers, indeterminate paintings of landscapes, and decisive portraits of the owner, General Vam Barong, Governor of the Province of Siemreap, in all dimensions, at every angle and profile, on the walls, the low tables, the tallboys. In came the general, carrying lightly his squat, muscular body, surmounted by a powerful, Napoleonic face, with full, margined lips darkly incised in the golden skin; full of energy, striding with an assumed brusqueness outlandish when he extended a small, charming, delicate, plump hand.

With him, weaponed to the eyebrows, came four bodyguards, and two secretaries in lounge suits.

'Cher Monsieur Multani,' said General Vam Barong, 'how glad I am to see you *again*.'

I've never seen you before, thought Multani, but he bowed. 'I understand you are not well, Your Excellency?'

'I am indeed very ill, monsieur. I have sugar in my urine,' said General Vam Barong. 'Fortunately, my doctor has flown out from Vienna to see me recently. I have to be careful, monsieur. But my heart is in good condition. How is your Writers' Congress proceeding? Unfortunately I could not address your first meeting.'

'A statesman has the duty to look after his health.' Multani thought he had turned the compliment rather well.

'Monsieur, you are too kind. I remember when I was Ambassador, before His Highness in his high wisdom promoted me here, it was fatiguing, very fatiguing...' His voice trailed. His round eyes looked amiably at Multani. He was obviously waiting. The bodyguards and the two secretaries disappeared. A servant materialized, crawling upon his knees, head well below the sitting general as he proceeded to deposit a tray of drinks between Multani and his host. It was champagne, iced, brimming in beautiful French imported crystal glasses.

'Your health, Monsieur Multani. And thank you again for your kindness in coming to see an old, sick man.' The general sipped, still keeping his round, very bright eyes on Multani.

Multani began to handle his coat lapels. 'I have here...' he said.

'Let me take your coat,' said the general, solicitously. 'It is indeed so hot in this room. Do let me, I pray you.' Two servants rushed in, but the general snapped a command and they disappeared. He carried Multani's coat out. Multani was left alone. Five minutes later the general was back, all smiles, Multani's coat on his arm.

'I hope you are not so warm now? Champagne is cooling, is it not? Do have more, I pray you.' Putting the coat down on an armchair: 'Ah, yes, those days in London ... I missed something very much in London, I missed my astrologer, the best astrologer in South-East Asia. I went to the Spiritualist Society quite often, but my astrologer was better. In fact, he is holding a seance tonight. He will indicate an auspicious day for me to ... aah ... to begin to feel better.'

'I hope this will be soon, Your Excellency.'

'It will be, it must be. Please leave your friends in no doubt about that. Tell them their trust is not misplaced. I am looking forward to some more kind visits ... say very soon.' He pursed his lips, placing his fingers together. 'It is so costly, to be ill as I am ... and to carry out my duties. You understand?'

'I understand.'

'You will tell your friends? Now,' he said briskly, 'this has been delightful, Mr Multani, but no doubt you must go to Angkor Vat to see the dancing. Our wonderful Royal Ballet. I am so sorry I cannot accompany you ... my health ... my astrologer ... tell your friends ...'

'Now you know what to do,' said Mary, giving her hair its final pat in place. 'Get going, Despair.'

'Oh, Mary, but I'm afraid.'

'Miss Faust to you now. There's nothing to be afraid of.'

'But I've never talked to a governor before.'

'It's time you did. And remember, start right in with our project. Don't stop talking until he says yes.'

'But we've got so many projects, Mary.'

'Idiot. Haven't I told you that the one we're pushing now is the Million Dollar Asian Intellectuals' Fund?'

'Suppose he doesn't want to see me?'

'He will. You're a woman, aren't you? Just say you won't go until you've had his O.K.'

'But he couldn't talk to us this morning because he was ill.'

'That's why we're going to see him.'

'I am, you mean.'

'You are. But you represent *us*. Don't forget to say *we* when you talk to him. You're no longer just *you*, Mabel Despair.

You're speaking in the name of Humanity, Progress.'

'The Intellectual Asians' Fund. All right, Mary, I'll try.'

Lederer turned to face the timid knock on his door. His eyebrow cocked in interrogation to the person sitting, immobile in the armchair, who rose, moved leopard-soundless into the bathroom.

'Entrez!'

He was not braced for the mild, hesitant Mabel Despair, peering at him with shy anxiety.

'Captain Lederer?'

'Yes, madame?'

'I wonder whether you could do me a favour?'

'I pray you, madame, do sit down. May I offer you a drink?'

Mabel glanced without seeing them at the two glasses on the table. She sat down in the armchair vacated. 'I don't know how to begin. I work for Miss Faust.'

'The "Death-to-the-Tyrants" lady? I've seen her.'

'Oh, I wouldn't describe her like that.' Mabel's giggle subsided. 'I have a husband and five children in Bangkok,' she explained, as if this meant everything. 'The baby is only a year old.'

'How nice,' said Lederer, grinding his teeth on the word 'nice'. His mind immediately leapt to sexual complication. He scanned Mabel; obviously the usual rebound from sexually unsatisfactory man to emotionally unsatisfactory woman. His interest dropped.

'My husband, Thomas, he's a technician with a firm. I wonder if you could take a letter to him?' She proffered a bulky airmail envelope. 'You see, I'm worried about the children. It's normal, I suppose?' She smiled bravely at Lederer. 'You're piloting the plane to Bangkok tomorrow morning, Mr Lee tells me.'

'Why don't you post this letter, madame? We are forbidden to take any correspondence or mail.'

'Because——' How could she explain that she did not trust the post? She had wanted to send a cable to Thomas, but Mary had caught her, and crushed her with scorn: 'What are you, Mabel, a grown-up woman or a child? You're too dependent, you've got a slave mentality. Let Thomas begin to appreciate and understand you. I forbid you to write.' Somehow Mary would find out that a letter was posted. Like the keys, the mail was spread out on the reception desk for people to help themselves. Outgoing letters were put in a large box with a lid. Anyone could lift the lid and remove a letter. Mabel felt that this large trust, this naïve confidence which seemed to imbue everyone in the hotel, so that even when the Prince was around no special precautions were taken and people went in and out, might result in Mary finding her letter, perhaps tearing it up. A little spurt of hate began in her against Mary Faust. But she couldn't say this to Lederer: only stammer and explain that the post, sometimes, took a long time, and if he would be so kind?

And Lederer knew that she spoke the truth, that she had five children, one a baby, was unhappy. 'I'll take your letter. Better give me your husband's office telephone number. I shall ring him and he can come to collect the letter at our Air Company's office.'

'Oh, you are so kind, Captain Lederer.' Mabel was suddenly quite pretty, with large soft eyes. Femininely she removed her thick glasses, wiped her eyes. 'You see, I'll be here for a week at least. I'm secretary to Miss Faust. And we're so busy, so many projects. For instance, tonight I've got to go out and see the Governor, General Vam Barong. A project of Miss Faust's.' She held out her hand to Lederer. 'Thank you, Captain. Wait, I'll just scribble my husband's office phone number. There. And thank you again. Tell him ... tell him I'll be back *soon.*'

'I will, madame.'

'Give me that letter.' It was Lederer's guest, now back from the bathroom.

'Why? It's a letter from a wife to a husband.'

'We take no chances.'

'Tell me,' said Lederer, as the other one folded up the letter slowly again, put it back in its envelope (the stick flap was still damp and had come off easily), 'what harm can this little woman's letter do?'

'We cannot take risks. This woman, we must keep tabs on

119

her, on her husband. They may come in very useful. Women are always more useful than men. We have quite a few in our net. Unknown to themselves, of course.'

Lederer paced slowly to the dressing-table mirror. 'There is one girl,' he said, 'I'd be obliged if you would not draw into any combinations, if possible.'

'Who?'

'The young blonde, Sheila Manley. I would not like her hurt.'

'But, mon cher, *nobody* will be hurt. Because nobody even *knows* how or why they are being used. Links, passing the current.'

'I would rather this one was not . . . a link.'

'Certainly, mon cher. But you will remember what I was telling you, won't you?'

'You can count on me. After all, I also believe in this.'

'Good. Then ring up the husband of the little woman when you get to Bangkok. It can do no harm.'

'What about the letter?'

'Say you've mislaid it. Never lie more than is necessary.'

Lederer paced up and down, up and down, then went into the corridor, knocked on Sheila's door. No one answered. He tried the lock. The door opened. Careless girl, she's forgotten to lock her door. He stood for a while, looking at the empty room, breathing the perfume of Sheila, and felt lost, empty, unhappy. He squared his shoulders and walked back to his room.

Multani stepped out from the lighted room in General Vam Barong's villa into the dark corridor, then into the moonlight, and back into the car, which started, passed the gate, turned to the right towards the ruins of Angkor, and stopped.

'What is it?' asked Multani.

In the car lights a figure had appeared, a woman waving a torch, who walked up and flashed the lit torch into the chauffeur's and then Multani's face.

'Oh,' cried the voice of Mabel Despair, 'it's you, Mr Multani. I say, can you tell me where is the villa of General Vam Barong? Miss Faust told me how to find it, but I'm afraid I got lost.'

'Ah, Monsieur Deroulede,' said Lee Souvan, 'you are here?'

'I've just arrived, the seven-o'clock plane from Phnom Penh, Souvan. Paulet gave me a room.'

'I hope it is comfortable?'

'It is, very comfortable.'

'We have the Buddhist Lay Ladies and the Roman Catholic Visiting Mission to South-East Asia tonight, monsieur, otherwise I would have attended to you myself.'

'Paulet did. You have a Writers' Congress on too, I understand?'

'Yes, monsieur. His Eminence Ulong Serap.'

'Dear Ulong Serap! I have not seen him for some time. But his affairs prosper, even when he meditates. How is my friend Reguet?'

'Monsieur Bernard went out with Mr and Madame Manley to eat at the Cantonese stalls in the market-place.'

'I'll have dinner here, Souvan.'

'Certainly, Monsieur Deroulede. In the smaller dining-room, if you please. The Prince is in the bigger one with the American Delegation. There is a ballet at Angkor Vat tonight, if you wish to see it.'

Lee Souvan watched Jean Deroulede walk towards the dining-room. Jean Deroulede, the planter, was one of the wealthiest men in Cambodia. A real gentleman, thought Lee Souvan. Deroulede had saved Lee Souvan's life during the Japanese occupation.

Lee Souvan checked the guest book. Yes, Paulet had given Deroulede a good room. It was unfortunate all the suites were occupied. The room was next to Mary Faust's suite. Lee Souvan smiled.

'Now,' said Ada Timberlake to Ibrahim Malek, 'I'd like to recapitulate the situation, since we're in this together.'

The other guests had left the market-place for the dancing at Angkor Vat. Das ordered coffee.

Ada began: 'I was travelling in the Middle East two years ago, doing a book on the desert, when I stumbled on the Trade. Opium, morphine, heroin, from the no-man's-land border regions between Burma, Laos, and Thailand, a traffic fanning out to Bangkok, Hong Kong, Singapore, the Middle

East, to Europe, and America. There are many ways in which opium gets out of were it is grown in Laos, in the valleys of the Meo tribes. It has its trade routes, its banks, its company directors, and its airline, Air-Opium. It is, in fact, a modern Big Trust, the biggest monopoly enterprise in South-East Asia, with the smallest expenditure in capital, and the largest profits. The Ring—that is what we call its top administrators—amiable, cultured men, live in Bermuda, the Riviera, or New York, and some are amiable politicians supported by the Western powers in South-East Asia.

'A kilo of morphine or heroin brings in something like ten thousand pounds sterling in Calcutta, and ten times as much by the time it reaches New York. One can finance anything with that. It's the sinews of many local wars. The war in Laos, for example, is also partly an Opium War, with strong men, generals, the chief dealers of the Ring, using its profits to finance their ambitions.

'The Meos who grow the opium remain poor, but the middlemen are Kuomintang Army officers from the old armies of Chiang Kai-shek, stalled in the vague frontier regions between Burma and Laos for the last twelve years, and they too make a lot of money. They have established their gangs to transport the opium to the first collecting stations, villages under their control, and there process it with equipment flown in under Aid schemes. The morphine and heroin produced go to certain shops in the towns of Laos. One of these shops is very well known in Luang Prabang, the capital; it has a sewing-machine outside its shop front, and it is run by someone called Jerry.

'The traffic is more swift, efficient, and profitable now than ever, because it's done by helicopters and planes. All that is needed for the helicopters is a few square yards of concrete, down in some valley. The pilots of Air-Opium are well paid, their contracts run six months at a time, renewable. They get in six months what in ordinary time would take them four years to make, plus a bonus of five thousand pounds sterling if they've lasted out three contract periods. They are recruited among the ex-airmen of the French Army, who know Indo-China well, who can fly this terrain almost blindfold . . .'

'Same batch that produced the O.A.S.,' interrupted Ibrahim

Malek.

'Right,' replied Ada. 'Yes, it is odd that the O.A.S. hadn't tried to muscle in on the Trade earlier, so many of the pilots being pro-O.A.S. Perhaps because of C.I.A. competition. Up to fairly recently one of the high officials in a certain pro-West country, in charge of Narcotics Control, was on the Board of Directors of the Ring, and very friendly with the C.I.A. He dealt with the Trade most efficiently. Usually let through three shipments out of four, then made arrangements for a smaller fourth to be captured by the police. It would be found in the luggage of some Chinese merchant, or in an abandoned car, or under the bellies of pigs driven to market by villagers, and confiscated. The merchants or villagers arrested as smugglers were made to confess that they were also communist agents, so that the political and the financial aspects of the matter were dealt with at one blow.

'I remember,' continued Ada, 'attending an opium liquidation ceremony some years ago. A holiday was proclaimed. There were fun fairs, orchestras, bunting and flags, lots of schoolchildren. I had a seat on the V.I.P. stand. All the high officials, even the Chief of Police himself, glistening with plumes, medals, and virtue, were there. The opium, in well-tarred, unleakable boxes, was piled on a barge painted black. The barge was towed a little way off, then sunk (to the accompaniment of music from the orchestras) by being shot by naval gunfire ... quite a number of shots before the barge was hit, not due to bad marksmanship, but to give the people their money's worth of bangs.

'The barge sank, amid shouts of joy, regattas began. Sailing boats, motor-boats, racing out on the sea. The first motor-boats to put out, of course, were the police, racing away ostensibly to start the regatta, but actually to rescue as many of the opium casks as could be rescued.

'That night an extra in all the newspapers announced that another death blow had been dealt to the Traffic and to communism. Occasionally the "communists and smugglers" are shot publicly, at night, in a fitting ceremony, to end the festivities.

'Now this high official, so useful in managing the passing of opium, was a great friend of the C.I.A. and also was related to the Governor of this Province, General Vam Barong.'

Ibrahim Malek said: 'My turn. The aforesaid high official died recently. Also some of the big shots in the C.I.A. were fired. This has temporarily disrupted the Ring and allowed the O.A.S. to muscle in.

'There is an organization called O.A.S. International, a network throughout Europe, now also in Asia among the French businessmen of erstwhile Indo-China. They come to Cambodia from Vietnam because they can't compete against the Americans who have taken over in South Vietnam, and also because they can't carry on business with the guerrilla war that's going on.'

'Everywhere in French Indo-China there is this rivalry between American and French interests. Acute contradictions between capitalists——' began Das, doctrinally.

'The French vote consistently against American decisions in SEATO,' said Ibrahim Malek, 'because de Gaulle's Europe is not Kennedy's Europe. The French Embassy in Cambodia three years ago tipped off the Cambodian Government about a United States sponsored coup prepared by the Central Intelligence Agency against Cambodia. And so it goes on, friend stabbing friend in the back . . .

'The French colonials and the ex-officers of Dien Bien Phu have not forgotten the war of Indo-China. Here, as in Algeria, they supported the pro-Nazi Vichy régime during the last war. Many have joined O.A.S. International, which is now getting narcotics through its own network. Locally, someone here in Cambodia is the brain behind this scheme. He has started a new system. The innocent passer. People are being used who don't even *know* they're carrying narcotics.'

'Sheila Manley,' said Ada.

'Yes,' said Das. 'Sheila Manley is an innocent passer. She was given a three-pound box of chocolates to take with her on the plane coming here. It was done in front of me, at the airport in Bangkok. I saw it without realizing at the time what was happening.'

The Algerian continued: 'Every chocolate in that box contains a pellet of refined heroin, total worth twenty-five thousand sterling. The box did not reach its destination, which was an agent of General Vam Barong, Governor of Siemreap. The box she handed over contained genuine chocolates. Did Sheila Manley discover the heroin in the chocolates, and make a substitution? Did someone substitute genuine chocolates unknown to her? I believe Sheila herself did not know and that the O.A.S. agent stole the chocolates containing heroin from her.'

'Sheila is in danger,' said Ada.

'From both the Ring and the O.A.S.,' agreed Ibrahim Malek. 'Both kill without compunction.'

Ada shivered. 'What a good thing you found us here so quickly. We had no idea you'd contact us.'

'I watched for you,' said Ibrahim Malek. 'Our intelligence network is efficient.'

'I wonder who he is,' mused Das, 'the O.A.S. brain I mean?'

'I don't know,' said the Algerian. 'It may not be a Frenchman at all.'

Eliza was back in her room.

My nerves are going.

She bent towards the mirror and was shocked.

My face, what is happening to my face?

She lay on the bed, put her legs up, closed her eyes, smoothing her face with her hands. Then she sprang up again. The electric light fell flat upon her and the hotel furniture, and shadows rampaged upon the floor. She went to the telephone.

'Give me Mr Anstey's room.'

'Mr Anstey is out, Madame Manley. He has gone to Angkor Vat for the dancing. Madame, Monsieur Reguet is downstairs. He is asking whether Madame can see him for a moment?'

'Oh.' Eliza threw a frightened look at her bag, standing on the table where she had placed it. 'Tell him to wait a moment.'

Bernard Reguet was waiting in the hall for Eliza Crawfurd when a hand was laid on his shoulder. He turned. It was Deroulede.

'Ah, mon vieux, nice to see you. When did you arrive?'

'From Phnom Penh by plane this evening. Join me in a liqueur?'

'No, I'm waiting for a lady.'

'My plane was full of ladies. A Buddhist Ladies' congregation. Is yours attractive?'

Reguet laughed. 'Always the same, Jean Deroulede. Will you never change? And you have one of the most charming wives...'

'There is nothing a wife appreciates more in her husband than a discerning eye towards other women.'

'Anyway, in my case, it is nothing of the sort. Mrs Manley is very charming, her husband very intelligent. But they are English. She seemed upset by something tonight, her husband let her go away alone, he stayed with his daughter. I came back to see if I could help.'

Eliza now walked down the stairs. She still clutched her bag. Bernard and Jean Deroulede rose. Eliza looked frightened.

Bernard introduced Jean Deroulede. Jean shook Eliza's hands, his eyes on her face. 'Madame, my homages.' Then to Reguet: 'Will you excuse me? Perhaps I shall see you tomorrow?'

'I am at your disposal. Any time in the morning.'

Bernard said: 'I am so sorry to disturb you, Madame, but when I saw you so upset I had to come.'

'It is nothing.' said Eliza. 'Nothing. That child's remark upset me. You see, I did lose a baby ... and it's the anniversary of her birth today.'

'Oh, madame! How sad.'

'Men don't quite understand how a woman feels.'

'I am so sorry. I did not mean to pry.'

'Please forget it. I'm feeling better already.' With an effort she started smiling, and said to Bernard: 'I have been worried about thefts. I must tell you, I carry this heavy bag because of my jewellery. I thought someone might take my jewels. So now I carry them about with me.'

> *'It's a good time to get acquainted,*
> *It's a good time to know*
> *Who is sitting close beside you*
> *And to smile and say hallo.*

> *'Good-bye to lonesome feeling,*
> *Farewell glassy stare,*
> *Here's my hand, I'm glad to know you,*
> *So put yours right there.'*

'Now,' Bud Kilton carolled, while the chorus cleared their throats, 'now, friends, once more—all together.'

Docilely the bespectacled pianist, a sallow girl with very thin arms and muscular hands, struck the keys.

> *'The more we are together, together, together,*
> *The more we are together,*
> *The merrier we'll be.'*

Sheila sang, splurted with laughter, sang and clapped her hands. Now she was wholly child, and Gion was full of tenderness. Never had he loved her so much as when she pushed her hair back, laughed like a child at a pantomime.

They were at Friendship and Trust Auditorium, she, Gion, and Charles. It had been a whim of Sheila's, saying to Bud Kilton: 'All right, we'll come,' taking a decision for all three of them. Now the two men framed her, she sat between them, and was happy; sometimes turning to Charles and sometimes to Gion, as if striving to share herself equally between them. Her hair brushed Gion's shoulder, and he wanted to put his arms round her.

Friendship and Trust Auditorium was a large room in a small house about a mile from the hotel. A few young Chinese boys, three Cambodian couples, sat and sang with application. Bud walked up and down, his arms spread wide, his smile all-embracing, in a determined attempt at good cheer. The pianist never smiled as she banged the keys hard, used the pedals. In between the songs she threw startled looks from behind her spectacles at everyone. A spinster, thought Gion. Probably converted to Christianity; gone out of her own Buddhist community through her conversion, she must be very lonely, nearly an outcast . . .

'Come on, folks, come on. Give all you got, let her go bust! Hi boys, hi gals! Give me your hand and say—all shake your neighbours' hands, c'mon, shake them,' cried Bud, putting his hands round his mouth as if he were hallooing towards a distant mountain:

> 'Hi friend, hi pal,
> 'I'm sure happy you could be here today.
> I know you're fine and dandy,
> You are so kind and friendly,
> So shake my hand and let's begin
> To have a happy time.'

Bud clapped himself vigorously, and then clapped his hands near the pianist's ears. The Cambodians and the Chinese clapped, got up.

'Thank you, thank you. Now that's over, do come again next week, Monday. Stay and have some coffee,' he said to Sheila and Gion and Charles. 'Oh, I know you've got to see the dancing. I'll take you there myself. When they say eight-thirty, they won't start before ten. No sense of time here, you know. Besides, they've got to wait for the Prince. His Highness won't be there before ten or ten-thirty. Have some chocolates. Maisie, Maisie—' he called to the pianist, 'bring the chocolate box.'

Maisie brought the chocolate box. Sheila took a chocolate, remarking: 'You get your chocolates from Bangkok, same place as I do, Mr Kilton.'

'Do I? Well now, this came in with the post today, I think. Maisie here, she's in charge of the post. Someone must have sent them to me. Probably a letter tomorrow telling me which friend. Post is a bit erratic here.'

'I think we must go, Sheila,' said Charles. 'The others must be waiting for us.'

'I'll get my jeep,' cried Bud. 'We'll all go together. Maisie, you come too.'

But Maisie shook her head, and walked away, her music rolled under her arm.

Gion wanted to get away, to be alone with Sheila. But Sheila had decided otherwise. She seemed determined to be with people. Well, he had started it, asking Sumipoon and Charles to come with them. Anyway, Sheila was in love with someone, she had said so. But the conversation he had overheard seemed so unreal, so theatrical, he was half persuaded he had not heard it.

I must ask Sheila who it is . . . Perhaps tomorrow.

Soon they were in Kilton's jeep, going towards Angkor Vat in the night.

'His Highness is still busy,' Bud said, as they passed the Suprême Hotel. 'Look, there's the royal car. And the show couldn't start without him, so we'll be at the dance too early.'

It was six o'clock in the morning, and the Suprême Hotel was already astir.

Waiters knocked on bedroom doors, opened them with master keys without waiting for sleepy grumbles from the beds. They shouted: 'Travail manuel sous la haute direction de Monseigneur' and 'Petit déjeuner, m'sieur, madame,' clattering trays with coffee and croissants upon bedside tables. There were curses, but the waiters paid no heed. They stepped briskly, smiling broadly above the trays, ignoring the mutters.

'Travail manuel, monsieur.' The coffee tray was put down by Gion's head.

He said: 'Oh . . . merci.' Manual labour, that was it. Today was manual labour day. By invitation from Prince Sihanouk. What did one wear for manual labour? Obviously one's oldest clothes. Sports shirt, drill trousers, tennis shoes. He swallowed his coffee, then remembered his dream.

In the dream he was walking with someone he thought was Sheila, along the banks of the river. A water-wheel rotated slowly, its axle creaked a tune. He said to Sheila: 'I remember this melody.' She turned her face to him, and it was not Sheila. It was no one he knew.

In the hall downstairs was Ada Timberlake, in short shorts, her muscular varicose legs courageously exposed; Das in puttees and a muffler—'I always sneeze in the morning'; Charles in impeccably worn baggy pants and check shirt; Multani in a Hawaiian shirt, saying: 'Anyway, I don't intend to work, I'll just take some snaps of you chaps training for the convict communes of China,' and laughing at his own wit.

'Won't do you harm to work for a bit,' said Ada dryly. 'I'm rather looking forward to manual labour.'

Multani detailed her legs with his eyes, but Ada stood her ground undaunted, and looked at him with a contempt which made him turn away.

The hall was suddenly filled with a stately flock of women, almost all stout, with the polished roundness of wealth and Buddhism on their faces, some in slacks, some in skirts, one or two carrying canes.

'Who are they?' Gion asked.

Lee Souvan, who was circulating, counting off the guests by fours for the taxis, and starting all over again whenever new arrivals entered the hall, explained: 'The Buddhist Lay Ladies' World Tour, monsieur. They came in last night on the plane from Phnom Penh.' Each one wore, pinned to her blouse, shirt or dress, a label with the country she came from: United States, Germany, Burma, Ceylon, U.S.S.R.

'I didn't know there were Buddhists in Russia,' said Charles.

'Mongolia, Japan, Laos, and Swat,' read Gion. 'Where is Swat?'

'North-west frontier, between Afghanistan and Pakistan,' replied Das. 'Beautiful valley. Alexander of Macedon was there.'

The Buddhist lady from Swat, who seemed in charge of the touring group, was counting her flock: 'Malaya, Malaya,' she called, 'where are you, Malaya?'

'Here.' A curved and dimpled woman in a long skirt, a jade in the shape of a heart round her neck on a gold chain, waved her hand. 'Meet my good-for-nothing nephew,' she said, pushing Teo forward. 'You rascal, we all thought you were busy studying. He is always running away from the university,' she explained affectionately, hugging Teo's arm. 'He's attending this Writers' Congress. My nephew a poet! What will your Papa say? How can you do business if you poet?'

'Madam,' said Peter, standing firmly near Teo, 'Teo is a very talented person.'

'A poet! I thought he eloped with a girl,' cried Aunty from Malaya. 'But it's good he is with you. No more writing business, Teo, you come back with me to Singapore.'

'I'll go back after this week, Aunty. I promise.'

'Your father will disinherit you if you don't stick to accountancy.' But she threw her nephew such a fond glance that the prospects of disinheritance seemed distant. 'Are you going to manual labour?' she asked. 'I can't stay too long in the sun, it would ruin my fair complexion.' Like many Chinese of the old type in Malaya, she stayed out of the sun as much as possible, for to be dark meant a lower social status.

'No harm go see,' said Teo. 'Carry your sunbrella for you,

Aunty.'

'Oh, this rascal fellow . . . he knows how to get round his old Aunty.'

Then Sumipoon and George arrived with Orion and Astarte, and Sheila carrying Laertes, cooing at him as a little girl with a doll. Gion went to her, forgetting everyone else.

'Good morning, Sheila. Are you coming to manual labour?'

'Not now,' she replied, smiling. 'I'm staying to look after Laertes for a bit. He's not well this morning. But you go. I'll come later. I've arranged it with George.'

'Sheila, I love you.' It was easy to say it this morning, light and easy.

'I know,' she said, looking at Laertes. 'But it doesn't make anything different, does it?'

Of course, she loves someone else. I'd forgotten.

'I mean, words are so worn out. And it's so important to make them real.'

That was what Ibrahim Malek had said, the previous afternoon. 'Who said that to you?'

She looked at him. 'I'll meet you at manual labour later.'

Sumipoon pulled Gion's sleeve. 'Gion, you're coming with us.' She sounded hurt, for in his haste to go to Sheila he had not seen her, had brushed past her without a greeting.

Ulong Serap, looking like an oriole, dazzling in saffron, approached the Buddhist Ladies, who bowed low while he blessed them. 'Good morning, my dear niece,' he said to Sumipoon. 'Shall we go together to the scene of our manual labour? I expect all of you will *want* to come. All the writers. Such a wonderful experience. So much more blessed, on a beautiful sunny morning, to work with our hands than with our tongues.'

'As you say, Uncle,' replied Sumipoon.

'Ah,' said Ulong Serap, 'by the way, George, someone asked after you last night. A Jesuit priest. One of the five touring delegates of the Roman Catholic group. They called on me after they arrived on the plane from Phnom Penh. You will doubtless meet the man at manual labour, if you have not yet seen him. His name is Father O'Dodder.'

'A Jesuit?' said George. 'I wonder what a Jesuit wants of me?'

'Have you been told about the coup, Uncle?' asked Orion.

'Orion,' began Sumipoon, 'don't start your tales——'

'My child,' said Ulong Serap, 'all evil doers shall be brought low.'

'Oh,' said Orion, 'then there's really going to be a coup? Who'll win, the Prince or the others?'

Said Ulong Serap: 'The stars are not ready. Not yet. But I ask you not to mention it, Orion. Justice will prevail, be sure of that.'

The guests filed into the cavalcade of taxis which had been commandeered to take them to the scene of manual labour. Sumipoon looked towards Gion as if she wanted to talk to him, then appeared to change her mind, and instead made comment on the landscape.

About five thousand people were all walking in the same direction on the elevated road-bed along which the new railway would run one day.

Cambodians, of all sizes and descriptions: large hordes of schoolchildren, singing hoarsely as they cantered in disorderly clutches with their schoolteachers; young women with curled hair and becoming *sampots* wrapped round their hips; young men, farmers, with bare feet and loin cloths and sweat bands round their heads, and their wives or sisters who in the free and equal manner of the women of Cambodia exchanged jokes with them of a verve and lubricity 'which should make me blush, but doesn't', said Sumipoon who translated in a whisper to George. The women wore their hair cut short, and though they walked behind the men, they grinned confidently, as if they too were taking out a posse of schoolchildren to a picnic.

'It's fantastic how young everybody always looks in Asia,' commented Charles.

They passed a dozen handsome girls, with shining hair, *sampots* of red satin and identical white nylon blouses. 'Look,' cried Sumipoon, 'the girls of the Royal Ballet Corps.'

The girls were made up as if on the way to another performance and not to dig in the mud of the rice fields for the day.

There were half a dozen amateur orchestras from the villages, blowing flutes, thumping drums, singers singing and turning somersaults in the road.

There were some corpulent government officials also walking along. They drew catcalls and jokes. 'Look at that one, rolling his grease along.'

'Hey, football, football!'

A woman cried: 'Hey, are you married ... ball of fat? Because if not, I'm a widow!'

To which the official turned round to reply, half in anger: 'Ho, grandmother! It's time you shaved your head and stopped thinking about lusty men like me ekuipped with ...'

This joke, in best village style, made the women hold their sides with laughter, while their husbands affectionately tapped their buttocks.

'I didn't realize your people were so uninhibited,' said Multani, to whom a Cambodian writer was translating the jokes. 'I thought you were religious.'

'But, sir, religion has nothing to do with love-making,' replied the Cambodian.

On they walked, the sun warming up. On both sides of the road-bed were paddy fields, clumps of palm, coconut, and kapok trees, and houses on stilts. On pathways winding between the fields women stood grinning, surrounded by children, their faces open like the morning.

'Isn't it extraordinary,' went on Charles, 'how the people here don't seem to have a care in the world? It does make one feel like retiring to a village. It's nearly idyllic.'

'It's a small country, only five million people, plenty of land. But they're poor,' said Gion. 'And it isn't true they haven't a care in the world.'

They caught up with a small battalion of girls in khaki with green ties and berets. 'Our Royal Volunteer Female Militia,' said the Cambodian writer, who seemed to have taken upon himself the duties of interpreter and guide.

'Nice hefty girls,' commented George.

'They dance beautifully,' said the youth, 'when they are not learning to shoot. They work in the new factories of Siem-reap.'

'Modern Asia.'

A soft roar came up from the crowd, swelling until it swept over them in a tide, and along with it came the steady pound of a helicopter, then the machine itself was above their heads.

'The Prince, Monseigneur,' shouted the Cambodian writer, dancing up and down with excitement as the helicopter swept over. Its door was wide open, and standing in the doorway, waving, smiling with a smile as broad as any of his subjects', Sihanouk went flying past over their heads. The helicopter swerved round, circling above them, and the crowds went mad with joy.

Gion found himself shouting, waving with the others, in a great tide of laughter that rolled up and down the rice fields as the country people sat down to slap their stomachs and groan with the excess of their mirth. Multani was not laughing; his eyebrows slightly contracted, he looked at the wheeling helicopter in astonishment, in dismay, unresponsive to the humour of the helicopter and its airborne Prince. He could not imagine a head of state acting in a manner which, to his eyes, was undignified, and he felt furious, indignant, and bewildered.

'What an exhibitionist that man is.' A bevy of schoolchildren running past, shouting and waving at the sky and colliding with him, did not improve his temper.

This made Sumipoon angry. 'Oh, Mr Multani! Don't you see that this is funny and wonderful? What other ruler in Asia dares to do these things?'

'Ah,' said George, soothingly, 'wait till you see this bit in the files of MESSO. It'll make our generals burst some blood vessels.'

'Then I think they're beyond humour and humanity,' replied Sumipoon, tartly.

They were now at the end of the already built-up track. In the fields to one side scores of men and women were working in the mud: men in loin cloths and men in uniform, men in lounge suits and men in dungarees; girls in skirts and girls in shorts, village women in black skirts; two cabinet ministers, shoeless, ankle-deep in the swishing rice fields, reared alacritous shovels, filling baskets which passed in a hand-to-hand chain to the new road-bed to be erected, its outline delineated by a row of widely spaced pickets. With whoops, as a school dashing into the sea at their first beach holiday, the ballet corps threw itself into another field, and grasping stacked shovels, of which small pyramids had been prepared every fifty yards, started to dig and scoop slices of slithering mud out of it.

All along the edge of the road-bed, as far as the eye could see, were people walking, arriving, then climbing down into the unused rice fields. Others emergent from toil, bespattered, sweaty, climbed back on to the dry road, or sat on the slopes or on the pathways. Orchestras planted themselves here and there, school-children filled all the interstices, clumped under trees to sing, or passed empty baskets in long crocodile chains.

A man in shirt sleeves and khaki trousers walked up, and Ulong Serap immediately went down on his knees. It took Gion a little time to do the same, recognizing in the figure brandishing a mattock His Royal Highness himself, streaming unroyally with sweat.

'Just in time,' shouted the jocund Prince. 'We have reserved a special sector of this ditch for the illustrious assembly of talent from the Writers' Congress. Allow me to show you the way.'

Briskly he guided the writers, gesturing and indicating the digging groups. 'Here we have our respected cousins, the Chinese, our trustworthy and sincere friends. See how skilfully they dig.' He lost himself in admiration before the group of diplomats from China, who went about the business of hauling off baskets of mud with a total concentration.

'They have been here since morning, even before We arrived,' shouted Prince Sihanouk. 'We believe that they are going to establish a great leap forward in digging.' He burst into happy laughter.

His Highness then stopped before the next group, who with streaming shirts occupied another stretch. 'Here We have placed our American friends,' he said, 'for We are convinced that they too will enjoy our Cambodian spirit of toil. In fact, His Excellency the Ambassador was telling me that he had been a coal-miner in his youth. We are lost in admiration.' His Highness waved his mattock about in tremendous spirits.

'But you are not in working clothes, monsieur,' he reproached Multani. 'We shall see to this. Our Minister of Education, who is in charge of the implements of labour, will provide you with working clothes if you wish.'

The writers were now at the plot reserved for them. Servants rushed forward, bowing low, presenting shovels.

Sihanouk went on to the next plot, and was surrounded, squeezed, almost suffocated by men and women, all trying to

136

touch him and to shake his hand.

Somehow, in the midst of all this laughter, the road-bed grew higher in uneven mounds, and villagers padded the mounds into place, evening them out to form a single upraised track. Under a tree Buddhist monks squatted, singing prayers to call blessings upon the work that was done, while next to them four Catholic priests, and one bishop recognizable by his purple belt, stood looking at the workers, upon their faces the longing of children. Finally the priests could not resist, and started to carry loaded buckets of mud to the track.

Gion, Charles, George, dug away at the mud, filling baskets. Here was a self-propelled, infectious activity, gathering strength from its own doing, inducing others not by exhortation but by example, making all those who worked brothers in a fellowship of sweat. Arms, legs, bodies, spades, shovels, mattocks, baskets, mud; out of it all an immense gaiety rose, as if all at once the earth was simple and kind, the myth of happy toil was no longer a myth, and fraternity was real ...

'It's a picnic, a picnic,' said Sumipoon, mud on her cheeks. 'I must write it all up.'

Even Multani was now passing baskets (his shirt had been changed to an old but clean khaki one) with a disdainful look, but he was passing them.

A boy and a girl, standing two yards away from each other in the mud, their hands swaying to the tune, began to sing a folk song, while an orchestra of flute and drums accompanied them.

> *'I went to the river*
> *To find my shadow there,*
> *But I found yours instead,*
> *Which you had left behind,*
> *Bathing this morning.*
>
> *'I went back to the river,*
> *To seek our shadows there,*
> *And I found nothing, nothing,*
> *For night had drowned them both.'*

Amid the laughter and the singing, Sihanouk's voice carried

on unquenchably, dominating the hubbub:

'Manual labour makes our intellectuals understand the peasant. Man doesn't understand unless he undergoes. Only when his own bones ache, his muscles cramp, the sweat pours off him, and he feels thirsty and hungry, does he begin to apprehend what it is like to endure this kind of life, day after day after day ... even half a day in the sun, like today, messieurs, more like a family picnic than actual work, with singing and music, begins to teach some of us what it is like. All his life the man who digs today remembers, because his muscles remember.'

He mopped his brow, threw his cherubim dimpled smile about, and shouted to a few of his officials: 'Harder, gentlemen! You must dig harder!'

The Buddhist Ladies shovelled in a group, unrecognizable now, so copiously mud-caked had they become. Aunty from Malaya had not forgotten her complexion, she had hired a little boy to keep an umbrella open above her head. The American delegation moved on to fresh muds, as they had dug themselves into a large pit. The Chinese also moved to another field. The Prince started cracking jokes in Khmer with the Militia girls, some of whom were so transported at his jokes that they threw themselves at him to embrace him. Sumipoon had given up, she sat on a pathway, the mud was drying white upon her legs.

'I shall become a Cambodian and stay with Uncle Ulong Serap, catch fish and drive oxen to market.'

Gion sat next to her and lit a cigarette. He found himself smiling, as if smiling had become a normal component of his face. He had almost forgotten Sheila, digging for the past hour. How puzzling the heart of man, with its intermittences of feeling, at one moment love so agonizing, tearing, overwhelming, filling all of one, at another, as at ebb tide, one's mind a flat mud field, caking in the sun, no trace of love's ocean anywhere; yet perhaps that was reality, that was an adequate knowledge of self, to know and especially to accept that it should be so, that intermittence, not constancy, was the way feelings lived, and to hold steadfast, steadfast to love even when it seemed to be gone, even when its smell and savour no longer existed.

> *And I found nothing, nothing,*
> *For night had drowned them both...*

He hummed the tune, and Sumipoon took it up. 'Ah, Gion
... yes, it is so, isn't it?'

'I was thinking of intermittence of emotion, Sumi. How
wayward love is...'

'So was I. I thought of Sheila and you.'

'Sheila,' said Gion. 'Has she said anything to you?'

'Yes,' said Sumipoon. 'I swore not to tell you, but perhaps I
should.'

'I see,' said Gion, thinking: even Sumipoon has been told
whom Sheila is in love with. But now, in the sun, it did not
hurt...

Sumipoon went on: 'I suppose it is consoling to know that
one isn't a straight line, but a zigzag? Think how dreadful it
would be if one felt all the time the same, about the same
things, pursuing an *idée fixe* all the time. Petrified, like the
stare of those great stone faces, pursuing a horizon they'll never
reach. Megalomania that never lets go of the image, the reflection of the self, a blue gibbon in a blue tree, permanently safe,
but how awful. Don't you think?'

Singers, sauntering across the mud, came to serenade
another group, along with an orchestra from another village.

> *'Oh the melons, the melons were heavy and golden,*
> *In the cart with the oxen,*
> *Heavy and golden as my loved one's buttocks,*
> *Whose love I bought with a smile.'*

'Courage, courage. Another hour, messieurs, then we can
rest.' It was the voice of the Prince, greeted with laughter and
shouts.

'Monseigneur, aren't you afraid something might happen to
you? You are here, quite unprotected...' Thus one of the
correspondents.

'Again?' cried Sihanouk. 'Why are you so afraid for me,
monsieur? With all my people round to protect me?'

A tall Jesuit with a crew-cut came up to Gion. 'I am looking
for a Mr Rolland, Cultural Adviser at MESSO. Do you know

him?' His eyes surveyed the fields with their thousands, hopefully.

'He is my husband,' said Sumipoon, contemplating her muddy legs with great satisfaction. 'Over there, working.'

'Thank you.' The Jesuit strode forward.

'Father O'Dodder. Must be. I wonder what he wants George for. It's ages since George has been to church.'

'They wouldn't be after him for that.'

'You never can tell. I had a Jesuit after me for years, trying to convert me. He used to send me cards at Easter and Christmas, "God remembers you". Then he tried the modern touch. Used to come for chatty teas and ask me to show him my dresses, talked to me of the horrors of family planning. I don't use family planning anyway. Then he tried to impress me with stories of ascetic saints, and you know how much we Buddhists *loathe* ascetics. As bad as lechers, but the other way round. So enthralled with their own personal salvation they never really take a good look at themselves or at the world. Quite the opposite of the Buddha, who never stopped being human and preaching the Middle Way.'

Now the Jesuit was coming back with George, who said: 'I must go to fetch Sheila, and see how Laertes is. Father O'Dodder is coming with me. We are going to have a little talk.'

'About what?' asked Sumipoon.

'I'll tell you later.'

'Bring Laertes with Sheila if he's better,' said Sumipoon. 'He'll enjoy it. Look at Orion and Astarte there, joining the band.'

Mary Faust, immaculate and surly, strode past, having just arrived by taxi.

'Have you seen my secretary, Mabel Despair?' she snapped at Gion.

'No.'

She snorted. 'Amusing yourself playing at manual labour, when there are millions who literally starve, who lift their poor, dumb hands, begging for food——'

'I don't think Cambodia does too badly,' began Gion. 'It does no harm——'

'Puts your true social consciousness to sleep,' retorted Mary

Faust. 'A crypto-fascist, that's what he is.' She looked scornfully towards the Prince. 'What we need is a clean sweep.' She strode on.

'She didn't get the interview she wanted,' Sumipoon said, 'Remember last night, Gion? How beautiful it was.'

Gion leaned on his spade, remembering the night before at the ruins, the dancing by moonlight. A ring of torches, and inside the ring, on mats, the dancers, slow, beautiful, with their pointed golden crowns, their hands with fingers arching back, slow, hieratic, deliberate. He sat next to Sheila, with Charles on her other side. Mary Faust sat behind the Prince. Multani and the Fumikaros took photographs by flash-light. When the ballet had ended and the Prince had risen, Mary Faust had gone up to him: 'Monseigneur, I would like to interview you for the papers I represent.' 'Certainly, madame,' the Prince had replied courteously, and called an A.D.C.: 'Please take down madame's name and the names of the newspapers she represents. We shall do our best to give satisfaction.' Mary had looked angrily at Sihanouk's retreating back.

Sheila, in the taxi returning with Charles, had put her head on Gion's shoulder, closed her eyes ... and that head against his had moved him so much that he had sat, still as a stone.

'Mabel must be somewhere,' said Sumipoon. 'Oh, I see Mary has caught Das again.'

'I wonder how you can stand that sexless communist,' said Multani.

'Sexless? Mary's full of sex,' replied Sumipoon.

'She told me that she was leading the Revolution in South-East Asia,' retorted Multani.

'How interesting for you.'

Gion walked to the road-bed where Ulong Serap was standing talking with the Catholic bishop. 'Ah, Mr Gion, enjoying your manual labour? I wanted to have a chat with you. I need your help.'

'You honour me, Eminence.'

'I wanted to tell you,' said Ulong Serap, 'that for me at times the past, which is the uncoiled flat road already trod, returns like the serpent's tail to be trod upon again. We met in a past life, you and I.'

'Possibly,' replied Gion. The singing, the villagers, the work, why was it that suddenly he felt that he had seen it before?

Of course, in my dream, I am one among many workers, in my dream building Angkor ...

'When the Bayon was not finished,' said Ulong Serap, 'already I was a priest there. And you too ...'

'I don't recall this.' The dream ... in the warm plain, with people digging all over the mud, it was silly to think that this was the past returning. Like a swift ghost besought by name, the name powerful enough to evoke a materialization of its body, the light greyed, the dream began. The singing, the singing, the same singing the workers in that other field, that other century, had sung, building Angkor to outlast the horizon. Hallucinatory, the Bayon hovered in the heat haze where the road-bed was being raised out of mud. Gion felt then what it was to be conscious on two levels at once, living at once two different spheres of sensation.

'Observe,' said Ulong Serap, his voice persuasive in the silence of the dream dimension, a silence as present as the present singing of this existence, 'that I too do not really recall until I let go the clutch of today's detailed anguish, let go of the clock sucking time into its bright and vacant face—I see you cover your watch with your finger—float back on the snake-tail of time, knowing all beauty lent, all consciousness freight of days, floating free from fact and reason, which is today's mud of the fields sticking to one's skin. You and I knew each other seven hundred years ago.'

'Perhaps.' The song fell about Gion's ears. He also felt his brain unclench itself from the actual scene, the life of now.

> *Oooooh, oooooh, the long and heavy stone,*
> *I have dragged it to the end of the day,*
> *And my life has been drained out of me,*
> *By the stone I have dragged all day.*

'I do not really remember. I am merely pretending to remember.'

'I wished to speak to you,' said Ulong Serap, 'for I believe that we are met again for a purpose. And when I saw you, I recognized you. My friend, you must help. There is evil about, and you must help me to undo it. The girl, Sheila, she is in danger. You must protect her.'

'I love her.'

'You think so. That remains to be seen. But you must help her, because you must redeem the past.'

'Redeem the past?'

'Yes, it is because of you that she died, many centuries ago. Of you and of me. Now we must protect her. We have a chance of undoing the past.'

'What is the danger? From whom?'

'How can I tell? I only know a little at a time. Remember that Right Motive and Right Intention are all important. Never forget that, and all will be well.'

And then Gion saw Sheila stepping down from a taxi with Laertes and George. She waved at him, and his heart found words remembered.

> *This no tomorrow hath, nor yesterday,*
> *But truly keeps his first, last, everlasting day . . .*

'You have come.'

'Isn't it a lovely day?' said Sheila. 'Did you enjoy yourself?'

'Yes, Sheila.' We shall be together all day, he thought. A first, last, everlasting day . . .

'Shall I do some manual labour?' said Sheila. Her eyes sparkled. She waved at someone afar, smiled. 'I want to get muddy too.' She had glad, animal movements. 'Can I have a shovel?'

She joined a jostling line, dragging Gion with her by the hand. Then suddenly she said: 'Did you really wait for me, Gion?'

'Centuries, Sheila, I have waited for you.' Beyond waiting, beyond myself, he wanted to add, but did not.

'Oh, don't say that, it gives me gooseflesh,' Sheila cried.

And then Charles came, and the black polished mirror in which the impalpable immobile shadows of the other beings which they might have been came crowding solidly, the illusions of memory placing them at the heart of time in the perfect ambush of the might-have-been become real, dissolved, smoked away as he puffed his pipe and said blandly: 'Oh, here you are, my dear. Have you seen Eliza? How's her headache, any better?'

They had lunch under a large roof of mats and bamboo erected for shade between big gum trees. To the left of them a village assembled its stilts, to the right was the green evenness of a pond where submerged buffaloes kept cool. Lunch was preceded by champagne, perfectly iced. A single slight fence of pickets, widely spaced and waist high, separated the diplomats and the Suprême guests from the villagers, who pressed forward as usual to touch their Prince, to pat his back, to shout jokes in his face, to squeeze his hands. At a microphone a young Militia woman sang.

The diplomats, the delegations from China and the United States, the cabinet ministers and officials, the Congress of writers, the Roman Catholic group and the Buddhist Ladies, helped themselves to Khmer dishes of dumplings and savoury rice and braised chicken.

The crowd roared, clapped hands, as some old ladies, shaven-headed nuns from a Buddhist nunnery, came to bless the Prince and receive gifts of cloth. Then the dance began. The villagers clapped hands as if giving the signal, and the Prince also clapped hands, and people began to dance the *lamtong*, the collective village dancing where men and women follow each other in an endless procession, never touching, their arms raised, their hands in motion, the extraordinary Cambodian hands with their fingers curving halfway back to the wrist. The bodies swayed very slightly, the feet trod a simple step while those magic hands and fingers described those tracings in air which are the lightness of the leaf and the glance of the fawn, the gaudy sun's joy and the hare's shyness, the bluster of the peacock and the soft down on the swallow's throat, evocation of flowers and entanglements of innocence, and sometimes, with a dragging, trailing finger, reptile of desire writing its hieroglyph in emptiness. On they moved, each dancer on his own, yet all together, winding their chains of people, and the dance made them whole with their past, for the gestures were the same as those carved, centuries ago, on the walls of Angkor.

And in this pageant, repetitive as the blind gaze of the God-

King encompassing a moving world within stony orbits, Sheila and Gion were also webbed, surrounded, sharing with all around the fluid enchantment to a music which linked them to all and to each other; until even the Catholic bishop, standing apart with a great cross defending his chest, began to move his hands about, while his face took on an innocence of pleasure, the pleasure of an innocence before Sin was invented, which erased the wrinkles etched upon his face by years of pastorate. Until even Multani, arms too extended, knees stiff, began to remember the gestures of his own country's dancing; his fingers loosened, forgot to grasp the air with hostility, swam in it with confidence; the camera dangling at his hip was put down on a chair, while he too danced, following a Khmer woman with hips smooth as oil, whose corpulence held the litheness of the leech, who smiled serenely unaware of Multani, who was now copying her gestures behind her.

After an hour the dancing slowed down. The Prince left in a buzz of cheering, his open Mercedes-Benz creeping down the crowded road. Children jumped into or hung on to the car for a last handshake and pat. Then the diplomats left, the Catholic bishop, the delegations. The Japanese couple photographed each departure. All morning they had taken photographs, of the diplomats, the officials, the Prince, the Ballet girls, the Militia, the shovels, the road-bed, the villagers, the buffaloes ...

'You must have photographed every basketful,' Das said.

Mrs Fumikaro was dictating something to Mr Fumikaro, who jotted down figures to her dictation in a small notebook. He grinned.

'My wife has calculated that today was done the equivalent of one day's work with two Japanese bulldozers and twenty men.'

'Does that matter? Everyone had a wonderful time. The psychological value of collective manual labour is more important than the actual work done, I believe.'

'Oh yes, undoubtedly,' said Mr Fumikaro, 'psychological importance is predominant. In fact, my wife and I will publish a poem about today's work. A joint poem, called "Collectively Building the Railroad Bed". May I show?'

'You read it to him, Teikon,' urged Mrs Fumikaro, blushing because she had been very daring and modern.

'Here I have it begun,' said Mr Fumikaro.

> *'Today, a Prince assembles a world of goodwill,*
> *Out of the ricefield rises new industry,*
> *In the hearts of thousands flowers brotherly love,*
> *In the mouths of myriads the music of happiness sings.'*

Said Das: 'Excellent. Top rate.'

'Socialist-realist and romantic, combination most efficient,' replied Mr Fumikaro. 'Tell me, Mr Das, are you a fan of Simenon? I read him always.' Mr Fumikaro hissed with happiness. Then he gave his visiting cards to Gion and to Das, for no Japanese travels without a supply. Gion scribbled his name and address upon a piece of paper.

The Fumikaros approached a waiting taxi, but could not avoid the enthusiasm of the Militia girls, now unemployed, who grasped both the Japanese bodily and transported them on their shoulders to the taxi. This enthused Mr Fumikaro even more, and he shouted 'Cambodia banzai! Cambodia banzai!' until his taxi disappeared in its own dust.

Mary Faust was talking to Ulong Serap: 'Mrs Despair had no right to go off like that and leave me in the lurch.'

'You must report to the police,' Ulong Serap replied mildly.

In the taxi Gion held Sheila's hand. The road was dusty and there were many ox-carts with villagers still singing, dancers on the roadside dancing the *lamtong* in long files, returning to their villages, musicians blowing trumpets a-pillion on bicycles.

Returning to the hotel in the late afternoon they saw Eliza sitting in the hall with Lederer, and a man Gion had not seen before, handsome, with massive shoulders and slim waist. Eliza waved.

'Sheila, my dear, do come here for a moment. Have you had a good time? Where is Charles?'

Both men rose. 'Monsieur Deroulede, Mr Gion, Captain Lederer you know already,' Eliza introduced. Deroulede looked at Sheila, and Gion could feel him stirred, saw his eyes rake Sheila's face.

'I'm *covered* in mud,' said Sheila. Her colour had heightened. 'Daddy's coming in another taxi.'

'I'll wait for Charles here. I want you to tell me *all* about it. I've had a wonderful time, buying the most lovely *sampots*, such wonderful bargains. Do come down and have a drink, both of you, when you've washed.'

Sheila turned to go up the stairs, and Gion followed her.

'Are you going to have a drink with them?'

'Did you notice,' said Sheila, not replying, 'Eliza is quite haggard. There's something very wrong with her.'

'Sheila, you didn't answer my question.'

She shrugged. 'I don't really care,' she replied indifferently.

'Shall we meet, in about fifteen minutes?' He would not let her out of his sight.

'Yes ... then we'll decide, shall we?'

But it was already decided. Gion knew Sheila had decided to go down and join the party, join Eliza she hated, Lederer she had slept with, because of that newcomer, Deroulede.

Tuesday Night

They were dancing the twist, the two of them, while around them Royal Militia maidens, writers, government officials, and hotel guests performed fox-trots or the *lamtong*.

The manual labour of the morning still held them in brotherliness, the music dragged its syncopated Khmer melodies without flagging, at intervals burst into loud jazz, then relapsed. Every fifteen minutes or so one of the Militia girls went to the microphone and sang. Ashley Basildon tried to grip one of the girls to him as she came off the microphone, and after that found no one to dance with him except Eliza, and Joan Warburton, his secretary. At ten o'clock he walked out.

Gion stayed on, stiff, watching Sheila dance the twist with Jean Deroulede. He hated her, hated himself, hated Deroulede. The Cambodians spiralled round them, as if the couple were invisible. Then Sheila and Deroulede walked back to the table. Sheila swept her hair back with her hand and laughed, excited.

'It is even more gay when Monseigneur is here,' the P.R.O. was explaining. 'Monseigneur is never tired. He is now receiving the Egyptian Ambassador. Tonight Monseigneur is flying to Kep to give a party to international correspondents at which

His Highness will play the saxophone and lead his orchestra. That will last till six in the morning. At eight Monseigneur will fly to Sihanoukville to open three schools, and at ten a.m. receive a delegation of scientists from the U.S.S.R.'

'Doesn't the Prince ever sleep?' Ada asked.

'Oh, certainly, from time to time, as we all do. But Monseigneur kills us all off,' said the P.R.O. cheerfully. 'That is why we relax when he is not here by dancing. Mademoiselle?'

And Sheila was off, dancing with the P.R.O., then with another Cambodian. Ada, whirled away in a cha-cha-cha by a handsome adolescent, came back: 'I thought he was twenty-one, but he is thirty-nine, a secretary of defence, and has fourteen children. If I stay here any longer my sense of proportion will go astray and I'll fall for a Khmer, wind a *sampot* round me, and stay in a village. This place grows on one.'

'I say,' Peter Anstey said to Gion, 'what's the matter with Eliza?'

'Is anything the matter with her?'

'I only wondered.'

Gion looked at Eliza. Now she was dancing with Jean Deroulede. Over his shoulder her face was ravaged.

The Buddhist ladies were being coaxed into dancing. Malayan Aunty did a fox-trot with her nephew Teo. Only the lady from Swat refused to dance.

And now Sheila was again dancing with Deroulede, as the orchestra struck up a waltz. Deroulede was a marvellous dancer. He dominated the floor. Around his left wrist was a triangular watch with a platinum bracelet, very expensive. He and Sheila did some intricate steps, their bodies moving with beautiful simultaneity, and the Cambodians, skilful dancers themselves, applauded.

'Another whisky, monsieur?' Gion was conscious it was his fourth. He would have a sour mouth tomorrow ... age, eroding away his youth, but chiefly eroding the intensity of passion, until he watched Sheila and Deroulede, and knew himself lost, not through intensity, but because he hated impotently, he could not get up and take Sheila away from Deroulede, take her in his arms, whirl her away in a dance (he was an average dancer, would look so ridiculous after Deroulede). He could not do what this young Cambodian was doing, tapping on

Deroulede's shoulder, taking a turn with Sheila, while Deroulede was now amiably asking a full-mouthed Cambodian to dance with him.

'For heaven's sake, Gion, don't just *stand* there. Why don't you dance?' That was Sumipoon, irritated, whirling past with Das.

And that only made it worse.

Bud Kilton materialized, a rumble of jollity, claps, and exclamations. 'Hallo, hallo, chin chin everybody. What a party, folks. This is the life.' He sat down on the chair next to Gion. 'Isn't this wonderful? Friendship, East and West meet. Thought I'd drop in. Just passing by, giving my assistant a lift back. Maisie's a very gifted musician, don't you think? Plays the piano with so much feeling.'

'Any news of my secretary, Mr Kilton?' Mary Faust was clad in a beautiful satin gown.

'Nope,' said Kilton. 'I inquired, as you asked me to. Did she take her things away?'

'She didn't have much. A suitcase, only half full. Her passport is gone. Also her handbag. That means she may have gone back, of course, leaving her suitcase behind, in case I'd object. I told her to go and call on a very important person last night. Either she's left, or something's happened to her.'

'Maybe she was kidnapped, ha ha ha,' laughed Ahmed Fouad. 'Cheers, everybody.'

Das, who had stopped dancing, asked: 'Whom did you send her to see?'

'General Vam Barong, the Governor of the Province.'

'Oh, the Governor,' said Das, sipping his drink. 'He's very ill, isn't he?'

'Yes. I rang him up, and asked whether she'd been there. The general does not see any visitors. Has not seen any for days. At least, that's what his A.D.C. told me. Says he's never heard of my secretary. I think she *may* have gone back to her husband. By car if not by plane.'

The orchestra played a tango. Deroulede and Sheila were again together.

Kilton turned to Gion conversationally. 'Ever heard about immersion?'

'Im ... what?'

'Immersion. True baptism by immersion. Total.'

'What on earth is that?'

'That is what I came to Cambodia for. To truly save. By total immersion.'

'Won't ordinary baptism do?' asked Ada.

'It's the abomination of desolation. Only total immersion, water over your head——'

'Excuse me,' said Gion, 'I'm going to bed.'

Sheila's head was on Deroulede's shoulder. His mouth was in her hair. Gion walked away, his back stiff. Ibrahim Malek was right. There was a whole range of emotions for which there were no words. Except perhaps in an African language. Some of the African languages were rich in feeling words, and now all feelings were intermittent and in-between. I shall have to learn one of them for these new feelings. It's because I have no words for them that I can't make up my mind what to do.

Sumipoon nearly captured him: 'Gion, do come with us to look at the moon?'

'No,' he said, knowing he was being rude. To hell with good manners.

Sumipoon's insatiable romanticism. She was sentimental about the moon like a young girl before the sputnik age. She bored him. Sheila too. Yes, no, yes. How the word 'Sheila' hurt, it hurt as a hedgehog in his breast would hurt.

The bed received him flatly. He turned off the light, through the mosquito net watched the moonlight, enter the open verandah doors, take over half the room. The music drooled on. He slept.

'Go on, tell me more.'

Ada composed a sweet interested face turned towards Bud Kilton, but in reality for the sake of Bernard Reguet, who had strolled in, pipe in mouth, shirt sleeves rolled up, as if torn from his working desk by the music and the mirth, and joining late but eager. The time was one o'clock.

'It's all in my book,' said Bud Kilton. '*My Asia and My God*. Translated into eighteen languages. Tried to get the U.S.I.S. interested, but would they touch it? No. Not since they've got creeping communism in now with that Ed Murrow fellow. Sad. Sad.'

'The good old days were better,' said Reguet, ironic.

'Well, we knew where we were, it was all black and white,' said Bud. 'Either you were a Red, or you weren't. We were fighting communism with everything we'd got then.

'Now I'm told this won't do. Got to be *subtle*. Even neutralism is O.K. now. But I don't believe in subtlety. It's the poison of doubt, corroding faith. I'm a true believer. The Bible, absolutely. That's why I'd like you to read my book, especially the chapter on total immersion, Lady Ada. I started it when I was in Saudi Arabia.'

'The Baptists——' began Das.

'Heretics,' said Kilton. 'Damned in hellfire for all eternity. Only the Saints on New Earth with Christ (that's the mission I belong to, SONEC) will rejoice in the promised Glory. Total immersion makes all the difference.'

'What did you do in the Middle East? Saudi Arabia, you said?' asked Ada. 'I've been there. Water's quite a problem. Any converts?'

'Oh, ye doubters that have no faith in the power of the Lord,' exclaimed Kilton triumphantly. 'Did we make any converts? Did we? I'll say we did. Our tanks were full of natives, thirsting for the Lord's Truth. Couldn't process them fast enough.'

'Tanks?' said Das and Ada together.

'Water tanks. The Eastbound with Christ branch of our Saints on New Earth flew in tanks full of water, under a special allocation worked by the vice-president of our board who's got a brother in the Economics for Under-Developed Countries section of the State Department. You've never seen so many souls flocking to the Lord. Especially the kids.'

Ada took a long pull at her Campari *à l'eau*.

'Now, why don't you drop in at our next meeting, Lady Ada? And you, Mr Reguet?'

'I'll drop in when I've found that missing object, Mr Kilton.'

'There you are,' said Bud throwing his hands up in the air, 'I've got to take the rap. Mr Reguet here believes I stole some curio or another, Lady Ada. An antique. It's absolutely ridiculous.'

Reguet gazed at the dancers. Lederer, his face very drawn

and tired, sat down next to him.

'It's always us, we get blamed for everything,' said Kilton. 'Like last year.'

'Last year a bomb was sent to the King of Cambodia from Saigon,' said Reguet to Lady Ada. 'Wrapped up as a present. It exploded in the hands of a young A.D.C.'

'And of course we were blamed,' said Kilton. 'Two days they interrogated me. I knew nothing about it, nothing at all.'

'The bomb came from Saigon,' said Lederer.

'Saigon isn't the United States, Captain Lederer. I'd like to remind you that South Vietnam is an independent country, at the moment subject to communist aggression. We're doing all we can to help maintain South Vietnam's independence.'

'Oh, merde,' said Lederer, 'South Vietnam's independence! You should have helped us when *we* fought at Dien Bien Phu.'

Reguet shrugged his shoulders. He rose, meaning to saunter to the dance floor, already with his eyes looking over the pretty Cambodian girls, some standing, some sitting and fanning.

But at that moment Multani came down. He did not see Reguet, went straight to Bud Kilton. 'Bud, I've got to talk to you. It's gone . . .'

Reguet turned. He saw Multani, saw Bud getting up. Quickly he put two fingers to his mouth and blew. As if by magic, men issued from a corner of the room, Cambodians, who converged upon the table. In no time at all there were handcuffs round a screaming, hitting Kilton, who was trying to choke Multani.

'You bastard, you idiot, you . . .' he screamed, 'you damn fool!'

'What's up?' Mary Faust asked. Mary had been talking mostly to the Cambodians, for tonight she had cast herself in the 'more Asian than Asians' role, and since Cambodians are polite, had not realized that they looked at her with astonishment and some fear as she hissed at them of Revolution; and since to Mary Faust conversation meant the sound of her own voice, uninterrupted and uncontradicted, she had the sensation of having made tremendous headway in her self-assigned mission at leading the Revolution of Asia.

It was Lederer who answered: 'I think Bernard Reguet suspects Mr Kilton of having stolen an antique. You know, we have very stringent laws about this in Cambodia. Possibly Mr Multani was his accomplice.'

'Will you dance, mademoiselle?' It was Deroulede.

'I'm talking to Captain Lederer,' said Mary Faust, 'don't interrupt.'

Deroulede slowly took his flat, gold cigarette case and selected a cigarette, and Lederer walked off abruptly and started dancing with a Cambodian. She danced beautifully. Mr Lee watched with great pride. 'My wife used to be a very good classical dancer,' he confided to Das. 'And she is also modern. I am a lucky man.'

'How many wives have you got, Mr Lee?'

'One Chinese, and Madame Shum,' he gestured towards Lederer's partner, 'who is a Cambodian lady, and perhaps another one if I can afford it, but the new ladies are very expensive and demanding and not hard-working. She might upset the family arrangements, so I must consider.'

'So she is on probation?'

'As you say, monsieur.'

Sheila was explaining: 'Kilton stole it and gave it to Multani, and he kept it hidden in his camera case, and now it's been stolen from HIM.'

'You are a detective, Mademoiselle Sheila,' said Deroulede.

'No, but I've got eyes. I notice things ... like chocolate boxes.'

'Are you sure you don't want to dance?'

'No, I'm tired.' She looked round. 'I'm going upstairs to sleep. Good night.'

Deroulede turned to Mary Faust. 'Will you dance with me now, Miss Faust?'

Mary nodded haughtily.

'Gion?'

He was awake, instantly, as if he had not slept, and the music came to him.

Sheila stood outside his mosquito net. The moonlight was so bright that when she raised her arm he could see it shine. Her face was hidden, only her arm was visible.

'Sheila!'

'Who else, stupid?'

He lifted the mosquito net, groped for his dressing-gown. 'Sheila, you mustn't . . .'

'Do you want me to go?'

'No. I . . .'

'You're *quite* stupid, aren't you?'

He switched on the electric light and the moon was abolished. He walked to close the verandah doors.

She sat, crossing her legs, fresh, glowing. It was two in the morning by his watch laid on the table. The music started again. Laughter, some feet stamping.

'Aren't you going to give me a drink?'

'Of course.' He went towards the bell button, but she said impatiently:

'You've got a bottle. Don't you remember? You bought it first time we met.'

He sat opposite her, glass in hand. Then he went to his bed, and pulled the mosquito net up and smoothed the sheet. She watched him.

'How funny you are.'

'Yes, I was born funny.' The brandy smouldered down his throat.

'I came to tell you that Eliza is up to something. And I'm going to find out *what*.'

'Oh.'

'D'you remember that remark of Orion, that she clutched her bag as if there were a dead baby inside?'

'Yes.'

'Well, I think there *was* something inside.' Sheila shook her head wisely. 'There's an awful lot going on. Under-cover things. People think I'm stupid, but I really know more than a lot of them. Did you guess at anything?'

He switched on the small bedside light and off the big light.

'Eliza's perfume. In my room. She leaves a trail of scent behind her, always. You wouldn't notice . . .'

Later, Gion was to regret that he did not, could not listen, because he was thinking of something else. He was overwhelmingly aware of his own body, roused from sleep, but also roused, maleness erect, demanding, and the woman, there in front of him, legs crossed. Lederer, so many others, perhaps

154

Deroulede ... then why not you, Gion, why not? How did she come into your room? She is here ... and so he did not listen.

'...I think she was mixed up in something quite shady ... I don't know if daddy knows...'

Sheila. Her mouth. Her breasts. Those legs, taunting him.

He rose and poured some more brandy, careful that the dressing-gown should not reveal him. His hand shook. His mouth was dry with desire.

'It's really because of her I suppose that I'm a nympho, or supposed to be. Though I really think that if I'd had a sister, someone like Mary Faust, I might have believed in something. But now I'm scared. Eliza really blasted my young life. My mother was her sister, you know...'

'Sheila, I'm not interested in Eliza. Let's talk of something else.'

'Of what? Of you, Gion? You're a writer, aren't you? You should be interested. So much going on. So many people playing a double role, so many faces...'

Where had he heard that? It was a dream...

'Everyone has many facets to their self, Sheila, everybody.'

'I know. That's why I get lost, but if only I get one clue the whole thing will come straight. I mean, people pretend there's good and bad, and proper and not so proper things, and they pretend they're this or that, but really it isn't like that at all. Take me. I think if I wasn't a nympho I'd like to be a nun. Really, at times I want to be a nun. Then I go to bed with a man, and then I want more to be a nun ... But I know what is going on. I'm going to try a little blackmail on my own. About chocolate boxes.' She grinned like an urchin.

And then he yawned. He could not help it. It was a yawn which started him wildly awake, throbbing with want of a woman, any woman, but it turned Sheila into a fury.

'I'm boring you. You think it's all nonsense. You're not listening to me.' Abruptly she wept, just as in the car on the Sunday morning, two hours after their first meeting.

'Oh, Sheila, please...'

'You don't like people,' she said. 'You aren't interested in anything except abstractions, like Humanity, Art, Mankind. Like Bernard Reguet. All he thinks of is stones, old stones and sculptures and *apsaras* of stone.'

He shook her arm roughly, and did not let go. 'Is it Reguet next, then?'

'You're not human,' she flung at him, 'you ... you prig. All you're concerned with is your precious integrity. Your self-contained sufficiency. You're worse than the others. Hypocrite.'

He knew it was true, and it infuriated him, for his body clamoured that he was like the others, and now he was fighting himself and fighting her; but she rose, and she was against him, held tight, then he had pushed her on to the bed (and later he was to know, in an agony of shame, that it was precisely because he had planned to do this that he had lifted the mosquito net).

And yet within himself someone prayed: don't let it happen, not to me, not to her. But already the deep satisfaction of his own power, proud as laughter, coursed through him. And she was moaning, in that demanding, importunating contradiction of pushing away what was most desired, as he found again habits of expertness unused in the last years of slight distaste and fastidious distance. And he could watch without shame, with the delight of rediscovery, his self going through the motions of inflicting pleasure with much effect, clearness, control. Yet all the time within him another self wept, horror-struck, whispering: what a pity, what a pity; another self which knew evil committed, knew evil to be the absence of love, the assertion of power, and even in his minute of pleasure he could feel thudding distantly in his brain, the pity of it, the devastation.

In a whirlwind of laughter timed by the drum beats of an invisible orchestra, among agile girls with jaws chewing phlegmatically, what in the confusion of cultural patterns he was sure was chewing-gum but turned out to be betel, Gion dreamt he was dancing the twist with an unknown partner whose face kept changing. It was Eliza, it was Mary Faust, it was Sumipoon and it was anyone else, but it was never Sheila that stood in front of him and wriggled desperately to the tune of the Friendship and Trust song:

> *For your biz is my biz ...*
> *And my biz is your biz ...*

Up and down waltzed Kilton, singing, in his arms a large chocolate box.

And then all at once again it was the withered plain, and he was alone, holding a stone lotus upright in his hand, and watching the Bayon, a leprous stone spider hand-walking its way across a world of trees ...

He woke, knowing the fester of guilt upon him, the odour of Sheila upon his hands, and the bed ambiguous, repulsive with indifference, not even untidy in the smug disorder of love.

His watch was laid upon the bedside table near the extinguished reading-lamp. It was eight o'clock, the sun shone, there was a hint of November coolness (the temperature had dropped to sixty-eight degrees Fahrenheit, according to the thermometer hanging in the bathroom). When he opened the wardrobe door a small cloud of mosquitoes eddied among his clothes.

The coffee was bitter.

I am getting old, everything hurts. Even sunlight.

His muscles were stiff and painful. The knowledge that he was now helpless in the face of small and trivial adversities, and all because of the inexorable attrition of age upon his muscles, bones, and blood, was unbearable. And worst of all was this startled horse exercise his mind did, leaping away every time the aspect of Sheila, the helplessness of Sheila a few hours ago, came clawing at him like a black panther out of the night.

He was unrefreshed by a shower, and irritably scratching, for he had been bitten because he had forgotten to put down the mosquito net after Sheila had gone. How abominable her disengagement, her rising in cold silence. In a state of hebetude, yet satisfaction, detaching him from the encounter, he had watched her. He had forborne to say anything as she walked to the mirror to look at herself, and only started a 'Sheila——' as she walked out. 'Sheila——' he had said again, anxious now, walking after her down the corridor as she returned to her room, 'what is the matter, Sheila?' But she had said: 'Good night,' and her door had shut, leaving him out. And he had gone back to bed and fallen asleep straight away.

Mary Faust was in the telephone booth, the door shut, and since the door was a wire screen, pervious to sight and sound, it fulfilled only a symbolic purpose.

'I'm telling you, she's not here,' she shouted. 'Yes, of *course* I've made inquiries . . .'

'Obviously the secretary's eloped with one of those personable young Cambodians,' Charles Manley said to Gion. 'Miss Faust within the booth reminds me of the young tiger in a chicken-wire net cage, which the curator, Bernard Reguet, keeps in his garden. Have you seen it? A beautiful beast, but I understand it's got a tooth abscess. Lower canine.'

'A tiger in a wire net cage?'

'Only until they get it shipped to a zoo in France. It's quite tame, and there's an extra enclosure in which they let it out. I go every morning to see it. A beautiful young beast.'

They sat down to breakfast together. 'Eliza will be down at any moment, I expect. And Sheila,' said Charles. 'So glad Eliza got over her headache. She has migraine attacks, you know. Fell her for days. How about a little walk before our morning session? Limber us up.'

Das and Ahmed Fouad now moved upon them, Das talking. 'I was just saying to our friend from Lahore that obviously one day Kashmir will return to Pakistan, and East Pakistan return to India. That would be a much more sensible arrangement

158

than the present one, don't you think?'

'Kashmir will come to us, but we will never abandon the east wing,' said Ahmed Fouad. 'Do not think that we shall sacrifice so many millions of Muslims into the bloodied hands of fanatical Hindus.'

Mary Faust shouted from the telephone booth: 'Das me boy, I can't make this chap understand. Come and tell him.'

'Tell who what, Mary?' Already Das was walking towards her, the mantle of meekness upon his shoulders once again.

'Tell that fool husband of Mabel that I haven't got his wife here. I don't know where she is. He's on the phone from Bangkok.'

The luggage of departing guests filled the hall. Charles tapped his pipe, and Gion saw him throw a look upwards at the windows. Sheila's window and verandah were on the front of the Suprême. He counted quickly: third one on the left ... the shutters were closed.

'Well, here it is.' In the garden of the Conservation Charles came to a stop in front of the tiger, burnished by the morning, prowling its enclosure, the empty wire net cage in the process of being cleaned by a young boy with a hose. 'Look at it. Only eight months and already such a brute. Can you see the swelling? Poor beast. It must hurt.'

The enclosure of stout sticks looked hardly strong enough for the rippling strength within it.

'A wire cage must be very cramping.'

They paced the tangled garden of the Conservation, passed Reguet's bungalow. Bernard Reguet, breakfasting on his verandah, waved at them. 'Come and have some coffee.'

'We were looking at your tiger ...' said Charles.

'The vet is lancing the abscess this morning.'

Unreality, hovering like the shadows of running clouds, was about.

'Cream, sugar, or black?' Reguet offered cigarettes. 'I suppose you heard about my fiasco? Kilton and Multani were released, both of them, almost immediately last night. I'm driving to Phnom Penh today, I must take up the matter there.'

'Isn't there a plane to Phnom Penh this morning?'

'The airport just telephoned. Something wrong with the plane engine. They're flying in a spare part from Bangkok. It might take the whole day. I prefer to drive by car. I'll be in Phnom Penh in five hours, six if the traffic is heavy, but it usually isn't these days.'

'What did Kilton do, exactly?' asked Charles. 'I'm not clear about it. My daughter Sheila seems to know, but I don't.'

'I'll tell you,' said Reguet. 'In our recent excavations I came upon something quite unique, a beautiful, carved gold belt, about thirty-five inches long. It has the most beautiful sculpture, actually one can call it that: it is sculptured gold, worked in depth, in the beautiful style of the ninth century—I'm sure it's over a thousand years old. Unique find, worth a fabulous amount as a collector's piece I would say, apart from the value of the gold itself.

'Well, Kilton stole it. I'm sure of it. I'll tell you why. We had in our museum a young man, who fell in love with a devotee of Monsieur Kilton's Friendship and Trust classes. The young man was persuaded to abstract this valuable gold belt and pass it to Kilton. Later he and the girl seem to have both been satisfactorily immersed. Then they married, forgot the Christianity they had learnt, and told me the story. I took a chance last night. Mr Kilton has friends in high places, and was released.'

'Disconcerting,' murmured Charles. 'Can't you let the Governor of the province know?'

'General Vam Barong? I'd rather not ... But I too have friends. I am taking the young couple with me to Phnom Penh. I do not wish anything to happen to them.'

On their way back to the hotel Charles threw another look at Sheila's shutters. Gion wanted to say: 'I love your daughter, and I wish to marry her.' But instead it was Charles who said: 'I must take you to the little village I've discovered, on our next walk.'

Gion waited for Charles to disappear into his room, then knocked at Sheila's door. He knocked and waited, waited and knocked, but there was no reply. He went downstairs, and looked along the counter for her key. It was not there, and that meant she was in her room, had locked herself in. Rapidly he wrote on a piece of paper, 'Sheila, I love you. I must see you.' He had begun to slip it under her door, when, once again, the pathos of his behaviour, the ridicule of his stance, crouched to slip a paper under a young girl's door, made him stand up, tear the note, and walk back to his room.

At nine o'clock the writers were once again in the conference room, a tired, tense, irritable lot. The two Chinese observers, the Rumanians, and the Americans remained stolidly in their previous places; Das, Ada, Ahmed Fouad, Charles, Ashley Basildon, and Joan Warburton sat in front; Father O'Dodder had now joined the ranks of the writers, and sat cracking his long jointed fingers in front of Gion; Gion had chosen a seat towards the back, for he wanted to slip out inconspicuously and go upstairs again to see if Sheila was awake. Behind Gion, unobtrusive, quiet, sat Ibrahim Malek; he had come in with the Cambodian writers who accompanied Ulong Serap; he nodded to Gion briefly, but he did not sit very long, for when Gion after a few minutes turned again to talk to him he was no longer there.

Captain Lederer walked into Bernard Reguet's bungalow as the latter was closing a small suitcase.

'Ah, mon vieux,' said Reguet, 'something the matter with your plane I understand.'

'The pump,' said Lederer. 'Waiting for a spare from Bangkok. Are you leaving?'

'For Phnom Penh. Yes.'

'Are you going to report the theft?'

Reguet was careful, non-committal. 'Perhaps.'

Lederer said: 'Reguet, you and I have never discussed ideas, but you're about my age, you've been here, you and your family before you, a long time. We are both French, patriots. I think I am not mistaken in thinking you a patriot. And we've both seen the name and the glory of France go down in the mud.' Lederer exhaled deeply. 'I was at Dien Bien Phu. And you?'

'I too.'

'Then what do you feel about it?'

'Nothing.'

'Nothing?'

'Nothing. We were stupid.'

'How, stupid?'

'Is this a political discussion?'

'Not a discussion. I would like to know, you understand, what you really believe in. In France, or in ... those bastards. Those who sold us.'

'I see.'

'Where do you stand?'

'I don't believe in glory. I believe in human beings. Equality. Fraternity. And Liberty. For others, as for myself.'

'And France? I know you're an intellectual. You're all the same, you intellectuals. You don't understand that it's either them or us. Either the communists, or freedom. Either France, or the Asian ant-heap.'

'Freedom is something we never gave them here.'

'And France? France tomorrow? We're not alone. It's time to put an end to it, everywhere. Them or us. I believe there's already one of them here.'

'An Algerian poet, yes. Attending the Congress. Is that wrong?'

'Poet my ... He fought in the guerrilla war. It jumps to the eye. One day he'll be here, on your verandah, and you'll be feeding the fishes in the lake.'

'I only hope that he will be sitting in Algeria one day, in as good a house as this one, sipping his coffee in peace.'

'You're with them.'

'I am for justice. It's time we stopped looking back.'

'You won't help?'

'Help?'

Lederer said, slowly: 'We are strong. Here also, in Cambodia, we're strong. We won't let France be dragged in the mud again.'

'I know that. Some of the French of Phnom Penh would be at ease among the *pieds noirs*. They have the colonial mentality.'

'Take care. Even if you don't think as we do, if we ask something of you, you'd better do it.'

'What, specifically, do you wish me to do?'

'It's simple. A small parcel. Take it with you to Phnom Penh. No questions asked.'

'What is in it?'

'I can't tell you, and if you open it we shall know. Someone will get in touch with you at the Royal, where you always stay.'

'I refuse. What has happened to you suddenly, Lederer? I've never known you like this.'

'I've been like this a long time. And now I've found myself. My destiny. The destiny of France.'

'You mean,' said Reguet, 'that someone has got at you, made you offers? It is a dangerous game.'

'You refuse to help us?'

'I refuse. It is madness.'

'We have our way with traitors,' said Lederer.

The desk he sat at, Gion noted, held a deep-etched obscene French word, and a charming picture of fishes entwined above it. Some artistic child had carved the fishes, and perhaps the same, hearing the word, had etched it in as decoration. The drawing purified the obscenity.

'Ladies and gentlemen,' said Ulong Serap, 'perhaps you would like to listen to my reading of the speech composed by His Right Reverend Eminence Bupta Prem, on the meaning of neutralism in the Light of the Lord Buddha's teaching? Then we shall call on Mr Charles Manley to report on the work of the two sub-committees.'

'I am sorry,' said Charles, 'our committees have not had time to debate these questions. Manual labour, the dancing—we shall probably be ready for this evening's session. I understand there will be an evening session?'

'Because we want to get out of here,' said Ashley Basildon. 'Ruddy Congress dragging on, you know. Other things to do.'

'Ah,' said Ulong Serap, 'I don't blame Mr Basildon for his hurry. He is a most successful writer. Perhaps Mr Multani, who has put his name down for a speech...?'

'Sorry,' said Multani, 'but after the insulting, the most offensive manner in which a certain incident occurred last night, I have decided to leave by the first plane. In fact, I would not be here, were it not that no plane is going this morning. I am expecting apologies from your government for the odious, the revolting manner in which I was dragged off last night. I want it clearly understood that I am attending this session only out of deference to my fellow writers, but that I repudiate all the proceedings as being communist-inspired.'

'Ulong Serap went on: 'It seems few of our delegates are prepared to speak before this evening's session, four-thirty to seven p.m., after which the hotel manager is offering you a dinner and dance soirée. Therefore I shall read the prepared speech, and pray that the Pure Light may guide you in your deliberations later.'

He folded his hands and intoned a prayer, and all the Cambodians there made a genuflexion, half seated, half kneeling, hands folded and heads bent to one side, achieving comfort and obeisance, worship, and ease at once.

'Buddhism, because of its transcendental power of viewing the world in impermanence, bestows upon its believers a tolerance, an ability to view contradictory ideas, with far more equanimity and understanding than any other religion. Buddhism faces *all* facts, discusses and reviews *all* realities, and knows them *all* transient. People have called Buddhism pessimistic, but that is false. Buddhism is entirely optimistic, since it teaches that the truth of the Noble Eightfold way is the way of understanding, and that through Understanding all pain, sorrow, and doubts can be dissolved.'

Gion looked round. The faces were inexpressive, Sumipoon's eyes were shut, Multani looked stern and drawn.

Ulong Serap went on, quoting Buddhist scriptures, reinforcing his discourse with quotations from the *Book of Gradual Sayings* and the *Book of Kindred Sayings*. Soon there were signs of restlessness. On and on, smoothly flowing, the unemphatic eloquence continued: 'The ultimately real is not and cannot be a personal God ... in the ultimately real all contradictions are solved ...'

Multani stirred, encountered Mary's frown, and the beatific smile of Chundra Das who, alone with the Chinese, did not look tired.

'Nothing is constant but change.'

The discourse rolled on, its page notes accumulated, a white heap upon the table. It was hot, the seats hard. Gion's mind wandered, and as usual when he was tired he felt all this had happened before. He let himself dwell in this nostalgic land of backward memory. *I was once here.* Thus he had sat, in time past, listening, floating on a drone of words. Thus he had sat, bewildered, doubting without being sure of doubt, his mind divided, and among the images of his mind the image of a girl like Sheila, but not Sheila, demanding attachment, particularization; putting a claim upon him, opening him again to pain and to passion, and to the bathos of passion, the dizzy shallow stumble from the tragic to the ridiculous; and below it all the notion of disaster, stalking him, disaster round the edge of his conscious mind.

'The evil of man returns upon him as fine dust thrown against the wind.'

The Rumanians had grown restless, the men shifting their new shoes bought in Siemreap market-place. Sumipoon sat transfixed by sleep, George was paging a book, perhaps one of those first editions he collected and stored in the cold vaults of MESSO, and from time to time solemnly nodded, to indicate his listening.

'Positive, active neutralism, right views, right resolve, right speech, right action, right living, right effort, right attention, right meditation ... leading through peace and goodwill towards all, to the extinction of suffering, and Nirvana.'

With a triumphant higher pitch of voice, flourishing the sentence like a final trumpet, Ulong Serap put the last sheet down. The Rumanians applauded vigorously, said 'Bravo, bravo'; Charles muttered 'Fascinating' round the stem of his pipe; indefatigably, the Japanese had taken copious notes. And Gion walked out. He must go to Sheila, marry her, make everything right, and then ... At one point, somewhere, they could have achieved something, but the time and the point in space had gone, floated past ... How could he put things right? Only by going to her, giving himself up.

Emergent as a dragon from the waters of oblivion came the phrase: the heart that thinks there is a tomorrow is as transient as the cherry blossom, for is there not the midnight wind?

The midnight wind, he thought, the midnight wind. Strains of long-winded Khmer music, sound of voices, of feet, and Sheila coming like a child, at night—and what had he done to her? Passion, he thought bitterly, passion unforgivable. A high wind in the branches of youth, and now only intermittence left, for with maturity no second wind, but only a sense too profound of one's self-exploration achieved, revealing insufficiency.

What would I not give for a moment of blind, eager passion, carrying me up, all of me, into her room, her arms?

In front of Sheila's room, aware only that no sun filtered under the door, as it should if her shutters were opened, he knocked. And when he heard: 'Who's that?' was so happy he shouted:

'It is I, Gion.'

Would she say, go away? He half expected it, and would stay pleading, till she opened. This time there would be no shame, no reticence, no carefulness——

'What do you want?'

'To talk to you.'

'What time is it?'

He looked at his watch. 'Ten-fifteen. Please open, Sheila.'

After a long minute the door opened, and he was plunged into night.

Sheila, fully dressed, stared at Gion. He had thought she would be in bed, but the bed was not made up. The room was neat. Only the shutters were drawn to, and the bed-light switched on gave the sensation of night.

'What do you want?'

He sniffed inaudibly, and turned into a wary, instinctual male, smelling the presence of another man ... or was it fantasy? The bathroom door was open, the wardrobe too small to admit an ensconced person. There was neatness. Even the chairs were devoid of any lingering cast-off garment. Something jarred.

In a rush, fearful of his purpose lapsing, the flame of passion which had carried him from Ulong Serap's discourse up the stairs to her door, to her, ebbing, he said: 'Sheila, I cannot accept that it should be like this between us. It means something, to me. I want it to.'

'Of course you would.'

'Please Sheila, please. Please let me say that it matters to me. I want to find what it means, I want to find myself perhaps. It seems to me that everything is wrong.'

'Why,' she said, very loud, 'are you in love with me?'

'I don't know. I don't know what the word means.' Although at that moment he did not care if he never saw her again when she said the word 'love' so bitterly, twisting it in her mouth like that.

She burst into laughter, long, forced, not amused. 'That's the funniest thing I've heard. Please go. You're too funny. Please go away. Don't bother me. Go.'

When Ulong Serap had finished his discourse, and the clapping had ended, Chundra Das had risen and called for half an hour's recess.

'I feel, Your Eminence'—to Ulong Serap—'as if I had been wrapt in ecstasy, transported to a Feast of the Soul without compare. I find, and I am sure my colleagues and all intellectuals worthy of that name, of the high calling to the service of Truth and Truth alone'—he scanned the back of Multani's head—'will find here ambrosial food for thought, indeed for re-thinking; for what, to use a journalese phrase, which I might be forgiven here, since after all in the noble calling of the Pen journalists are not excluded, and here at the Congress they sit with the poets and drink deep at the fountain of wisdom, for there are no untouchables where wisdom is dispensed so liberally and so fruitfully'—here Multani essayed a 'haw-haw', but it fell awkwardly and sounded as if he were deriding Ulong Serap rather than evincing his contempt at Chundra Das's garlanded sub-clauses—'to use, then, a journalistic phrase, each and every one of us is called, at this moment, to an agonizing reappraisal of our motives, our intentions, nay, to a search for our *inmost* soul.'

Here Chundra Das paused plangently and people naturally fell into Rodin attitudes, while the Cambodians and the Rumanians and the Chinese, thinking the speech over, began to clap. Chundra Das raised his hand, and continued, brisk yet charming: 'I move that we adjourn for half an hour, to savour this delicious repast for the spirit, and at the same time refresh our bodies, the humble slaves of the soul, for they too need proper recognition, as the Lord Buddha pointed out in the Noble Path.'

He said to Ada: 'Let's find Gion. He must be with Sheila.'

They met Gion coming out of Sheila's room.

'Now, Gion,' said Chundra, as they were sitting in his room, waiting while he made some English tea, practically unobtainable in Cambodia, boiling water in his small electric kettle plugged to the lamp (which was forbidden), 'I think the time has come to talk with you.'

'What is it?'

'It concerns Sheila. And Sheila concerns you. Relax.'

'She won't have anything to do with me.'

'Because of last night?' said Ada. 'Sorry Gion, but I couldn't sleep with that dreadful music and sound.'

'Does everybody know everything that goes on in this hotel?' Gion said bitterly.

'I'll put it all in a nutshell for you,' said Das, looking at Gion's face. 'There is a plot on. A political plot.'

'Orion and Astarte talked about it.'

'Plots always sound so ridiculous, unreal, comical, especially in South-East Asia where everything always sounds a bit like comic opera. There was a plot here a few years ago, mysterious messages, gold bars flown in from Bangkok, ambassadors exchanging notes. You must know that Cambodia's neutralism irritates a lot of people who can't leave well enough alone.'

'I thought it was "love that neutral" now?'

'It is. But it hasn't penetrated everywhere. There are any number of agents abroad, now called independent agents, whose livelihood depends on trouble-making. Look at Laos. There the war really goes on between the American Embassy, trying to carry out the State Department dicta to get a neutralist government going, and the U.S.O.M. and M.A.A.G., still addicted to the good old Dulles days and methods, quiet and ugly Americans, the lot.'

'Like Kilton.'

'Like Kilton. But it's not the political angle that we are interested in. It's the narcotics angle, where our young Algerian friend also comes in,' said Das, pointing to the immobile young man in the chair. 'And Sheila. She has to pass twenty-five thousand pounds sterling worth of heroin wrapped in chocolates in a three-pound chocolate box from Bangkok to someone here. He or she never got it. We think the O.A.S. got it.'

'The O.A.S.?'

'Yes,' said Das. 'O.A.S. Where there are Frenchmen, there

are some pro-O.A.S. French.'

'A chocolate box?' The images began forming. 'She mentioned a chocolate box.' Where was it?' 'At Kilton's place, Bud Kilton. Friendship and Trust Auditorium. He passed round some chocolates he had received in the post, and Sheila said she had a similar chocolate box.'

'We thought you might warn her. Protect her.'

Ulong Serap too had warned him, and Sheila had been talking last night. What had she said?

'I'll try. I'll try. But she won't listen to me. Can't you tell me more?'

'What more? She is in danger ... all of us, in fact,' said Ada. 'Sheila is a fine girl, a beautiful girl. Innocent. You know that, don't you?'

'Yes, I do.'

'No one has ever cared for her, or so she believes, so she tries all sorts of things. But this is murder. She'll get herself killed, if someone doesn't look after her.'

But I've killed her too, thought Gion. I've also murdered. What happened was like murder, and I am ashamed.

'I'll go now,' he said, 'I'll find her.'

Whatever she said, he would not leave her side.

Sheila, Sheila, Sheila—but the door was open, and she was not in the room.

Downstairs, Mr Lee Souvan said: 'Yes, Miss Manley has gone out. Yes, in the direction of Siemreap. She was walking.'

The small village of a few houses was at a turn, its main path a zigzag among the wooden houses upon stilts. Ulong Serap walked to his house at the end of the village, where a small *stupa* shrine, newly painted, reared upon a platform of stone. Near it the remains of an old laterite wall enclosed a few ruins, old as Angkor but more defaced, remains of an old temple now containing a new statue of the Buddha, freshly painted, hung with flower garlands. Next to it was Ulong Serap's house, also a wooden one on stilts. And standing in front of the shrine was Charles Manley.

Ulong Serap said: 'I see you know the place well. You come here, I know, to find peace. Your daughter will be coming here too.'

'I don't think it's any use,' said Charles.

'My friend,' said Ulong Serap, 'we must cure her, and you. You are both diseased.'

'Diseased?'

'Rotten with hatred and pain. One day you will explode.'

'I am quite calm, you know. Placid,' said Charles.

'Your pipe looks placid. Your fixation upon your obsession, your daughter, gives this appearance of calm. You are immobile round your own turmoil. But there is danger. And Gion loves her.'

'He's hurt her,' said Charles, 'like the others. I know. I always know everything about her. I tell you, he's hurt her more, because she loves him. And he's over forty, she's twenty-one. I can't stand him.'

'Alas, yes,' said Ulong Serap sadly. 'Alas that the past should repeat itself. Gion confused a movement of the body with an attitude of love. But I have asked your daughter to come here. Let us wait for her. She said she would come.'

'Mr Lee,' said Ashley Basildon, 'any pretty girls? Any night clubs? I went out last night and couldn't find a thing. And that female militia frightens me.'

'Houses of prostitution are not permitted in Cambodia, monsieur.'

'I'll have to go reconnoitring on my own.'

'As you please. Shall I call a taxi?'

'I'll have my lunch first. When is the next plane to Phnom Penh? I might go there for a bit.'

'Monsieur, the plane is damaged today, and tomorrow there is no plane.'

'Oh, Christ,' said Ashley, and walked away.

Mr and Mrs Fumikaro conversed with Lee Souvan.

'My wife and I compiling manual on Siemreap. My wife doing statistics on birth, death, infant mortality, annual income per head, chief industries, and making Fumikaro poll of opinions. I myself ambitiously translate Cambodian folk songs to acompany statistics of my wife. So far 99·99 per cent of people here *for* the Prince. Only great person not interviewed so far is General Vam Barong. We are requesting interview with Governor of Province. Tomorrow perhaps.'

'Tomorrow?' said Mr Lee. 'I do not think so.'

'Ah, so so?'

'The stars are not good tomorrow, monsieur.'

'Ah, so so so,' said Mrs Fumikaro.

'Another picture please.' Mr Fumikaro snapped Lee Souvan against the reception desk.

Mr Fumikaro took a paperback out of his pocket. 'Accept, please. Translation of Simenon in Japanese. Done by unworthy self.'

'I am indeed grateful,' said Lee Souvan.

'We already have 3,072 photographs,' announced Mr Fumikaro, returning to his subject. 'We plan to take 117 of General Vam Barong, his villa, his staff. We have obtained plan of villa from architect in Paris, now retired Frenchman. General Vam Barong has extensive wine cellars, is not so?'

'We shall make a list of the wines he collects,' said Mrs Fumikaro. 'This will complete knowledge of Siemreap town, the Suprême Hotel, Angkor.'

Mr Lee Souvan said: 'If the stars are auspicious.'

'So so so,' said Mr Fumikaro.

'Ah, mon vieux,' said Deroulede, 'I seem to have caught you just in time.'

Reguet was already at the steering-wheel of his car. 'In time for what, Jean? I'm going to Phnom Penh.'

'An archaeologist in a hurry! Look, there is no plane as you know, and the telephone line to Phnom Penh seems out of condition. Can you take this letter to my wife? I promised to ring her up some time today, and she may worry.'

'What is a chap like you doing, lolling round Angkor? I've never known you stay here longer than three days.'

'It's only my second day today,' replied Deroulede, laughing, 'and there is the beautiful Mary Faust.'

'A revolution who's lost her secretary.'

'A challenge. I'm also here on business. With Fumikaro.'

'Fumikaro? I thought he was a poet.'

'And a banker. Nephew of Yoshida, biggest textiles monopoly in Japan today.'

'I see,' said Reguet. 'I suppose the deal will be closed soon?'

'No doubt, with a moonlight banquet at the Bayon,' replied Deroulede. 'The Japanese have kept a wonderful sense of aestheticism, even in business. You cannot imagine what we businessmen have to put up with to swing a deal. With the moon, and writers' congresses, and fire-spouting beauties like Mary Faust.'

'George,' said Sumipoon, 'I've thought of something.'

'What, my darling?'

'That the contempt for manual labour goes hand in hand with the contempt for women. I must work that out in my next novel.'

'My dear, is that true?'

'Yes, it is. I've been thinking about it since this morning. Actually, I was thinking about Mary Faust.'

'What about her? She wearies me, my dear.'

'She wearies me too. She got Das to tell the husband over the telephone that Mabel wasn't here. He rang up from Bangkok. Afterwards I tackled Mary and she said: "I'm not responsible for a mere menial." So I give her up. Anyway, Mary is angling for Deroulede, because he's very rich. Rolling in wealth, I'm told.'

'You don't think she'll lead a revolution?'

'No, I don't. Anyone who behaves like that towards other human beings can't really love them, and without any love for others it's only a power-complex she's trying to satisfy ... and then she and Deroulede. They were dancing together last night.'

'Sheila was dancing too. And in a much more intimate manner.'

'But Sheila is *innocent*. A saint, with a halo slightly askew, but a saint. Mary isn't. She's got lashings of perfume on today. You didn't notice.'

'I thought you *liked* her?'

'She has a convincing presence.'

George said: 'In all this, there's one thing we haven't worried about.'

'What?'

'Mabel Despair. What has *really* happened to her?'

'But I do worry,' Sumipoon said. 'I wonder what has happened, but what can I do?'

'Sometimes,' Ulong Serap said to Charles Manley, 'the past returns, if one meditates long enough.'

'I wonder whether Sheila is coming?' said Charles, not listening.

'Only Gion can save Sheila,' said Ulong Serap. 'You must stop hating Gion. You must accept him. Then she will be happy.'

'I am myself an expiator of a crime committed in the past,' continued Ulong Serap. 'Many will smile and think it insane, even boring. Actually, if it is an illusion, it is the illusion of limpid-eyed children and convalescents, for whom time has lifted its fences a while so that they become attentive. The child still knows the continuity between his silence and his dreams, he is at the heart of time, and space is ambushed in his body.

'For Gion and I murdered Sheila when she was not Sheila, I through what I called love and he through jealousy, both equally vicious. I was her half-brother, and loved her more than a brother should, but hid it from myself. She was married to an old man, more a father than a lover, and took Gion as her lover, and we killed her in the name of virtue.'

'And the old man she had married ... was me?' said Charles, polite, frozen, a hand rubbing his chest.

'Yes,' said Ulong Serap, 'you. Thus was it revealed to me. Since then I have expiated. In this life I continue to expiate by building pagodas and temples, and soon I shall withdraw completely from action, give all my money to the schools and stay in this village, living on alms. I have built three hundred and fifty-two shrines.'

'In the present,' said Charles, 'my daughter can't leave men alone. I don't think the past matters one bit.' Then he heard quick stamping steps and, his heart lurching, he saw Gion and a Cambodian come running towards Ulong Serap's house.

'Ah,' said Ulong Serap, 'doubtless Sheila is coming.'

'Sheila. She's gone,' Gion cried from below the house. 'In Reguet's car.'

'Reguet?' said Ulong Serap. 'Reguet is a good friend, trustworthy. Perhaps she is coming here.'

'Are you sure?'

'I saw her this morning early. She was unhappy. I asked her to come here. She promised.'

The Cambodian spoke in Khmer. 'I followed her, Eminence, as you asked me to. She went to some shops in the town, looking at things. I kept about fifty yards away. Then a car came by, stopped, and honked. I saw it was Bernard Reguet's car, so I did not run up. I stopped where I was. She got in and they drove off.'

'If it is Reguet, there is nothing to fear,' said Ulong Serap.

'But you were afraid,' cried Gion, 'you warned me. You asked this young man to follow her. What are you afraid of?'

'The past,' said Ulong Serap.

Gion turned to Charles, very still and grey in the face, with a hand on his chest, as Gion had seen him before. 'Mr Manley, did you know your daughter was in danger? That she is involved with the drug traffic? Did you know?'

Charles did not answer. Then a moan came from him, he clenched both hands to his chest, and toppled forwards on the floor.

At the Conservation the tiger cub lay on its side, tied with ropes. In a white coat the veterinary surgeon bent over the animal.

'Is Mr Reguet back?' Gion asked.

The veterinary surgeon turned. 'Monsieur Reguet is gone to Phnom Penh.'

'To Phnom Penh? Where can I find him in Phnom Penh?'

'His servant may know.' He spoke to one of the two boys with the ropes. The boy signalled to Gion to follow him into Reguet's office.

Upstairs, on the desk in the small private office, was an address book, black. The boy indicated this. Obviously a routine for visitors looking for Bernard Reguet. Well organized, he would leave an address or telephone number behind.

Gion fingered the book. It contained lists of names, with telephone numbers. Phnom Penh 629. Phnom Penh 820. Phnom Penh ... at least a dozen Phnom Penh telephone numbers.

Gion asked: 'Do you know if Mr Reguet is staying in Phnom Penh tonight?'

'Hotel Royal, Phnom Penh,' the servant said.

Gion glanced round him. On the floor was an envelope. The servant, noticing it, picked it up and placed it on the desk. Gion automatically straightened a rumple of the blotting-paper pad, and turned to go. Mad, awful Sheila. Going off with Reguet, going off to Phnom Penh, six hundred kilometres away ... so it was Reguet ...

The tiger snarled, claws outstretched, as he passed again. The vet was washing his hands in the basin.

Gion went to the hotel. 'Mr Lee, I want a long-distance taxi. To go to Phnom Penh.'

At the Bayon, dead stone in the before-noon's flat light, Eliza posed for Peter Anstey, looking up at the towering faces as if peering into their shadowy nostrils. Their Cambodian taxi-driver amused himself shooting small arrows from a cross-bow of the kind that pedlars sold to tourists. His presence was obviously exhilarating to Peter, who suggested to Eliza that an interesting photograph would be the youth shooting an arrow, with Eliza entranced following its upward course, bending backwards in the light wind, the Cambodian *sampot* she wore buffeted into becoming folds by movement and breeze; behind them the stony faces would stare frozenly.

'Such a marvellous picture, darling,' said Peter abstractedly, eyeing the young chauffeur's face. 'He's really got a face that's come straight off the walls of Angkor.'

'All right,' said Eliza, 'but do hurry, I'm so tired. It's nearly twelve.' She added, malicious: 'I wish Teo were here.'

Peter did not reply. It was all over, as Eliza knew.

Eliza saw Ibrahim Malek walking towards the Bayon. As she looked up at Peter's command, bent like a sail, *sampot* draped, a louder commotion of bats made one fly out blind, hit against one of the faces and fall dead between her and Peter.

'Oh dear, why can't we work in peace? Here, boy, hold my camera, will you?' Peter approached the bat, and with his foot shoved it out of the picture.

Eliza closed her eyes.

Ibrahim Malek was now climbing the Bayon steps. Soon he would be on their terrace.'

'Turn, darling,' ordered Peter. 'Right shoulder forward, please.'

She turned. And she saw the Terrace of Elephants, the trees beyond. She gazed, wide-eyed, absent-minded.

After lunch the hotel's inmates retired to their rooms and to bed. With the night's dancing everyone was tired out.

Except Mary Faust. Looking at herself in the mirror, Mary did not know whether to wear her usual well-cut slacks, or a skirt. Her suite was large, the bedroom held a triple mirror. While she changed she could hear the ash tray being moved by the man waiting for her in the sitting-room, separated from the bedroom by long blue curtains. The odour of his cigar, definitely pleasant, mingled with the scent she used, the subtle, expensive perfume she placed between her breasts.

If Mary had not belonged to a culture where sexual excitement masqueraded as intellectual attraction, the moistness of her lips and certain other physical warmths would have warned her as preparatory stages of sexual excitement, elicited by conversation, lunch close to a physically desirable man, a man sure of his maleness. Jean Deroulede had an arrogant unconsciousness of his own attraction to which Mary responded. Among the men of her country maleness was whittled, pared out of them. The fact that Jean Deroulede had wide shoulders, narrow hips, a disrobing look, and the assurance of the upper class, yet seemed unaware of all these advantages, fascinated Mary. It was irresistible. She must change him, dominate him, conquer ... Their words might seem at variance, their minds were tuned to the same exploitation of others' needs; though opposite in attitude, they were both dedicated to the same end: power for themselves. The look Jean threw upon her body between dessert and coffee had set her nerves singing with an excitement which she told herself was the highly moral purpose of converting him from capitalism to socialism, but which was actually the natural one of conquering him for bed.

'You won't have those expensive cigars when your plantations get nationalized.' She issued from the curtains, throwing this insult calculated to stir him, in a voice already altered, one register lower.

'I started life on the docks at fourteen,' he said. 'Work does not frighten me.' His hand was steady as he held a match to her cigarette, and he looked at her breasts, appraisingly.

Nonchalant, pacing an exhibition of her beautiful body, she walked to the verandah, surveying the space below with its dormant taxis and *samlos*. 'Well, are we going out to that temple you wanted to show me? Or are you tired?'

'I have been thinking.' He put his cigar down carefully on the ash tray, walked to her and caught her wrist.

'Let me go.'

'I am going to have you.'

'Don't be ridiculous. I shall scream.'

'But not very loudly,' he said. 'You *know* that you want me to make love to you, have wanted it some time now.'

'How dare you——'

He pushed her on the big settee, and was upon her.

Mary screamed, but not too loudly, tried to bite at his mouth came near to hers, but her jaws snapped on air for he pulled her back by the hair. Then she knew that it was going to happen at last. This time there would be no holding the man back, none of the contemptuous tongue-lashing, the wrestling out of which she usually emerged victorious and unscathed, holding power over the man, power over the furious excited helpless male...

'You are like that,' he said. 'You excite men, then you play the virtuous, outraged hussy. I bet you did it to that Indian, Das. But you won't do it to me.'

'Let me go.' Already the syllables dragged, her body acting the procedure of resistance with singular weakness, her threshing hips an invitation disguised as rebuff.

He slapped her in the face; then again, with the side of his hand, stunning her. And now she was really crying, really hurt, helpless, yet at the same time knowing the slow exquisite change that went on, growing from pain to pleasure, until she screamed again, but in a different voice, knowing a body far away, astonished, moaning, invaded, lost, all refusal receding into a blur of pleasure which later she would strive to erase from her memory, but never succeed.

'We don't know our terrible minds well enough,' Ibrahim Malek was saying. 'In them only murder is authentic and incorruptible.'

Ada Timberlake, Chundra Das, and Ibrahim Malek sat together in Das's room.

'Now,' said Das, 'you are beginning to use words again to describe the states of mind, the inner weather.'

'If I were to try to describe our state of mind now,' said Ada, 'I would call it a state of sleepy tension. What are we waiting for?'

'For things to happen,' Das said. 'Where is Sheila? Where is Gion? When is the coup? It is rather terrible not to dare be able to do anything for fear of precipitating something.'

'Except keep together. In case something happens to either of us when alone.'

Ibrahim Malek said: 'Find out anything with that concealed microphone?'

'No,' said Das.

'No mechanical gadget ever works with Das,' said Ada.

'Our Das is in love with Mary Faust. I think he tried to sleep with her, and she made him feel guilty,' said Ibrahim Malek. 'One day someone will have to write a history of the influence of sex on politics.'

'I said that the other day at lunch,' Ada replied. 'Only I said it better.'

'Where are you going now?' asked Das, as the young Algerian rose.

'To the astrologer,' said Ibrahim Malek. 'Don't leave each other, you two.'

'That was clever of you, finding him,' said Ada.

'Not me. It's like that all over South-East Asia. Nothing is ever begun without consulting the stars. Certainly not a war.'

At four-thirty p.m. that Wednesday the plane from Siemreap to Phnom Penh was repaired, and took off under the command of the co-pilot, because Captain Lederer, feeling suddenly indisposed, remained at the Suprême Hotel.

It was a greatly diminished Writers' Congress which met that afternoon, for the Rumanians, the Chinese, and the Americans went on the repaired plane, as well as the Roman

Catholic and Buddhist delegations; Teo went too, with Aunty; Father O'Dodder remained behind. Ahmed Fouad, Ashley Basildon and John, Mary Faust, Das and Ada, Sumipoon and George assembled in the hall when Mr Lee Souvan came in with the news of Charles's illness. A heart attack.

'Poor man,' said Sumipoon. 'Let's go to see him at the hospital.'

Four Cambodian writers arrived. They presented Ulong Serap's apologies. He was at the hospital with his friend Charles Manley.

'Eliza and Sheila must be there too,' Sumipoon said to Ada.

'We'd better find out,' said Ada.

'Gion isn't here either,' added Sumipoon.

'Well,' said Das, 'though we are few, we might as well proceed. We were talking this morning about the meaning of——'

Mr Lee Souvan reappeared, accompanied by a small, dark man, holding a leather jacket in one hand and a small suitcase in the other.

'Miss Mary Faust, this gentleman wishes to speak to you.'

'Thomas!' Mary said. 'You here?'

'Yes. Where is Mabel, where is my wife? If anything's happened to her, I'll kill you, Mary Faust. I'll most certainly kill you.'

At four forty-five p.m., outside the hotel, the passenger bus ground its gears, starting for the airport with a full load.

Well, thought Mr Lee Souvan, carefully checking the departures in the hotel register, that clears matters up a little. The hotel was emptying. Now we shall see . . .

Out of the Congress room now trailed the writers, Mary Faust at their head, with Thomas on her heels still mouthing threats. 'I'll kill you, if we can't find her.'

Das and Ada went to Mr Lee. 'Mr Lee, is it not possible to see the Governor, General Vam Barong?'

'Impossible, monsieur. Mr and Mrs Fumikaro have asked to photograph him, but he refused.'

'This gentleman's wife disappeared on the way to his villa. We must see him. Tell him a delegation of writers will call on him.'

'I ... monsieur ... I will ring up again.'

He disappeared and then after a few moments came back: 'Monsieur,' he said to Das, 'General Vam Barong is unwell, but he says since you insist, and since the stars are auspicious, he will receive you briefly, for ten minutes, so that you can reassure yourselves that the body is not there.'

'Well, now ...' Das looked round. Who should he take with him? The husband, of course, and Mary, himself, and Ada ... They would have to take two taxis.

'Please,' said Mr Fumikaro to Das, 'may I and Mrs Fumikaro come with you? Possibility we photograph General on bed of disease ... yes?'

'Truly,' said Mr Fumikaro, as they rolled towards Vam Barong's villa, 'this is lovely country. Most suitable for development of industries, as Mr Deroulede tells.'

'You have business contacts with Mr Deroulede?' inquired Das.

Mr Fumikaro became prudent, and replied evasively that Mr Deroulede was a good business man.

'Villa of Governor,' announced the taxi-driver.

'Beautiful villa, such style,' Mrs Fumikaro murmured.

'Style uncertain of period,' remarked Mr Fumikaro.

'Indeed,' replied his wife.

They pointed their cameras.

The visitors were ushered in, save for Mrs Fumikaro who refused to enter. 'I shall stay outside, photograph villa,' she said.

She strolled, examining the gate, the wall, crossed the road to the other side, adjusted her camera, squinted in the view-finder. A small laugh made her turn. Behind her two little boys, naked but for very ragged shorts, brown with sun and dust, struck a photographic pose, holding hands. Mrs Fumikaro smiled. She photographed the villa, then turned round to the little boys.

'Photo?' she asked.

They stiffened, suddenly serious, and she snapped. They relaxed, laughing, and she snapped again. The smaller of the two put a hand upon her arm.

'What name?' Mrs Fumikaro asked them in her halting

Khmer. 'What village name?'

'Kampong Siu,' said the elder, pointing vaguely into the forest behind him. Then he added, mysteriously: 'There is a woman who cries.'

Mrs Fumikaro looked round. 'A woman? Where?'

'Woman from hotel.'

Mrs Fumikaro became wary. This was dangerous ground.

'Where is the woman?'

'Cellar underneath villa. My brother tells me.'

'Your brother?'

'Brother of a brother.'

Mrs Fumikaro already knew that family relationships were extensive. Brother of a brother might mean a friend...

'Have you seen her?'

'No, but my brother says she weeps.' He mimicked: 'Uh—uh—huh.'

Mrs Fumikaro stood rock still. Then she walked back, near the taxi, eyed the villa anxiously, waiting for Mr Fumikaro to return.

'Mesdames, messieurs, I give you my word of honour that I will do my best, do the impossible, to find the lady whose disappearance causes you disquiet.'

The general lay in his bed, a huge affair of gilded brass with French lilies and a baldaquin of purple embellished with oval shapes in which his initials were embroidered with gold thread. An entire wall of the bedroom was coated with mirrors; a cheval mirror stood at the foot of the bed, placed at such an angle that the general could watch himself in it, and at the same time watch the reflection of its reflection on the wall.

The general wore a Chinese silk purple dressing-gown; he had many pillows behind his head. Servants came in, walking on their knees, bearing trays with cups brimming with iced champagne.

'If this lady has encountered misadventure on her way to my house that night, it is my duty, my responsibility as Governor of this Province, to do my utmost to retore her to the arms of her spouse, to her hearth, her children. May I say that I should have been apprised of this earlier? Why was no complaint made to me at the time?'

Mary said: 'But I did notify the police.'

'You didn't bother,' Thomas said. 'For you no one exists in the world, except to serve you. If anything has happened to Mabel, I will kill you.'

General Vam Barong extended a podgy hand. 'Monsieur, I give you my word. I shall do my utmost. In our happy, peaceful land, we have not had one murder for the last three years.' He consulted an expensive gold clock. Cupid swathed, on a bedside table, and pressed on a bell button. 'Time for my medicine. Ask the doctor to wait.'

Das said: 'We are deeply grateful to your Excellency for receiving us when you are so obviously unwell.'

'It is our duty,' said the general affably. 'I myself delight in the company of intellectuals, of literati. Proust, Hugo, how'—he waved an intellectual hand about—'they delighted me in my youth.' He collapsed backward with a sigh. 'Alas, I have worn myself out in service of my country. You may go now. I shall see to it . . .'

'Tell me, monsieur,' the taxi-man said to Gion, 'why you wish to go so fast to Phnom Penh?'

Gion had been staring vacantly at the flat ricefields, with their clumps of separating kapok trees. He had not spoken to the taxi-man, and now looked at him. He was a young man, as most Cambodian taxi-men seem to be; of the new generation first acquainted with machinery and enamoured of engines, spending their evenings polishing cars, talking mechanics, and reading machinery textbooks. 'I am looking for a girl who has gone off to Phnom Penh. Is this funny?'

'Not at all,' said the taxi-man. 'Always it is a girl. Is it the blonde girl that went out with you the first day, and cried on the way back?'

'How do you know?'

'We talk to each other, monsieur, my brothers and I. Everybody is the same. We all have feelings.'

'Yes,' said Gion, 'it is that girl.'

'My name is Bok. I am the best driver of all, that is why Monsieur Lee gave me to you.'

'Very good of him.'

'He is a good brother. We Khmers like to help people in need of help. It is our village custom. The blonde lady is a nice girl, but she will not make a good wife.'

'Perhaps not, but I love her.'

'Yes. Always it is love. Did she run away with someone else?'

'She has gone to Phnom Penh with Monsieur Reguet.'

'Monsieur Bernard?' cried the taxi-man. 'It is impossible! Monsieur Bernard would not run away with someone else's woman.'

'He may just have given her a lift.'

'Oh, well,' said the taxi-man confidently, 'at the next village we stop for petrol. The police post there check all cars on this road, write down the numbers and the names of the people travelling, because of the opium smuggling. You understand? Our enemies are trying to corrupt us with drugs.'

'I heard something about the opium.'

'We have many enemies, monsieur, because we are peaceful and independent and neutral. Even now, they are plotting ... but we, the people, will stop them at the right time.' He passed a cigarette to Gion. 'We, the people,' he said, 'we won't let them turn us into slaves. We know what we want. We are independent.'

Gion said: 'Yes,' and felt happier. It was true, there were the people, all around him. He was not alone.

'My name is Bok,' said the taxi-man. 'Call me Bok.'

'No,' said the man at the police post, going for the third time through his register, 'Monsieur Bernard did not come through this morning.'

'Well,' said the taxi-man, 'what about it, Monsieur Gion?'

'I know Monsieur Bernard,' said the policeman. 'He goes up to Phnom Penh once a month or so. How could I miss him?'

'Is there any other road to Phnom Penh?' asked Gion.

'No. This is the only one.'

'I will tell you now,' said Bok. 'I think Monsieur Bernard may have taken the lady for a drive to the ruins of Banteay Sray, about eighteen miles from Siemreap. It's a bad road. Shall we go there to find out?'

They went to Banteay Sray. The pink and lovely temples were deserted. There was no one. They returned. It was two o'clock.

Bok said: 'Gion brother, I think we must go back and mobilize the masses.'

'What is that?'

'Tell all my brothers. Everybody will look. Only in this way we shall find them.'

By four o'clock every *samlo*, every taxi-driver in the town of Siemreap was being told that Gion was looking for Bernard Reguet and Sheila Manley.

Gion was back at the Conservation. The tiger was asleep in the small cage, now in the shadow, a soft inoffensive hunk of brightness in the penumbra of leaves.

Gion walked to the bungalow, and saw Reguet's servant asleep on a mat in the shadow of the verandah, a fan dropping from his hand. The siesta hour. Crouched under a tree, a boy and a girl also watched, smiling expectantly. The girl had a bundle tied in a checked cloth by her side.

'Who are you waiting for?'

They both smiled.

'Monsieur Reguet?' he said. 'Bernard Reguet?'

'Monsieur Bernard, yes,' said the young man.

Gion's hand reached for the servant's shoulder, and shook it.

'Oh,' said the girl, 'he is asleep.'

Gion again shook the man, who woke, yawned, stretched, looked at the sun, then at Gion reproachfully: 'Not yet time.'

'Wake up. It is past four o'clock. These two'—he indicated the boy and the girl—'they are waiting for Mr Reguet.'

'Mr Bernard gone to Phnom Penh.'

The boy said something, and the servant shrugged his shoulders.

'What does he say?'

'He say he go to Phnom Penh with Mr Bernard. Mr Bernard forget.'

'Did Mr Bernard promise to pick them up?'

'Yes. They wait. Mr Bernard forget.'

No, thought Gion, it is not like Bernard Reguet to forget them. He remembered. This must be the boy and girl Bernard

Reguet had said he would take with him to Phnom Penh. Because they were the witnesses in his case against Kilton and because he did not want anything to happen to them...

He walked out of the Conservation, walked back to the hotel.

At the bar there was only Jean Deroulede. Automatically Gion moved towards him. Then he stopped. A waiter came up, and he realized he was very hungry. He had had no food since breakfast. He said: 'A brandy, and a sandwich.'

Jean Deroulede looked at Gion in a friendly way. He said: 'Are you also looking for Mrs Despair?'

'No,' said Gion, 'I'm not.'

Now Lee Souvan approached him. 'Monsieur Deroulede is a great friend of Monsieur Bernard, perhaps he can tell you.'

'Bernard Reguet?' said Deroulede. 'He was going to Phnom Penh this morning. He was just starting when I saw him. In fact, I gave him a letter to take to my wife.'

The astrologer lived on the third floor of a small Chinese hotel, in the smallest and darkest room, right under the roof. He was old, not very successful. Like all astrologers, he spied on everyone, and sold information for money.

'Tell me more,' said Ibrahim Malek.

'There is not much more. My illustrious friend the General's personal astrologer has predicted the auspicious day, as I told you. The only thing that may make him change his mind is a catastrophe: a falling star, the death of a woman...'

'So General Vam Barong has decided to become healthy again?'

'Yes. Even today, the personal astrologer allowed him to receive visitors.'

'And tomorrow is the day?'

'It is.'

Ibrahim Malek emptied his billfold, walked downstairs, walking in the way he had been taught as a guerrilla, effaced, invisible in visibility.

He twice circled the avenues round the town, went into Chinese shops to buy knick-knacks. When he neared the cinema he perceived Ashley Basildon talking to a Cambodian waitress in one of the open-air restaurants where Coca-Cola and Pschtt were sold. He saw Father O'Dodder pacing the walk near the river, reading his breviary, watching the children throw themselves with delighted shouts in the water; and then he saw Eliza, walking alone, looking so old . . . He waited a little, to be sure she was not being followed, then set off after her.

The time was six o'clock.

Monsieur Paulet's dinner and dance party that evening was a failure. Valiantly the music poured itself out to a nearly empty floor. Peter Anstey danced gracefully with Madame Shum. At the bar, Lederer explained to Joan Warburton that the next day at ten a.m. he would fly to Phnom Penh and Saigon. He felt better.

'That's fine,' said Joan. 'I'll start packing tonight. Ashley has decided to go to Phnom Penh. He can't write here. Absolutely deadly, this place. Only ruins.'

Multani and Kilton also told everyone that they were leaving.

'I want to catch a connection to Hong Kong from Saigon,' said Kilton. 'But I'll be back. Meanwhile, this little girl will keep things going.' He indicated the pianist, Maisie, who had come with him, but stood, refusing to dance, darting fearful glances about.

'I did not know that you were leaving us, Mr Kilton,' said Jean Deroulede.

'Must report to headquarters in Hong Kong.'

'I thought they were in Bangkok?'

'Both places.'

At eleven p.m. the party came to an end.

'Tell me, Das,' said Ada, yawning, 'why is that you're afraid of Mary Faust?'

'I'm not afraid,' said Das. 'I wither when she's around. It's got to do with the Raj.'

'The Raj?'

'The British Raj. Shades of Brooke's "Grantchester", E. M. Forster's *A Passage to India*. We never get beyond Brooke, Forster, and T. S. Eliot, we Brindians. The last eminent Victorian is a present-day member of the Delhi Gymkhana Club . . .'

'And the last British viceroy is Nehru. I've heard it. But Mary is American.'

'That only makes it worse. She is THE White Memsahib, in all her arrogance and peremptoriness. And all at once I am transported back to my childhood. Did I ever tell you about my childhood, Ada?'

'No, Das, not that far back. Only how you became a writer. Because you went to jail for throwing a bomb.'

'Our bombs were so inefficient, when I think of plastic. But as a child I was put in an English school, and there taught by Miss Fawny. She was auburn-haired, an imperious do-gooder. She taught me to *rebel*. "Don't agree with me," she said, "Why don't you protest?" I had not understood the concept of loyal opposition; I did not realize that in order to avert a real revolution the British have always had the genius of stimulating "revoltees", particularly among the English-educated élite in Asian colonies. I became one of them, and Miss Fawny showed me the way, and so I was subservient, soul-bound even in my rebellion.'

'I wouldn't call throwing bombs a fake revolt.'

'It was, though I went further than Miss Fawny expected. By that time Miss Fawny had gone home, and I remember thinking of her, so vividly, when my bomb exploded, killing no one. She belonged to a very good family, a very good family,' said Das, and suddenly the whole snobbery of the caste-conscious Indian, than whom there exists nothing more snobbish except his English equivalent, was in his voice. Ada recognized the intonation, and her mind squirmed. We'll have been responsible for a lot of things, she thought, and one of them is the preservation of the caste system in India. 'Now I find in Mary Faust a physical resemblance to Miss Fawny, and it holds me in thrall.'

'First love always does,' said Ada. 'Shall we go to bed?'

'Yes, Ada. Good night. I only wish our friend Ibrahim Malek was back.'

'And Gion, and Sheila. I don't know what to do now. This waiting makes me nervous ...'

'Got to stick it. Sure you'll be all right alone?'

'Positive. Besides, I'm on the front of the hotel, the safer side. And remember, it's not known that we're on the trail.'

'Sorry I sound nervous. But it's Gion and Sheila. Monsieur Lee said Gion had not gone to Phnom Penh.'

'That's what I'm worried about. Why should Sheila go to Phnom Penh with Bernard Reguet?'

'So now what to do?' said Mrs Fumikaro to Mr Fumikaro. They were both in their room, whispering to each other.

Mr Fumikaro considered. The banker, the poet, the prudent businessman, the sleuth, were fighting each other in his spirit.

The businessman said: 'Better not meddle. You have come here to investigate business possibilities.'

The banker said: 'Get out as soon as you can.'

The poet said: 'You must rescue her.'

The sleuth longed for adventure.

Finally, the poet won. 'We must tell Miss Mary Faust, since the prisoner may be her secretary.'

'I don't trust her,' said Mrs Fumikaro. 'She is a very haughty lady.'

'Whom else do we know?'

'You know Mr Deroulede. You might talk to him.'

'Business,' said Mr Fumikaro, 'does not mix with other things.'

They cast in their minds, and rejected, every person, including Mabel's own husband. 'Too emotional,' said Mr Fumikaro. 'You did right not to say anything when we came out of His Excellency's house. Who knows, it might have been very dangerous.'

'Perhaps Princess Sumipoon...?'

'Yes, that is the best. Let us go.'

But the Rolland family were not in their suite. They seemed to have vanished.

Mr Fumikaro left a message, and the couple went to bed, setting the alarm clock for 6 a.m.

Drowsily Mary said: 'It's odd, you and I.'

Deroulede, naked torso rippled with muscle, had a very thin gold chain with a gold medal round his neck. To Mary this was more erotically fascinating than any other aspect of her lover at the moment. Fancy making love with a medal of the Blessed Virgin round one's neck...

'It's not odd. It had to be. You and I, we are born to rule. Over the others, the not-so-well-equipped.'

'I don't approve of this "superior race" complex.'

'Not race. Individuals. In every country there is an élite. Born to rule over the others. You and I belong to the élite.'

'But...' But at the moment Mary's hastily acquired egalitarian doctrines were confused to her. Besides, obscurely, she had always felt that she knew better.

'Do you really think that your silly little secretary is as good as you are? Physically, mentally?'

'No,' said Mary, 'but she's a human being, like me.'

'Of course,' said Deroulede. 'A human being, born to obey, as you are born to command. Believe me, she would not be happy, except in subjection. That is why she came to you.'

'I wonder what's really happened to her,' said Mary. 'I've tried not to worry, but I am worried. Very.'

'Tonight,' said Deroulede, 'let's worry about ourselves. Tomorrow I'll find her for you, I promise.'

'Wait, wait,' cried Das, 'I'm coming.'

He opened the door upon which the thumping had wakened him, and Joan Warburton, Ashley Basildon's secretary, entirely naked, fell into his arms.

Das half carried, half dragged Joan to one of the twin beds of his room, noting she was stockier than he had thought. She pressed her hands with their silvered nails over her breasts, sobbing and gasping, and Das took the top sheet from his own bed and threw it round her. She wrapped it tightly and began to sob in earnest.

'He kicked me out. He got that woman in, then he kicked me out. The brute, the stinker, the ...'

From which Das understood that Ashley Basildon had been successful in rounding up a Cambodian girl for the night, had brought her back to his hotel room, met with Joan's protests and thrown Joan out of the room.

'He tore my nightgown off ... I didn't know what to do. No wonder his wife can't stand him. Always bringing back women, he always wants two at one time.'

It was before midnight on that same Wednesday that Gion

189

found Sheila.

He and his new friends, Bok, the other taxi-drivers, the *samlo*-pedallers, their wives, their children, human beings whose faces he would not remember, whose names he would never know, had searched the ruins, the temples, combing bit by bit the whole enormous area of Angkor, looking for Sheila, for Bernard Reguet.

It was in the amethyst light of six to seven o'clock that the peasant woman with one eye a stone gave the first clue. She had been fishing that morning, about the time before the sun was highest, on the lake shore for small sand crabs at a place she knew. She had seen with her one good eye (and it was being filled by fog too) a big car, something closed (her hands enclosed a square of air) pass on the other shore.

'It was a big, big car, something like a bus.' But the point was, this big car was going through at a place where there was no good road, only a track. She had seldom seen a car along that track.

'There are four alleyways to Angkor Thom, and one of them is not used by cars. It is overgrown, not tarmacked. It leads to the lake. That is where she saw the big car.' Thus Bok, when at nine o'clock that night the woman's words were reported to him.

Once again Gion went through the gate crowned with the four faces. They rounded the Bayon. Behind it, a misshapen saffron moon was rising, berthed by trees.

'This way,' said Bok. And he drove the taxi to the overgrown, scarcely visible rough track at the end of the large square with its monuments.

Here was another four-faced gate, unrepaired, still a tumble of stones. The taxi jumped on the potholes. At one moment the road dipped into a large, sandy rut and the wheels were helpless to drag the car up again; Gion and Bok got out, put stones behind the taxi. Bok went into first gear and roared the taxi out.

It was then Gion saw the tyre marks. 'A car has been here.'

Bok drove the taxi one yard ahead, switched the lights on, and peered. 'Yes, two. One van, one car.' He put on the long-distance lights, and the tracks were visible, running forward.

They drove a few hundred yards, and suddenly Bok exclaimed, for now instead of two tracks there were three.

Gion said: 'I don't understand.'

Bok lit a cigarette, and said: 'How can two cars make three? And two of them the same tracks? And why do the tracks begin here, as if a car had dropped from the sky?'

'Let us go on, and see.'

They drove on. Now there were three tracks, sometimes riding on each other, at others diverging and overriden by the broader space between the wheels of the van.

Bok stopped. At their right a gap appeared among the bushes, as if a heavy object had crashed through the curtain of vegetation.

And now the moon, free of the horizon, was small and clear, slightly time-warped, the light strong enough, so that after twenty yards of walking through the undergrowth already battered by the passage of some big object—'like an elephant,' said Bok—they found the car, and its occupant at the steering-wheel, crashed against a clump of trees and stones.

'Bernard Reguet,' said Gion.

Bok turned and ran.

Gion looked at the dead man, sitting up with his head resting upon the wheel. Upon the head was a driving cap with a visor. The hands were threaded through the wheel.

There was a sudden burst of gay music blaring very loud. Gion walked back to the taxi. Bok was in it, doors shut, the radio turned on loudly to a jaunty marching tune. He opened the door for Gion, and immediately shut it again and drove off, the radio still blaring.

'Ghost. I am afraid. I make noise to chase away.'

And now there were only two tracks, the bigger and smaller. Another four hundred yards and the trees cleared. On their left, below them, was the lake with its sandy beach. The tracks disappeared where a tarmac road began.

Bok stopped, and rolled down the windows. 'What do we do, Brother Gion?'

Gion said: 'We go back.'

'No, no. I am afraid.'

'Bok, suppose the cars had come from this road and driven towards Angkor Thom, and not the opposite way, the way we came?'

'I don't understand.'

'Let us go back. We'll understand.'

'No,' said Bok. 'Gion, I will do anything for you, but not stay near the dead.'

'All right. Then I shall walk back.'

Already Gion was getting down from the car. Then Bok said: 'Get back in. I'll drive you. You have no lights without me. But I must keep the music on.'

They drove back, in a rush of music, and once again Bok sat in the car, hermetically shut, while Gion walked into the gap and looked at Reguet once more.

'Let us get back to the Bayon,' Bok pleaded.

'It's no use driving, Bok, I must walk, and you must follow me slowly, with the car lights on.'

'I usually have a torch,' said Bok, 'but not tonight. It's always so, isn't it?'

For another hour they searched, Gion walking slowly. From time to time, if he thought the undergrowth on either side disturbed, he walked into it, pulling apart the thickets.

Once again they neared the ruined gate, the sand-pit where the taxi had nearly stuck. And now, on the other side of the sand-pit, they perceived the tracks which they had missed, but very blurred, for here was much sand. Only by following the crushed grass edges could they still make out that the van had been there too.

'We did not look, coming out,' said Bok. 'We are stupid.'

Back in the old city of Angkor Thom, with its monuments, enormous, square, the Bayon in its exact centre, four large avenues going off from it. No track marks could be seen because of the well-kept surfaces. On the Bayon small glow-worms of fire flitted slowly—they were the torches of the searchers, Bok's friends, village people, searching for Sheila.

'The van must have come in here, or left from here.'

'I think now it could have been one of the vans of the Museum workers. They are working here, behind the Terrace of Elephants, on the Palace of Kings. They have vans stowed here, to take stones to the museum. I will go and take a look at the vans,' Bok said.

Gion said: 'I'll wait for you here.'

The moon threw a clear light as he walked to the Terrace of Elephants sprawling its great length like a rampart. He walked across it until he came to the Terrace of the Leper King. The statue of the Leper King was pale with moonlight, its face with its Dali moustache insipid. And, round its neck, he found the scarf, knotted gaily. He undid the scarf, started automatically straightening its wrinkles. It was much wrinkled, as if it had been wrung, twisted as a rope.

He looked round, and suddenly he cried aloud: 'Sheila, Sheila, O my love.' No echo answered.

Then, half consciously, he walked down from the Leper King, down the twisty narrow steps which led into the earth, into what was called by the tourists the Corridor of Women.

For here, six yards below the surface and open to the sky, was a zigzag tunnel, walls lined with statues, rows upon rows of smiling, lovely-faced stone women. The tunnel was too narrow for more than one person at a time.

Of course she was there, at the first turning. He felt that he had known it all the time. As he had known the manner of her death before he bent down.

Here, unlike the scarf now straightly folded in his pocket, could be no unwrinkling, no smoothing restoration of neatness.

He wiped the tangled hair away from the cold forehead, and took her in his arms, more careful of her in death than in life, taking care not to hit his burden against the stone faces and breasts that protruded from the walls. He walked up the stairs again, and laid Sheila by the side of the Leper King, took out the scarf from his pocket, covered the staring eyes, the bruised neck, the purple lolling tongue.

At five a.m. the guests of the Suprême Hotel were wakened by shots, crash of glass, screams, a rumble of military vehicles, the stamp of feet.

Chundra Das, Jean Deroulede, and Mr Fumikaro found themselves at the top of the stairs at the same time, asking each other what was the matter. Coming up from the hall twenty soldiers in camouflage battledress, armed with Sten guns, made them raise their arms. The soldiers proceeded into each room, pulling out the occupants. The prisoners were driven into the hall.

A corpulent officer with a list in his hands checked the names, looking hard at their faces, sometimes asking a name and ticking it off his list. He gave some orders. Three soldiers leapt up the stairs again. The crash of furniture was heard, and doors banging. They came down without any new prisoner. Other soldiers went into the garden, towards the kitchens. They returned, shaking their heads.

Mr Lee Souvan was nowhere to be seen, but Monsieur Paulet was dragged out from the manager's office, crying: 'Messieurs, I protest, I protest. I will complain to His Highness . . .'

'Attention,' the officer barked in French. 'Mesdames, messieurs, attention. In view of the peril of communism in our beloved country, Cambodia, General Vam Barong, Governor of the Province of Siemreap, true patriot and great statesman, at the urgent demand of the Cambodian people oppressed by the tyranny of——'

'Is the fellow quite right in the head?' muttered Ashley Basildon.

'—in an alliance,' continued the officer louder, as if reciting a lesson, 'with all the true democratic forces of anti-communism, groaning under the dictatorship of a despot——'

At that moment Mrs Fumikaro was seized with a fit of giggles. One soldier came up to Mrs Fumikaro and tried to shake her, but Mr Fumikaro, suddenly transformed into a ferocious little man, glared.

'Don't touch my wife, don't touch the lady my wife, preese!'

His spectacles glistened, and the soldier remained behind in air.

'Take them away,' shouted the officer. 'We'll look for the others.' He brandished a fist at the prisoners. 'Messieurs, 'dames, you will be held at the pleasure of His Excellency. If you obey, nothing will happen to you. If you do not, you will not escape the just anger of His Excellency.'

The prisoners were marched out of the hotel. An open truck stood at the entrance. Its back was let down, and Das was prodded to climb into it.

In the truck a man sat.

'Gion!'

Gion looked up. The body he held crosswise on his lap did not move. Its face was covered. Das stared, his eyes widened.

'Sheila?'

'Yes.'

Das was pushed forward to allow room for Ada, Eliza, the Fumikaros. Eliza also stared. She buried her face in her hands.

It was Joan Warburton who screamed. Still wrapped in the sheet Das had thrown over her, she shrieked, went on shrieking, stopping abruptly when Jean Deroulede slapped her.

The truck moved, rolled away.

'Listen,' Jean Deroulede said, 'I have the habit of coups. I was also a prisoner of the war. Listen to me. We must organize, otherwise we shall suffer more than necessary.'

'I agree,' said Das. 'We must keep up our morale. This may be a long-drawn affair.'

'The first thing is not to panic. This is a coup directed against the government. Temporarily prisoners we are, but there is no need to fear for our lives. Not unless we are communists, and I don't think any of us are.'

The truck had brought them, not to the jail (which they passed, and to which they could see files of Cambodians, men and women, tied to each other by ropes, being pushed), but beyond it, to the outskirts of Siemreap, to a square, large building, with a tiled roof, cement floor, with the words 'École Primaire', primary school, on a board. The windows were merely apertures, spaces closed by roughly fitted wooden bars.

Outside a number of desks were thrown in a heap.

'At least, there's space and air,' said Jean Deroulede. He had become, without argument, their leader. His calm, reasonable voice, the manner in which he had stopped Joan Warburton, helped Eliza by putting his arm round her, the tangible adoration of Mary, elected him. They clung to his quiet authority. Without a word he had indicated a corner to Gion where Gion now sat, isolated by his burden, a halo of emptiness round him. Even Das, squatting nearest to him, had left a space between them. Most of the prisoners were in dressing-gowns or pyjamas, except Joan in her sheet; only Deroulede was dressed, in a loose shirt and pants, his sleeves rolled up. This too reinforced his prestige.

'First of all, let us count ourselves, see who is missing, and why.'

'I've counted,' said Mary. Her auburn hair cascaded over a black nylon dressing-gown and nightgown. 'Sumipoon and her family, Mr Multani.'

'You know Charles is in the hospital,' Eliza said in a muffled voice, without looking at anyone.

Deroulede looked round, frowning: 'I seem to recollect others?'

'I don't think so,' said Ada, 'unless you mean the Chinese, the Americans, and the Rumanians? They left last night for Phnom Penh.'

'No, no,' said Mary, 'he means someone else. But who?'

A voice spoke up: 'Deroulede, can you explain what happened to Sheila Manley? Why is she dead?'

'No, Lederer. All in due course, my friend. I am as upset as you are about this ... this tragic event. Doubtless Mr Gion will know. But first, let me parley with the guards. Prisoners need three things above all; food, water, and latrines. Nothing will be arranged if we do not arrange it now. Let me see to it first.'

He advanced to one of the windows, and started calling in excellent Khmer to the soldiers. These at first did not heed, but as Deroulede went on talking, one of them approached. Some money changed hands. Another soldier came, more money circulated.

'Latrines,' said Deroulede. 'This is a school, and there

should be outside latrines. They will take us there in turn.'

Docile, one by one, the prisoners went. Deroulede did some more parleying, and two pails of water, tin cups sailing their surfaces, were brought in.

'Have you any money on you?' Deroulede asked.

Only Mrs Fumikaro had brought her bag with her. 'All our money we brought,' said Mr Fumikaro.

'Excellent,' said Deroulede, 'we shall be able to organize.'

There was a commotion at the door. Then Ulong Serap stood in front of them, robed and dignified. The door shut behind him. He walked straight to Gion.

'Alas, alas,' said Ulong Serap, 'the pity of it, that once again I should have been responsible for her death.'

'I want to know,' said François Lederer again, 'who murdered Sheila Manley?'

'Is this the time?' Das said.

François Lederer repeated: 'There is a murderer among us. I have my suspicions. If we do not immediately demand an explanation of this man Gion, Deroulede I shall start——'

'Yes,' said Ada, 'he is right. We cannot sit like this, knowing that someone has murdered Sheila.'

Everyone turned and looked at Gion. 'I found her...' he said, 'like this.'

'What happened? Tell us,' Lederer said.

'Your Eminence,' Deroulede said quietly to Ulong Serap, 'it seems there is a wish to establish an inquiry.'

'Inquiry?' said Ulong Serap. 'Inquiry? But we do know why she died ... the past.'

'Sir, it is the present that concerns us.'

'Is this necessary?' said Ahmed Fouad. 'It isn't at all sure that the murderer is with us. It might be some soldiers. After all, there are quite a few of us missing, Multani, Kilton, others ...'

Lederer said: 'Gion, did you kill her?'

Gion lifted his head, looked at each of his fellow-prisoners. They seemed so unreal, so far away. 'I did not kill her,' he said.

'Well,' said Deroulede, 'let us have an inquiry.'

Ulong Serap said, sighing: 'I do not wish to do this, but I must. The court of inquiry is open. We shall begin with burning the body of Miss Manley, that her soul may have release.'

But he was again interrupted as once more the door opened, and Multani and Kilton were catapulted among them.

'Well, well,' said Ashley Basildon, 'of all people. And I thought you were such pals of General Vam Barong?'

From outside smoke assailed their nostrils with the exhalation of burning flesh. Joan sobbed on the shoulder of Ashley Basildon.

Sheila's body was burning, under and upon a pile of school books in the courtyard of the primary school.

It was Ulong Serap who had initiated this, going to the window, where a respectful soldier immediately appeared; for Ulong Serap was still a Buddhist Eminence, treated with respect even in jail. The soldiers knelt to be blessed when he spoke to them.

Soon a pyre had been built.

Gion had carried Sheila outside. The sun had pricked his eyes. He had felt giddy with lack of sleep. Tenderly he had deposited her on the bed of school books, children's copybooks, chopped firewood. He had taken the scarf away, and seen her naked face.

Ulong Serap had recited prayers, the soldiers had struck a match and lit some rags soaked in gasoline, the flames took, burning swiftly, gaily, had flashed in the fresh morning round Sheila's head, had seemed to make the cheeks live again. Her hair caught fire and spat and hissed.

It takes a long time for a body to burn. It had taken all of an hour before Ulong Serap took Gion's arm, and said: 'Come,' and led him into their prison room again.

Now the pyre smouldered, the body had disappeared in great part under the heaping of half-burnt wood, but the smell was with them.

'Let us pray.' Father O'Dodder rose in his pyjamas and prayed for the soul of Sheila Manley. Ahmed Fouad prayed to Allah, kneeling facing Mecca with hands outstretched, Mrs Fumikaro poured a cup of water on the ground for Sheila's thirsty spirit.

'Ladies and gentlemen,' said Ulong Serap, 'now that we

have released the spirit of she who was, we can proceed with the inquiry.'

Ulong Serap sat in the lotus position in the middle of the classroom jail, Deroulede on one side of him, and on the other side Father O'Dodder.

'We have among us,' said Ulong Serap, 'people who knew her and may elucidate the manner of her death. Although in my view this was as it was to be, for she was already known to me some centuries ago, when I was responsible for her oblivion. This time, I was given a chance to save her; but it did not happen, the forces of evil were too trong. And so I must await another rebirth, to fulfil my expiation towards her.

'We have also among us,' said Ulong Serap's quiet voice, piercing the stridency of the morning crickets, 'the restless soul and body of her murderer, hovering in the mists of wrong-doing and fear, perhaps plotting another killing——'

'Yes,' said Lederer, 'another killing. But why did you burn her, if not to make sure that her murderer cannot be found?'

'We shall hear each one of you in turn,' said Ulong Serap, 'and who shall speak first?'

'The one who found her,' said Lederer. 'Let him speak first.'

Ulong Serap said to Gion: 'Start with the first day, the first moment. Tell everything.'

'I met Sheila on Sunday morning, for the first time. We went to Angkor Vat together.'

'When did you sleep with her?' That was from Lederer.

Ulong Serap raised his hand: 'You need not answer that, Gion.'

'I wanted to marry her,' Gion said. 'Not that it makes things better, but I did want to marry her.'

'How did you find her?' said Deroulede. 'How did this happen?'

And then Thomas also broke in: 'Gion, have you seen my wife? Do you know anything about her?'

Mrs Fumikaro said: 'Mr Thomas, I must tell you. I think I know of your wife.'

'Proceed, Gion.'

'My wife,' muttered Thomas, now squatting near Mrs Fumikaro, 'tell me, tell me.'

So Mrs Fumikaro whispered to him while Gion went on.

'Sunday morning we went to Angkor Vat. Sunday evening, Sheila went out with me to dinner at the market. Monday morning, we were both at the Congress, sat together at lunch with all the others'—Das nodded confirmation—'at the hotel. Afternoon, she first agreed to go swimming with me, then changed her mind. Evening, we went to dinner again, at the market, with Princess Sumipoon and her family. There her father and ... Mrs Manley joined us. Kilton appeared and asked us to his singing meeting. We went. We stayed half an hour, then we went to the ballet at Angkor Vat. Tuesday was manual labour. We returned together. At night Sheila was at the party. You all saw her. I went to bed.'

He was sweating now, and mopped his brow with his shirt sleeve. 'I went to bed, I went to bed ...'

Lederer said: 'Speak, imbecile, speak. You went to bed with her?'

'Then Wednesday morning,' said Gion, 'I wanted to talk to her and twice went to her room. But she would not speak to me. Then I heard ... something from someone, she was in danger.'

'Elucidate, please.' That was from Ulong Serap.

'I cannot,' said Gion, 'I cannot. Forgive me. All I know is that I suddenly realized she was in great danger. Owing to a chocolate box.'

There was a sudden tenseness, and Kilton uttered a hoarse moan.

'A chocolate box ... and Sheila said Mr Kilton had offered her a chocolate from a box exactly the same as the one she had brought from Bangkok for someone else.'

'What was in the chocolates?' That was Deroulede. 'Drugs?'

'Heroin,' said Gion, 'so I was told.'

'May God forgive her,' said Father O'Dodder. 'Poor girl, poor girl.'

'Wednesday I realized she was in danger because of this drug business. I started to look for her ... and I found that she had accepted a lift from Bernard Reguet, the museum curator, who was on his way to Phnom Penh.'

'Reguet,' said Lederer. 'Ha ha ha.'

'But then I discovered that Reguet did not go to Phnom

Penh.'

'How did you find that out?' asked Ulong Serap.

'I——' Gion was going to answer, and then out of his fog of tiredness something made him stop. What was it he had forgotten? Someone had said something about a murderer ... a murderer among them.

He looked straight at Ulong Serap. 'I found out because I went out in a taxi to the first police check post. No one had seen Bernard Reguet or his car there. So he had not left Siemreap. Then we began to hunt for Sheila.'

'We?'

'Myself and some Cambodians. Drivers, taxi-men...' The lights at the Bayon, he thought, torches twisted by little boys, resinous torches, going about in the night looking. They had helped him. And he had seen the files of them, brought roped to prison. 'They killed Bok,' he said, as if they all knew who Bok was. 'The soldiers.' And this also he could not speak of. Bok, Sheila, Bernard Reguet, a solidarity in death to remain with him for the rest of his life.

'Did you find Bernard Reguet?'

'Yes. He is dead too.'

'Aaaah,' said Lederer, in a voice full of pain. 'He made love to her, then he killed her. I knew it. I knew it.'

No, thought Gion, no. But again, out of his fog of tiredness and hunger, wariness was born. He did not reply.

Deroulede said: 'Bernard was my friend, my great friend. I don't believe he could kill a woman. Where did you find him? How?'

'There is a disused track,' said Gion, 'one of the four roads radiating out of the ruined city of Angkor Thom. He had gone off the main road, in his car, into the bushes.'

'He killed her,' said Lederer. 'And I was thinking ... but it was Bernard Reguet, all the time.'

'François,' said Deroulede kindly, 'you are too excited. Please collect yourself. Bernard would never do this. Possibly Vam Barong ambushed Reguet and Sheila and killed them both.'

'No,' said Eliza suddenly. 'It was Reguet, I think. I saw him. That Wednesday morning, walking about the Elephant Terrace.'

'Where were you?'

'At the Bayon. Being photographed by Peter Anstey.'

Gion drew the scarf from his pocket, smoothed it. And he heard Peter say: 'But that's my scarf.'

Eliza said: 'Don't be a perfect idiot, Peter. There are lots of scarves like that.'

'But Eliza, my dear——'

'It can't be, it can't be.'

Ulong Serap again raised his hand for silence. 'Mr Anstey, will you tell us about the scarf?'

Kilton ceased moaning and raised his head, as if he too were beginning to listen. Father O'Dodder cracked the joints of his hands. They were large hands, Gion thought, strangler's hands ...

And now Gion watched each person in turn, noting down reactions, what they said. Any one of them could have murdered Sheila ...

'I came here, let me see, Sunday evening, by the afternoon plane from Phnom Penh. I'd met Teo in Hong Kong. Malayan Chinese, a poet. I persuaded him to come to Angkor for a few days. I'm mentioning this because, you see, I had this scarf, and this scarf had been given to me by Eliza Crawfurd—Eliza, darling, you don't mind my saying this, do you?—for my birthday. I thought it so utterly sweet of her. I do so love silk next to the skin, you know. And I loaned it to Teo.'

'Where is Teo?'

'Gone back to Malaya, with his Aunt.'

Lederer said contemptuously: 'Are you accusing someone else of killing Sheila?'

'I'm not accusing anyone. I'm just saying that I loaned the scarf to Teo, and when he left he told me he'd put it with the skirts, the silks that Eliza bought.'

'I never saw your scarf,' Eliza said, 'I didn't have it. Don't try to accuse me ...'

Ulong Serap said: 'Will you, Mr Lederer, tell us about yourself?'

'I met Miss Manley briefly in Bangkok, at a party. She was on the plane. Many of you saw her come to the cockpit to watch the landscape. I thought her charming. On Sunday we had a drink together in the afternoon, before I flew on to

Phnom Penh. Since then I haven't seen her alone or talked to her alone. That is all.'

Ulong Serap said gently: 'Did you, at any time, feel that Miss Manley's life was in danger?'

Lederer did not reply at once. His face was rigid, drawn, the skin, like that of an opium addict, stuck tightly to his cheekbones.

'Danger? No, I don't think so, but I was worried. She was imprudent.'

Then Kilton said: 'She knew a damn sight more than you did about everything. She was passing heroin and she knew too much. That is why she died.'

'My name is Bud Kilton. I love God, and God loves me. He knows that Bud is devoted to His service. I've been three years in this God-forsaken country, and I've done my best to make His Word known to the natives.

'Now this Reguet said I stole something valuable from the museum. It isn't true. I did not *steal*. The Lord put something valuable in my keeping, that's how it was. Bud always does what the Lord tells him to do.'

Father O'Dodder cracked his joints.

'All heretics shall be damned in hell fire, but Bud will be saved, for he follows the straight and narrow path,' cried Kilton, throwing out his arms in true revivalist fashion and nearly singing, 'Yea, Lord, though they bring their thousands and ten thousands against me——'

'Stick to the point, my friend,' said Das. 'You stole a valuable antique, then passed it on to Multani, your accomplice. What has that got to do with the drug traffic, or Sheila Manley?'

'Oh Lord, Thou seest how my enemies——'

Ulong Serap interrupted: 'Mr Kilton, you took something from the museum.'

'I was trying to restore an antique to its rightful owner, the Governor of Siemreap, General Vam Barong. It had been unlawfully stolen by that pro-communist Frenchman, Bernard Reguet, a fellow traveller. I found out that he had been to a congress of archaeologists in Moscow, and he was planning to go to China, ostensibly to do archaeology. I asked God, and

God told me what to do.

'But the enemies of God are everywhere. The man I called friend'—he pointed a shaky and accusing finger towards Multani—'cheated me. The antique disappeared. I had left it in his charge.'

'Stuff and nonsense, sir, stuff and nonsense,' said Multani, in a weak, hoarse voice. 'A pack of lies. It was stolen from me, I don't know who by.'

'I'll tell you who by.' Kilton pointed solemnly at Jean Deroulede, and then at Lederer. 'You two. The French. You hate us Americans. Do all you can to throw a monkey wrench in the works. You're both fellow travellers. You stole the antique from Multani. And you also, you ... yes, you'—he pointed to Deroulede—'you took the heroin which was in a chocolate box carried by Sheila Manley, and then you tried to get me in a jam by putting a chocolate box in the post for me.'

Deroulede took a cigarette case from his pocket and opened it. He extracted one cigarette, lit it, and then laughed. He turned to Ulong Serap: 'Your Eminence, need I answer?'

Ulong Serap said: 'Yes, Mr Deroulede.'

'To begin with,' said Deroulede, 'may I point out that I do not know these gentlemen. I knew nothing about antiques being stolen. I arrived Monday evening from Phnom Penh. Mr Fumikaro, here, will tell you that I discussed business with him that night, and the next day after he returned from manual labour.

'As for chocolate boxes, I could not possibly substitute chocolate boxes when I was not there, could I? To place a chocolate box in Mr Kilton's post so that he would get it on Monday, I would have had to do so on Saturday or Sunday. But I was in Phnom Penh on those days. And I don't eat chocolates. Need I say more?'

'Give me a cigarette,' said Ashley Basildon.

'No,' replied Deroulede.

Ashley lunged towards Deroulede's cigarette case. The next moment he was writhing on the floor, two feet away.

'Ah,' said Mr Fumikaro appreciatively, 'judo. Good.'

Deroulede went on smoking.

Ulong Serap said: 'Mr Basildon, just now when these two gentlemen'—he pointed to Multani and Kilton—'joined us, you said they were friends of General Vam Barong. How did you know that this was the case?'

'Find out for yourself,' said Ashley. 'I'm not joining this farce.'

Mary Faust said to Deroulede: 'Jean, give him a cigarette, on condition he talks.'

Joan Warburton said: 'Just hold it in front of his nose, Mr Deroulede. Don't give it him until he's come clean.' She rearranged her sheet, leaned back against the wall. 'The great Ashley Basildon. Haha, if I only told what I knew about him . . .'

Ashley inhaled from the cigarette that Deroulede lit for him. After he had taken two puffs, he smiled. 'Well, since this seems to be one of those public confessions meetings, I'll do my bit. I didn't know anything about these two until Wednesday night. I came back with a girl. A nice girl. Cambodian.'

'He threw me out——' Joan began.

'My dear, you were appalling. Of course I threw you out. Anyway, I met those two, decided to have a little party upstairs. Only Joan wouldn't co-operate. Very unsporting of her.'

'It is forbidden,' said Monsieur Paulet. 'The good name of my hotel, monsieur. Immoral behaviour ... Monsieur Deroulede, mon colonel, I shall bring an action against them as soon as we are released.'

'Calm yourself, Paulet. These things happen in the best hotels.'

'Very well, mon colonel.'

'Ah,' sneered Lederer, 'another of your old soldiers, Deroulede. I didn't know.'

'Lederer, you are not doing yourself any good.'

'I want to find the murderer, Deroulede.'

'I too want justice. Let Mr Basildon proceed.'

Ashley Basildon, mollified, went on. 'Candidly, I don't see any harm in a mixed party, so long as no one's hurt. I found this Cambodian girl, a waitress in the open-air restaurant just off the cinema on the main street of the town. Of course I took her back to the hotel. Joan had no right to object. Joan, you're interfering with my creative impulses, d'you know? Too possessive. I won't have it.'

'You were planning a gay party with Mr Multani, Mr Kilton, and two ladies?' said Ulong Serap.

'Oh, how the mouths of men twist the truth,' cried Kilton. 'A party? Nothing of the sort. I was trying to bring these creatures to the light of God and total immersion.'

'Come off the Bible, Bud, who d'you think you're fooling?' said Ashley Basildon. 'Let's have some of the facts, shall we? I brought the waitress, Joan ran off, we had drinks, you were both congratulating yourselves about being released and arguing about the antique you stole. Multani swore he'd had it with him, in his camera case which he kept an eye on, except for about ten minutes while he danced with Madame Shum. You told me the whole story, my dear fellows, both of you drunk ... and you told it to Sheila when she came along. Kilton went off with my Cambodian waitress,' continued Ashley Basildon, 'and Sheila stayed with Multani. That's the last time I saw her.'

At four o'clock soldiers brought in water, some gruel made with rice and a few floating vegetables. The air was cooling, the sun darkening. Deroulede opened his eyes and said: 'I smell rain.'

All the prisoners ate, except Ulong Serap who went out, respectfully escorted by the soldiers, to the pyre, no longer glowing, to pray. A scuffle of wind began, and ashes flew up. They entered through the windows and settled in the room, on the gruel. Only Gion noticed, and put his bowl down.

Kilton suddenly started a violent quarrel with Peter Anstey. 'I say, you can't do that, take all the cabbage.'

Mary made an effort to talk to Thomas. 'It's wrong of you to keep on saying "I'll kill you". It wasn't at all my fault that this happened, don't you see?'

'I'll still murder you,' said Thomas, 'if Mabel is hurt.'

The sky darkened and there was a short burst of thunder, wind whipping trees, and distant shots.

Multani went to the window, took the bars in his hands and shook them. Immediately a shout went up, and two soldiers started hitting at his hands with their rifle butts. He screamed: 'You bastards, you bastards, wait till I get out, there'll be hell to pay.'

'I've noticed,' said Ada, 'that the percentage of clichés in our friend's conversation rises when he gets upset.'

'And I notice,' said Das, 'that we still haven't had any explanation why such good friends of General Vam Barong should be here, in jail with us.'

Then Lederer turned to him: 'And I still haven't an explanation why you climbed into my room that Sunday afternoon.'

'I told you.'

'Yes, you told me an unbelievable story. But I have my own explanation.'

'Indeed?'

'Yes. You are a communist. You were putting a microphone in my room. Luckily I found it, stuck under the armchair where you sat.'

The wind gathered strength. From incidental swoops, rising and then relapsing into a heavy stillness, it became a steady roar. Darkness fell, then thunder set in, and crackles of lightning, until the rain, precipitate, impetuous, splashed its curtains round the classroom in the new night, establishing a fury of water and wind almost theatrical in its gusts.

The shots and the screams were already near when the prisoners heard them, and the downbeat of rain was like the machine-gun bursts which now could be distinguished, now merged with the crackle of lightning.

'Shooting,' said Deroulede. 'Lie flat, don't go near the windows.'

The door opened with a howl of wind, and two soldiers appeared, their flashlights dancing upon the prisoners. They shouted something.

'They want us to march out,' Ulong Serap said, and picked himself up.

'Don't,' said Deroulede. 'Here, Lederer, Paulet, stop His Eminence. We don't go out to be machine-gunned. Lie down, all of you.'

More soldiers came in and started pummelling the prisoners to make them stand up. The corpulent officer reappeared, an aide held up a hurricane lamp by which his face could be seen.

'We are taking you to a place of safety,' barked the officer. 'March, otherwise we shall have to shoot you here, all except you, Eminence.'

'I go with them,' replied Ulong Serap.

'No.' The officer put his hands together. 'I pray you, Eminence, come with me.'

'No, I go with my friends.' And Ulong Serap led the way out into the rain.

A soldier hurried forward with an umbrella for Ulong Serap. Then the file moved out, the Buddhist monk in the lead. Deroulede let all the others pass in front of him, counting them, like a good officer. 'Quick,' shouted the officer, 'quick.'

A truck came by, the soldiers pushed them towards it, only to find that it was full of soldiers and did not stop.

The officer shouted: 'Forward, we march,' and set off along the road.

The rain threw itself at them, beat them, blinded them. In ten seconds they were soaked, their hands lifted to wipe the water off their faces.

'Where are we going?' Mary Faust shouted to Deroulede.

'Towards the airport, I think. The coup has failed.'

More trucks came by, filled not with soldiers but with furniture, trunks, bundles covered with tarpaulin, while soldiers scrambled behind, trying to get on, slipping in the mud and throwing their rifles on to the road.

Deroulede stopped walking. 'Mary, when I give the signal, break and run.'

'Run where?'

'Anywhere, dearest idiot. Run and hide in a ditch. Don't you see the coup is over? They're trying to get away. Taking us with them, as hostages. We've got to run.'

He walked forward, pretended to fall, nursing his knee, gripped Das. 'Break and run for it at the next turning, clump of houses on your right, trees on left. Tell the others.'

Das turned to Gion. 'Deroulede says run.'

More soldiers trundled by on motor-cycles. A truck's engine stalled in the middle of the road. Das fell, stumbled, suddenly ran crouched, rolled, picked himself up, ran. A shot rang out. No one could see in the dense rain more than ten yards.

Ada also ran towards the houses, following Das. Suddenly

there was a clamour, more shots, as soldiers issued from between the houses to bar the road. Ada was surrounded, her arms gripped. Around her high-pitched voices cried: 'Friend, friend.'

'Oh,' cried Ada, 'it's you.' She wept with relief.

Madame Shum, for it was she, in battledress and beret and Sam Browne belt, put an arm round Ada. Two more Militia girls came and helped Ada into the shelter under a house, laid her on the straw, pushing aside the family bullock. It was suddenly dry, suddenly quiet.

'Oh,' cried Ada, 'we're saved, aren't we? Thank God.'

'Yes,' said Madame Shum. 'All bad people collapse, nobody killed, very good.'

Thomas said to Mr Fumikaro. 'I'm going to find Mabel. Will you come?'

'Yes, certainly,' replied Mr Fumikaro. 'Simenon idea, I am enthusiast.'

The rain stopped, abruptly as it had begun. Armed with hurricane lamps the Royal Militia scoured the woods, the ditches, called: 'Mesdames, messieurs, troupes loyales du Prince Sihanouk, vous êtes sauvées.' Before the moonlight of ten o'clock they had found and brought all the prisoners back to the Suprême.

Thomas tramped along the road against a ragged trickle of trucks, cycles, the remnants of the forces of General Vam Barong, now trudging to surrender at the road barrier erected by the loyal troops. No one paid heed to him or to Fumikaro, and they walked on. Behind them were shouts, as Vam Barong's troops fell into the hands of the militia, but they were shouts of laughter. Grinning with relief, the soldiers of Vam Barong surrendered and immediately mixed with the loyal troops, drinking coffee and joking. The coup was over.

'Buddhists don't like to kill,' said Fumikaro. 'It is much more sensible this way, isn't it?'

Houses were opening, faces peered, furtive, fearful, then reassured.

In the darkness a patrol of soldiers were upon the two almost as soon as the sound of their feet squashing the mud with their sneakers.

'Soldats Prince Sihanouk,' shouted the soldiers.

Thomas and Fumikaro shouted together: 'Banzai, banzai Sihanouk.'

The officer flung a light in their faces, and they were hugged, patted, offered hot coffee.

'My wife,' Thomas said. 'She is a prisoner at Vam Barong's house. I am going there.'

'The traitor Vam Barong's residence has already been taken over by our loyal troops.'

'But I would like to go,' said Thomas, 'to see if my wife is there.'

'I will give you six soldiers and a jeep to go with you.'

They passed the Suprême Hotel. The electric power had been cut, it was in darkness. There were trucks, soldiers, motor-cycles in front of the hotel, a coming and going.

And then they were at the villa, and there Thomas found his Mabel, sitting in the bedroom of General Vam Barong, a bed-room denuded of curtains and hangings which had been ripped off and taken away in the trucks, along with the portable furni-ture, the chandeliers, the clocks, the statues. All that remained was the huge bed, and its enormous mattress. Two Militia maidens sat on the mattress with Mabel, feeding her cham-pagne in a tumbler. She sipped and wept, looking young, thin, and to Thomas very beautiful.

'Oh, darling, you're here at last,' she cried, when her hus-band came in, as if it were the most natural thing in the world that he should be there, and the many mirrors multiplied their glad rush into each other's arms.

'It's always like that in South-East Asia. Tragedy sounds comical, political plots resemble Gilbert and Sullivan operas, and even real shots with real mortars sound like off-stage bangs. Even when people get killed, the gore does not look real ... oh, I'm so sorry, Gion.' Thus Das, suddenly realizing that Gion was near.

'More brandy, monsieur? It avoids colds in the head.' Lee Souvan, a bottle of Courvoisier in each hand, was pouring brandy in the tea cups and odd glasses rescued from the wreckage of the Suprême Hotel.

In the main hall, on mattresses, pillows, chairs, settees, in the jumble left after the half-hearted looting by the departing bodyguards of General Vam Barong, the guests of the Suprême, enveloped in an odd assortment of blankets, sheets, and dry clothing, congregated, eating ham and cheese sandwiches, drinking an assortment of coffee, brandy, and liqueurs. Around them, candles mounted on empty bottles threw a dim light.

They kept together, happy to be safe, already beginning to worry again about their clothes, money, and jewellery, wondering what was left after the passage of Vam Barong's soldiers.

Mr Lee reassured them. 'Have no fear, messieurs, 'dames. I have done my best to protect your property.'

A few hours before the coup Lee Souvan had removed the hotel registers, the safe money, and hidden himself, only to reappear, during the afternoon just before the rain, clad in battledress, with a small posse of soldiers, and lead a counter-attack upon the rebels guarding the Suprême Hotel.

'They surrendered very gladly,' said Lee Souvan. 'I paid each of them five hundred *riels*. Some more brandy, Monsieur Deroulede?'

'Lee Souvan, you are a clever man,' said Jean Deroulede.

'Oh, monsieur, if I am here today, it is due to you. Monsieur saved me from the Japanese,' he explained to the assembled guests.

'Darling . . .' That was Mary, whispering softly, proudly.

It was again Deroulede, with the help of Das, who stopped a rush towards the tumble of clothing, luggage, and objects which the soldiers were carrying into the larger dining-room to be sorted out.

'We must obey orders. Some things have been taken away. The soldiers are trying to recover everything. If you insist on looking for your belongings now, you will make things difficult. By tomorrow, all will be cleared up, and you can then pick out your own property.'

When Thomas and Mabel returned together, Mary walked to them gladly, hands outstretched. 'Oh, here you are. I'm so glad nothing's happened to you. At least, no more than to us.'

'No thanks to you, Mary.'

'Don't be silly, Mabel. We've all suffered.'

211

Mabel said: 'That man.' Her finger pointed to Multani. 'Mr Multani. He knew. I saw him. I was in front of Vam Barong's villa that night and I asked him the way, he was coming out of the villa in a taxi.'

'Stuff and nonsense,' replied Multani. 'Stuff and nonsense.'

Thomas sprang at Multani, and hit him in the face.

Peter and Das came to Multani's rescue. Mr Lee Souvan also attempted to control Thomas.

'Monsieur, monsieur, do not use violence. Justice will be done. All will be made clear.'

'Clear?' cried Kilton. 'You bet it's got to be clear. He's the guy who brought the money from Bangkok for the coup. All in his precious camera case. And who killed the girl, because she knew too much. You bet things have to be cleared up.'

'All in good time,' said Lee Souvan. 'Actually, messieurs, 'dames, you are all under restraint. No one is allowed to leave the hotel. However, you need not be frightened. Our Cambodian hospitality, during this unfortunate detention, necessary due to the recent events, will not be wanting. Any more brandy, anyone?'

'You know, Joan,' said Ashley, 'we'll get married as soon as we can. An experience like this, together, means something.'

'Oh, darling, how lovely of you to say that.'

'And I want to write this. It'll make a wonderful play.'

'Quite a difficult thing to act on the stage, darling, a coup.'

'Oh, that? No, not that. Much too untidy, even for a novel. Imagine anyone trying to write it up as it happened. It's like the war in Laos. No, I thought of the Sheila—Multani angle.'

'Sheila—Multani, Ashley? What do you mean?'

'Sheila, who's just offered herself to this man, Gion, thinking she loves him ... Then he falls asleep, and she goes off, desperate, looking for someone else, and falls on these two, Kilton and Multani ... I'll have to give them a background, of course, and of course I'll put myself in, as an English writer come East in love with an Asian whore.'

'Darling——'

'Do stop interrupting. And then, of course, it happens. Multani asks her to do something beastly with him, and she does.'

'Did she? What thing?'

'If you can call that kind of thing beastly. Though I'm told it's quite common. Multani likes to play doggie.'

'Doggie?'

'He's got a wide, broad collar, with a chain, in his suitcase, likes to put it on and be led around saying woof woof. Can't ask his wife to do that for him, I suppose, so gets it done by other women. A common vice among company directors and business executives. Harms no one.'

'How disgusting. I prefer your perversion, Ashley. More natural.'

'Kilton goes off with the Asian whore (I must be careful there, or it'll sound like *The Quiet American*), and the girl goes off with Multani, and I'm left alone ... I wander off, then meet the girl again. She, having plunged to the depths, feels dirty, dirty ... nothing but death can cleanse her, so she asks me to strangle her ... and I do ...'

'Beloved ...'

'Oui, ma chérie ...'

'Say you'll always love me.'

'Always? Non, ma chérie, but I'll love you well, and look after you.'

'But what will happen to me if you leave me?'

'I will not leave you for a good while yet.'

'But after ...'

'You must stop trying to organize the future, my dearest. It is a very bad habit. As bad as His Eminence explaining everything in terms of the past. It brings disaster.'

'That is what Sheila said.'

'Sheila? I did not know you were friends.'

'No. Not really friends. I felt sorry for her. She was a nymphomaniac, you know. I felt she should be psychoanalysed.'

'Shall we stop talking about Sheila? I scarcely knew the girl.'

'Isn't it terrible, her being strangled? Who do you think did it?'

'I don't know. Possibly Reguet, possibly Gion, possibly me ... possibly ...'

Mary laughed: 'Stop making fun of me. I think it's the Algerian poet.'

'The Algerian poet? Who is he?'

'Oh, you haven't seen him. A chap called Malek. Very elusive. I only saw him in the guest list, and once at the Congress. I kept on thinking this morning in jail, we've forgotten somebody. Someone who should be here, among us, but isn't.'

Multani lay on the sheetless mattress, then rose, paced, lay down again.

Deny, deny, you must deny everything.

Curse that Kilton. Curse Sanger in Bangkok. Curse them all. Why couldn't they see to it that their information was accurate, their plots fool-proof? We are the laughing stock of the world, he thought bitterly. Organizing these coups here and there, and failing miserably. I would never have trusted that Vam Barong. One could see he was incapable of anything well organized. He's probably gone off with all the money, purposely let the coup fail, left us in the lurch. So he can now blackmail us, threaten to publish his memoirs, reveal secrets ...

Career ruined, reputation wrecked, possibly jail in Cambodia for years. They were Buddhists here, they didn't shoot one ... but they might put me in a labour camp, make me work, as they do in China ...

Feverishly Multani made a mental list of some Big Shots he knew who might help him out. But Big Shots were funny people. They dropped you like a hot potato if you failed.

Ruined. He was ruined. And all for a ridiculous, twopenny opera of a coup, which had fizzled in a day.

Ulong Serap was ceremoniously escorted back to his small village by a young captain and ten soldiers.

The village was not asleep, it waited for his return. Torches were lit, people stood outside their houses. They had erected small altars, with photographs of the Prince, garlands, piled bananas, and flowers. When Ulong Serap arrived the drums sounded, the flutes played, the village danced ...

Sumipoon, George, Astarte, and Orion and a very sleepy Laertes were standing on the verandah of Ulong Serap's house.

'Uncle, uncle, we have been worried for you. Is all well?'

'My dear nieces, nephews, Sheila is dead, and also Bernard Reguet. Alas, alas, I could not prevent the evil of the past from repetition...'

'Oh, uncle,' said Sumipoon. 'Sheila, Bernard Reguet ... how terrible. How did it happen? And what about Gion?'

'Gion found them both, and some think it was he who killed them,' replied Ulong Serap.

Lederer did not sleep.

Rigid as if already dead, his dry body burning as with fever, he propped himself up on the bed, determined not to sleep.

He tried to chuckle. He, François Lederer, wasn't going to be trifled with. He wasn't going to be assassinated while he slept.

He had been very clever.

It was Mr Lee Souvan who had opened the door of the room for him, Sheila's room.

Lederer had gone to Lee Souvan after the others had entered their former rooms, and three soldiers had been posted in the corridor to watch. 'Lee Souvan, give me another room, you must have empty ones. In front, not at the back.'

'Non, Capitaine, some officers are quarterd here. Why, do you not like your previous room?'

'I don't know whom to trust any more, whom to believe. Someone might want to kill me, Souvan. I suspect that man Das. He climbed into my room last Sunday. He might try to kill me while I sleep.'

Lee Souvan had nodded, as if it was perfectly natural that Das should try to kill Lederer. 'There is a room vacant, that of the demoiselle, you know...' He stopped, emotionally upset. 'Ah, monsieur, and to think that in Cambodia we have not had such a crime for *years*. For years no one has been killed like this, and now, the poor demoiselle, so pretty, so gay——'

Lederer said: 'Lee Souvan, stop it.' In these flat words Lee had conjured up for Lederer a Sheila more real than she had ever been.

'If you are not afraid of a gentle ghost, perhaps, who knows, the spirit of the demoiselle will be happy to see a friend in her room.'

So now he was propped up in Sheila's bed, devoid of sheets, on the mattress hastily put up by the waiters who had returned, his shutters wide open to the night.

Sheila. Yes, if there was an after-life, perhaps her ghost would come to him. He hoped it would.

Then perhaps we could really talk, really begin to understand each other.

If it is true that spirits return to earth, Lord send her spirit back to me.

He would begin thus: 'Sheila, I have sinned against you. But I love you. Forgive me.'

I have sinned. He shook the words off, angrily. Sin. He did not believe in Sin. He was anti-clerical. No such thing.

But I have sinned, the small voice within him protested. Through lack of love. Absence of love is worse than any other sin. I hurt her, hurt her.

Foolishness. Buddhist foolishness of Ulong Serap. Christian absurdity. He had done nothing which she had not wanted, herself.

I will avenge you, Sheila. This is all I can do for you. Avenge you. Find the murderer.

The murderer could be one of two or three probable people. It might even be Gion, that insipid, tame person with his quietness, his irresolution. One never knew, with these Asians. They were so deceptive, so deceitful...

Charles lay propped up, in his hospital bed, propped up on many pillows; on his face was clamped an oxygen mask, going into two bottles, one of which made bubbles as his breath came and went.

Now he was conscious of the pain in his heart. It hurt, hurt every time he moved; and the name of the pain was Sheila.

In waves, consciousness floated in and out of him. He could not tell whether the shots, the screams, the doctor standing in front of his bed, were part of that dream in which Sheila came to throw her arms round him, saying: 'Daddy', then went away, in a car, with someone else who had no name, a man who was every man...

No, Sheila had not gone, she had returned in a black Ford taxi while Bernard Reguet opened drawers, saying: 'Let me show you some of our latest finds . . .'

Then time went back, licking itself back as a wave does, and he was not with Eliza, there was another woman there . . . but her name, persistently, escaped him. All he knew was that she was Sheila's mother and she was in bed with someone else. And it hurt, astonishingly, impossibly, it hurt until his whole chest was sore with pain.

And Sheila was a little girl, small fragment of life, ridiculous, laughable, pathetic. He would always remember her bare, thin legs, in that tumbled bed with Harley, his colleague whom he had trusted.

Charles felt like shaking his head over the comicalness, the unfathomable, pointless, impossible, bizarre dislocation of all these images, coming up at him like waves of the sea; but it hurt to shake his head.

Eliza. The first night, sleeping with Eliza, he had not looked at her body. Shut his eyes and pretended it was the other woman, the women whose name he could not think of . . .

But it's natural, it's natural. Everyone has got carefully concealed tragedies, horrors, vices, carefully put away, suppressed, sat upon . . . never to explode into the sun.

But now something had exploded, inside him. His heart was all over the place, bubbling irregularly in a ridiculous bottle next to his bed.

He wanted to laugh and shake his head and laugh, but all he could feel was water running down his face; he did not know if it was sweat or tears, and it was too much trouble finding out, his hands were both so heavy, so heavy . . .

As in a dream he saw, standing in front of him, beyond the bottle where his chest and its contents bubbled outside of him, the doctor preceded by this extraordinary upturned smile of his, the smile of Angkor, the same smile he had had from beginning to end, even when the soldiers were round the bed and there was the sound of shots.

And with the Cheshire cat doctor stood a very thin young man, with dark, mobile eyes, pale. He had seen him, his face was familiar, but he could not remember where, when. The young man spoke, very quietly:

'Does he know?'

Then Charles recognized him. The Algerian poet. Funny

217

fellow, almost invisible. One of those who had not slept with Sheila. At least, not yet.

Does he know? Know what? That he was dying? Know what? He tried to speak. The bottle bubbled ferociously.

The doctor came forward. 'Mr Manley, don't worry, everything is all right, don't worry ...'

He would not worry. The doctor lifted one of his hands, then later he heard the ampoule breaking by his side, his arm moved, a prick, not even painful ...

Then he remembered the name of the woman ... Jacqueline, Eliza's sister, whom he had loved ... but she gave herself to other men, and then there had been nothing to hold on to, except Sheila, and Sheila was like her mother.

Gion found his old room bereft of his clothes. Only the mattress back on the bed, but no sheets, and the mosquito net torn but enveloping the bed. The lamp on the bed-table was untouched, but the wardrobe door hung half off its hinges, miserably yawning into the room, the empty wardrobe like a coffin erect. At any moment, it seemed, something would step out of it ...

He shook back the phantoms. That was tiredness and perhaps pain.

I haven't had time yet to feel surprised or horror-struck at everything that has happened, so quickly, so quickly.

Finding Sheila, carrying her out of the labyrinth, laying her by the moonlit Leper King, waiting for Bok. And Bok had returned, and wanted to run away again to his taxi.

He should have let Bok run away. If he had stayed by Sheila, like a stone statue, like the Leper King, transfixed with immobility, Bok would not have died. Bok would have gone away in his taxi and would still be alive.

But he, Gion, had run after Bok, caught him by the arm, said to him: 'We must carry her back to the hotel.'

'Back,' said Bok, 'to the hotel? What will Lee Souvan do with a ghost in his hotel, I ask you? No, no, my brother, leave her here, with the ancestors and the gods, in good company.'

But he had forced Bok to wait, with the taxi, in the name of their brotherhood, and Bok once again had given in; shivering with fear, groaning at the steering-wheel, radio pouring music, he had allowed Gion to carry Sheila inside the taxi. His love greater than fear, and for this he had lost his life.

They had run into the patrol, almost immediately on leaving the gate with its faces staring at their backs.

'Halt.' The patrol levelled rifles.

Bok had pressed on the accelerator.

The officer had shot him in the head.

Even then, Gion had not understood that it was a coup, that these were the soldiers of General Vam Barong. Only later.

Now he was back in his room. With the mosquito net. He would never be able to bear the sight of a mosquito net again. He ripped it off, threw it in a corner. It stayed there, a malevolent white heap, a witness against him.

He wandered round the room, opening drawers, shutting them, impelled to these meaningless openings and shuttings by some unconscious urge, as if he could discover some clue, some answer, some solution, as if he were looking for something he had lost. In the desk drawer, the central, flat one, was Suprême Hotel paper and envelopes. He stared at them, as if they could yield ...

And then, things fell into place. He sat down, as the frail construction began to solidify, charged with certainty, precise as the Bayon itself, with all its faces pushing themselves forward, faces of the others, those round him, among which was the murderer's face.

Now he knew, knew without knowing everything, knew against reason, logic, and facts, he knew the murderer's face.

It was one a.m. when Gion opened his room door. Immediately he heard the drag of the rifle butt as the soldier in the corridor came towards him.

'Brother, I want to talk to Lee Souvan.'

The soldier hesitated.

Gion said: 'It is very important.'

'I will ask.'

Gion waited with the other two soldiers, heard a door open and knew someone was looking. The murderer? In the shadows peopling the corridor in front and back of him it was impossible to tell.

'Come with me.'

Lee Souvan lay on a settee in the hall, a candle by his side. He looked at Gion: 'What is it?'

'I want to go to Bernard Reguet's office. I have a clue. To do with his murder.'

Lee Souvan looked at him. 'Monsieur Gion, you know about——'

'The drugs? Yes. And the O.A.S. too.'

'She was passing drugs, was she not?'

'Yes, in all innocence.'

'Whom do you suspect?'

Gion sat down by Lee Souvan and whispered a name in his ear.

Das said: 'Something is happening.'

Ada said: 'Don't go, Das.'

'My dear Ada, nothing will happen if I merely peek.' Das opened the door, and looked down the corridor. There was a candle, two soldiers, someone whose back was turned to him.

He looked towards the other end of the corridor. Something had moved, in the darkness. But he could not pierce the darkness. That way was Mary's suite. Mary Faust. Das sighed. Heavily, feeling old, he returned to his room.

'Das,' said Ada, 'someone has gone out of the hotel. I heard footsteps.'

They listened. Very faintly, they heard the steps receding.

'Let us sleep,' said Das. 'Tomorrow the arrests will be made.'

Throughout the tangled garden of the Conservation, not a shadow moved. No presage of dawn lightened the cloud-covered sky. It would rain again before dawn.

The tiger gave a brief roar. Gion heard it rubbing against the wire net cage restlessly. Had it been fed?

The soldier that accompanied him remained downstairs in the garden as Gion climbed the stairs, finding the steps with a torch borrowed from Lee Souvan, and went to Bernard Reguet's office, to Reguet's desk.

Perhaps he would not find what he looked for. The bungalow might have been ransacked by looters . . .

Gion lit the candle he had been given by Lee Souvan, placed it on the desk. Nothing seemed to have been touched. Here was little to tempt a soldier. The drawers, full of stones and statues, had not been opened, the glass cases not smashed. Perhaps reverence and fear of the old gods, the ancestors, the stones of Angkor, had made the soldiers of Vam Barong by-pass the Conservation. Perhaps, also, respect for Bernard Reguet. Pen, ink-stand, paper-cutter, even the blotting-paper pad, all were there.

Gion moved the candle over the desk, searching, lifting the pad.

Very quietly, someone said: 'Is this what you are looking for?'

Gion turned, braced for the murderer, and saw Ibrahim Malek, gun in right hand, and the plain envelope, the envelope similar to those of the Hotel Suprême, the one which the servant had found on the floor and replaced carefully on the desk, in his left hand.

'Well,' said the Algerian, 'is it?'

'Yes.'

'I thought so.' Ibrahim Malek put his revolver back in his belt, sat in the swivel chair which Reguet had occupied, motioned Gion to sit down on the chair opposite. The candle stood between them, motionless in the still air, smoking towards the ceiling. 'What a circus, isn't it? Have you got it all taped?'

'No, but I feel I know.'

'The thing about wars, murders, and all violent things, is their revolting inefficiency,' said Malek. 'So inept, so untidy, so stupid. Always. Nearly always kill the wrong person, do the wrong thing. Same with this coup. Utterly silly, yet I'm sure it cost millions of dollars and involved a lot of what is called high-level planning among some war planners abroad.'

Gion kept silent.

'You're quiet,' Malek said. 'Not like Das.'

'Tell me all that I don't know,' Gion replied.

The Algerian shook his head. 'First, we've got to carry out justice.'

'We have to? You and I?'

'Who else? If we leave it to the Cambodians, they are a sweet people, hate to shed blood, they will refer it to the courts. There will be lawyers, advocates ... justice will never be done. It will be like the Salan trial. Not real justice. We've got to be the maintainers of Justice. Executors.'

Gion looked at the young man, and thought: he is right. I must choose. Whether I walk the path of justice with him; whether I choose to act, myself, since legality, justice, cannot work properly, since what happened cannot be determined by the normal processes of legality. Or else, I abdicate in favour of Abstract Justice, and do nothing.

Malek said: 'History is made by those who did not wait for Justice to arbiter, who took things in their own hands. So are Revolutions, my friend. We can no longer wait, and be tricked.'

'I will come with you,' Gion said.

'Good. Remember, we act on our own. The Khmers will not hinder us, but they cannot render us aid. However'—he smiled in the shadows, for now he had blown out the candle and was walking downstairs, soft as a tiger—'we may obtain a few volunteers ... but they must remain anonymous.'

Once again Gion walked in front of the hotel and raised his head, looking towards the verandah on the first floor that had been Sheila's room. There was someone on the verandah, a small, thin shadow, darker than the shades around.

Malek also had noticed. Gion heard his pistol being cocked. He raised his flash-light. It picked out a face with staring eyes looking at them.

'Who?'

'Lederer. He'll be dealt with later.'

They went into the hall. Lee Souvan, waiting for them, gave orders briefly to two young men.

'Our volunteers,' said Malek to Gion.

Lee Souvan said: 'Bon courage. Kill clean.' He turned away.

They went upstairs, walked the length of the corridor, straight to the door. Malek tried the master-key which Lee Souvan had given him. The key was in the lock, inside the room.

'Shove it in.'

The two men had brought with them something like a sawn-off short tree trunk. They swung it against the door, which crashed open at one blow.

Mary Faust screamed: 'Who is it? Jean, Jean.'

Three flash-lights explored the bed, with Mary in it, the vacant room.

Malek said: 'He's gone.' He walked to the verandah, an ample one, giving on to the corner of the hotel. Down below was a bush, bruised from the man's fall. 'He's jumped down.'

Mary was furious, clamorous. 'How dare you? How dare you? Where is Jean Deroulede?'

'When did he go?'

'I was asleep, how do I know? What is it? Why ...?'

No one answered.

'Where can he go? He may hide anywhere, last for weeks, he's clever,' said Malek.

Downstairs Lee Souvan said to them, when they told him: 'To the airport? Monsieur Deroulede knows the country well, he has trekked here for years.'

'He may have some hide-outs,' muttered Malek.

Gion's memory stirred. He said: 'Near the ruins, in Angkor Thom, there are some vans. Used by the archaeological unit.'

'Yes,' said Malek, 'transport. He must have transport. He may go there.'

'I think he will.'

'He's gone on foot. That means sticking close to the road, through the forest. If we follow him by car, he'll hear it. We must go on a bicycle. Safest. Can you cycle?'

'Yes.'

'Two bicycles, Souvan. Requisition them.'

They got on the bicycles. Lee Souvan handed Gion a gun as he got on to his bicycle. 'Monsieur, tell Colonel Deroulede ... Lee Souvan is very sorry ... if you have time to speak.'

Once again they were in Angkor Thom. With them four Cambodians, naked to the waist, chained their bicycles by the Terrace of Elephants. Malek had taken off his shirt, and wore only his dark trousers. As did Gion.

It was dark, the sky still clouded for more rain. They reached the Terrace of the Leper King, the entrance to the Corridor of Women. Malek turned, clasped Gion's arm, whispered in his ear:

'Go down there. We'll try to drive him towards you here. Keep your gun ready.'

'But——'

Already Malek had gone.

It seemed to Gion the sky had lightened, as if layer after layer of veiling had rolled off, and light seeped through. Now he could see. Almost at once, as the birds began at the same time as the light, the murderer was there.

He was there, with a soft plop, having jumped into the Corridor of Women from its dead end that had no steps.

He was there, beyond the zigzag, the first turn, where Sheila's body had lain. He did not walk, but there was a shuffling sound, as if he were grinding something underfoot. Then, a faint metallic tinkle, almost covered by a bird louder than the rest, then silence.

Gion, flattened against the wall, raised his gun.

Jean Deroulede was in front of him, broad-shouldered, naked to the waist, handsome. The sight of his beauty weakened Gion's arm. Jean's shirt was in his hand, wrapped round some object.

'Let me pass,' said Jean Deroulede, as Gion stood, barring the stairs.

'No.'

Jean smiled, his smile attractive, at ease, not at all frightened. 'You will be hurt.' His arm, holding the bunched shirt, came up.

Gion wanted to press the trigger, knew he must press the trigger.

But when the shot came, it was in air, for Jean had struck his arm upwards; at the same time his other fist had come crashing towards Gion's face, but Gion had turned his head backward and it glanced off his cheek. He would have fallen, his back hitting the steps hard enough to break his spine, had not his left hand, flung against the wall, gripped a projection, one of the smiling women's heads jutting out, and broken his fall.

Already Jean's foot was on the steps. Gion flung his arms round his leg, throwing his whole body into the grip. Hatred and rage came to help him, to make him hold hard, while Jean gave him a blow across the ear which made his eyes threaten to pop out of their sockets. He screamed with pain, and then bit hard, in the calf, hanging on with his teeth like a dog, while his hands sank into the muscled thigh, sought the tender back of the knee, squeezed.

Jean's fists came crashing down on him, but Gion's teeth did not let go.

And then it was over. Suddenly, there was another pair of feet there under his eyes, and he heard a singular sound, half snarl, half croak, warm liquid, blinding him, poured upon his head.

When he could see, opening his eyes, wiping the liquid off his face, clenching fists to his bursting head, he saw Jean Deroulede's body sprawled upon the steps, and Malek turning it over with his foot. Jean was still breathing. Froth, dark in the grey dawn, bubbled from his mouth, his legs were working. Malek stood, knife in hand, waiting. The breathing stopped.

'Its over,' said Malek. 'Are you badly hurt?'

Gion spat out blood, shook his head, spat some more blood.

'You'll live,' said Malek.

He bent down, tore from Deroulede's neck the chain with the little medal, looked at it.

Two of the Khmer volunteers came down the steps silently. They began to drag the body out.

'What shall we do with this medal?' said Malek. 'Give it to his girl friend?'

Gion shook his head. He could not speak.

Malek clapped his shoulder. 'Think I'm cruel? You don't know what real cruelty is. We'll burn him now. It's best.'

They passed the Leper King, and Malek stopped. He took the medal, wound the chain round the Leper King's neck, grinned. 'Suits him, don't you think?'

Gion leaned against the stone parapet and vomited.

Down from the Terrace of Elephants the volunteers were carrying Deroulede's body into the bushes.

Malek sat down by Gion, companionably, and with gentle, experienced fingers, felt his bones, his stomach. Both watched the dawn come lifting corners off the sky to show the sun, while from some distance the small wind of morning brought the odour of smoke, and that other odour, that steady exhalation of flesh consumed by fire, so definite, so clinging.

Chundra Das was in his element: a sea of talk. His mind, agile like the dolphins of his Indian Ocean, with its blend of imagination and logic, recapitulated for his audience the events of the past six days. Thus put into words, they began to assume solidity.

Not that Das did not realize that his version was but one of many, and that other explanations were possible, but he was a master of the sinuous, flexible sentence, lassoing speculation, and giving it, like the rope trick, direction and purpose concrete as a staircase.

'Truth is the most elusive item in our stock of values,' he said. 'Ten witnesses to the same event will give you ten different versions. But I have done my best to assemble all the facts from many different sources.'

As usual in real life, different from the detective story which reunites all characters in a grand finale, the participants, those on whom action had devolved, were not there. Gion, Malek, Lederer, Eliza, were absent when Das set up his edifice of words.

They sat in Ulong Serap's house, quietly away from turmoil. Sumipoon, George with Laertes fast asleep on his knee in the morning freshness, Ada, and Ulong Serap himself. Too small an audience, perhaps, for Das, who glanced questioningly at the village road below, hoping that Malek or someone else would turn up to listen to the magic fusion of the puzzle pieces accomplished by his agile brain.

But Ada, who knew Das and his moods better than he did, said: 'Come on, Das, don't wait. If Gion were here, or Eliza, there are lots of things you couldn't say at all.'

'True,' said Das, 'all too true. So I shall begin. Our story begins in Bangkok——'

'No,' said Sumipoon, 'not really in Bangkok. Begin with the other plot, the political one.'

'Very well. Actually we are facing a story with two plots.'

'Three,' said Orion.

'Four,' said Astarte.

'Children,' said Sumipoon, 'go out and play.'

'Mamma, really, you are *so* old-fashioned.'

'Never mind. Go out and do some sleuthing on your own.'

'To begin with,' said Das, a little irritated by these interruptions, 'there is the political coup. General Vam Barong, Governor of the Province of Siemreap, is a corrupt, ambitious man. Precisely the kind of person that colonial powers prop up in the name of democracy in order to perpetuate their own power.'

'They're giving it up,' said George.

'No, alas,' said Das. 'Syngman Rhee, Chiang Kai-shek, Phoumi, Boum Oum, they go on doing it, and it always ends the same way, in a fiasco, with bloodshed, lots of money spent, and the people more communist than before.

'Vam Barong received money and help to stimulate his ambitions. He was thought to be a likely person to organize a *coup d'état* and upset the government of Cambodia.

'I don't know why it is that Westerners suffer from such poor judgment where Asians are concerned, fall for the "strong man" who already stinks in the nostrils of his own people. Vam Barong had no public support, only a suborned, heavily paid small army of mercenaries. But he was thought to be powerful, influential, a good bet. So they bet on him. They sent him money, for he needed a lot of money to pay his troops, he said. Every month or so someone or other, ostensibly a tourist, came into Angkor with either a big fat cheque, or cash, or both. The latest tourist to bring in a half-million dollars was our friend, Muni Multani.'

'That was silly,' said Ada. 'Multani's sympathies and ambitions are well known.'

'Not all that silly. Multani came to attend the Writers' Congress, his presence was legitimate. The last person entrusted with cash disappeared with the lot. Multani was too ambitious to be tempted by mere cash. Ulong Serap, Your Eminence, you must tell us later your own version of the Writers' Congress, and your explanation of what happened,' said Das, half respectful, half teasing. 'I confess I am no Buddhist.'

Said Ulong Serap: 'I accomplished destiny in this world of illusion.'

'General Vam Barong is a many-sided man. He is also a

trafficker in opium,' continued Das.

'That's quite normal in South-East Asia,' said George.

'Don't interrupt,' said Sumipoon, seeing Das frown.

Das continued: 'Although modern enough to motorize his bodyguards, and to use the anti-communist jargon which pays well, he was entirely in the hands of his astrologer. He never made a move without consulting the stars.'

'Like Hitler.'

'Yes. Hitler also became the victim of astrology. General Vam Barong had a well-paid astrologer, whom he consulted nearly every day.

'In Asia nothing is secret. The Cambodian government was aware of Vam Barong's ambitions, knew he was being paid by certain foreign agents to mount a so-called anti-communist revolt. It had in front of it the example of Laos, where the war bears no relation at all to the Laotian people, whose only concern is to avoid fighting each other. It kept watch on what was going on, but did not move before the time was ripe. It was decided to let the general have his coup; to minimize its effects as much as possible by subverting his own mercenaries, and especially his astrologer.

'A precipitate move might have had the effect of Vam Barong subsiding his activities, or mounting a counter-coup to show his own loyalty. Then it would have become more difficult to deal with him.

'The coup could not succeed, not only because everyone was warned, but because of the astrologer. The astrologer, through a friend of his, also an astrologer, passed information to the government. This other astrologer could not be consulted openly by any Cambodian, as this might have been reported to Vam Barong, who has his spies. That is where our Algerian friend stepped in, ostensibly to consult his destiny, a thing which surprises no one. He is well trained in the arts of this constant war which is embodied in the most innocent comment, the most artless and inoffensive-looking picnic, which takes place over jovial drinks at a bar.

'This is where we came in, Ada and I.'

'I always wondered,' said Ulong Serap, 'why you and Lady Ada were working in the anti-narcotics organization?'

'Me,' said Lady Ada, 'because I can't stick evil. I am well

qualified to help. Travel a lot. Well-to-do. Trained to observe. Who better than a writer to do the sort of thing I do? Everyone does intelligence of one kind or another in this political century.'

'Me,' said Das, 'to make clean money. I can't make money out of my books.'

'I arrived in Bangkok on the trail of the drugs traffic. Ada came from Hong Kong. We were to meet at your Writers' Congress. We had been told that here, lately, had been set up another centre of traffic. We knew about Vam Barong being in the Ring.'

Said Ada: 'We found that Sheila was an innocent passer. A box of chocolates sent by a Siamese princelet, to give to a relative of his in Angkor.'

'She is a Buddha,' said Ulong Serap. 'I have consulted her horoscope, I know she had to suffer for others. She gave to all who asked of her, profligate in compassion. I shall erect a shrine to her memory.'

'Sheila received the box at the airport on the very morning of departure. She left her father, with whom she was sitting at breakfast in the airport restaurant, went outside, collected the box from a young acolyte monk, one of those watching the planes. The acolyte possibly did not know what was in the box, he may have been only a servant of the princelet. I saw the transaction by pure accident, but half our job is lucky accidents.

'When she reached the Suprême Hotel that Sunday morning, Sheila placed her luggage in her room, then went to Gion's room. It was impulse. She had noticed him looking at her in the airplane. She went to him.'

'That was her way,' said Sumipoon. 'When she was unhappy, that was her way.'

'Gion took her for a walk. He made no advances. I think she fell in love with him. His lack-lustre reserve, his negativeness, made her feel that he had stores of strength, which he did not have.

'While she was away with Gion, someone went into her room, took from her luggage the chocolate box with the heroin and substituted another box, with real chocolates.'

Sumipoon, face set, stroked the sleeping Laertes's hair.

'On Sunday, at lunch time, Sheila gave the chocolate box to someone. But it was the wrong chocolate box.'

'Plot number two,' said George. 'Like a Chinese puzzle.'

'Correct,' said Das. 'Now we come to plot three. For some time another organization was getting into the drugs traffic. Formed by the O.A.S., and for the same reason. Opium the sinews of war.

'There are still embittered Frenchmen who have not forgotten Dien Bien Phu, for whom Algeria was an occasion to restore the "glory" of France.

'Jean Deroulede was such a man. Popular, wealthy, influential, in many ways honest, he thought of the world in terms of the rulers and the ruled. To some he will always be a hero, to others a criminal. He saved Lee Souvan's life during Japanese times. He was liked by many. Yet he, too, was poisoned with the bitterness of defeat. He became the head of the O.A.S. organization here.

'Deroulede began to think of the drugs traffic. He had to be careful. He could not hunt openly, he could only recruit secretly, content himself at first with what was left over of the lion's share in the Trade, slowly infiltrate the Ring with his own people.

'He had unconscious allies in every Frenchman who deemed himself patriotic, and the French are patriotic. He had an ally in Monsieur Paulet, the manager of the hotel, who had fought under him in his regiment during the war.

'Deroulede did not arrive, as we all thought, on the Monday afternoon by airplane from Phnom Penh. Even Lee Souvan was deceived. He arrived on Saturday night, before any of us. He concealed himself in the van he uses when he goes out on safaris throughout the countryside. You will see this van, it is hidden in the ruins behind the Terrace of Elephants. There are an enormous amount of odd corners for concealment in the ruins. Two other vans belonging to the archaeological department are parked there. Deroulede's van is the same build and colour. He also has something else: two licence plates, one for Phnom Penh, one for Siemreap. The Cambodian workers excavating the ruins are not mechanically-minded; even if they noticed the van, they probably thought it one of theirs. Bernard Reguet was the only one who would have known the van was not his, but he happened to be busy in another place, restoring old ramparts, which does not entail transport. It would be easy for Deroulede to know this. Reguet talked to all and sundry about his work, because he loved Angkor, lived for Angkor. He would tell everyone, minutely, every step of the process of restoring the monuments. Deroulede had paid a visit here about four weeks ago, chatted with Reguet, who thought Deroulede progressive and liberal. Even if Reguet had found the van, Deroulede might still have explained his presence without arousing Reguet's suspicions.

'Deroulede contacted Paulet, and told him that he was on a mission for France. Paulet took his small car out to the ruins, brought Deroulede back to the hotel at night, through the back door and up the fire escape, to his own rooms on the top floor.

'And there Deroulede was, on Sunday morning, waiting for Eliza Crawfurd, and also for Sheila Manley.

'We have our informers in Bangkok, so did Deroulede. He knew the Siamese prince in the Trade; knew that he was going to use Sheila to pass some drugs. The prince went himself to the shop where chocolates are sold, and bought a three-pound box. In Europe such a purchase would go unnoticed. Everybody buys chocolates, everybody eats chocolates, everyone gives everybody else chocolates.

'But in Asia, and especially in South-East Asia, in the hot tropics, chocolates are a rarity. Very very few Asians eat or give chocolates. Perhaps not more than one in a hundred thousand eats any chocolate. And in Bangkok there are only two shops selling hand-made chocolates. Deroulede had his intelligence agent in that chocolate shop, since it is French-run.

'He got his agent there to purchase a chocolate box, exactly the same as that of the prince. But Deroulede would not have thought of waiting for Sheila here at the hotel, if he had not known Eliza.

'He had known Eliza when she was a model and he a young Free French officer in London. Both Eliza and her sister Jacqueline went out a great deal. Jacqueline was married to Charles, but marriage did not make much difference. She was so afraid of losing her good looks that she did all the wrong things to persuade herself of her own attractiveness ... drink and men. Both sisters escaped National Service by taking secretarial jobs with the foreign embassies or missions in London. Charles was away with the Army. Jacqueline, working for the Free French, had an affair with a French officer, a friend of Deroulede. And it was her sister, Eliza, whom she had trusted, who arranged that Charles should know of it when he came home on leave.

'There was a divorce. Charles never knew it was Eliza who had stolen the cable sent to Jacqueline to inform her of his return, so that he caught her, with her lover. But Deroulede and his friend guessed. Jacqueline's lover did not marry her. Charles divorced Jacqueline, and married Eliza. Jacqueline killed herself . . .

'When Deroulede read in the newspapers from Bangkok which are flown here daily that Eliza Crawfurd was coming to Angkor, and that her husband Charles Manley was the celebrated economist, he thought he would see Eliza, and blackmail her into serving his organization. For he had conceived a plan, that of employing innocent passers, people who would carry drugs without knowing. What better passer than Eliza, with her fame, her profession, her many travels?

'How he must have wondered at fate, or luck, which put in his hand both Sheila and Eliza, and possibly Charles too, since Charles might later also be blackmailed through Sheila . . .

'He saw Eliza that morning, and while Sheila was out Eliza went to Sheila's room, took the box of chocolates containing the heroin, and substituted the other one. Then she went to lunch.

'Deroulede gave the box to Paulet to hand to Lederer, since Lederer was flying to Phnom Penh that afternoon. Lederer also did not know what was in the box of chocolates. He did not know that Paulet was acting under orders from Deroulede. All this became clear to him only later, after the coup.

'Lederer's flying schedule included a trip from Siemreap to Phnom Penh and Saigon on Sunday afternoon, a return flight to Siemreap on Monday, a round trip flight to Bangkok on Tuesday, and a flight to Saigon on Wednesday.

'Monday was the day that Deroulede chose to "arrive". He had already accomplished his main object, got the heroin on to Phnon Penh and Saigon through Lederer. Why did he remain?

Because he had learnt about the coup, and planned to see what he could make out of it. And also he had to organize a system of passers, preferably in Angkor, a tourist spot. He had also found out about Multani and Kilton.'

'Plot number four,' said George.

'A very small one,' said Das, 'but it kept Deroulede here. Kilton stole a gold carved belt, a treasure, from the museum. Reguet suspected him. Kilton passed it to Multani to keep for him. Like a fool, Multani accepted. On Monday night Multani went to give the money to General Vam Barong; Eliza tried to go into his room (with Deroulede's master-key, borrowed from Paulet) to find the gold belt, but she lost her nerve.

'She did not collect the belt. Instead, she piled her jewels in a big bag, because now she was frightened that Deroulede might rob her of her own jewels, and went to dinner. But a remark of the children upset her. She came back. Reguet came to call on her, he thought her attractive. Deroulede also hunted for the belt, but could not find it, because Multani, you may remember, had taken his camera with him. He made a great play of taking pictures of the Ballet at Angkor Vat that night, after he had called on Vam Barong and given him the money for the coup. Deroulede realized then that the camera case had a false bottom, and that the belt was concealed in it. Previously the fake bottom had held the money given to Vam Barong.

'But meanwhile, what about Sheila? On Monday afternoon, after the lunch where all of us talked so much about writing, she was on the point of going out to swim with Gion when she found the person to whom she had passed the chocolate box in her room.'

'It was a woman, of course,' said Sumipoon. 'Who was it?'

'Give you a guess,' said Ada. 'I guessed. I guessed because I was the only one who saw her twice.'

'I give up.'

'The pianist.'

'The pianist? Which pianist?'

'Kilton's pianist. Maisie. The thin little woman with glasses and frightened, darting looks. Hers is a real tragedy. Maisie is a convert, one of the few that Kilton made. Actually, she is Vietnamese. How she became a drugs passer I don't know, except that she seems to think it holy work against the communists and the Devil. On Sunday she got the chocolates from Sheila, and that night they were given back to her by Vam Barong's agent. Wrong chocolates. No heroin in them. She was threatened. She must find the right box or ... She was terrified. She did not know where to put the box of genuine chocolates, so she pretended they had come in the post for Kilton. Kilton has a sweet tooth, and chocolates are not obtainable in Siemreap. Then Maisie panicked more, and went to see Sheila at the hotel. She rang up Sheila from downstairs, and at that moment Sheila was in her room, preparing to go out to swim. Maisie said it was terribly urgent, and she sounded so frightened that Sheila told Gion she could not go out with him. She saw Maisie instead. And Maisie told her that the chocolates should have contained heroin, but did not. Had she, Sheila, changed them? Maisie did not tell Sheila that this was a brutal, dangerous thing to get involved in, and that her life was in danger.

'Then Sheila began to think, and the first person she thought of was Eliza. Because of what she had noticed, which she told to Gion, but to which he paid no attention, a few hours before she died. She said to him: "Eliza's perfume. In my room. She leaves a trail of scent behind her, always." When she had returned to her room that Sunday to collect the chocolate box and give it to Maisie, she had sniffed Eliza's perfume in her room...

'On Monday night when she saw Eliza with her big bag, heard the children's remark, saw Eliza run from the market, she laughed. She was beginning to guess that Eliza had changed the chocolate boxes. At the song-meeting in the Auditorium she was excited, pleased; like your children, Sumipoon, she loved a thriller. She made a remark about the chocolates, and Kilton, who is quite innocent about drugs (he confines himself to other misdeeds), told her what she knew already. Maisie was frantic. She was at the Suprême again on Tuesday night, with Kilton, at the party. She knew that both she and Sheila were in danger, if the box with the heroin was not found.

'On Tuesday morning, while all of us were at manual labour, Sheila confronted Eliza, who was in bed with a headache (or so she said), with the accusation that Eliza had been in her room on Sunday morning. "I smelt your perfume in my room," she said to Eliza.

'And then she began to remember other details. Lederer. You will remember that she was with Lederer on Saturday night, in Bangkok. And Lederer was drunk. Now when we questioned Lederer yesterday, asking what he and Sheila had talked about, he said: "Her father." "And what did you, Lederer, talk about?' Lee Souvan asked, and Lederer said: "I think I spoke of France, my war memories." So Lee Souvan pressed him: "Did you mention Deroulede?" And yes, now he thought, he might have mentioned Deroulede, who was such a wonderful type, had a charming wife, was a hero.

'Sheila on Tuesday afternoon returned with Gion from manual labour and dancing, and met Deroulede and Lederer with Eliza. And she felt almost immediately that there was something between Eliza and Deroulede.'

'That is where Gion was so stupid,' interrupted Sumipoon. 'He thought Sheila sexually attracted to Deroulede. He behaved like a nincompoop at the party that night.'

'Reticence plays a role in our lives as frightening as vice,' said Das. 'If only, instead of standing about drinking himself silly, watching Sheila dance with Deroulede, if only he'd spoken to her. Remember how he sulked? Unable to go away, refusing to dance, watching Sheila with a sour and angry face. And then he went away, to sleep he said. All around him was intrigue, innuendo, agitation; there was Sheila, caught in a net, a foolish, brave child who thought she would single-handed uncover a narcotics ring. But Gion was unaware of all this, completely wrapped up in himself.'

'Gion was always too reticent,' repeated Sumipoon, and there was an edge of bitterness in her voice.

'Sheila, noticing Gion had left, went to him in his room. She wanted to talk to him, tell him her suspicions. But she could not avoid playing the mysterious, hinting, evasive role she thought would evoke his protectiveness ... and they were alone, a man and a woman, half in love with each other. What happened had to happen, I suppose, given the time, the place, the occasion. Sheila left. Somehow it must have been awful, because for the first time she felt herself in love. She went to Multani's room.

'Bernard Reguet had accused Multani and Kilton of the theft. Reguet moved too rashly, too impulsively. Though he was sure of his facts, legally he did not have enough evidence. He took Kilton and Multani to the police station, but they were immediately released on orders from Vam Barong. Then Reguet understood that this was no longer a mere question of the theft of an antique, but that, as usual in South-East Asia, there were wheels within wheels. Multani and Kilton were both involved with Vam Barong, and so it was he, Reguet, who was now in need of protection.

'So Reguet decided to go to Phnom Penh, taking with him the two young Cambodians who were witnesses against Kilton. He told this to Charles Manley and Gion on Wednesday morning, on which he was preparing to leave by car for Phnom Penh.

'But, meanwhile, what about Deroulede? When Sheila on Tuesday night talked maliciously about chocolate boxes while dancing with him, he realized that she suspected something, knew more than he had thought. But *how much* did she know? He could not take a risk. He must eliminate her, if she knew too much.

'And what about Mary Faust? Mary Faust might also be used. She was a challenging, exciting woman. While he thought how he could deal with Sheila, he danced with Mary Faust, and already, in his mind, saw how he could use Mary Faust for the drugs traffic, as well as for other purposes.

'Then there was Reguet. If he could recruit Bernard, it would be excellent: Bernard was the last person one would suspect. If not, since Bernard was also in a tricky position owing to Multani and Kilton, he might engineer something so that Sheila's death might be ascribed to Reguet. All this must have gone through Deroulede's mind that night.

'Of Eliza he was not frightened, nor of Paulet, nor of Lederer; but Sheila was a danger, and if she and Bernard Reguet got together, the danger would be enormous. So he moved.

'On Wednesday morning the plane to Phnom Penh did not leave because Lederer on orders from Deroulede deliberately removed a part in the engine. I'm not an engineer, I can't tell you what it was. A spare had to be flown in from Bangkok.

'With Lederer here, Deroulede asked him to go to Bernard Reguet and to ascertain, once and for all, where Reguet stood politically. Reguet was offended by Lederer's proposal to aid in an O.A.S. conspiracy, and refused. Then Deroulede decided to act. Since Reguet felt so strongly against the O.A.S., he was dangerous and had to be eliminated. He went to Reguet ostensibly with a letter for his wife in Phnom Penh.

'Reguet had considered Deroulede his friend. But when the letter had been given to him, and Deroulede had gone (in reality, he turned the corner of the bungalow, then climbed over the verandah and hid), he did something which showed that actually he did not trust Deroulede as much as it appeared.

'For we know that Reguet went back to his small office, picked up the telephone, rang the telephone operator and asked her if it was true that the long distance telephone to Phnom Penh was out of order as Deroulede had told him. The telephone operator said she would check. When she rang up again, she could not get a reply. She decided that Reguet had gone out without waiting, and did not report the matter at the time.

'What Gion found, later that morning, was this: a blotting-paper which looked as if it had been rumpled, and an envelope on the floor.

'What most probably happened, since Deroulede who could have told us is dead, was that, as Reguet replaced the telephone and waited for the operator to ring him up again, Deroulede, who had come up (remember how soundlessly he moved), seen and heard Reguet telephoning, struck him on the back of his neck and killed him. He was very strong, remember, an expert at Judo, a complete athlete.'

'A real hero, the kind that do much harm,' said Ada.

'His intention at first must have been to take Sheila to the Conservation, and kill her there, so that people would think she and Bernard had had an affair, that Bernard had murdered her, then killed himself. Post-mortems in Cambodia are not common; crime is rare, and doctors too; there were only four doctors in Cambodia in 1955, and there are only twenty-three doctors today.

'Then he must have seen Sheila walking out of the hotel, from the windows of Bernard Reguet's office, and decided on another plan.

'He put on Reguet's motoring cap, jacket, and dark glasses, the way Reguet dressed for long-distance driving. He packed Reguet's body in the luggage compartment of the car. He drove to Siemreap, saw Sheila, honked. She came to the car. He must have said to her: "Want to come for a drive?" Or perhaps he said: "I'm going to fetch Reguet." We don't know. All we know is that she climbed into the car.'

'It seems to me,' said George, 'that if she was suspicious of him, she would not have climbed into the car.'

'You don't understand her,' said Ada. 'Sheila was suspicious, but not of *murder*. To her this was an exciting story of drugs and detection. She always was the child who has to put her hand into the fire to see if it really burns. She lacked all sense of caution. Remember how she wandered into people's rooms? She got in the car, delighted perhaps to confront Deroulede with her suspicions, delighted like a child telling a story, triumphantly. "See how clever I am, I've found you out..."'

'And also,' said Das, 'think how stunned she was. Gion, whom she loved, had taken her as if she were a common whore. Then Multani asking Sheila to lead him round the room, for that was the way Multani took his pleasure. She was desperate, unhappy, excited ... perhaps she longed for a kind of death, then, and it was death she found.'

'Ah,' said Ulong Serap sadly, 'we are born part of the way death goes...'

'A character is only an entire character when its elements disagree, when it contradicts its expected behaviour,' continued Das. 'That is the essence of the success of the English and the Russian novelists. A character who is always in character is no character at all. Neither in fiction, nor in real life. So Sheila's contradictions are explained by the very fact that one facet of her personality engendered its opposite...'

'Stick to telling the story,' said George. 'You'll write it later. Sheila climbed into the car, and then?'

'Then,' said Das, 'Deroulede took her to the ruins. Nobody will ever know what they said to each other, but he strangled her with Peter Anstey's scarf. And he did this deliberately, to compromise Eliza. He had picked up the scarf in Eliza's room among her *sampots*, Monday evening or night, before she could return it to Peter Anstey.

'That is why Eliza said she had not picked up the scarf. What else could she say? But she had. Teo had left it among the *sampots*, in his careless, spoilt little rich-boy way. And so Eliza *knew* that Deroulede had murdered Sheila, and that is why she said that she saw Bernard Reguet in the ruins. She was terrified that something might happen to her, that Deroulede might kill her. She wanted to show she was on his side . . .

'When Sheila had been strangled, Deroulede did something else. He buried the gold belt, which Kilton had stolen, in the Corridor of Women, near Sheila's body.'

'How did he get the gold belt?'

'Easily. Multani was dancing, he had left his camera case in his room upstairs. Deroulede borrowed Paulet's pass-key. It would take him four minutes to go up into Multani's room, get the belt, come out. Apart from its own value, he could use the belt to blackmail both Multani and Kilton.

'When he had strangled Sheila, buried the gold belt, he tied the scarf round the neck of the Leper King. That was bravado . . . but then he was like that, Deroulede. He liked to cock a snook at fate. He played dangerously, but not for himself. He was doing this for a cause . . .

'Now, a question comes up: how could he drive Reguet's car on the road to the Bayon, to the ruins, passing so many places where Reguet would be known, without being recognized? The answer is, he didn't. He went, with Sheila in the car and Reguet's body in the boot, the long way round the lake, where there are no houses; then up the unused track into the big square of Angkor Thom, through the side gate. Possibly he strangled Sheila while they were in the deserted track, among the bushes. He continued with the car till he came behind the Terrace of Elephants, put Sheila's body in the Corridor of Women, then drove the small car into his own van which he had kept parked with the working vans behind the ruins. He drove the van out, on to the unused track, retracing the way he had come, got the small car out of the van; then about half a mile along the track he sent the car crashing into the undergrowth. He arranged Reguet's body round the steering-wheel, drove the van out the way he had come in, round the lake and on to the main road to the airport.

'The airport was deserted at that hour of noon save for a few men guarding the plane. The repair crew had not yet reached it. From there he telephoned Paulet to come to fetch him. Paulet is not too bright, and is used to obeying orders from "Colonel Deroulede" implicitly.

'At the hotel he met Mary Faust, lunched with her, spent the afternoon with her. It did not make an alibi, only half an alibi. But he would have her on his side. At the same time, I think, he now fell in love with Mary. He was living at such a pace, taking so many risks, that his whole being was energized, stimulated, as in war. Love, murder, cram a lifetime of emotion in a few hours ...

'In the afternoon he saw Gion looking for Sheila, and there made a mistake. He mentioned the letter to his wife which he had given to Reguet that morning.

'Then came the coup, on Thursday morning, perhaps sooner than Deroulede expected. Deroulede knew that he would not be hurt. The coup might be unpleasant, but the hotel guests were not in danger.

'And here is where Providence, Destiny, Justice, were preparing their comeback. In the shape of our friend, the young Algerian poet, Malek. Remember how Deroulede began to count the prisoners to find out "who was missing"? And all, all of us forgot to mention Ibrahim Malek. We simply forgot.'

'I didn't,' said Ada. 'I was dead scared you or someone else would start mentioning him, Das.'

'My dear Ada,' said Das, peevishly, 'what do you take me for? Of course, when I say we all forgot, I don't mean you or me. *We* knew. But we kept quiet.

'Deroulede forgot Ibrahim Malek, or perhaps had never known of him. Otherwise he would not have remained in the hotel on Thursday night to be trapped.'

'No,' said Ada, 'I think he did fall in love with Mary. That temporarily dulled his keen perception of danger.'

'So Deroulede was with Mary Faust on Thursday night.' Das fell silent, suffering over his face like a greyness. Then, with an effort, he took up the narrative. 'Meanwhile, our Algerian friend had been busy. He was in the confidence of the Cambodians. He called on Ulong Serap and heard from him about Sheila and Reguet going off to Phnom Penh, and Gion pursuing them. He went to the astrologer's friend and was told that Vam Barong would start the coup on the next day because it was an auspicious day for war. When he left the astrologer he saw Eliza, walked after her; finally, he cornered Eliza.

'Eliza was already on the edge of a nervous breakdown. Ibrahim Malek is observant. He knew there was something wrong. She had deteriorated so much physically in the last few days. He pretended that he knew everything: "Come on, own up, otherwise you'll be arrested right away."

'It worked very well. He promised that she would be safe, whatever happened. So she talked. Of course, she knew nothing of Sheila's murder, or Reguet's. She talked of herself, of Deroulede making her take the chocolate box.

'And that is why Eliza, when Deroulede began to count the prisoners, never mentioned Malek. Everyone else forgot him, even Mary Faust, although she remembered later, at night ... Deroulede did not know that he had aleady been betrayed.

'Malek had found Reguet's body. He went to Reguet's office, found the envelope with Deroulede's writing——'

'Ah,' said Sumipoon, 'here he comes. Ibrahim Malek.'

'And Father O'Dodder,' cried Das. 'Welcome.'

'Oh,' groaned George, 'I don't want to see him.'

Sumipoon said: 'George, I've been thinking——'

'Hallo, there,' cried Father O'Dodder, 'may we come up?'

'Please do,' said Ulong Serap.

Ibrahim Malek sat on the mat and removed his shoes. He offered cigarettes.

'Well,' said Das, 'what news?'

'Everything all right,' said the Algerian. 'Ça va.'

'Yes, but what's happening? I mean, Multani, Kilton, Lederer, Paulet?'

'Deported tomorrow, all four.' Laconic, Malek seemed to shrink within himself, away from the gusts of prolixity which Das emitted.

Father O'Dodder said: 'Well, Mr Das, my friend here was telling me that you know everything.'

'Oh,' said Ada, 'don't, or he'll start all over again.'

'It gets better every time,' replied Das, somewhat vexed.

'Matches?' said the Algerian.

Ulong Serap gave an order, and a young acolyte came forward to light his cigarette.

Sumipoon looked at Malek. He was very thin, weighing no more than a hundred and twenty pounds. Not a spare ounce of fat, not a spare word. He had killed Deroulede neatly. 'Are you going to break the O.A.S. ring?' she asked.

'Yes. There must be more of them. Must stop it. And also up there, on the border, I think there's an opium dump. I'd like to blow it up ...' He blew the smoke, watched it with a pleased smile, engrossed in its spirals.

Father O'Dodder said to George: 'I shall have to leave soon. Will you think again about what I told you? Please.'

'No,' said George.

'Yes,' said Sumipoon, 'yes, George. I want you to leave MESSO. I don't like tricks like this one. And I suspect MESSO is in this.'

'But I'm only in the Cultural section. I don't know anything about the political side.'

'You can't separate things any more,' said Sumipoon. 'We can't pretend our hands are clean. I don't know how far moral responsibility can go, but I won't have you stay in MESSO now I've been through this.'

'But, darling——'

'George, I won't.'

George was silent. 'All right,' he said to Father O'Dodder, 'we'll talk about it, this afternoon.'

'By the way, Father O'Dodder,' said Ada suddenly, 'you must have known that Deroulede was lying when he said that he was on the Monday evening plane, and he wasn't. Because you were on that plane.'

All eyes turned to Father O'Dodder.

'Yes, Lady Ada,' said Father O'Dodder, 'I knew.'

'Why didn't you speak up then?'

Father O'Dodder lowered his head. 'Because, Lady Ada, the priest is bound not to reveal ... what the pènitent has said in Holy Confession.'

'You mean to say——'

'Jean Deroulede confessed his sins on Wednesday night,' said the priest.

In the silence, Ulong Serap spoke: 'Ah, my friends, how I

wish I had been clear in my vision! All is to do again in another life. Let me tell you what happened, in the past...'

Ibrahim Malek knocked on the door and entered.

Gion was packing his retrieved shirts. All morning the Militia, under the energetic Madame Shum, had been carrying back from hiding places the loot taken by the bodyguards of Vam Barong. The guests of the hotel had found a pile of clothes, jewellery, objects, from which they had picked out their own belongings.

'Leaving tomorrow, Gion?'

'Yes.'

'Any idea what you're doing next?'

'I don't know.' Gion walled himself in an opaque, dumb pain.

'Odd lot, you writers,' said Malek. 'Not really aware until you've written about what's happened.'

'Not me,' said Gion. 'Nor do I talk as much as Chundra Das.'

'You ought to do something,' said Malek. 'Action, not Words. Kill the rats. Get rid of them. I hope to mount a small expedition. All volunteers, of course.' He grinned. 'Go and wipe out a dump which, I suspect, is manned by some O.A.S. guys in the no-man's-land up there. One napalm bomb on the lot, a burst of machine-gun fire, a lot of history made or unmade. More than you can write in a lifetime.'

'I know,' said Gion. 'Don't rub it in. When I couldn't even fire at Jean Deroulede because he was so handsome that it hurt to kill such beauty, I knew how useless I was ... But I can't go now with you and throw bombs and machine-gun enemies. I'm too old.'

'Pity,' said Malek, rising. 'Never too old to learn. Hope you get on. Maybe see you one day, somewhere.'

They shook hands. Then Malek said, grinning: 'If I were you, I'd go and see Mary Faust. Fine girl. Needs consolation. Pity I haven't the time...'

Eliza sat by the bed where Charles was being divested of his bottle and the tubes that came out of it.

'He is much better, much better,' the doctor said, 'but it will take six weeks.'

Charles opened his eyes. He saw Eliza, and she was an old woman, a woman he no longer hated or minded. He said: 'Sheila?'

Eliza looked towards Ulong Serap. The latter said: 'Your daughter is reborn ... as all of us will be. When you are better, stay with me, Charles, in my village which you like, which has already given you peace, until you are whole.'

Eliza said: 'But I can't stay, I'm afraid. I have many commitments, my job ...'

Charles closed his eyes. He felt completely detached, except from that heaviness in his chest which kept him from soaring, flying, very high. He lapsed into a dream again. He was in the village, and everything was clear, everything was exactly as it ought to be, he understood it all. He had no doubts. He knew Sheila reborn someone else, and he had only to soar, throwing out the stone in his heart, in order to meet her. So he dreamt, while his heart, slowly, carefully, wrapped itself round its own wounded flesh, and his body began the long, slow process of healing.

'And so, Gion,' said Sumipoon, 'we shall be seeing you, sometime?'

'Yes. I shall call on you ... on my next visit or so.'

'Can't you tell us when? Because we might not be in Bangkok. George is leaving MESSO.'

'Oh?'

'Yes. He's selling his collection of erotica to the Vatican.'

'The Vatican?'

'Yes. They have the biggest collection in the world at the Vatican. The best kept. Father O'Dodder is negotiating with George. They're talking in the bar at the moment, even Jesuits are more amenable over a glass of liqueur brandy. George doesn't like to part with his books, but Father O'Dodder is offering him the job of research worker for the Vatican Library.'

'What do they do with erotica at the Vatican?'

'Keep it safe, so nobody can read it. We might not be settled for a bit. Anyway, I feel like a change. I didn't like the coup, Gion, I don't like all this messing with countries, trying to provoke crises.'

'I wonder how the Vatican came to know about George's collection?'

'An error,' said Sumipoon. 'Our secretary was to pack a collection of Asian folk songs for the Vatican Missionary Society. It's nearly impossible to preach religion now if one doesn't add local colour. The girl sent off some erotica instead.'

Gion looked at Sumipoon as she chattered, and felt detached, far away. What stood between them now? Nothing ... except that he had participated, even in a remote, ridiculous, and incompetent way, in some event, and that she had not ... she was as he himself was yesterday. Today he was different. He was no longer untouched. He could not go all out, like the Algerian, to fight, to kill, or be killed, but he would have to do something, he would have to take sides.

And Sumipoon, as if guessing, said: 'It's the cold war, isn't it? Even if we think we cannot possibly be involved, we get sucked into the maelstrom.'

'Everything gets involved, everyone. Motives, intentions, personal temperament, ideals, sex ... it is as if a film company's stage props suddenly became a real battlefield, a kindergarten, a school for training in murder. Everything is out of focus, unreal, crass idiocy, yet it happens.'

'Yes, it does.'

'Gion,' said Sumipoon, in a rush, 'my dear, I'm so sorry. You know that she loved you, didn't you? She told me, but she asked me not to say it to you.'

'No,' said Gion, 'I didn't know. I didn't know ...'

'Would it have made much difference, Gion, if I had told you?'

He said: 'The worst thing I did was not to ask her, that first day in the taxi, why she wept. And the second worst thing was to take her, without love, through lust, when again she came to me ...'

'I'm so sorry, Gion,' repeated Sumipoon.

Gion smiled, his smile meaning nothing, a vacancy. Sumipoon was not guilty. Only he had wronged Sheila. I am worse than Deroulede, he thought. He died because he stayed to make love to Mary Faust, when he could have fled earlier. I was not capable of such carelessness.

And then he remembered the afternoon when he had heard Charles and Sheila quarrelling, heard Charles's contemptuous voice: 'A pseudo-intellectual,' and Sheila's reply: 'I love him.' They were talking of him and he did not know it ... A pseudo.

'Good-bye, Sumipoon,' he said. 'Please don't be sorry. It wouldn't have changed anything, because I'm not capable of changing anything.'

The airport was more crowded than usual for a departing plane. Madame Shum and the Militia girls were supervising the search of the outgoing passengers' luggage, far more thorough than usual. Kilton, Multani, Lederer, and Paulet, under armed escort, were kept apart from the other passengers; they were going in different directions, Lederer and Paulet deported to Saigon, Multani and Kilton to Bangkok.

Lederer alone of the four talked, laughed aloud, crushed cigarettes underfoot. The co-pilot had come to see him off. 'T'en fais pas, mon vieux. François Lederer isn't going to let himself be done in by a small thing like that.'

'Sure, sure, you'll get a job easy as anything.' The co-pilot, knowing that Lederer would not get a job in South-East Asia, except perhaps in Air-Opium, gave Lederer a cigarette, lit it for him. 'After all, it wasn't your fault.'

'You,' said Lederer, 'you've always been scared of your own shadow.'

'Sure, sure,' said the co-pilot, 'I don't understand.'

'One day, they'll come and sit in your house and sleep with your wife.'

'Who?'

'Those. Like that one. There.' Lederer spat as Malek passed. The Algerian did not turn his head.

Multani and Kilton spoke neither to each other, nor to anyone else. Multani had his camera case with him. Everyone was looking at it, he felt. Certainly Das, a few steps away, voluble as usual, seeing off Gion and Sumipoon, had noticed it.

'I still don't understand why Multani and Kilton were put in jail with us,' said Ada, 'when they were such friends of Vam Barong.'

'I asked Ulong Serap,' replied Das, 'and he told me: because Sheila was killed. You may remember the astrologer saying that Thursday would be an auspicious day, provided no crime was committed? Crimes are extremely rare, so Vam Barong thought himself quite safe. And then what happens? Gion is found, with a dead woman in his arms. At first Vam Barong was not told, but they could not keep the news from him long. Then he got terribly angry. Somehow or other he got the idea that Multani and Kilton were responsible for her death. So he put them in jail too.'

Thomas and Mabel sat with Ashley Basildon and Joan Warburton. Ashley Basildon's producer had driven in from Phnom Penh the night before, had been told the story of the coup by Ashley Basildon, had only understood one thing, that Mabel had been kidnapped and jailed, and this he felt was material for a most successful film screenplay by Ashley Basildon. Mabel Despair would play herself. 'But you'll have to take off fifteen pounds,' he warned her.

'They are going to make screen tests of me in the ruins next week,' Mabel told everyone.

The Fumikaros had come, to photograph everybody off, Madame Shum, the deportees, the airplane, Mabel ... Suddenly Madame Shum remembered that photographing at the airport was forbidden. However, as this was a day of joy, she decided to forget it again.

A taxi was perceived, speeding towards the airport.

'Ah,' cried Ahmed Fouad, 'Miss Faust has arrived.'

And such was Mary's personality that everyone stood still, watching her entrance.

Dramatic in a vivid red dress, beautiful, alive, indomitable, her head held high, her copper hair glowing in the morning sun, her face masked by sunglasses, Mary came down from the taxi and immediately started giving orders.

'Hand me this bag. Careful, those are my manuscripts.'

She approached Sumipoon, who stood, a little hostile, shielding her children. 'Sumipoon, will you take my books with your luggage? They'll be confiscated in Bangkok otherwise.'

'Well——' said Sumipoon, wavering, but George intervened.

'Of course we shall, Mary. Leave it to me.'

Superb, Mary turned to Mabel Despair. 'I understand you've got a job with a film company, Mabel. My congratulations.'

And Mabel, cowed, said: 'Yes, Mary, thank you.'

Only Thomas was not overwhelmed. He held out his hand. 'We'll let bygones be bygones, Miss Faust. Wish you luck.'

'Thank you, Thomas.'

And now it was Chundra Das, who was not leaving, but staying on with Ada Timberlake.

'Good-bye, Das. Give my love to Ulong Serap. And don't give up writing, will you? The world needs you.'

'My dear...' began Das.

But Mary continued: 'I blame you for not taking me in your confidence earlier. You should have told me.' Her lips quivered, but she went on. 'Everybody can make mistakes. I'll be writing to you. From Singapore. I'm going there, if I can catch a plane connection in Bangkok.'

Das sighed. Always, always, this woman would make him feel small, incompetent; whatever she did he could not find it in his heart to blame her. How strong, he thought, the images of childhood ... if only we knew them all, for each person, we would understand so much more about life, we might predict ... At that moment Das, who never lost himself because he could always explain others to themselves, was once again a little boy, listening to an imperious voice that held him in thrall.

'I want to know, Das,' said Mary, 'that Sunday when you ran away from your room, ran into the next room, was it *really* because you were frightened of me?'

'Yes and no, Mary. Actually, I was on the point of going into the next room, to set up a small magnetic microphone, because I was very suspicious of Lederer.' He said this in a very low voice, so that no one else could hear. 'But please don't tell anyone. I failed. Lederer was in his room, when I thought he was out. I did set up the microphone, but he took it away.'

'How silly you are,' Mary said, crushingly.

Ada said: 'Well, m'dear, look after yourself. You need a good rest. Don't try to start anything too big, will you? I don't think somehow you've got the hang of things yet. Revolutions are made by people, common, ordinary people, people who work with their hands, like these...' Her hands took in the Cambodian landscape. 'They can't be made by clever, ambitious intellectuals, to please themselves.'

'I don't think you are qualified to talk about these things, Lady Ada.'

'True,' said Ada, 'I'm not. But what I'm saying is that

you've got a lot to learn. Never mind, you're young, you'll learn.'

When the plane landed in Bangkok a posse of journalists, photographers, and correspondents assaulted the passengers. Gion found a newspaper thrust into his hand. Automatically he read it:

'Communist take-over of loyal province.'

'Massacres of tourists by Cambodian troops.'

'General Vam Barong, staunch democrat and friend of the West, flees for his life before onslaught of Reds.'

Ahmed Fouad was surrounded. 'Will you give me an interview, Mr Multani?'

'I'm not Multani,' said the Pakistani indignantly, 'and you have the wrong idea——'

The journalist was off. Multani and Kilton were identified, photographed, photographed again.

A group formed round Mary Faust. 'Here, sister, hold it.' Photographs. 'Now tell us, were you imprisoned by the Reds?'

'No.'

'You were not imprisoned?'

'Yes, but it was General Vam Barong who started a coup against the government——'

'We don't want to hear about that, sister. We've heard the correct story from Vam Barong himself.'

'Vam Barong himself? He was here?'

'Came three days ago. A great man,' said one correspondent, putting back his notebook and looking Mary up and down. 'Now what I want is *your* story, when you were jailed.'

'It's as I told you. Vam Barong started a coup. He took us all and put us in jail, but we were saved——'

Already the correspondent had turned away.

Kilton was surrounded. 'Come on, tell us all, we know you were working for a democratic take-over.'

'Not a word, not a word.' Gion suddenly recognized one of the three Americans he had seen at the Writers' Congress. The American moved to Kilton, said sternly: 'Not a word, d'you hear, till you've cleared with us. You're coming with me.'

Ahmed Fouad lunged forward. 'Here,' he cried, 'was this man your agent?'

'Not at all. An independent agent. Nothing to do with us.'

'Nothing to do with us. This man acted against our policy. He'll have to clear himself,' said another.

And now Multani was alone, confronted with the correspondents. 'I went to Cambodia purely on cultural matters,' he announced, 'to attend a writers' congress. Purely cultural. I have had nothing to do with its internal politics. Whatever happened had nothing to do with me. I have nothing to say.'

Mary Faust and Gion were on the plane connection from Bangkok to Singapore that afternoon.

They did not sit together. Mary had on her dark glasses, and read a book steadily.

Gion had been given a newspaper by the hostess when the airplane took off. In it he read that General Vam Barong, strong man of democracy and a most popular leader in South-East Asia, had been the victim of a 'pro-communist plot' in his own country, had fled, and was now engaged on a tour of the free world to explain his case to the western democracies.

On the back page, last column, he read a message from the U.S. State Department denying that the United States had had anything to do with any coup, and saying that General Vam Barong would not be officially invited to the United States.

On the second page was a declaration by a Pentagon general saying that such people as General Vam Barong were 'true champions of democracy' and should be supported.

And on the fourth page was a statement by MESSO denying any knowledge of General Vam Barong. 'We do not have this name in our files.'

Under the Stock Market news he read that there had been a general rise in tone, due to 'some uncertainties of the situation' in South-East Asia. Industrials were strong, and 'in view of the possibility of certain conflicts developing' rubber and tin both had seen an upswing in prices.

Gion put down the newspaper. He closed his eyes, and remembered Sheila.

Already she was dissolving, fluid, impalpable, dissolving yet filling the landscape of his future, an essence, a persistent dream.

He had loved. Of that he was sure. He had loved Sheila,

otherwise he would not be, as he was now, completed and helpless. He had held the body of his beloved, in life and in death. Could anyone have more?

And through this brief contact, fortuitous, unpremeditated, he had had to come to terms with his own reality, had faced himself, his insufficiency, his poverty of emotion, of action, his ineptness, his age.

The face of Ibrahim Malek came to him. The man stripped for action, who no longer lived by the legal euphemism which, at the moment, were injustice and not justice. The man who had gone back to take justice in his own hands, to deal out justice, himself, since legality was a farce. Was he right or wrong?

He pictured to himself those fields where the opium grew its lovely, deathly flowers, where in barns was stored the deadly poison that paid for war. Oh yes, the Algerian would do what he had said he would do. If not he, someone else like him, some other one of those who had had enough of being pawns in the terrible grave of war. He would go and burn up those poppy fields one day.

Gion thought: I must go there. Perhaps it is futile, but I must go.

If only he had enough strength, enough resolution. If only a fatal ebb of emotion did not strangle in him this new, young foolishness.

Yet he could see them, the valleys where the deathly lovely nodding poppies of opium blew, where helicopters came out of the sky to carry the drug away, where a traffic with international ramifications, with political implications, went on, where guns and armaments were exchanged for a drug that killed more slowly, ruined its thousands, in the big cities, because unscrupulous and stupid men wanted power, wanted to keep power.

I must commit myself. I cannot escape any more. I must be committed wholly to a total humanity.

When they landed at Singapore, Mary walked in front of him. And he knew that she had wept, alone, behind her dark glasses, which she kept on although it was now evening and the electric lights were bright.

He said: 'Mary, will you stay long in Singapore?'

She threw back her shoulders, ready for hostility, defiance. 'I'm ringing Teo. He gave me his telephone number. I might stay a week or two.'

While they waited for their luggage and the health and passport examinations, Mary, imperious, and obeyed as ever, obtained a telephone. She returned with anger and a certain childish hurt which Gion noticed for the first time.

'I got Aunty. She's quite stupid, that woman. Says Teo is busy with his accountancy. He's going into Papa's Bank. They have no room in the house for me.'

Gion said: 'Let me look after you for a while. I think we shall need each other.'

She reared like a young colt. 'What d'you mean? If you're insinuating——?'

'Stop it,' he replied. 'I'm not insinuating anything. I don't want anything from you. I am going to a hotel. Let us go there. I will pay for your room, if you are short of money. Later, we shall talk. I don't want anything else from you.'

Her mouth quivered, and he knew her eyes were again filling with tears. She pushed a handkerchief under her dark glasses, and wiped her eyes.

A selection of titles by Han Suyin available in Panther Books

To order direct from the publisher just tick the titles you want and fill in the order form.

All these books are available at your local bookshop or newsagent, or can be ordered direct from the publisher..

To order direct from the publisher just tick the titles you want and fill in the form below.

Name _____

Address _____

_____

Send to:
Panther Cash Sales
PO Box 11, Falmouth, Cornwall TR10 9EN.

Please enclose remittance to the value of the cover price plus:

UK 45p for the first book, 20p for the second book plus 14p per copy for each additional book ordered to a maximum charge of £1.63.

BFPO and Eire 45p for the first book, 20p for the second book plus 14p per copy for the next 7 books, thereafter 8p per book.

Overseas 75p for the first book and 21p for each additional book.

Panther Books reserve the right to show new retail prices on covers, which may differ from those previously advertised in the text or elsewhere.